I0708532

the GraveyardShift

VALENTYNE

COVER DESIGN & CHARACTER ART:

MAC

Copyright © 2023 by Valentyne King

Paperback ISBN: 979-8-9897670-0-7

Cover Design & Character Art: *Maybemacdc*

 @maybemacdc

Editor: *Conan Ray Graves*

 @scrambledeggs_n_stuff

This is a work of fiction. Names, characters, places, and incidents either are the product of the author's imagination or are used fictitiously, and any resemblance to actual persons, living or dead, businesses, companies, events, or locales is entirelycoincidental.

Except Nox, Nox is real.

DEDICATIONS

The Graveyard Shift has been the most challenging project I have ever faced. Never before, or since, have I given up on a novel. Back when I started writing *The Graveyard Shift* in 2016, I felt defeated when I had to step away from it, and that feeling only grew with every subsequent attempt, every total rewrite, that fell short in the years following. It was my elephant in the room, the novel that bested me. No matter how many others I wrote, Igor's story haunted me, unfinished. However, now I know that I was just not ready to tell the story I wanted to yet. I had more colors to meet before I could bring justice to Igor's.

This book would not be in your hands had it not been for the profound patience of my roommate, **Kyle**, who was randomly assigned to me in college five years ago and has continued to live with me and listen to my desperate ramblings about this damn story, ever since. It wouldn't be here without the **Beta Reading Team** that I have been so lucky to work with, without the amazing brain of my editor **Conan Graves**, without the encouragement of **Felix**, the love of my life, and the support of my **Patreons**.

This also goes out to my **coworkers** who brave the front lines of retail with me. You helped me find myself when I felt as if there was nothing left in me. The gift of your inclusion, kindness, and support over the years has forever changed my life. Thank you to those who make an appearance in the pages to follow, I'm sure people are going to love you as much as I do.

Thank you everyone, it is due to the kindness and support of so many that I am able to chase this dream. **I won't let you down, I promise.**

-Valentyne

- Beta Readers -

Conan Graves | Airic Fenn | Michelle Emmina | Kate Dojan | Allyamber

- Patreons -

Simprince | **furby** | Vi Vanattia | Jai Howard | Nic Kelly

Sheena Vancleave | Imp | Ciara | Ally | Stray

Samantha Saulsgiver | Samson

MISSING

On December 10th 24-year-old Igor Francis left work to walk home. On his way, he stopped at the graveyard on 12th street.

IGOR FRANCIS

The reason he stopped is unknown, though witnesses claim they heard the faint ringing of a bell moments before his disappearance. Igor was last seen walking toward a grave with a shovel. One witness returned to the scene to find an unearthed, empty grave, and no sign of Igor, or the corpse. Igor continues to not show up for work and has not contacted his family, as if he vanished into thin air.

OBIT

Cyrus Glory

There's the s____ and ____coms of g___ father glory b____in. Who would ____ders ____ those ills we have, there's the thousand n____al ____cks that m____ ____ ____ traitor ____ long a lif__, for who would bear, to grun__ and lose the mind to ____er the ____, and their currents turn awry, and ____rprises of troubles and ____

UARIES
HAEP
ATTACK
VAMPIRE
FINNEGAN VAN SERIFINO

... witch ...

... who hanged ... to grant and lose the mind to suffer the will, and their ... and enterprises of ... and storyteller ... this the ... and enterprises of ... suffer the ... of outrageous fortune.

Nox

There's the slings and ... of ... fortune ...

They call it the graveyard shift.

Watching as the hand on my watch ticked to 2:50 a.m., I reached for the intercom to read the closing announcement.

It was a common turn of phrase for a time worked through the night.

The automatic doors creaked open behind me.

Turning, hand still extended before me, my eyes met a teenage boy as he walked in on the tail end of a blistery December gust. Staring at me, arms crossed over his chest, clad in a red and white letterman jacket, his black hair a bit of a mess from the wind, it really made the blue of his eyes stand out.

He dropped his head and started into the store. Eyes slowly tracking him as he passed the front end, I waited until he disappeared around a display to reach for the radio clasped to my hip.

The lights above flickered orange.

Pausing before my finger met the radio, I glanced up as the lights hummed back to their usual corporate off-white.

Finger pressing the talk button, it beeped in the piece that sat looped over my ear. "We have a customer."

I heard my manager's sigh turn into a groan from across the store.

Legend had it that, once upon a time, it wasn't unheard of to be buried alive. So, to combat this, the peoples of old would tie a string to the wrist of the deceased, feed it six feet up, and attach it to a bell so that, in the event they woke up, the person working the graveyard shift would hear the ringing and exhume them.

As I leaned against my register, adjusting my bowtie, I tried not to yawn.

An occupying thought, though snobs will say the phrase was coined much later and held no such connection.

"Man." Venecia approached the front end, stopping on the other side of the counter from me, a stack of newspapers in hand. "What could he possibly need this time of night?"

Watching her as she reached forward to slide the papers into their slot next to the register, the yellow of her sunflower print shirt and matching hair ribbon managed to remain bright, even in the fluorescent lights.

"God, who knows." Amy said as she picked up a shirt that was on the floor next to a nearby rack with a vengeance. Her sage green sweater complimented the cedar of her eyes as she slid the shirt back onto a hanger. "I just hope he finds it fast, Nicholas needs to close the fitting room and run the rack, but he can't with a customer in the store." Walking toward us, her manager clipboard in hand, the green gem in her rectangular woven metal pendant caught in the light as she approached the counter. Leaning on it, her eyes stopped on the papers Venecia had just placed. Brow raising, she took one in hand. "Holy shit, did you guys see this?"

As Venecia leaned around Amy, her high, umber ponytail that curled up at the ends bounced with the movement as her eyes widened. Leaning a bit over the counter, my eyes met with the headline, too.

Young Man Jumps in Front of Train, Dies

Eyes scanning down the story, they caught on an image. Grainy, it was difficult to see, as his photo stared back at me. Wavy hair and a wicked smile, a young man no older than twenty, he seemed to have a personality that was loud enough to jump off a page. Staring into his eyes, a breath sat, suspended in my chest.

The light of my register flickered from white to red.

"Damn." Amy turned around, leaning her back against the counter as she held the paper up for us to see. "They can't identify him, the ID in his wallet was a fake."

"That's awful." Venecia straightened away from the paper, "I wonder if they're going to brush this one under the rug, like they did with what happened to Salem at Juniper High."

Taking one last look at the young man, I stepped back into my station. Picking up a duster, I brushed it around my register as the faint holiday music played from the speakers above, filling the beat. As my coworkers stood with the quiet, the jingling of sleigh bells in the moments between us, I could sense the unease in the air. But as I paused in my dusting, staring down at the worn check-out counter, I waited for something to stir within me, too.

Though, nothing did.

Resuming dusting, I let out my breath.

Nothing ever did.

Venecia leaned against the counter next to Amy. "What is going on. First Salem and his friends are killed in some like, satanic ritual, and now a random jumps in front of a train. This stuff didn't use to happen in Blazing Star."

"Right? And they still don't know who killed Salem." Amy folded the paper. "Though, a lot of people think it was the quarterback. He beat Salem for years."

"But." Venecia pushed herself up off the counter. "Wasn't he killed, too?"

"Oh yeah, you're right." Amy slid the paper back into its place at my register. "Remember when he was stalking Salem and came into the store? I had sent Igor to scare him off when-"

Someone cleared their throat.

While Amy and Venecia both jumped, I did not.

The lights above flickered purple for just a moment, but it was a moment long enough for the young man to look me up and down before it returned to white. When my eyes met his, he looked away. Starting toward the register, two fake plants in his hands, he didn't even look up to Venecia and Amy as they stepped out of his way. Placing the two fake plants on the counter between us, he continued to stare down, shoulders tense in his letterman jacket.

"Which one do you like more?" He looked up to the plants. "They're for a friend, the real ones keep dying in this cold." Bringing up his hand to his hair, he ran his fingers through it with enough force to appear painful. "I just, I just want something that will look nice, and I know it's stupid, but it's the best I could come up with."

Looking between the two fake plants, one a plastic elephant ear and the other a plastic bird of paradise in bloom, I looked back to the young man that stood between them. Eyes catching on the patch on his sleeve, the insignia was that of the Juniper High Devils football team.

The lights above flicked blue, startling everyone but me. And while the young man had an excuse, my coworkers did not. This had happened as long as I had worked there, and no matter how many times they put in a work order about the lights, the problem was never resolved.

Gesturing to the bird of paradise, I looked up to him.

Slowly looking down to me from the lights as they returned to white, I could see the tears in his eyes. Staring at me for far too long, something lit in his gaze, something that softened it until his eyes lowered to see my gesture. Jumping, he shook the look he had on his face as he smiled. "Thank you." Reaching toward the plastic elephant ear, he looked away. "I'll go put this one back."

"It's alright," Amy called as she pulled out some carts from the line of them next to the doors, "we can take care of that for you."

The young man appeared as if he wanted to argue, but I took the fake elephant ear into hand by its pot and set it behind the counter. No words exchanged between us, I scanned the barcode on the bottom of the bird of paradise's pot as Amy pushed the carts to block all but one of the doors.

As the young man inserted his card into the PIN pad machine, he looked up to me. When our eyes met, he looked away. As I pressed a button on my screen, I looked away, but when I looked back, I found him staring at me again.

What was he looking at? Was it the bright yellow of my button down or the nine years of service pin attached to my nametag? Maybe he thought my eyes were too brown, so dark they matched the bags beneath them, or that my black hair looked wrong with my complexion. Or perhaps he thought my black bowtie was stupid, I got that one a lot. Whatever it was, whether it was the flat line of my mouth or my darkly rimmed rectangular glasses, his gaze on me intensified.

When we both looked away, the lights above flashed red.

Looking up at the lights as the PIN pad beeped at him to remove his card, it took him a moment to notice it. Jumping, he took the card out. Taking his wallet out, he fumbled with it. When it hit the ground, he tensed. Laughing a little, he dropped to his knee to grab it. Springing back up, he just shoved his wallet and his card separately back into his pocket. Staring at me for a moment more, he reached to take the plastic potted plant into hand.

As he turned away from me, red in the face, the lights above flashed yellow.

All but running out the doors, as quickly as he had arrived in our store, he was gone into the cold December night. I had worked at this store for nearly ten years, and in all my graveyard shifts, I hadn't had a customer quite like that one.

Snorting as she locked the doors behind him, Amy turned to look at me, and though it seemed as if she wanted to say something, she didn't.

The graveyard shift here was lacking corpses, other than mine, I suppose. Removing my radio, I turned it off and wrapped the cord around it, placing it with the others. The only bell we ever heard was that of the jewelry case needing assistance. Picking up the fake elephant ear plant, I glanced out the doors at my reflection in the night.

No one was coming to exhume me.

"Good job tonight, everyone." Amy locked up the doors as we stood outside the store. "Thank you for your hard work."

"What did he even buy?" Nicholas started off the sidewalk, his long dark brown hair pulled into a top-knot ponytail on the back of his head above a sharp undercut, a few wisps framing his tired face as he stretched.

"A fake plant." Amy pulled on the doors to make sure they were locked.

"Interesting." Nicholas yawned, his voice only haunted by the Greek accent he had when we were kids. "Have a nice night."

Watching as he walked toward his car, I could see it, the angle of his head turn down as his eyes met the ground.

Every step quietly jingled because a little bell on a necklace he always wore. Nicholas Garland, we had gone to school together, though never really spoken. The only thing I knew about him was that he adamantly believed in Santa, swore up and down he had met the man. As he unlocked his car in the darkness, I wondered if he still did, or if the years of relentless bullying beat that out of him. Miserable as one could be, our coworkers often compared us, but miserable was something, something more than me. When he got in his car and closed the door, the sound echoed against the store.

"Goodnight!" Venecia started off the sidewalk, the yellow light of the store's massive sign casting her shadow on the road before her, but as her eyes drifted past me, she stopped. "Oh, Igor," her high ponytail bounced as she turned to face me, her brown pleated skirt shifting with her. "Would you like a ride? You walk right by the graveyard on your way home, right? I wouldn't want you getting kidnapped by a zombie or vampire or something."

Looking between her smiling eyes through the dissipating cloud of her breath, the sign above us grew brighter, the yellow more intense. The sweetest person I had ever encountered, I wondered if she knew she was everyone's favorite person in the store. Somehow never fazed by me, hers was the only smile I met that felt genuine, despite how I was.

"He'll say no, I'd know, I ask him every night." Amy hopped off the curb as she put her store keys in her back pocket with one hand and pulled out her vape with her other. "Igor isn't afraid of anything." Glancing back at us, she brought her vape up to her mouth, "That one jackass spit on him and he just stood there."

Humming, Venecia looked back to me, brow lower than before. "Are you sure?"

Nodding, I averted my eyes.

Obviously not a fan of my reply, Venecia stood there for a moment longer before sighing, a smile returning to her face. "Okay." Hopping off the curb, she ran a few strides to catch up with Amy, falling into step at her side. "Get home safe, Igor!"

Amy waved. "And give my number to any vampires you run into."

Standing there, watching them walk toward their cars as they sat, parked next to each other, the clouds of their breath catching in the moonlight as they laughed, my feet felt heavy. I could have been up there with them, laughing at whatever Venecia had said, if I wasn't like this. Shadow before me, cast by the store's yellow sign, the light around it flashed blue for a moment. Letting out my breath, it didn't cloud like the others.

Taking out her car keys from her pocket, Amy accidentally pressed a button on the fob. Alarms screaming into the night, I watched them both fly out of their skin, Amy's car flashing.

Standing there watching as Amy fumbled to disarm the alarm, that should have drummed up a startle, made my heart race, conjure even something as simple as a jump. But as her car fell silent, the air buzzing with the absence of a horn blaring, I felt nothing.

Absolutely nothing.

Calling an apology out to me, Amy laughed and waved again as she got into her car.

Unable to will my arm up to even wave in return, I just stood there.

How long had I been this way?

Turning, I started down the sidewalk and out of the light of my store's sign.

As long as I could remember.

Walking around the corner of the store, I started out of the deserted outlet mall, not a single car left in the lot. Hand raising up to my face, my fingers met the corner of my mouth. The way my coworkers smiled at me, I wondered what that would feel like, if my muscles were even capable of it.

Walking along the sidewalk beneath streetlights, as I passed under each one, they flickered.

When we went to Salem's funeral, everyone cried.

The streetlight above turned blue.

When a customer yelled at one of us, everyone got fired up.

The next streetlight turned orange.

When we started to get holiday decorations in the store, everyone was excited.

The next turned green.

When a man threatened to rob us, everyone got scared.

The next, purple.

When I got promoted to the front-end supervisor, everyone was happy.

Then yellow.

When I got a secret admirer letter from a regular, everyone made a whole thing about it.

Stopping under a streetlight as it turned red, I stared down at my shadow.

Everyone but me.

Glancing back at the line of colorful lights behind me, they flickered again and a moment later, they all went out completely.

It had been so long since I felt anything, so long since her heart flatlined and stopped mine. Perhaps a choice at one point, as I raised my hand up, running my fingers through my hair, sighing in the dark, it no longer was. Though there were times, times as I stood before a raging customer or in my little brother's embrace, that I wondered what it would take to bring me back to life.

Standing in the darkness, a gust of wind rushed by, taking some of me with it.

A creak split the air.

Slowly looking up to the side, my eyes met with a gate as it groaned open. Intricate, metal, it was usually locked this time of night. Staring through its open threshold into the graveyard that slept just beyond, I stood in pause. Headstones against the night sky, they sat, silhouetted by the nearly full moon. Though I had been there just about two months ago, it felt like Salem had been gone much longer.

Turning to the graveyard, I stood there as the light above flicked back on, bathing me in white.

A gust of wind crashed into my back, so strong it made me stumble forward through the threshold.

The gates slammed closed behind me.

Tripping over my own feet, frozen grass crunched beneath my shoes as I gathered myself. Straightening, I glanced at the closed gate through my messy hair. Bringing my hand up, I raked my hair into place.

Turning back around, I looked out into the graveyard. Eyes meeting the tree line that separated it from my neighborhood, I pocketed my hands as I took my first step.

I could get home this way, too, I guess.

Mindful to not step on any plots, I wove my way around headstones. Passing a small gardening shed, silence sat in the air. It was still, too still, still enough that as I ascended one of the many rolling hills, I could hear my own heartbeat. Slow, steady, unchanging, it never raced, never stopped, never skipped, just continued at the same, predictable, pace.

Passing a line of headstones, I stopped mid-step. Gaze drifting down, it met with a name. Tall, expensive, a premium plot, it was a gift from an affluent family in the area. Glancing around at the other five headstones of the same nature, I hadn't been back since the funeral. They all cried so much, my coworkers. Barely eighteen, my eyes returned to his headstone before me. Raising my hand to it, the cool stone met my palm. He had been fired shortly before he died, and while the two seemed completely unrelated, I wasn't so sure. Killed in what appeared to be a ritual at his high school alongside four others, there had always been something off about him, so while the news was devastating to everyone else, it wasn't the strangest way for him to go.

Though, of all my coworkers, he was the only one who seemed particularly interested in getting to know me. Unfortunately, there wasn't anything there to come to know, but he never did stop trying.

Fingers drifting down the stone, they traced over his name.

Salem Willow

Eyes drifting over the line of headstones, they met with those of his friends who had died with him, but then landed on the headstone at the end. I had been to two funerals here. Walking toward it, my hand fell from Salem's headstone. Stopping before the last headstone, older than the rest, the name of the only person at school who ever paid me any mind stared back up at me.

Kasper Kloven

I didn't cry at that funeral, either.

I couldn't.

Deep breath escaping me, it filled the silence. He was sure that ghosts existed, started an entire club about it. I spared the headstone one last moment before looking out over the graveyard. Perhaps this was where I belonged, I had more in common with the corpses. They couldn't cry, either. It was as if I was one of them, one of the many who had fallen motionless.

The ring of a bell broke the silence.

Turning, I slowly looked around.

It rang again.

They call it the graveyard shift.

two

Beyond Apathy

Stepping back from Kasper's headstone, I hesitated as another ring sprinkled the air. Eyes meeting the headstone down the line from Salem's, the smallest glint of something silver near the base caught my eye. Walking around it, the unassuming stone lacked much note, especially compared to the six behind it. Though, as I stopped, my eyes caught on the bell as it rang again.

Flipping on my phone's flashlight, I knelt to inspect. Hanging from a swirly metal post, the little silver bell caught the moonlight. A string, thin like silk, pulled tight, ringing the bell. Eyes following it down, they stopped where it fed into the recently disturbed ground before the headstone. It rang again, more violently this time. The corpse must have been getting impatient.

As I reached out, tapping the cold metal of the bell with the pad of my finger, I wanted to credit that occurrence to my coworkers, but it was doubtful. While they were creative and clever, it was unlikely that even they could conjure something like this.

It was about then that reality made its way through my haze of perpetual indifference and I grasped the potential severity of the situation in which I was standing. What was I even supposed to do? Dig the grave up? I'd prefer to not exhume some random who somehow managed to bury themselves six feet under. But if there was some person suffocating down there, it would be unfortunate for me not to save them.

My phone's flashlight flickered once, turning purple for a moment, then died, leaving me in the dark with no way to call for help.

Looking around one last time in search of my coworkers, I saw no one. It became obvious that I'd have to do something as the bell rang again. My eyes caught on the gardening shed I passed on the way in. Walking back toward it, I didn't go out of my way to hurry. If they had been fine up until this point, it probably wasn't a matter of life or death.

Stopping at the shed, my eyes lowered to the handle. Yawning as I reached for it, my hand met the cool metal. To my dismay, it opened. Had it not, there was realistically nothing I could do. But now that it had and my eyes had met the shovel that sat within reach, I had literally no excuse. Taking the shovel, I dragged it behind me. As I approached the grave, pulling the shovel in front of me, the thought faintly crossed my mind that digging up a grave could be illegal. But as another ring took the air, a cloud floating in front of the moon, it didn't matter.

Lifting the shovel up, it was too dark without the moon to read the name on the headstone. I hesitated, the shovel hovering above the ground that had recently been broken, as I felt something ever so slightly stir inside. A moment later, I plunged the shovel into the ground. As mound after mound of dirt piled at my side, my athletic incompetence became readily evident.

My shovel hit something hard.

Staring at the shovel as my shortness of breath caught up with me, I tried not to cough.

That was an unusually shallow grave. As the handle reverberated, the clang stinging the palms of my hands all the way down to my bones, I stared at the damp dirt dancing with moonlight.

Losing my breath faster than I could catch it, I cleared the dirt from the lid of the mahogany casket and tossed the shovel to the side. I was barely able to wonder why the casket had only been buried a little over a foot under as my hand found its way to the side. Fingers meeting nothing more than a latch, I paused. Was it just not locked in any way at all? Pulling the latch, it clicked open. Hand lingering on the side of the door, I knew all it would take was a serious tug with great intent to free its captive.

The bell rang once more.

Eyes on the string that commanded the bell, I came to the idea that it resembled silver spider thread.

A gust brushed past my skin as I yanked the door open, the audible breaking of the airtight seal relieving to even I. and I wasn't the unlucky one suffocating. Falling dirt passed between us, obscuring the air in the moonlight as the lid fell to the side with a thud. Coughing met me from the casket, the dirt starting to settle, but still clouding my view. The first thing that broke through the haze was a glow, crimson like a fine wine, aged but robust.

Though I am unsure what I had expected to see in that casket, it wasn't a handsome young man. Sitting up, some dirt fell from his wavy, sun blonde locks and rolled down his toned figure, catching in the tasteful folds of his suit. One hand up to his mouth, the other wafting away the dirt, he coughed again, eyes closed beneath well-kept brows as he sat all the way up. As the cloud dissipated between us, he opened his eyes.

That glow I had caught moments before struck me again as the truest red I had ever seen emanated from his iris. Eyes wide, brows raised, he started to lower his hand from his mouth as it sat half-way to a smirk that appeared intended for someone else. As his eyes looked me up and down, I could see it, his disenchantment with me. He appeared to be expecting someone, and a young man in a bowtie probably wasn't them. But then, as his eyes finished tracing up my every line and landed on mine, it was as if something had lit in them as they glowed brighter, his smirk turning into a smile.

"It's you."

His voice was made of the sort of color one would expect to see in the fading lights of a forest fire, flecks of the vigor it once held shining through, but overall mellow and vibrant in its undertones.

Brow furrowed as I stared down at him, the last dirt particles catching in the moonlight as they fell between us, I realized I had seen him before. Though the newspaper claimed he was dead after jumping in front of that train, he most definitely wasn't.

I didn't know what to say, so I just extended my hand instead. Eyes lowering to it, his gaze held, his mouth slightly open, as if he wanted to say something but couldn't. Though just as quickly as he had been taken by that pause, alarm took its place. Looking around, he accepted my hand. The moment we made contact, the bell rang, trapping me in the beat. His sunny locks bounced with his movement, the red of his eyes reflecting off his wavy, middle-parted bangs. His skin warm on mine, it must have stung, making contact with someone as cold as me as I pulled him up. Feet meeting the grass, he straightened to be eye-level with me, perhaps an inch or so taller. Not a lot, but enough that if he wanted to lord it over me, he could.

His hand tightened on mine as I stood, staring up at him, the stars above growing a bit dimmer in comparison. Though I had never met him before, though we had never touched until that moment, his hand felt like home, and something in me didn't want to let go. When he smiled at me, his wavy blonde hair catching the moonlight, drifting about in the December breeze, I almost let his warmth taint my hand, but then I came about myself and yanked it away.

"You're not a zombie."

A light breath left him, turned up by his smile as he bent over a little to look me in the eye. "Why would you dig someone up if you were expecting a zombie?"

The way he spoke to me made me take a step back. It was as if he were speaking to an old friend, a closeness that I didn't consent to as his Brooklyn undertones ruled the moment. Eyes askance, I put another step's worth of space between us. "Perhaps I should put you back where I found you."

He laughed, but it was cut short when the air spiked cold.

Jumping, it was as if he too were looking for someone who hadn't arrived. Feverish, his scanning of the surrounding area was relentless.

"Man, do I love you, but you really have the worst timing." Looking back to me, his smile maintained despite the furrowing of his brow. "You need to get out of here before they show up. If they find you in this state, they'll-"

As if his words had already jinxed me, his eyes widened and a moment later, the sky turned purple. A swell of smog grew, pouring around us as the light of a single star pierced through the haze, warping. As if the air itself ripped, the screaming tear flattened the moment. The young man looked back to me, eyes scanning mine for the answer to a question I didn't even know. Though when they caught behind me, it appeared he had found it. When his hands made contact with me, spinning me around, my mind stalled and it took me far too long to realize I was falling. Landing in the casket, the air was knocked out of me. The door slammed on top of me, the creak ruled my world as I was plunged into darkness, coughing. A silver string was but a wisp above me in the few inches between the tip of my nose and the padding of the inside door.

Vibrations disturbed the casket, some dirt shaking loose from the lid. Placing my palm up against the padding above me, my vision crooked with my glasses, I could feel his warmth fading from my skin. A shock rattled the ground, shaking more dirt onto me, as if a shell had fallen from the sky. Pressing against the lid, I struggled with it. Had I been buried? The seal broke, air pouring in from the outside with a bit more dirt from the crack.

"Imprudent immortal," the world shook with the voice, so deep and muddy it was as if congealed the air, "you have gone too far this time."

"Really?" the young man I exhumed laughed, his nerves so visible from the darkness that I cringed a little, "I thought that one was pretty theatrical, all things considered. Though, the train did hurt like a-"

"How long do will you insist on doing this?" another voice said, one that rang in my ears. "Your search is futile, he is gone."

The zombie didn't reply.

Pushing up on the lid a little more, I tried to peek through the crack.

"Though your intentions are well-meaning, we can't watch you continue to do this to yourself," a third voice said, and though I understood it, something about it sounded backwards, as if it were echoing back into itself, "give up your search and return to Netherside."

"Now why would I do that?" the zombie said, his tone far too comfortable in the company of the others. "I'm having a grand time up here. And you sure do think you know everything, don't you?" He held the world hostage in his pause as I pushed up on the lid a little more, still unable to see anything over the dirt outside. "I will find him again. I've found him every time."

"If he is still walking among the Pulse, it will end the same. You heard his wish," the voice that shook the ground said, causing dirt to fall into the crack onto me.

"I don't care." The audacity of the zombie, it made me wonder if he was buried for a reason.

What sounded like a scoff boomed, shaking the ground further. "How can you say that-"

"There is no use trying to reason with him," the voice that rang cut them off, "he would rather suffer for all eternity than accept Nox's wish."

"Yeah, and I have more suffering to do," the zombie said, his pause filled with his footsteps, "so what do you want? It's an honor, a personal visit from The Three, but I am a busy man and I have lives to live and a king to find."

As I pushed the lid up more, slowly as to not make it creak, the scene playing above me started to come into view. The zombie's dress shoes stood, back to me, though I couldn't see the shoes of anyone else.

"We come with a word of warning," the backwards voice said as a shadow on the ground hovered closer to the zombie, "if Nox did manage to incarnate again, this one will be strong enough to destroy not only Flipside, but all of the realms."

"I know." The zombie took a half step back, his shoe not fully meeting the ground behind him. "Your point?"

"If we must, we will not hesitate to grant his wish in your stead," another shadow drifted toward him on the ground as the voice that rang went on, "we will not allow your biases to endanger the realms any longer. We are too invested in the characters this time to let you ruin it for us."

"If the last incarnation didn't banish himself," a third shadow cornered him as the deep voice shook more dirt free, "we will."

When the zombie's shoes were yanked up from the ground, he choked, dangling there, though he didn't struggle. His voice was strained but I could still hear it, his smile. "Not if I find him first."

"What do you think you can possibly do that you haven't already done?" The ringing voice may have laughed, I wasn't sure. "You've had tens of opportunities and you have failed him each and every one."

That's when the zombie started to struggle, a word trying to escape him, but it was choked out.

"Your selfishness will bring him nothing but suffering." the backwards voice said, the darkness outside growing darker.

Any fleeting hope that this was simply a prank was suffocated when a cough attempted to conquer me. Free hand flying to my mouth, eyes shut, I fought to uphold my silence. A flash of light bleached through my closed eyes, the air burning in my lungs as a sharp chill stung my every inch. An explosion blew the door of the casket open, though the dirt thrown into the air drowned out my sight as my eyes opened.

"If you love Nox, let him rest."

The deep booming voice faded as a shadow darkened the dirt in the air above me, obstructing the moonlight. As it grew closer, it took a form. Breaking through the dirt, I only saw him for a moment, the young man coming crashing toward me. Tie flailing out to the side, wavy hair suspended in the fall, the glass in his crimson eyes reflected their glow as they met mine.

Crashing into me, the impact knocked the air from my lungs, my ears deafened by the cracking of wood as the casket gave from behind me. Sweeping suction, a rush of cold, it culminated to the shattering of something as I fell back. Dropping through the hole we created in the back of the casket, where I had expected to meet the dirt, I was met by nothing. Free fall took me as I dropped. Tumbling through clouds, I had just been in the ground and now I was in the sky. Shattered shards of wood fell between us as the young man struggled in the air above me, a hole in the sky behind him.

Teeth grit, brow furrowed, his hair blown back, he reached for me. Passing through another cloud, I was blinded by it. His hand missed me as we fell, air ripping by us with such force that I couldn't breathe. Crashing through another cloud, it turned purple in the impact before fading away in the dark sky behind him. Reaching out again, he dropped in the sky above, his hand meeting mine. Pulling me up into him, the zombie wrapped his arms around me. Trapped in an embrace, despite the air that tore over my every inch leaving me with a profound chill, he was warm.

Though we were falling, in that moment, I was suspended in a sky full of stars.

My heart probably would have jumped, if it were capable.

Turning us around, he pulled himself below me. As the wind crashed into my face, eyes watering behind my crooked glasses barely hanging on, I saw the quickly approaching ground. A castle in the distance, a surrounding town expanding out until it disappeared into hazy obscurity, the structures were black, the stone shimmering, the sky without a moon. Stacks leaked smoke into the air, the tallest tower of the castle touching the sky, embedded beyond it.

His arms tightened around me as he buried his head into my shoulder.

My eyes met with the impending ground.

We were about to die.

Crashing into brick, skidding, we brought up dirt as we tore through the ground like falling space debris. Tumbling, catching on stone and soil, we slowly came to a stop. The momentum dissipated, leaving numbness in its wake as dirt hung in the air around us. Ears ringing, laying on his chest, my glasses nearly knocked from my face, my vision came back into focus. A cough came from below me. Arms shaking, I pushed myself up. Palm meeting something wet and warm, my eyes dropped to the ground.

Blood.

Sitting up, I looked down to the young man laying in the crater below me. Messy bangs obstructing his eyes, black blood poured from his hairline, pooling around us. Dust started to settle as I stared down at him, vision blurring in and out of focus, black blood dripping down my arm from my hand. Pulling myself off him, I knelt in the blood at his side as shadows started to obstruct the dust around us. Murmurs grew, as did the numbers of shadows.

Coughing, a smile found its way back to his face as the zombie opened his eyes, glowing from under his disheveled hair. Shaking as he sat up, blood poured down the side of his face, staining the white shirt under his blazer as his hand came to his head. Running it back through his hair, he pulled it out of his face, his raised brow bringing life to his tattered features.

"Welcome back."

Opening my mouth to take a breath, I was about to ask him if he was alright when my heart thumped so hard, it sent a jolt through me. Chest seizing, ears ringing, my lungs caught fire as I doubled over on my knees, coughing. A hand on my back brought warmth to me but I couldn't hear what he said as numbness raced through me, hands up to my mouth as I choked on the air. Each breath left me emptier than the last, taking some of my consciousness with it.

I didn't feel it when I hit the ground.

Eyes opening, it was as if I had blinked. Surrounded by white as far as I could see, the space I stood in had no beginning or end, an abyss. Taking a breath, I ran my hand through my hair, staring forward through my glasses. The eternal white, while objectively intimidating, inspired no such rise in me, as if I had been there before. Something shifted behind me. Turning around, my eyes met with another. Scruffy white hair, his back was to me as he stood but a step away. As he turned, my eyes met with a notebook in his hand, his other paused in writing with a feather quill. As my gaze drifted up a white, bellowing poet shirt, the line of his jaw led my eyes up to his face, drifting over his frown on the way. But before they made contact with his eyes, I blinked and everything went black.

The first thing I felt was a warmth on my chest, alleviating the burning in my lungs. Laying somewhere hard, my senses slowly started to dull back into my world. A faint yellow met me through my closed eyes as that warmth spread from my lungs to my throat. Mind spinning, it tried to pull anything into focus.

"I don't know why this is happening," the zombie's voice broke through the ringing in my ears, dull and muffled at first until my hearing regained its clarity as he went on, "his powers should counteract the effects of being down here, they always have before."

"Are you sure it's him?" A feminine voice said, directly next to me as the sensation of a hand on my chest came to me, "I know you've never been wrong, but something feels off about him and he's way older than the others were. They have never made it this far before-"

"It's him," the zombie said, cutting her off, a light jingle of a wind chime filling the beat, "I know it. Though you're right, there must be a reason. Maybe they're repressed and that's why he's being poisoned." He paused, the creak of a chair filling the moment. "But the powers were emotion based. There's no way he doesn't feel anything, right?"

"I sense nothing in him," the feminine voice said, the swell of her accent pulsing on the vowels, "I've never felt someone so completely still before. Something must have happened that sealed his emotions off." When she paused, so did the warmth emanating into my chest. "But if it is him, what are you going to do? You know what he wants."

"I won't do it." The young man's voice was almost unrecognizable, the spark in it had gone out. "I'll find another way."

"There is no other way, we have to-"

Eyes opening, I tried to tame the dizziness my mind had cast upon me. A blurry ceiling met me, my glasses absent as my eyes fought to stay open.

"Oh hey," the zombie said, his voice lighting up again as he sat, a blur moving in my vision, "I hope you're alright."

Cool metal found the sides of my face, meeting the bridge of my nose as my glasses were slid back into place. The first thing my world zeroed in on were his eyes. I never really thought much on colors, as they had never stood out to me. But there was definitely something to be said about crimson. Scuffed up, he didn't appear to be bleeding any longer, though the stain remained on the collar of his button down. Disheveled hair falling forward from where it had been brushed back, he stood at my bedside, smiling down at me.

Trying to sit up, a hand shoved me back down and that's when my world expanded to hold the young lady sitting directly at my other side. Hair nauseatingly yellow, like a highlighter, eyes a disturbed communion of orange and green like a molding pumpkin, her rainbow painted, lengthy nails dug into the fine fabric of my shirt as her glare tightened.

I blinked at her, squinting a bit as my senses were assaulted by her loud color scheme.

With an eye roll, she released the pressure and ran her free fingers through her voluminous, bluntly cut hair. "If you want to live, I'd suggest staying down." Her other hand pressed down on my chest and a moment later a dull yellow glow grew from it, the light traveling through my blood as it made it easier to breathe. I stared at the glow, wondering if I had fallen asleep in the graveyard waiting for my coworkers to come running from the shadows in sheets.

Shifting into my view, the zombie leaned over to be closer to me. "How do you feel?"

Taking a shaking breath, I couldn't look away from him. "I think I'm alright, though." I looked him up and down, every fold of fabric complementing his form. "Are you? You were bleeding."

"Oh me?" He straightened, smiling as he pocketed his hands, "I'm fine. Hurt like hell, but I can't die, so it's whatever."

About to ask him what he meant, a sizzling made the young lady jump. Stiffly moving my head to the side, I took in the room. Floating colorful orbs meandered about, their glows reflecting off the stone walls and the glass of display cases. Their shelves were home to jars of eyes, mice, and other indeterminate items suspended in vaguely yellow liquid. Faint meows made their muffled way from a door across the small room left ajar, a shattered mirror the only thing I could see through the crack. A cauldron boiled over behind the young lady, its contents sliding over the rim and down its bulbous body until vaporizing upon its marriage with the rainbow fire below. Colors weaving around one another as the flame burned, I watched as the young lady wove her hand near it and the flames shrunk.

Sighing, she turned back to face me, the clean cut line of her bobbed hair so sharp it could have probably sliced me. "You have some nerve, coming back again after what you put us through last time. You really need to have the decency to just banish yourself already."

My words died in my throat, because even though I had no idea who she was, something about the way she said that made me feel as if I deserved to be scolded.

"What's your name this time?" The zombie said, sitting down on the foot of my bed, arms crossed over his chest, head tilted, smile the brightest thing in the dimly lit room.

Staring up at him and the colorful orbs that floated around behind him, the bubbling of the cauldron filled the beat. Eyes dropping to my nametag, I wondered if he could read. Shaking, my arm lifted up from my side, his black blood staining my sleeve. "Igor Francis."

"Igor?" He laughed, eyes dropping to my extended hand, "I haven't heard that name in a hundred years." Uncrossing his arms, he took my hand, his grip stronger than I had anticipated. "Cyrus Glory, I'd say it's nice to meet you, but we've met many times before, so," tilting his head, some of his wavy hair spilled over as the excitement in his voice calmed into warmth, "it's nice to see you again."

Hand lingering in his, my senses settled back into my skin, my mind slowing down in the beat. And though I tried to make sense of it all, the string of events that led me to that bed, as my brow furrowed, gaze narrowing on him, I couldn't.

"You don't know that," the young lady said, taking her hand from my chest. "And for his sake, we can only hope that it's not him."

The moment her hand left, cold raced through me, and when it made it to my heart, it exploded over my entire body, lungs burning. Sitting up, coughing, I brought my hands to my mouth, shoulders tense as I tried to stop.

"And besides, if it were him, this wouldn't happen." She put her hand on my shoulder and a moment later her warmth washed over me, calming the fit that had taken my body. "He must be a regular Pulse, he's not supposed to be here." Looking back to Cyrus, her hair sliced the air with the movement. "You have to take him back." When Cyrus didn't reply, she just sighed, though it didn't sound out of exasperation, it was sharper than that as her eyes returned to mine, searching them. "Maybe he really did get his wish with the last one."

"Say, Igor," Cyrus said, disregarding her entirely, "do weird things happen around you a lot?"

I was about to shake my head no, eyes unable to look away from his as they stared into me, expectantly, but the floating orbs of light around us flashed red so brightly, it washed everything else out for a moment.

As the light faded away, Cyrus came back into my vision. Reeling from the flash, he looked around at the orbs for a moment before a smile look him and he looked to the young lady. "There's only one way to know for sure."

"No." she stood, though she kept her hand on my shoulder. "You can't take him to the castle."

"Why is that, Valor?" Cyrus stood from the bed, walking around it. "I know you're a competent witch, you could absolutely make a charm that would last long enough." Taking his blazer up from a chair behind Valor, he tossed it over his shoulder. "And if it's not him then I'll take the gate back with him and I'll be out of your hair until I get in trouble again."

Standing there, nails digging into my shoulder, Valor said nothing, jaw tight.

Clearing my throat, I gathered their attention, startling them as if they were so busy talking about me that they had forgotten that I was there. "I'm sorry to interrupt, but I think you may have the wrong person." My eyes drifted away from the floating orbs to Cyrus. "I've never met you before, nor do I have any idea what you two are talking about." Looking down to my watch, I was thankful that it didn't crack in the fall. "I'm not sure what's going on or where I am, but I have a shift that I can't miss soon, so I'd like to get back."

"A…" Cyrus turned to fully face me, his smile fading. "Shift?"

"Yes." I straightened my bow tie. "I work in retail, and we are understaffed." Standing from the bed, I swayed a little but caught myself, Valor's hand remaining on my shoulder. "If I no-call no-show they'll probably burn the store down without me."

Staring at me, the two stood in silence.

This had to be a dream. I must have been sitting, back up against some headstone in the graveyard, asleep. It was unusual though, I had never had a lucid dream before, or a dream so creative. I could only hope that I'd remember it when I woke so I could write it down,. It had the beginnings of a good story.

"You're a bit," Cyrus said, smiling again as he shifted his weight, "blasé about this whole thing."

"Well." I pocketed my hands, looking back to Valor's hand on my shoulder, a yellow light emanating from it. "This is a dream."

Cyrus blinked at me.

About to open his mouth to say something, he was cut off by Valor. "That's right, this is all a dream." She yanked me with her, causing me to stumble across the room as she approached a wardrobe next to the cabinet of jars. Opening it with her free hand, grip tight on my shoulder, she looked over a collection of cloaks and jewelry that hung inside.

Plucking a ring from a tray of them, she closed it in her fist. Turning to me as her fist began to glow, her intense eyes locked on mine. "Now take this ring and don't take it off until you're back home." Opening her fist, she extended it to me, the simple silver banded ring emanating a slight glow sitting in it as she looked behind me. "He'll take you to the gate and then you'll wake up and forget this ever happened."

Accepting the ring, I looked down to it before looking back up to Cyrus. He stood there, brow lowered, annoyance evident on his features despite his smile remaining, though it was sharper than it had been before, clipping his tone. "Valor, don't be this way."

Sliding the ring on, the moment it met the base of my finger yellow deposited in me, making my next breath less labored. Shoving me with her hand on my shoulder, Valor sent me stumbling across the room toward Cyrus. Catching myself, I straightened, a few steps away from him as I looked back to her as she turned away from us.

"That's not him, he must have destroyed himself the last time. You need to take this poor Pulse home, he has nothing to do with this." Starting for the door that sat, slightly ajar, she pulled it open, her back to us. "He's gone, Cyrus. That's what he wanted. You should be happy for him."

Cyrus' breath hitched as he stood, unmoving at my side.

"You know what the last incarnation said." Stepping into the door, her hand lingered on the knob. "Get over it already."

Slamming the door between us, she left Cyrus and I in silence.

I slowly looked over to him to see him just standing there, staring at the door, expression frozen in place.

Laughing, he broke it as he pivoted around, hand reaching for the other door on the wall behind him. "Don't mind her, she's actually pretty nice, she's just mad at you."

Turning, my eyes met his back as his hand landed on the doorknob. Though this was a dream and I couldn't have cared any less as I just killed time until I woke, I supposed it wouldn't hurt anything to play along. Walking up a step behind him, my eyes drifted back over the room. "Why?"

Pausing at the door, he didn't turn to face me. "I can't blame her, I'm a little mad at you too." Opening the door, he didn't pull it all the way. "But it's alright, we can talk about that later after we know for sure."

When the door opened, a town square met my eyes. Bustling, figures rushed past one another, a fountain spewing silver colored liquid sitting in the heart of merchant booths. The hum of conversation and the light music of buskers met my ears as a cool front brushed in with the air. The aroma of flowers took my senses, so sweet it felt sad.

Lifting his head, he looked to me from over his shoulder. "Welcome to Netherside."

Stepping outside, I followed him. Shoes meeting the brick street below as the door closed behind me, I looked around at the passing figures. People who looked more avian than human, with feathers for hair, passed us by as they chirped in what sounded like laughter. Staring at them as they walked along, I wondered where all this creativity was when I was awake.

A hand met my wrist, pulling me forward. Gaze jerked back to Cyrus, my eyes were suck to the back of his head as he dragged us through the crowd, weaving around others. Nearly crashing into someone as they raced by us, I only caught a brief glimpse of them, but that was all it took to see that they were covered in scales. Rounding a corner, we stepped onto a sidewalk of amethyst tiles. Leaving the populated square, we entered a calmer street, lined with shops. I looked into the windows as we passed, trying to take it all in. Hats floated in one, another displayed shirts with six sleeves. As we passed one window after another, I was met with flying books, bubbling potions, wands, swords, and cloaks, as I glanced into each sliver of world.

Suddenly coming to a stop, I stumbled into Cyrus' back. I was about to ask him what happened when my breath was stolen from me. Staring up, I watched as a horse drawn carriage made of smoke passed us, the horse without its head. Pulling me across the street with him, a step behind him, my eyes locked on the carriage. Someone sat inside, long snowy blonde hair spilling over their shoulders clad in a fine black vest decorated in a deep emerald velvet pattern, a cream ruffled jabot rested on their chest, boasting a matching viridescent brooch. Their eyes glowed green as they read a book in the cabin, face propped up on their hand, elbow on the windowsill. The embodiment of elegance, I only saw them for a matter of moments, but I don't think I'd ever forget them, even when I woke.

"Who was that?"

"They have gone by many names, and surely will go by many more. But as of now, they're Finnegan van Serifino." The way he said that name, he made it sound like much more than just a name. "A vampire…" we stepped up on the sidewalk as he glanced over to the carriage. "And someone I would like to avoid."

A vampire? I stared at the carriage. Listening to my little brother ramble about vampires had finally made its way into my dreams. As we stepped into the shadow of a building, the castle started to grow closer before us. "Why would you want to avoid them?"

A light laugh took him as he looked to me. "When you've been around as long as I have, you tend to, uh." He looked away, "make rounds, a few too many times, if you uh, know what I- anyway." He paused far longer than would normally be called for. "Vampires are just a whole thing, never sure if you can trust them. And nobody knows how to kill 'em, either, a well-kept secret, I guess. Though we both can live forever, they bite people about it, and I don't like that."

Though there was no visible source of light above, the entire area glowed, a lively hum lacing the air. For a dream, it really engaged my every sense.

As the carriage left my sight, continuing down the path, I looked back to him. "You called this place Netherside?"

Grip tightening on my wrist, I saw him flash a smile before he turned forward again, a spring to his step. "Yup." We were met with a staircase winding around dark bark trees, leaves purple as they loomed above us like a canopy. "There are several realms." Starting up the stairs, he didn't let go of me, an underlying urgency to his every step, "There's Flipside, that's where you're from, and Limbo, both in the middle. Above is Upside and we're below in Netherside." Reaching the top of the stairs, I was out of breath, but he didn't stop, dragging me toward the castle as it grew against the sky in front of us, but a few blocks of shops between us. "Netherside was created by the true king when he wished for somewhere all us magic folk could be safe, since it is so dangerous for us Flipside. A nefarious little snow globe of a world, it is perpetuated by the power of the king. Though, the current one is just a proxy while we wait for the person who was always intended to wear the crown."

Rounding another corner, his every step sped up, starting to leave me behind but dragging me all the same. "While powerful, the current king is just barely able to maintain the realm." We started across another street. "If he falters even a little, the realm may collapse, and since we're on the bottom, the rest will fall with it." Cyrus gestured to the sky. "And like, nobody really vibes with him, either, so it would be rad to dethrone him."

Looking up to the sky, I had never once considered that it could fall. "Where is the one you believe to be better suited?"

"Missing, but." He looked back to me, eyeing me up and down. "I've been looking for him. Though," he laughed, looking away, "some people believe he's gone forever and that my search is pointless."

I was never one for movies, lacking the suspension of disbelief required to take the fantastical seriously. Nothing had changed, though the way Cyrus spoke threatened to paint pictures in my mind, almost causing me to forget that this was all a dream as I followed a bit closer behind him. "What happened to him?"

"I'm not sure." As we crossed the last street between us and the castle, he came to a stop. After a moment of pause, he looked away from me. "I know he died, but somehow, he keeps coming back, over and over, trapped in a cycle of reincarnation." Eyes holding on the swirling sky above, they narrowed. "He was profoundly powerful in his first life, and with every new incarnation, his powers only grows, so much so that his body can't contain them and they, inevitably, destroy him just for him to come back and go through it all again." Bringing up his other hand, he raked it through his shimmering locks, eyes drifting down. "It's like they grow exponentially, but whether is because the older his powers become, the stronger they become, or if his soul is picking out people who were already to be born a witch to reincarnate with and he's just collecting their powers too, I haven't been able to figure out, but, I do know one thing." A clump of hair fell over his forehead from between his fingers. "None of his incarnations live past twenty, the age he was when he died originally. Each one dies a little younger, the last one didn't even make it past ten." Looking to me, he raised a brow. "How old are you?"

"Twenty-four."

The spark that lit in his eyes, it made the depth of his crimson swirl as he dropped his hand from his hair. Turning back toward the castle, he looked up to it. "Is that right?" A beat floated between us, faintly filled with chimes and the muffled sounds of the town behind us. Looking over to me, his hair fell back down and over his face a bit, obstructing one of his eyes, "You're pretty levelheaded, aren't ya?"

"I suppose that's one way to put it." I looked away from him and toward the castle, wondering how long this dream was going to drag on. It wasn't all that tall, not as tall as a castle ought to be. But upon inspecting the tallest tower, I watched the way the darkness above flowed around its point, breaking the sky. That wasn't a compliment to the castle, but a disservice to the sky that was so low a mere tower could scrape it. "Some would suggest that my apathy is a shortcoming."

"A shortcoming?" Cyrus' grip tightened. "I disagree."

Eyes lowering from the castle, they met with the moat that surrounded it, a few steps before us. Silver liquid similar to what came from the fountain in the square sloshed around, viscous and thick, it shimmered like mercury but moved like molasses. Grinding took the air, metal groaning as the drawbridge began to lower. It was profound, the fact that even in my dreams, the most fantastical couldn't move me. Watching the dark wood lower, the chains clinking as it did, I didn't look to Cyrus as I spoke.

"Why?"

He looked over to me. "Why what?"

The drawbridge met the ground, throwing up dust in the impact.

"Why isn't it a shortcoming?"

"Oh," he laughed, pulling me along with him toward the lowered bridge. Our shoes left hollow thuds behind us as we crossed over the silver moat, "feelings are the worst, real dangerous."

Stepping off the drawbridge and onto the path on the other side, we passed under a gate. Two statues that stood guard on either side bowed to us, the creaking of stone taking the air. Staring up at them, I stopped for a second before I was pulled forward. Entering a courtyard, hip level square hedges lined our way, the black leaves shifting about despite the air being still. The grass was well kept, lined with purple glowing flowers that were the source of the sad, sweet scent. My steps struggled, getting snagged a bit more with each one. Looking down, I watched the blades of grass slither onto my shoes, grasping on and fighting with me as I tried to step away. Yanking my shoes up, I stumbled onto the path below the outer ring of the castle, a half-inside hallway surrounding the courtyard.

"Okay, so here's the plan," Cyrus said, grip firm on my wrist, other hand in his pocket, his white button-down still stained in his black blood as his wavy blonde hair brightened even the shadows we stood in. "I'm going to request passage through the gate to take you back Flipside. In the same chamber that the gate lives in, there is an artifact that I'd like you to take a look at." Looking over his shoulder as distant voices echoed down the hall, his gaze narrowed. "Leave the talking to me. We don't want the king to get suspicious." He looked back to me. "It's technically a capital offense, bringing a Pulse down here. And while it wasn't my fault, they'll blame me anyway."

"Correct me if I'm wrong." He pulled me behind him down the corridor. "But didn't you say something earlier about being unable to die? Why do you care about capital punishment?"

"You're observant." Smiling at me over his shoulder, he exercised caution before taking me around the corner with him. "While I am but a simple Immortal who can't die, they could banish me. A fate worse than death, no one knows

what is beyond banishment, but it is considered the greatest

ultimate end."

Entering a grand hall, stained glass climbed the

cathedral like stone walls of the castle, light pouring in them

despite there being no sun in the sky outside. Our steps

echoed as we walked down the middle of the vast room,

purple velvet carpet beneath us, running tables piled with

food at our sides, glowing orbs floating above. There was so

much air in there that it was suffocating.

Meeting steps like an altar, we climbed them and

were met with a door so large, I couldn't imagine how it

would even open. It must have been fifty feet tall, reaching

all the way to the top of the vaulted ceiling. Free hand

meeting the wood, Cyrus smiled as the door flashed red.

Creaking, the door slowly opened, having to push against all

the air in the room to do so. The creak was so loud that its

echo echoed as Cyrus took a step back, taking me with him

as he looked up and watched. Eyes lowering from the door,

they met the young man at my side. What was it like, to be able to smile like that? I was busy staring at him as he stared up, maybe that's why we didn't notice the man until he spoke.

"Cyrus?"

Though he didn't jump, his grip tightened for a second. Slowly looking down, Cyrus' smile was unfading, though I could tell that his eyes no longer were. Following his gaze, I saw him, the owner of that exuberant voice. A man of bright colors and well-kept graying hair, his tie was that of a thrift store that was abandoned for a reason, his blazer boasting a clashing pattern. A rosary around his neck, its black beads stood out against his pastel button down as the silver crucifix caught in the light when he shifted. The sort of man that would come into my store and proudly embarrass his teenage daughter with inappropriate comments about her figure, he already grit on me and he had said all of one word.

His footsteps made no sound as he approached. "I heard that you had a run-in with The Three, are you already heading back Flipside?" Slinging his arm roughly around Cyrus, he yanked him about with a full-bodied laugh, breaking his grip on me. "It's like you want to be banished or something."

When he laughed, it sounded like a laugh track, a combination of tens of laughs, warped as they all came from one man.

Ducking out from his grip, a nervous laugh oddly placed on his breath, Cyrus turned around to look at me. "Yeah well, I have some business to take care of, King Anton."

My eyes slowly drifted from Cyrus to the man. The King of Netherside looked like a used car salesman? A realm of misfit creatures and magic, I guess the ruler was no exception. But I suppose I had expected him to be some wizard or something, I don't know. Anything more interesting than just a creepy man. And hadn't Cyrus said something about him being powerful enough to sustain the entire realm? He didn't seem capable of that.

My eyes drifted to Anton's.

I heard my heartbeat in my ears when his eyes locked on mine.

They were so black, they swallowed the light. A slight smile found him, but I only saw it for a moment before his gaze returned to Cyrus. Reaching for his head, Cyrus managed to avoid the King as he stepped back to my side.

"I want to request passage through the castle gate." Cyrus took my hand in his, not my wrist, as he turned to look at the King. "If you'd excuse us."

Dragging me forward, Cyrus' grip iron, I could feel it, or rather, I couldn't. There was an absence of something, easily missed if you were to get caught up in his warmth. He didn't have a pulse.

"Why are you boys in such a rush?" The volume of the King's friendly tone made it far more threatening as he followed us into the round chamber. "I haven't seen you in decades, and you can't even stay to catch up?"

Standing beneath a stained-glass dome, tapestries surrounded us on the walls. They depicted angels and demons, transparent people and dragons, forms made of static and hooded beings, they must have detailed an epic tale. Before us stood a metal garden gate, the woven rods rusted but still standing. The craftsmanship that of an expert with a liking for flowers, they sat about, wrapped out of metal on the handle of the gate. Below the tapestry, behind the free-standing gate was a pedestal, something siting on it, too small and far away for me to see clearly.

"I apologize, King Anton." Cyrus stared forward, not at the gate, but at what was beyond it. "But I'll come visit soon and this time, I'll stay." Looking over his shoulder, he smiled at the King. "I promise."

The King stood, his figure that of someone who enjoyed the spoils that came with a position of power as he propped his hands on his hips, huffing. "I get lonely you know, the least you could do is come to the ball tomorrow night. If you attend, Finnegan will too, and I'm sure they'd give you a warm welcome, y'know, in the way that they do."

Cyrus didn't reply, his back to the king.

Turning, Anton started for the door, his shoes hitting the floor hard but still making no sound. Stopping in the door, his hand met it, turning it black as he glanced over to us, his tone smiling but his face flat. "Careful with that one there, boy, Cyrus is trouble."

The door closed with a thundering thud, shaking the entire room and leaving us in silence.

Scoffing, Cyrus rolled his eyes away from the door. "I thought he'd never leave." Yanking me forward, he took us around the gate and toward the pedestal. "This is what I wanted to show you."

Sitting on the pedestal was a silver, circular brooch resting on a velvet pillow, the sole subject of a precise, black spotlight. Gems embedded into sections on its silver base, they surrounded a star shaped center stone. All of the gems were clear, though not like diamonds, but as if the color had been drained from them.

Letting go of me, Cyrus brought his hand up to the brooch but hesitated before touching it, "This is the artifact that he left behind, the true king." Looking up to me, his hair was darkened by the spotlight, "He was a witch named Nox, hanged by a wicked holy man over six-hundred years ago. Perhaps the most powerful being to ever be, he belongs here, the ruler of Netherside." Placing the pad of his finger on the brooch, nothing happened, "He owned this in life, a gift forged specifically to funnel his powers, it will only react to him. It just sits here, waiting for its owner to come and claim it, to come back and save Netherside from collapsing." Picking his finger up, he looked to me, "Isn't that cool?"

As I looked down to the little brooch, something about it felt familiar. Perhaps we had sold one like that in my store. Or maybe it was the story that felt like an old friend, reminding me of one my Mum used to tell me as a child. Though it was faded in my memory, the more Cyrus spoke about it, the more I heard his words in her voice. Perhaps it was my subconscious trying to remember what she had said, as if it were important. Dreams were like that sometimes, I suppose. Bringing my arm up, I looked to my watch, "As interesting as this dream has been, I really should be waking any time now."

Standing there, smile frozen on his face, Cyrus visibly deflated, "Do you really think this is a dream?"

"Of course," I lowered my arm pocketing my hand as I shifted my weight, "while it is unusually vivid and creative for me, it is likely the result of falling asleep outside in December and being too cold." Looking up around the dome, I stepped back a bit, "Though it is really something, this whole world. My mind doesn't usually conjure up images so…" my eyes drifted back to him, "enticing."

Sighing, Cyrus ran his hand through his hair, one wavy lock falling through his fingers, "Would you still be this coy if this weren't a dream?"

"Probably," I forced my eyes away from the way the colorful light caught on his hair as I shifted my weight, "work in retail long enough, nothing really phases you anymore."

Hand dragging from his hair over his face, his impatience was palpable as he studied me. Heart on his sleeve, he was like an open book. As quickly as his annoyance had painted him, it snapped back into a smile, his eyes lighting up as he dropped his hand, gesturing to the brooch, "You're right, you have been asleep, and it is time to wake up. All you have to do is pick up this brooch, then you'll wake, and this time," his eyes searched mine, his brow lowering just enough to give way to something behind his smile, "this time I'll save you."

Staring back at him, something in the back of my mind itched, as if I had seen this sight before. Eyes lowering from him to the brooch, my gaze rested on it. Stepping forward toward the podium, I glanced back up to Cyrus, his white shirt purple in the black light above. "Why didn't you say that first?"

Looking away, he lowered his hand, "I did."

As I brought my hand up, I reflected on the dream. Exhuming a handsome young movie star of a man from a shallow grave, free falling into a realm of magic, I met a witch, crossed paths with hybrids, and witnessed a vampire. If something that exciting couldn't get a rise out of me, well…

My eyes met with Cyrus.

I guess nothing could. As he smiled at me, a part of me didn't want to touch the brooch. Because when I did, I'd wake and never see him again. And while I knew he was but a figment of my imagination, my brain simply processing the headline I read earlier, there was something interesting about the way he wore colors on his features.

When the pad of my finger met the middle of the brooch, it lit up.

I only saw it for a moment, the way Cyrus looked at me, glass in his eyes, smile taking him, before lights exploded from the brooch, blinding me in colors. Unable to yank my hand back, my body locked up as the lights spun around me, creating a tornado of muddled rainbows. Mixing until they turned into a messy brown, they sped up, blowing my hair around. The ground shook and as it cracked beneath my shoes, I wondered what it would take to make me feel anything if something like this wasn't enough. Even though it was a dream, it didn't feel like it.

Closing in on me, the vortex of messy colors collapsed, turning my world black.

The last thing I felt was the brooch, its cool gem pressed against my fingertip.

three

Orange

I could still feel it, the water dripping down my arms, the sting of broken glass.

I could see it, the overwhelming richness of red as it dripped to the carpet, her lifeless body in my hands. I could hear them, the yells, my sobs, my mother's calming voice, it was all so long ago but felt just a moment behind me. She was so cold as she died, the water staining my pants as I knelt, holding her.

Margo.

Her name was soft yellow, one that would greet you at the budding of spring.

A wall between us, I could never fully reach out and embrace her, not until the end.

Grass tickled the back of my neck, the first sensation to return to me. The next was a tightness. A shaking breath took me, fighting on the way down. Cawing of December birds met my ears, bringing the world back in around me. Eyes barely able to open, they were met with the muted winter sky. Hand shaking as I raised it from my side, it met with my shirt collar. Why was it so tight?

Sitting up, my body creaked despite my youth. Glasses sliding down my numb nose, I was too cold to shiver. Crossing my arms over my chest, I looked around. Met by rows of headstones, they stretched over the horizon, dew clinging to the stone. Hand finding the ground behind me to steady myself as blood dropped from my head, it was met with recently disturbed dirt. Turning, I stared at the headstone I laid beneath.

Cyrus Glory.

What an obnoxious name.

Struggling to stand, I yawned, cold body fighting the whole way. As I stood, something felt off. Hand meeting my bow tie, I paused. It felt tighter, too heavy around my neck. Taking out my phone, I tried to unlock it to get to the camera, but its battery had died. Staring at myself in the reflection of the darkened screen, my eyes met my bow tie. As if it had been restored to new, the silk of its fabric felt more like the cape of a wizard than my retail uniform. Though that was strange, the most peculiar thing about it was the brooch that now sat in the middle, making a home on the knot. Small and dull, it was made up of several grey gems surrounding a darkened star, embedded in silver. Fit for a king, it was something I'd definitely remember putting on, however, I did not.

There was something else I didn't remember. Looking around at the graveyard, I lowered my hands to my pockets. Why was I here? Heading forward, back to the headstone I had woken beneath, I shivered, starting to warm a bit. Maybe I'd be able to remember once I got home. With each step, my body came alive, as if I had been dead on my feet before. Nothing ached, not even my feet after working nine days in a row. Taking a breath, my exhale made a cloud in front of my face. Meeting the cemetery gate, I looked up to it.

"Igor!"

Stopping mid-step, a voice echoed out behind me, one so warm, it made me forget how cold I was as I turned. Running up to me, a young man stopped, not out of breath despite the fact that he must have sprinted there. Wavy blonde hair glistened in the morning light, casting soft shadows onto his lightly freckled skin as his raised brow and smile animated him. Though he looked flawless at first glance, as my eyes took him in, I saw the tattering around the edges, the dark stain on his wrinkled button down beneath a torn-up blazer. The crimson of his eyes as they locked on mine lit a match in my mind, the flame catching on the corner of the haze that had taken it. As the fog ignited and burned away, a clear image pulled into focus.

"Cyrus?"

Nodding, he raised his hand up, running in through his movie star hair, "Yeah, are you alright? I stepped away and when I came back, you were gone."

Taking a step away from him, images raced back in waves, exploding in my mind. An exhumed immortal, falling from the sky, a whole different world full of mythic people, it couldn't be real. It all culminated, overwhelming me until one last thing took over my senses: the ring of a bell. Static drowned out my thoughts as I stared at him and his glowing red eyes. He was an untrue statement, an impossibility. But there he stood, smiling before me. Staring at him, I waited. This was where I cared, where a rise bubbled up inside me, where I felt something, anything. When nothing came, not even the smallest twinge of surprise in my chest, my eyes drifted away.

The impossible had become possible right before my very eyes and yet, I couldn't be bothered.

"It wasn't a dream?"

Laughing, it was too damn early for Cyrus to be so energetic, "Yeah, but it's a dream come true," stepping closer to me, his eyes dropped to my bow tie, "I knew it was you."

Staring down at his mop of golden hair, I thought back, wading through hazy memories to no avail, "What do you mean?"

Straightening, his eyes locked on mine, a smile taking him as he stood, a step and a half too close, "I've been looking for you." Bringing up his hand, his finger extended toward my neck, hovering a moment away, "Remember what I said?"

Bringing up my hand to push his back, my eyes caught on my watch before I could. Eyes wide for a moment, I lowered my hand and turned from him. "I have to get home before my next shift."

Walking from him, I left Cyrus below the gates of the cemetery and the way he looked at me as I turned made it look like I had left him at the altar. I almost thought he wasn't going to follow me until his racing footsteps came stumbling from behind on the sidewalk. Nearly falling over himself, he stopped at my side.

"Your shift? Igor, you can't be serious."

Continuing on my way, I was thankful that the walk home was short as I didn't reply. Maybe he'd just go hop back into that grave where he came from.

A groan escaped him as he bent over to catch my gaze but I looked away, "You have to come back to Netherside with me." Extending his hand to me, he tilted his head, his hair catching the light, "I can teleport us there, just take my hand."

"I politely decline," I dug my keys from my pocket, turning down the street to my house, "but thank you for the offer."

Cyrus stopped, and I had hoped he'd stay that way until he came barreling to my side again, walking backwards to face me, "You can't just refuse, you have a crown to claim."

Though I felt nothing, that did make me stop walking in my driveway, "What?"

Stopping, he extended his finger out towards me again, "Do you not remember what I said about that brooch?"

Slowly bringing my dead phone from my pocket, I looked to my reflection in it, the brooch on my bow tie catching my eye. Staring at it, my eyes widened, only a bit, as hazy words resurrected in my mind.

"Yeah," Cyrus said, his suit, while well fitting, started to look a little silly on him as he sighed, "see? You can't go back to retail," he bent over, smiling at me, "you're the one Netherside has been waiting for. The brooch proves it."

Lowering my phone, I looked up to him. Without saying anything, I turned away and started toward my house, my keys the only sound between us, "I'm not your witch of legend. Take the brooch back, it must be a mistake."

Footsteps followed me, "What? No," stopping at my side, Cyrus watched as I unlocked the front door to the faded pink humble abode, wood worn and paint chipping onto the crumbling sidewalk below, ""I can't just-"

"I apologize, Cyrus," turning to look at him, he stared at me, eyes wide, mouth still open after I cut him off, "I don't have time for this, nor do I want my family seeing you." Bringing my hand up to my bow tie, my fingers met the pin, "I will gladly return the brooch."

About to pull it off, I was stopped when Cyrus' hands landed on mine.

The front door flew open, freezing our struggle.

"Igor?" My little brother, Ross, stood in the threshold, floppy orange hair above his young face and shocking blue eyes, guitar strung over his back, "You're okay!"

Standing there, I stared at him for a moment, frozen, Cyrus' hands on mine keeping me from ripping the pin from my bow tie.

Opening the door more, he looked to Cyrus, youthful eyes bright, unclouded, "Hey there-" When he stopped, smile frozen on his face, his eyes began to widen, "Your eyes," stepping forward, Ross made Cyrus let go of me and take a step back, "they're red. You look just like a-" the gasp that took him as he bounced, I could only wonder what it felt like to be excited like that, "are you a vampire?"

Cyrus blinked at my brother, the other of the most animated people I had ever had the displeasure of encountering, before his brow dropped, "No."

"But your eyes, they're red," Ross turned, his orange flippy hair bouncing with the movement as he rushed inside, "I saw a vampire just like that in one of my books," his voice became muffled as he ran down the hall, leaving the front door swinging on its hinges, "hold on, I'll grab it."

Watching the door creak closed, we stood in a silent beat filled by the metal groan. Looking back to Cyrus, I wanted to care, to be moved by the fantasy before me, but I wasn't. I never was. Tone lowering, I looked away from him, "Why can't you just take this and leave me alone?"

"Trust me," his eyes rolled away from the door where they had remained for a moment too long, "I would if I could. Of all your incarnations, so far this one is definitely my least favorite." Turning away from me, his eyes dropped, "You can't take it off, every time you have, your powers got out of control and killed you. I think there's more to it too, though," Pocketing his hands in his slacks, he kicked a bit of the distressed sidewalk, "you told me about it like six hundred years ago, but I don't think I was listening."

"Powers?" The porch light flickered turning purple, "I don't have-"

"Don't just whisper outside, come in," Ross' voice cut me off as he called for me from the house.

The porch light flickered back to white.

After staring at Cyrus for a moment as he stared at the porchlight, I started into the house. He followed, though his footsteps made no sound. As soon as the front door closed, Ross lunged from his open bedroom door, book in hand. Jumping toward me, he trapped me in a hug, his little arms holding as strong as he could. A child's strength, but stronger than I could ever hold another.

"I was worried when you didn't come home last night."

Eyes dropping to the carpet, the bright colors of the house were too much as I stood, stiff in his embrace, "I apologize, I fell asleep reading."

Gasping, Ross looked up to me, his chin digging into my chest, "Outside? Did you see any other vampires?"

Green eyes pierced my mind, a headless horse drawn carriage, passing through my thoughts before I chased the image away, "No."

Cyrus lingered behind me, "I'm not a-"

"Oh honey," my mum's voice came from around the way as she left the living room, entering the hall, "you shouldn't sleep outside, it isn't safe." Walking up to us, her floral dress painted in oranges and yellows, it echoed the warmth of her rolling curls and smiling eyes. One green, one blue, when they met Cyrus, they widened. She stood in a moment of pause for a moment too long before opening her mouth to speak, but even then she hesitated, the line of her lips twinging up, just a bit before she said, "Goodness, I didn't realize you had a friend here with you. Hello," the way my mom smiled could convince you she had never frowned before, erasing the nuance previously etched into her expression, "I'm sorry I was so surprised, Igor has never had a friend before."

Staring at her when Cyrus snorted, turning away, a sigh escaped me, "Mum, please."

Eyes drifting back to me, they caught, a bit lower than my face. Holding near my neck, one of her fine brows raised, but only for a moment before she looked back to my eyes. Reaching up, she brought her dainty fingers to my hair, trying to tame that one tuft that always misbehaved as she laughed, "How was work?"

Trying to pry myself free of Ross, my voice strained, "The same as usual."

"You sound like you hate it," my father laughed from the loveseat across the living room, setting down his newspaper, his heavily tattooed arms coming into view.

"Quite the opposite," I freed myself from Ross, leaving him laughing as I started down the hall, "I have another shift so I'm going to go get ready then head back again."

"Already?" My mum huffed, cheeks puffing as she crossed her arms over her apron, "Well, make sure to be home for dinner. I'll have a place set for you." Eyes drifting to Cyrus, there was something that shifted in them as they looked my resident zombie up, a gleam I had never seen in her before, "You can bring Cyrus, too."

Stopping mid-step, Cyrus froze. Eyes widening, they flew to my mum. Not a single word exchanged between them, the silence roared as she winked at him. Stiff as all hell, Cyrus' hands flew to the sides of his head as he stepped back. Looking between my mum and I as I walked away, I watched a million things flash over his features from the corner of my eye.

It should have mattered to me, that my mother knew his name without having been told, but unfortunately it didn't.

Waving to my mum, I didn't reply, leaving Ross to whine at me. Back turning to them, that's how it always was. They had probably seen me walk away more than I had ever walked toward them. Cyrus bolted down the hall, stumbling forward as he followed me like a trespassing puppy, eyes on the ground, hands in his pockets, silent.

Ross ducked back into his room, his voice muffled through the wall as it was accompanied by things shuffling about, "Wait, I just have to find the right book."

I closed my bedroom door.

Silence sat between Cyrus and I, punctuated by the metal click of the lock on my door.

"Your family seems…" his voice trailed off when his eyes drifted up, taking in the grey of my walls, bedspread, and furniture, "colorful."

Setting my keys on my grey dresser, they landed between my two picture frames, "They've always been that way."

"Your mother," Cyrus leaned against the wall, looking away as a certain stubbornness took his tone, "her name isn't Sierra Bell, is it?"

My eyes rested on the color of the dresser. Not void of tone, not black, not white, just desaturated, faded, "Bell was her maiden name, but yes, it is," I opened a drawer, "why?"

A downward hum taking him as his hand found its way to his face, that was the only reply I got from Cyrus as he stood with that for a moment. A moment later, he jumped, eyes flying up to me as a realization visibly crashed into him.

"You said you're twenty-four, right?"

I opened my closet, "Right."

"When's your birthday?"

Pawing through my clothing that all looked the same anyway as it hung before me, I turned to look at him, "August 16th."

Hands dropping from his head, he turned from me a bit, muttering numbers under his breath as he counted on his fingers. First, he counted back ten months from August, then he started counting years as he rabidly counted backward from the current one until he reached twenty-four years previous. After adding ten months to that with his fingers, he squinted off at nothing, things going on behind his eyes that were beyond me. Repeating that year a couple of times, he stared at his fingers. Closing his eyes, hand finding its way back into his hair, he pulled his bangs out of his face. After a pause, his eyes flew open again, this time locked on the ground as a sigh of relief took him, his panic melting away from his frame.

If I had been capable of caring, I would have asked him what that had been about, but at least it appeared to have resolved favorably. What could have been so important about the year I had been conceived I'd never bother to know.

Taking pants from my closet, Cyrus didn't say a thing to me as I excused myself to the restroom to get myself together. Though, I had caught a bit of him muttering about my last name and my father as I stepped through the door. The faint strumming of Ross' guitar floated through the walls, muffled but still warm. He must have given up on the book. Cyrus was right, they were colorful, my family, and I was not. They laughed, they smiled and cried, they must have been so happy. My mum loved to tell stories, my father showed us little magic tricks, Ross was obsessed with vampires. They were people, whole humans. Looking up to myself in the mirror, the bags under my eyes were gone, my tone less grey than usual, I almost looked human too.

But there was no way, no human would be like this.

"Hey, Igor?"

Turning, I barely looked to Cyrus over my shoulder as I entered my room, "Yes?"

Eyes drifting to me over my room, his brow furrowed a bit, the line of his mouth flat, "I've been meaning to ask you, but," his hesitation held me hostage as that moment lasted longer than a moment should, "do you feel anything? Valor said she sensed an unusual stillness about you."

My eyes lingered on him before I turned back around, eyes meeting one of the framed photos, Margo's warm orange taking me as I stared at her, "Not a thing."

His steps carried him to my side, looking over my frames as well, "You look happy in these, though."

Eyes drifting between the photo of my cousin and I, her orange hair pulled back in a bun as we smiled at her birthday, and the photo of me holding a bag, my goldfish I won at the elementary school fundraising fair event inside, I could only look at her orange for a moment before looking away, "I was once capable." Turning from him, I walked to my closet, "Though it was so long ago, I don't remember what feeling even feels like."

I heard him take a picture frame into hand, the wood sliding against the dresser, "What happened?"

Stopping at my closet, I started to unbutton my yellow button-down, back to him. Hands meeting my bowtie, I was about to take it off when I stopped. Something so slight, so, I don't know, fleeting, came to rise in the muscles in my fingers, something dissuading, something that made me pause. Cyrus wasn't looking, he probably wouldn't have even noticed if I removed my bowtie and the brooch along with it, but something about how much he cared resurrected in my mind, leaving me to ponder in that moment what it was like to feel ever so compelled about anything. Hands lowering from the clip at the back, they met the collar of my shirt. Popping it, I slid my bowtie up, but not removing it from my neck, "Death does strange things to people."

"She die-" when Cyrus' voice hitched, I turned to look at him. Eyes wide on me as I slid my shirt off, they dropped to the bowtie still around my neck. Eyes landing on the brooch, his panic faded, but transmuted into something else within a moment. I didn't understand why he looked at me like that before turning away completely, hand up to his face as he went on, "She died?"

Staring at him for a moment longer, I turned back to my closet, setting my button down in the hamper as I reached for a clean one, "When I was nine."

"I'm sorry, losing someone you care about can really mess you up." I heard him set the picture frame back down, though I didn't know which he had been holding, "Everyone in your family has such lovely orange hair except you."

Tucking in my shirt, I ran my hand through my hair as I turned back to him, "I dye it."

A moment passed between us.

Turning his back to me, he snorted as he tried to muffle his laugh.

Stepping by him, I took my keys from my dresser into hand, "I need to get back to work."

Turning, he looked to me, his hair bouncing with the movement, "You can't." Rushing to land between me and the door, he extended his spindly hands at his side, the sleeves of his blazer pulling up, "If this is like any of the previous times, the longer you stay here, the more dangerous you become."

Stepping right up to him, eyes on his through my rectangular glasses, his height didn't matter to me, "Please step aside."

Looking between my eyes, the ruby in them started to glass over, something about this moment feeling bigger than itself, bigger than us. His arms faltered for a moment, as if to oblige me, when he stopped himself.

"No," moving his hand forward, he extended his finger toward my bow tie, "I'm not losing you again. We've played this game over and over, but it has to end here." When his finger met with the gem, a spark shot through me.

A flash of light exploded around us, bleaching our surroundings. But as they faded back in, I was met with something different. In that moment, just for a moment, my room, my world, wasn't grey. Surrounded by lights, they danced through the air, colors meeting my eyes that I had never seen before, not that I could remember. Taking a step back, when my foot met the floor, it sent a rippling ring of rainbows out around us. When the rings collided with my dresser, it turned orange, when they met with my bookshelf, it turned green. One object after the next, my bed turned red, my lamp purple, the walls yellow. As the glow poured over us, painting Cyrus in colors as he looked about, they almost felt like old friends. Slowly looking to Cyrus, his hair blowing about in a wind I couldn't feel, it was as if I had seen this exact sight before. Like he was bathed in the light pouring through the stained-glass windows of a church, that image of Cyrus almost did it, almost brought a rise to me. For a moment, but a moment, I felt it, the line of my mouth threaten to pull up into a smile.

The sensation of water dripped down my hands like her blood did.

The colors stopped.

Fading away around me, they dripped down the walls, taking every color from our surroundings with them until we were trapped in grey. Looking around, I took a step back. Smoke erupted from the walls, as if the grey had caught fire, corrupting the air. Eyes meeting Cyrus, that was when even my blood stopped.

Eyes wide, brow quivering, I could see it, how disgusting grey looked when it was reflected in his ruby.

Storming around us, the grey smoke spun, the air going cold as our hair whipped. Rushing toward me, I had nowhere to run as I stared at the smoky grey cloud, so I didn't. I had embraced this color for years now, it was all that I could be. There was no use running from it. Crashing into my chest, its metronomic monochrome shot through my body, pins and needles taking me with an explosion of air as I was thrown back. Crashing into my bed, my shoes caught on the frame, keeping me from hitting the window above it. Thrown into the door, I heard the crack when Cyrus hit it. Books flew from the shelves, my photos were thrown to the ground, closet door flung open.

As the pressure drained from the air I was left, laying on my bed, staring at the ceiling as my vision blurred in and out. Hand shaking as my mum's muffled voice approached down the hall, it met with my lips. I had no idea what he had just done to me, but I did know one thing. Struggling to sit up, my eyes were met with Cyrus as he sat on my floor, back up against my door, disheveled hair thrown into his face. I wanted him to never do it again.

"Are you okay?" His voice strained as he struggled to stand, sliding his back up my door.

I did not reply as I stood. My mum called through to door asking what happened, knocking but not barging in.

"Everything is alright," I called back to my mum, stopping in front of Cyrus, eyes locked on his, not backing down, "I dropped something, I was just about to head to work."

Looking between my eyes, Cyrus didn't move.

A moment passed, one that would have killed anyone else under the weight.

The light flickered orange.

Stepping to the side, Cyrus lowered his eyes.

Opening the door, I brushed past him. Assuring my mum that everything was alright, I started for the front door. Leaving that house without looking back, it was like any other day. As my mum called to Cyrus, saying that it was nice to see him again and to come back soon, he didn't reply, eyes on the ground. Cyrus followed me, a few steps behind, not saying a word as we started down the driveway. Looking to my watch, I was only barely going to make it in time.

"You're the worst, you know that?"

I didn't reply, my pace holding ahead of him as we approached my store.

"Six-hundred-and-three-years. Forty-eight reincarnations. I have found you over and over, watched you die younger every time, just to have you show up now, this old, giving me hope and shit. You can't do this to me." When I didn't reply, his tone grew in volume, though not in sharpness, "I know you're in there, I know you can hear me, Nox."

I stopped walking, though not of my own will. Standing there, eyes wide, I couldn't move as Cyrus came to a stop at my side, leaning over to look into my eyes. He searched them, as if he could see beyond them, beyond me.

"It's not my fault that you can't get rid of me," Straightening, he crossed his arms, "you're the one who cursed me to live forever."

The lights above us beneath the sign of the store flickered.

The automatic doors rolled open.

"Igor," Amy yawned, eyes closing as she turned her head away, a couple of her oak curls falling over her shoulder, "seems like you didn't die."

Cyrus jumped back around the corner of the building, hiding, before Amy's eyes opened again. Stopping in front of me, she looked like she was about to say something else, the nametag hanging from her lanyard catching the morning light, when her eyes met with my bow tie. They lit up a little, in that way that a dapple of sun finds the forest floor in a slight breeze, "I like the brooch." She shifted her weight, her green and brown flannel shirt shifting with her as it sat open over a white tank top and above brown pants, "Anything exciting happen at the graveyard?"

The spell that had held me broke, allowing me to breathe as my eyes lingered on the corner of the building where Cyrus had disappeared, "No."

Laughing, she turned back toward the store, flipping the sign to 'open', "I guess that's for the best. Come on in, you're working the sales floor today."

Staring at the doors as they closed behind her, I took a moment before I looked back to Cyrus as he stepped around the corner again. The number of objectively concerning and strange things he had said just kept growing, but even with their swell, my care did not follow. Why didn't I care? Did I want to care? Did I want? Bringing my hand up to my bow tie, I looked away. I didn't care, but he definitely did.

The light above me flashed red, just for a moment.

"What would happen if," I watched as he leaned up against the wall, crossing his arms over his chest, "I continue to ignore you and pretend that this brooch is just a new pin?"

"You'll end the world," he turned to look at me, "I'd imagine, anyway." Walking up to me, his every step was slow, with leisure, "Now that you have that brooch, it's really just a matter of time." lifting his hand, he extended one finger up toward my neck, "You will succumb to the powers lying dormant within you that have been stirred, effectively destroying the realm around you without me there to lessen the blow," lowering his hand, he pocketed it, "I've played this game forty-eight other times, but this has to be the last one. The powers you possess are exponential. If you melt down, it will be the end." His movie star smile broke through the clouds of his reservation as the sun broke over the tree line, "But, I won't let it end that way, not again."

Extending his hand, I saw the young man lying in a casket for just a moment as Cyrus smiled at me. Turning from him, I don't know why I asked. It wasn't like it would drum up any urgency in me, obviously nothing would at this point. Starting toward the door, I didn't reply. They opened, their squeaking the only sound in the air. When I stepped into the doors, Cyrus spoke, stopping me in the threshold.

"You can hide from me all you want Nox, but, doing so will only harm Igor."

I stepped inside, the door closing behind me, cutting me off from him.

Clocking in, I tried to ignore what he had said.

A reincarnated witch, a king, powers of magnitudes untold? The brooch on my bow tie weighed as I walked into the store. Mindlessly picking up pants from the floor, I folded them over my arm. That wasn't my world, not the grass that held onto your shoes, not the vampire riding by, pulled by a headless horse. This was, this dead-end place we all ended up somehow, wasting away our hours on the linoleum floor of broken dreams. But I had never paid it any mind, I didn't have any dreams. My world dulled into the faded blue of denim and off white of security tags.

This was my world, my only world.

So why?

When I blinked, I saw it, the town square with so many mysteries.

Why?

When I passed mirrors, I saw my reflection in the potion shop window looking back at me.

The crisp clink of hanger against rod wasn't satisfying.

Staring at the shirt I had just hung up, my hand lingered on the fabric, a tremble starting to bud beneath my skin.

The lights above flickered, turning blue for just a moment before returning to off-white.

"You're going to crack any moment now."

When Cyrus' voice came from my side, I jumped away, stumbling over my feet and into the shoe wall. The lights above flickered purple, just for a moment. Staring at him as he stood, not looking at me, I believed that was the first time in over a decade that I had been startled. Slowly looking up to me from the floor, hands in his pockets, his hair shifted in the light, "If you stay here, you're going to level this whole store and kill everyone inside."

Pushing myself up from the shoe wall, I straightened some I had knocked loose, voice lowering, "What are you doing in here."

"When it hits," he walked up to me, "you're going to need me," he stopped at my side, reaching forward to straighten a shoe, "if you want to not be banished by your own powers, that is."

"I don't have powers," turning to him, I shoved him behind a display of shirts to hide him from sight, "and you're talking too loud. I don't want my coworkers to see me with you."

His eyes on the ground, it took a moment but his actor's shine returned as he looked up again, "I have all the time in the world, I'm not going anywhere."

Looking around to make sure no one was near, I lowered my voice even more, "Can you at least wait outside?"

"Nope," Lifting a finger, he slowly moved my glasses back into place, the tip lingering on the frame for a moment before lowering it with a smile, "I can't leave your side, and while I'm sure you're not thrilled about that, trust me, the feeling is mutual."

Stepping back from him, I adjusted my glasses.

"Even with that said though," Cyrus looked to the clothing rack at our side, pushing shirts down it, "I don't think this is who you really are. You have feelings in there somewhere, and with them your powers will return," he slid another shirt down the rack, "or perhaps it's the other way around, your emotions will come with your powers." Stopping on a shirt, he looked it over, "Either way, they are there, just dormant, for some reason."

Staring at him, for the first time, something he said had waded through my haze of indifference, "My powers or my emotions?"

A beat passed as he took out a shirt and inspected it.

"Both."

"Igor do-" Amy stopped, eyes wide and on the shirt Cyrus was holding.

A customer bumped into her, taking her attention away for a moment.

Cyrus jumped, letting go of the shirt before stepping behind the display to my side, hiding. Catching the shirt mid-fall, I stared at it as Amy turned back to me.

Her redwood eyes studied the shirt I was holding up for far too long before she looked to me, "Do you want to go on your break first?"

"My break?" My eyes darted to my watch as I held the shirt out in front of me, how had two hours already passed? "No, I can do the last one, I'm fine."

Eyes on the shirt again for a moment, she nodded before leaving with a laugh, "Alright, well I'll go on mine then. Until I'm back, you're in charge."

I stared at her as she walked away with an urgency indicative of her youth until she was out of sight.

Putting the shirt back on the rack with a dull clink, I turned to Cyrus, "What are you doing?"

Shoving his hands in his pockets, his eyes slid away, "I'm a dead man walking in these parts, can't let myself be seen after they blasted my face all over the news." Leaning around the rack, he looked out, "It was in bad taste, really, publishing my picture. But I guess if your suicide is theatrical enough, taste gets thrown to the wind."

Staring at him, I didn't have anything else to say. As I started to the next area I needed to clean up, he followed closely. After a slight glance about, I looked to him, "What did you mean by dormant?"

"What?" Blinking at me, it took him a moment but then he laughed, "Oh right, yes, powers. They are tangled, so if one were to wake, the other will too. They've been sleeping, I could barely sense them in you when we met last night. But now?" He looked me over, "Now there's no question. I speculate that the death of that girl in the photo with you made you this way, and while that may be the only reason your powers haven't destroyed you already, it's going to make this reawakening a whole lot more painful." He may have seen it, the color start to drain from me.

I didn't care.

I couldn't care.

I wouldn't care.

"But," he smiled, raising his hand, "while I may be of a boring breed of immortal, I was really something in life, so I do have some power myself." A red light began to glow from his palm, "I'll be able to absorb some of the blow." Lowering his hand, he shifted his weight, "And unfortunately for the both of us, that means until every gem on that brooch holds a color and you're capable of controlling them, you're stuck with me."

Turning from him, I ignored the shaking of my hand as I picked a shirt from the rack that was in the wrong size. Walking down the way, I hooked it into place, hand lingering on the fabric to hide the tremble, "It wasn't the girl in the-"

"Hey Igor," Venecia's voice came through my earpiece, "would you mind coming to the front? The line is getting long."

Hand lowering to the radio hooked to my hip, I couldn't hide my fraying as my finger met the button, "I'll be right there."

Turning from Cyrus, I didn't spare him another glance.

"Wait," I heard his scrambling footsteps behind me, "what are you doing?"

Snatching up a random empty hanger from the rack at my side, I didn't turn to look at him, "my job."

The lights above flickered orange, but this time, they held the color a bit longer.

I heard his footsteps stop.

The signs hanging from chains above, connected to the industrial ceiling, started to sway despite the still air, their shadows dancing over me below. With the quickening of my every step, my heart rate followed. Shoes falling from shelves on the walls as I passed, the clothing slid away on the racks, hangers screaming against the metal bars. Jaw tightening, my eyes locked on the mounting line at the front. A cardboard holiday display fell as I passed. Walking by customers as they looked around, their concern reminded me of the look my mum gave me that day, of water and broken glass and blood on my hands.

Of Margo, her cold body.

Turing the corner into the front, I walked up to my register. Stopping at my station, I reached forward to the switch. Flipping it, the click split the air with its volume. When the light came to life, it was orange.

Calling to the next customer, I found I ran out of breath faster than before.

Scanning item after item, removing the security devices, bagging each as I went, I could feel my quickening pulse right beneath my skin. Almost as quickly as it had grown, between Venecia's friendly small talk and my few words, the line went down until there was no one left.

Taking a breath, when it left me, it felt harsh against my throat.

Slowly turning from her register, Venecia's eyes scanned me up, "Are you alright?" Turning to face me, she leaned up against the counter in a pink floral shirt, taking her matching hair ribbon into her fingers, "Something seems," she paused, staring at me, "like, wrong?"

It was absurd, her words, nothing was ever wrong with me because there was nothing with me to be either which way.

But, as I opened my mouth to reply, a burning met my next breath.

Someone cleared their throat. Shrill and without any class, it made my heart jump. Jaw tight, I slowly looked over to the side to see a woman standing in line. Eyes meeting

Venecia's for a moment more, I didn't know what to say to her before turning back to my register.

Nothing was wrong, right?

Waving to the customer, I summoned her to my register. As she rolled her yellow cart up, something behind her caught my eye. Peering around the sunglasses stand, Cyrus' eyes met mine for a moment before he jumped and hid behind the stand. Staring at it for a moment more, my eyes drifted back to the customer.

Setting down a pink-tinted, rose shaped perfume bottle on the counter between us, it was over half empty. Glancing back up at the customer for a moment, I remembered checking her out just a couple days ago. She had tried to argue with me about a discount on that perfume because it was out of season, but ended up buying it at full price, anyway.

Short, messy, dull blonde hair sat atop her head, the haphazard chunky highlights reflecting the orange of my station's light. She crossed her arms over her chest, taking the flaps of her sweater with each hand as she stiffened. "I'd like to return this, it smelled awful."

Staring at the bottle for a moment, I listened as Amy asked Venecia to cover the fitting room so they could go on their break over the headset. With Amy on her break, I was the second in command, the next acting manager. As I looked back up to the customer, I tried to take a breath, "Upon purchasing this item, ma'am, you were informed of the store's no-return police on fragrances."

Scoffing, she threw her head up a bit, "No one told me that."

"With all due respect, ma'am," I shifted my weight back, each word coming faster than the last, "I sold this to you and did inform you of the policy."

Dropping her jaw, dignity didn't appear to be in her wheelhouse as she shook her head at me, "I cannot believe how disrespectful you are. I want to talk to your manager."

The lights flickered orange again, holding the color even longer than before.

Brow twinging up a bit, I stood in that moment as the customer jumped, looking up and around at the lights.

"That would, unfortunately, be me, ma'am," my eyes drifted down to her cart to see a few more items there, "and while I can't accept your return, I can get the rest of your items checked out if you would like to place them on the counter."

Still shaking her head at me, it slowed, her dead, unblinking blue eyes locked on mine until she snatched something out of her cart. Tossing it onto the counter with no regard, she averted her eyes from mine. Tossing her next item onto the counter, then the next, and the next, I just stood there, watching her tantrum. Huffing, she scooted the items around into three separate piles. Still refusing to look at me as I started to scan the items from the nearest pile, she pulled out her wallet from her purse. Tossing some money onto the piles, she didn't say a thing.

As I finished scanning the last item from the first pile, I placed it in the bag at my side. "Will this be three separate purchases, or all together?"

Crossing her arms, she ignored me, looking literally everywhere but at me.

Standing there as the running timer on my register began to ruin my stats for the day, I took a breath, "Will this be three separate purchases, or all together?"

Smacking her mouth, she sighed, looking up and around, rolling her eyes.

Brow twitching again, it had a mind of its own as my heartbeat faster in my chest. "Ma'am, will this be three separate-"

"You have asked me that three times."

Mouth open, words dead in my mouth, the corners of my vision began to darken as I couldn't even blink, staring at her. Bringing my hand up to my bowtie, as it raised in my vision, I saw it, the shaking.

"Yes ma'am, that is because you have not answered me."

With a huff, she snatched up one of the bills from the counter, eyes snapping to mine, "I don't speak English."

Throwing the bill at me, it hit me in the face.

Something screamed through me, a flash of acid, burning my insides.

Eyes wide as I lowered my hand from my bowtie, I could see it shake as I took the bill into my grasp.

Slowly raising the bill up toward the light to check its validity, I didn't even look at it, I couldn't, not as I stared at my trembling hands. My hands hadn't done that since she died in them. Breath shaking as I lowered the bill, I brought one of my hands to the touchscreen of my register. Vision blurring in and out with every deafening pound of my heart, the darkness taking it at the corners grew. Typing in an amount on the screen, I pressed enter, but received an error. The lights above flickered orange. Typing it in again, I fought with the tremble of my hands until input it in properly. The cash door dinged, flying open into my chest. The signs hanging from the industrial ceiling began to sway again, chains creaking above us. Making her change with shaking hands, I counted it, and with every count, I got a different amount. The screen of my register flickered. Handing her the change, as she snatched it from my hand, I noticed how sweaty my palms had become. I slammed the cash drawer closed and with its crack, the lights above turned orange and this time, they didn't turn back.

Eyes darting up, I stared at the lights as they buzzed above.

What was happening?

Another bill hit me in the face.

Slowly looking down to the customer, when my eyes met her smirk, something snapped in me.

I wished she'd get the fuck out of my store.

A crack from above split the air and a moment later, the large sign that hung from the ceiling to mark the check-out fell before my eyes. Crashing into the floor between us, it made her fall away, screaming as she dropped to the ground. As dust settled in the air between us, my eyes on hers, I watched the color drain from her. Amy's voice came over the headset but all I heard was vaguely concerned static as my head crooked to the side.

Scrambling to her feet in a mess of herself, the woman blubbered as she snatched her purse from her cart. Watching, the line of my mouth threatened to move, threatened to do something, as she ran toward the doors faster than they could open. Crashing into them she screamed, pounding on the doors until they opened. Tripping as she ran into the parking lot, she was almost hit by a car, its honk taking the air.

My heart pounded so hard in my chest, my ribs felt it.

Every muscle in my body tensed.

The doors slammed shut so hard the glass cracked.

My heart plummeted into the acid of my stomach, taking all the blood from my head with it. Turning from orange to purple, from purple to green, from green to red, from red to blue, the lights flickered, turning the store into a rave. An incredible weight dropped onto me. Hand landing on the counter as my knees gave out, I kept myself from falling. Teeth grit, eyes wide, I stared at the ground. Other hand grasping at my chest as my heart raged, my ears rang. Another wave of pressure collapsed onto me, threatening to take me down. A blur threw itself over the counter, but I couldn't see what it was as my hand slipped.

Dropping, I anticipated the hard floor against my knees, but then, something caught me. Arms, they wrapped around me, warmer than I had ever been, as they tightened.

Voice soft, Cyrus' head hovered next to my ear, "You need to go on your break right now."

Barely able to open my eyes through my crooked glasses, my vision blurring in the flashing rainbow light, I saw Cyrus. Shaking hand raising to my earpiece, my finger was too numb to feel the button as I pressed it down, "Actually, Amy," trying to keep my voice even as the pressure started to fade a bit, I pushed myself up from Cyrus, "Would I be able to go on break?"

He kept his hand on my back as I braced myself against the counter, straightening.

"Yeah, are you okay?" Her voice came through my earpiece, muffled by static as it engulfed our line of communication, starting to drown them out again, "I'm on my way up now."

"Yes," my voice strained as I forced myself to my feet, "I'm alright."

Sweat taking me, it stung as I stumbled back into the counter. Cyrus' hand on my shoulder, his grip tightened as I looked up to him. Eyes meeting through my crooked glasses, they held for a moment until I ripped mine away. Why was he looking at me like that?

Pushing myself up from the counter, I started out of the front end and toward the outer path of the store. As I passed the doors, they screamed open and shut, open and shut, over and over, cracking more with each close. Stumbling but not falling, I bumped into a display as I started into the outermost aisle. Following me, not letting go, Cyrus looked around as things flew off shelves around us, the lights humming to a roar above, sounding as if they were about to explode.

When his grip tightened on me, it grew warm on my shoulder. Glancing over to the side, it was hard to tell in the flashing from above, but his hand emanated a light. With every step the pressure grew, slowly building, deepening my tremble, until it reached all the way to my bones.

Pressure snapping, heat that was so hot it felt cold ripped through me.

Knees threatening to buckle as I turned down the housing aisle, every muscle tensing, Cyrus' grip on me tightened. Hand on a display to keep myself from falling, a customer spoke to me but I couldn't hear them. Stumbling forward, my tunneling vision met with the back door in the distance.

Vision blurring, the lights flashed faster, the colors like a roulette, just waiting for the chamber to align and trigger the shot, a slot machine spinning in anticipation of a jackpot. Dragging myself forward, the pressure made each step harder than the last, my breath burning up in my chest, leaving me more breathless with each one. Meeting the door to the back room, my shaking hand reached up to the keypad, fighting the whole way under the pressure. Finger shaking, I struggled to type in the code. It beeped at me. I had typed it in wrong. Another wave rushed through me, causing me to grit my teeth, knees fighting me as I leaned my forehead up against the door. The canvases on the back wall fell to the ground. Typing in the code again, the lights got even faster, so fast that the colors started to bleed together, warping the surroundings.

It beeped.

A hissing breath escaped my clenched teeth.

A vase fell from the shelf behind me, shattering. Eyes wide, body locked up, the sound brought it back, the feeling of broken glass, of the cold water, the last move she made in my hands. That's right, that was it, the last time I felt anything, I promised it would be, it had to be, because if it wasn't, it would happen again.

The colors stopped flashing, painting the world in a rich amber.

The door flew open. Keypad sizzling, it fell apart as the door sat, lodged in the drywall. Staring as dust fell from the air, amber painting my world, I could only dwell in that pause for a moment before the pressure dropped back onto me. Stumbling inside, Cyrus followed me, about to say something when I cut him off, slamming the door. Standing there, staring at the door, I was taken over by something. Starting in the acid of my stomach it boiled, roaring until it overflowed, poisoning me.

All at once, everything that hadn't fazed me came screaming back. When customers yelled at me, called me obscenities, slurred at my coworkers, waved me off or demanded things, when they'd threaten to relieve themselves on the floor in front of me when I told them the bathrooms were closed because someone rubbed their feces all over the walls, when they'd get in my face or say something creepy about Venecia, when they'd watch me clean up a section then take something off the rack and throw it over right next to me, so many things, constant tantrums and threats and raised voices, but none of it had ever gotten to me though, not until now.

A million moments venomous lived in me in that singular one, so many, too many.

The warmth of Cyrus' hand on my back pulled the world back into focus.

I was barely able to unclench my jaw as I looked back to him, "What's going on?"

Brow furrowing, his eyes glowing more red by the moment, he smiled a little, "You're mad, Igor."

"I'm wha-" my word was cut off by another pang of pressure, ripping through me, causing a groan to escape my clenched teeth as I nearly fell from my feet.

I heard it, something start to crack.

Why was this happening.

Eyes flying open, they locked on him.

I was feeling.

What he said earlier came to me through the steam about to burst from my core.

"This is your fault." Storming from him into the break room, I left him standing near the door. "If I had just left you buried, this wouldn't be happening right now." I heard his steps as he followed me into the break room, and every single one served to escalate me further, "I don't feel things, Cyrus, I can't, I'm not allowed to. The last time I did, I-" turning to face him, my feet moved before I knew what was happening, my grip found his shirt before I even realized we were so close, his back was shoved into the wall next to the vending machine before I could even feel the fabric in my grip, "You have to take this brooch and get away from me, because if you don't…" my grip tightened on him as the corners of my vision darkened, leaving nothing but him in my sights, "bad things will happen again."

Hair disheveled from the shove, he just stood there beneath my grip, back to the wall, head tilted just a bit, eyes on mine. And despite my tone, despite the amber light above and the pressure, Cyrus Glory still smiled at me. Vision blurring, I was no longer in this musty place. For a beat, I was in tens of settings all at once. They changed from the forest to an alley, from a bedroom to a park, they were all different seasons, places and times, but in every vision, no matter when or where, one thing was the same: Cyrus, smiling at me.

I wanted to let go of him, to back up, to silence the roaring in my chest. I wanted to open my mouth, I wanted to ask him to make it stop, to save me from whatever had taken over. But as my grip tightened on his shirt, my jaw clenching, brow furrowed and eyes locked on his, the feeling only swelled.

Mad?

I was mad?

Why was I mad?

As another wave of pressure crashed into me, I shoved him further into the wall, no space between us.

A campfire flashed in my mind, stars and a cabin. Shaking my head, I tried to fight them off but I couldn't as the visions continued to take me. Children and trees, a little

town and a church. Crimson and emerald and tangled sheets,

flowers and chirping birds, the visions felt as if they should

bring calm to my storm, but they were simply gas on the fire.

Bells rang in my ears, warping with screams. Red, so much

red, it was all I could see as I brought my hand up to my face,

pushing my glasses out of place as my grip tightened on

Cyrus. A slow walk, a crowd surrounding, words were yelled

at me, dizzy in the ringing in my mind. Staring at someone as

they stood in the front the crowd, wearing all black, a

rectangle of white on their neck, their face was obscured by

the glass taking my eyes as their hand met a lever. Three

steps up, a wooden platform, the branch of a tree, a rope. It

was rough, around my neck, tight like the bow tie. The

person before me, obscured in my mind's eye, pulled the

lever.

I felt it, the drop.

Another wave crashed into me, buckling my knees

but I caught myself before I fell.

Free hand flying up as the visions drained from my eyes, they burned, tears budding in the corners of them. This was too much, so much, I couldn't stop it, I couldn't win. Free hand shaking as I raised it, my trembling fingers met with the bow tie.

Hand flying up to mine, Cyrus' grip tightened on my hand, pulling it down. Raising his other hand, he was slow despite the chaos, collected as the lights began to hum, the pressure swelling, the vending machines around us beeping, lights flashing. Bringing his hand to my glasses, he slid them from my face. Folding them, he tucked them in the chest pocket of his blazer.

Smiling, he lowered my hand and let go, "You look," when his voice cracked, glass took over his eyes, "just like him." Bringing his hand back up, it hovered over my chest, not making contact yet, "It's going to be alright, you just have to get through this, all you have to do is survive and I'll take care of the rest." Placing his hand on my chest, his eyes lit, the red growing brighter as he clenched his teeth. A wince taking him, he tried to maintain his smile despite his body

locking up, despite the furrowing of his brow, despite the

glassing of his eyes as his hand glowed against my chest.

"You're doing so good," his voice strained, he looked up to

me through his disheveled wavy hair, "I believe in you."

With my next heartbeat, I felt it, his red race through

me.

And for a second, all was still.

Crimson pulsed through me, getting into every crack

in my chest, filling them, making me feel almost whole. As

his glow grew brighter against my chest, his hand trembling

as he took on the brunt, I was taken. If any color could

unravel me, it would be red.

Another wave crashed into me, shattering the still.

Muffling my yell, I tried to pry myself off him when he

yelled out too. It was too much, I could see it in his eyes. I

was too much, I was always too much. I couldn't do this, not

to another. My hand wouldn't listen to me, refusing to

unclench from his shirt. Another wall crashed into me, leveling me and taking me to my knees as I ripped my hand from his shirt. Doubled over, one hand to my mouth to muffle my pain as it swelled, the absence of his red stabbed me, stealing my breath.

Red deposited into me again, his hand landing on my back, his voice barely audible through the violence in my ears, "I'm not going to lose you again."

When his other hand met my back, he yelled out, the pressure lifting from me. Turning my head to the side, I stared up at him, eyes wide through my bangs. He was a bit blurry without my glasses, but I could see it, the pain he was in.

Just when Cyrus had brought relief to me, another pang took the air, crushing us as our yells warped. Collapsing over my back, he held me, his grip unwavering despite the way he trembled, despite the crack in his voice as he yelled. He needed to let go of me, I was hurting him.

That was all I ever did.

Face shoved into the floor by the pressure, my bangs spilled on the concrete before me.

Mum's unfading smile as I walked away from her, my father as I just tolerated him showing me his magic tricks, Ross as he was left, standing outside my closed door, book in tow, Margo as she died in my hands.

My eyes closed as another pang pushed us down, cracking the floor.

A sob shook through Cyrus' stifled breath.

Colors flashed, the world blurred into a rainbow around me. Warping, distorting, the break room became a pool of oil in the rain. Outlines snapped, colors from one object bled into the next. Turning from concrete to abstract, our surroundings were rendered nothing more than their colors as the world deteriorated around us. Teeth grit, face against the floor, arms wrapped around my chest, bow tie around my neck tightening, I couldn't breathe, I couldn't move, all I felt was hot white as it pulsated through me, burning beneath my skin.

"Help him," Cyrus' voice cracked as he shouted, arms wrapped over my back as I knelt, doubled over on the floor, "Please, you can't do this to him." The pressure grew, cutting his next word off, turning it into a yell before he tamed it, "I know you can hear me," his grip tightened as another pang washed over us, cracking the floor beneath us further, and while the sound of that was deafening, Cyrus' yell was louder, "Nox."

Everything stopped.

My ears rang out, my world falling from focus as my eyes closed.

The ringing in my ears warped into laughter as my eyes flew open. Still doubled over, paralyzed by the power racing through me, the floor was no longer the concrete of the break room, but pure white, void of texture.

"Look at you," a voice said from above me between laughs, "pathetic."

Shoes stopped in my vision. Eyes barely able to focus, jaw so tight sharp pains shot through my skull, bangs falling in my face, I forced my head to the side. Eyes trailing up from the black boots, they were met with black pants and a white, bellowing poet shirt that clung to a spindly frame, one so delicate it looked as if merely laying a finger on him would shatter his every bone. Shifting my head to look up further, brow furrowed, trembling with the pain as my breath hissed through my teeth, my bangs fell from my eyes. A leather notebook sat, closed in his hand, a feather quill lounging between fine fingers. Gaze met with a sharp jaw, it trailed up to fluffy hair so white it reflected light, a sickly completion dusted in freckles and bushy white brows. The smirk that pulled on the line of his lips, it led my eyes up to his. Dirty brown like mine, the way the surrounding white reflected in them shifted as he crooked his head.

"Help you?" The breath that escaped him was poisoned by his smirk, turning into a scoff, "As if."

Bringing up his boot, he kicked me, throwing me away. Landing on my back, the air was knocked from me as I laid on the ground. Hand to my chest, grasping the fabric of my shirt as I writhed, I could barely keep my eyes open on him as amber seared through me, rendering me incapable. Leisure in his every move, the young man no older than twenty started around, circling as he looked down on me.

"Unpleasant, isn't it?" clumps of his fluffy white hair bounced with his every step, like a vulture waiting for me to die, "You shouldn't exist, you're too powerful." Stopping above my head, he bent over, upside down in my view, "I even tried to suppress your powers so he couldn't find you, but you went and walked right up to him. You did this to yourself." Lifting his shoe, he pressed my face to the side, but didn't put much weight on it, "Stop fighting it, just give up. Maybe you're the one who could do it, finally destroy me. You just have to let it."

Shaking my head under his shoe, my grip tightening on my shirt, my jaw was too locked to speak as a groan left me, another pang crushing me.

"Oh? You want to fight it?" Increasing the pressure on my face, he leaned forward, his words so sharp I felt them, "How selfish, you're nothing but a danger." Another pang tore through the air as he pressed into me further, my ears ringing, my body burning. "You could have lived a normal life, had Cyrus not come out of nowhere are ruined it. But he's good at that, destroying lives." Bending down, he tugged on my bow tie, pulling the brooch into sight, "Now that you have this, they've been woken. I took your emotions away from you, made it so you felt nothing to keep them at bay. But now it's too late, just a matter of time before they destroy you."

Glaring up at him from beneath his shoe, through the parted curtain of my disheveled hair, jaw tight and brow low, I could see my reflection in his eyes.

The white room around us flashed another color, far too quickly for me to process what it was.

My grip on my shirt struggled to loosen.

The reason I was this way.

Letting go of my shirt, my hand started to travel up.

The reason nothing got a rise out of me.

My hand trembled as it passed by my face.

The reason I couldn't build a relationship with my family.

My hand met his ankle above my head.

This was him, the person Cyrus was looking for, the person strong enough to wear the crown, the one everyone thought was gone, the owner of the brooch around my neck.

Nox.

He was the reason.

My grip tightened on his ankle.

The white around us flickered amber.

A shock raced up my arm, its orange light blinding as it shot into him. An explosion threw us away from each other. Sent tumbling, I rolled on the ground, every place I touched turning amber beneath me. Coming to a stop, the air hummed. Laying there for a moment, my muscles relaxed some, no longer paralyzed. Coughing so hard I tasted blood, I shook trying to pull myself up to my knees. Straightening, I looked up through my messy hair to see Nox picking himself up some way away.

Surrounded by endless white, we were in an abyss.

Bringing myself to my feet, I took a breath. Running my hand through my hair, despite the brief reprise, the swell started to build again, burning under my skin. With my first step his way, the white floor beneath my shoes turned amber. Looking up to me as he sat, hands splayed behind him on the ground, the smirk was absent from his face. Jaw too tight to talk, my muscles began to fight with the next step, but I continued, my shoes echoing endlessly. Fists clenched at my sides, an upward tilt to my head, amber stood around me on the floor like a shadow as I stopped above him.

Scooting back, as his eyes locked on mine, I could see it, the amber reflecting off the white of his hair as it grew brighter around me.

"You're a monster," scrambling to his feet, he took a stumbling step back, hands up, "Or do I need to make you kill someone else to remind you?"

My eyes widened.

The abyss turned amber, the color raging as far as the eye could see, white completely gone.

Tension ebbing, it allowed me to loosen my jaw, "What did you say?"

Looking around slowly, eyes growing, Nox stood, the only white remaining growing from where his shoes met the floor when he stepped back, "Your powers, they killed her. They'll kill again." Looking back to me, a slight tug on his mouth, my amber reflected in his eyes, "In fact, if you can't get a hold of yourself, you're about to have more blood on your hands right now."

I was about raise my voice, but then, I heard it, echoing through the veil of the amber, a yell, no, a scream. I looked up and around, though all I could see was the amber that took me for all eternity.

Cyrus.

"You're too much, Igor. You always have been and always will be." Nox took a step forward making me take a step back as my eyes dropped to him, "You're better off gone, just let it happen."

Better off gone?

The way Ross remained outside my door, his shadow not leaving for a few moments more, even after I had closed it in his face. The way my mum hugged me even though I never hugged her back. The way my father sighed when he thought I couldn't hear him when my mum mentioned me. The way Venecia looked at me when I did something reckless, with little regard to myself.

I was hurting them.

The abyss flickered white.

Looking around, Nox's smirk grew, "That's right," his eyes locked on me, "you're a burden. Give up, everyone will be better off that way. You won't hurt anyone anymore, and I'll finally be free."

He was right.

Ross, my mum, my father, my coworkers, Margo.

Every day was the same, doing so much but doing nothing, it never changed.

The click of a hanger against a rack.

I took another step back.

The abyss flickered white again.

"You could do it," extending his arms, Nox stood, resembling a crucifix before me, "you could free us," lights flashed at his sides, racing down in a line. As each faded, a wall of people appeared. They started out similar in age, young men of varying appearances, but as the lights extended down further, the boys became younger, shorter, until the last light flashed, revealing a little child. Back mostly turned, I could see but his profile as he stood, head hung low. Looking down the line, my breath struggling to come to me as amber sat in pause in my core, I realized something. While we all looked different, there was one thing we shared.

Our eyes.

"It's a vicious cycle, Igor," Nox stepped froward from the line, "please," he stopped a step away, looking down to me, "I know you don't understand, but, you must end it before it ends the world."

Exploding into yells, the line of young men called out to me, and while I couldn't understand what they said, their words colliding with one another, some in languages I didn't know. I could sense it, what they were asking of me. Colors flashed to life on each of them, the brooch appearing on every person. The oldest who had been at Nox's side wore it pinned to his shirt above his heart, the circle of gems nothing like the desaturated brooch I knew. Each held a color, glowing brightly, except the last one that remained desaturated, the circle incomplete. As my eyes trailed down the line, I could see it, every few incarnations having less colors on their brooch than the ones that came before until my eyes landed on the youngest, the child who looked away. He didn't have a single color on his brooch as he held it, barely grasped in the length of his limp fingers.

My mind flew back to Netherside, to the story Cyrus had told me. The brooch around my neck weighed, the bow tie tightening. If what Cyrus said was true, if I was an incarnation of Nox, then I was doomed.

Taking my hand in his, Nox was cold. Closing my fist in his grip, he tightened his on mine before releasing it, opening my palm. As my fingers uncurled, light poured from between them, illuminating the space between us. A ball met my eyes, resting in my palm. Its amber churned, burned at the touch. Staring down into it, I could see it in the orb, every time a customer was mean, every time they trashed the section I was cleaning right in front of me, every time they threatened to call corporate. The orb began to hum, orange electricity snapping off it as I couldn't look away. Every time I watched my family laugh and I couldn't understand, every time I walked out of my room to find them all playing a game or watching a movie together, without inviting me. Of course they wouldn't invite me, who would want to be around someone like me. As the feeling drained from me with every passing image, the orb in my hand grew brighter, hotter, churned faster.

"Destroy yourself," he looked up to me from our hands, "do that, and you may be able to end the cycle. If you do it here, you won't affect the outside. Our powers will explode in this realm and not that one."

The abyss turned white.

Looking up to Nox, our faces lit up by the amber, I could see it, my reflection in him. Had he been shorter or I taller, his hair darker or mine lighter, we could have been twins, the most similar of all the incarnations. Emptiness met me again, screaming in the absences of the amber, a white noise, radio silence. I didn't think I could experience something more overwhelming than amber, but as I stood there, eyes wide as the pins and needles of numbness took me, I realized I was wrong.

Sure, amber was searing, a color capable of possession. But as my eyes lowered to it burning in my hand, I didn't mind it.

It hurt.

But that was something.

And something, no matter what it was, was better than nothing.

Bringing my hand up in his, he moved the orb in my grip closer to my chest, as if he couldn't push it all the way, like he needed me to.

"Do it," Nox's smirk returned, eyes trailing up me, "before you destroy Cyrus too."

Though he wasn't there with me, as I stared down at the orb in my hand, far too hot to be so close to my face, I could feel him. It was faint, his arms wrapped around me as he knelt next to me on the floor of the break room, his grip unwavering. Eyes jumping up, images raced behind them as they passed over the line of young men. With each one, I saw him again, Cyrus, smiling at me. No matter when, no matter where, he was always there.

No matter how much it hurt.

Cyrus didn't give up on him.

My eyes returned to Nox.

"Look at you," yanking my wrist from him, I brought my free hand up to his shirt, taking a bunch of the fabric into my grip, pulling him forward, "pathetic."

Eyes wide, he stood, frozen.

"You have obviously never been the only cashier during a holiday rush ten minutes after closing," I raised a brow, bringing the orb in my hand forward, "sometimes you can't just give up." Closing my hand over the orb, I crushed it, making it smaller before opening my hand again. Eyes met with the smallest orange light, in this form it was hard to believe it held so much power. If Nox wanted me to break the cycle, then I would… just not his way. "I'm not going to run away."

Nox jumped, reaching for my arm.

When my hand made contact with the brooch, amber exploded.

In that moment, the moment in which the only thing I could see was amber, I was at peace with it. I had run from it, but as I stood there, in an orange embrace, it reminded me of the fierce flash of warmth in the sky before the fall of night. Thrown back, I didn't lose my footing as my shoes skid on the ground, leaving an orange trail. Amber blinding, the air searing, but it didn't burn me. Panting as I straightened, something washed through me, burrowing into my bones, making a home in my core. Shoulders dropped, head low, I fought to remain standing. Pulling my head up, my gaze raised through my disheveled hair. Eyes wide, my breath hitched.

A splash of amber so large, it reached into oblivion, staining the abyss in a huge, messy slice screamed out from the floor where I stood. Laying on the ground some way away, Nox stood out in the orange, his light clothing and hair free of the color. The other incarnations gone, in their wake stood piles of glitter, catching on the orange light as it faded. Hand raising to my brooch, I could feel it, the warmth now emanating from one of the gems. Gathering myself with a breath, I ran my hand through my hair.

Anger.

Perhaps it was a good thing I didn't have that while at work.

Taking my first step his way, the abyss turned orange beneath my shoes, but this time the shade was softer, lighter, a tamed pastel tone of amber. With each step, my core stilled, though it was not completely empty, now home to a hum. Stopping above him, I looked down to Nox as he laid, staring up through messy hair.

"I have never seen so much pent-up rage before," Nox continued to stare up at the amber stain around us, "where did it come from?"

Shifting my weight, I looked around the stain, "Retail."

A beat passed, one in which his brow furrowed.

"Why must you fight." His eyes rolled down to me through his shining bangs, "Why can't you just destroy me."

"While I don't care about anything-" Extending a hand to him, I would have smiled at him if I had known how, "Cyrus does, and he wants to save you."

Eyes wide, locked on me, a sudden sharpness took him.

The abyss flashed red.

"Leave."

Opening my mouth to say something to him, I blinked, and when my eyes opened again, I was met with the color of the concrete floor of the break room. A wave of pressure crashed into me. I think I yelled out, the taste of blood ripping through my throat would suggest that, but all I could feel was the fire as it ate away at me, all I could hear was the electrical buzzing around me. The floor below my knees returned to the concrete, then a moment later, like a wave rushing over the room, one item affecting the next, everything regained their lines, their color, shape and shadows as they returned from the abstract.

The world clicked back into place.

Beeping, sizzling, cracking, humming and alarms, they took over my world. Breath shaking on the way in, my bangs sat, spilled over my face. Sitting up, my every muscle shook, the weight on my back lifting as I did. Eyes meeting him, Cyrus sat, hand on my shoulder, eyes on mine as the world around us hummed. Eyes lowering, they met my neck, the amber emanating from the brooch reflecting in them. For a moment he smiled at me, his gaze rising back to mine, but then his grip loosened, his brow furrowing as the light dimmed in his eyes. Falling forward, he crashed into me, going limp in my arms.

Staring forward, my breath caught in my throat. He was so warm. As my hearing blurred in and out, the tattered break room cracking and groaning as the pressure faded, I looked down to him. Turning him in my arms, resting him up against me, I couldn't breathe enough to speak. Bringing my hand up to the side of his face, it was met with the remainder of the tears that had streamed down.

As if I had seen him tens of other times, the echoes of him I had seen with Nox haunted me.

I didn't know him, but I did.

Somehow.

Looking up and around, I took it in, what I had done to my surroundings. Table knocked to the side, the ceiling panels loose, smoke tinting the air, the papers posted to the walls singed. I had done this to my store. My eyes lowered to the unconscious young man in my arms. I had done this to Cyrus.

Pulling him up into me, my eyes closed as my grip tightened.

The light above flickered red.

Amber roused behind my eyes, my jaw clenching.

I had harmed him.

A hand met my back, taking the rise of amber with it. Eyes wide, breath snagged in my throat, I pulled back. His eyes struggling to stay open, exhaustion evident on his every feature, despite it all, Cyrus still smiled at me.

"You did great." His hand sliding from my back, it met with my chest, pressing up against it. Smile exploding on him, he was like a balloon, no matter what pulled him down, he always floated back up, "you tamed it, your first color. Just a few more to go and," he took my shirt into his grip, "then you'll be complete again."

I opened my mouth, an avalanche of things wanting to come out, but then my eyes focused up behind Cyrus. Grabbing onto him, I yanked us backward, rolling on the floor. A crash of metal and glass groaned through the air, deafening as I held onto Cyrus. The quiet that followed felt numb, buzzing in my ears as I pulled myself up off Cyrus. On the ground below me, his hair spilled around his head, he didn't struggle. Laying there, looking up at me, I had never been looked at like that before.

A hissing crack sliced the air.

Looking to the side, I was met with the vending machine, face down on the ground, electricity humming and snapping. Glass all over the floor, the way the dim light caught on the shards sent me back to the day I lost her. A hand met mine as it sat on the ground, holding me up above Cyrus. Breath hitching, I looked down to him. His eyes regaining their glow, they must have been reflecting on his face because it appeared a bit red too.

Taking his free hand, he reached into his blazer pocket, taking my glasses from it. Swinging them to the side, he opened them with one hand before carefully sliding them back into place on my face, bringing him into striking clarity, the only thing in my world.

"That wouldn't have killed me, I'm immortal," his grip tightened, every word livelier than the last as he regained his edge, "though I appreciate the sentiment."

Staring down at him, something about the dusting of red on his face made me pause before looking away, pulling myself off him, no longer pinning him to the floor with my weight, "But it would have hurt you."

Standing, my body shook. Using the side of the toppled break room table to help myself up, a hiss escaped my clenched teeth. Taking a breath, I turned to look at Cyrus, but he wasn't there. Eyes dropping, they met him as he remained on the floor. Approaching him, he reminded me of the zombie in the casket. Extending my hand, I stared down at him.

Staring back at me, he didn't take my hand.

I looked away, "What?"

"It's just…" taking my hand, he startled me, almost pulling me over because I wasn't expecting it, "no one ever considers that."

Standing there, hand in mine, Cyrus smiled down at me.

His wavy hair falling into place, his movie star softness and life to his glowing eyes, his hand was warm on mine.

The light flickered red.

The door swung open, knocking me into the wall behind it. Ears ringing, world blurry, I slid down to my knees, hand to my face where my crooked glasses sat. In the moment before my senses returned to me, the moment before I snapped back from the daze, I saw them, the line of young men standing in the abyss, staring back at me.

"Are you okay-" Amy came into my view, kneeling at my side, hands hovering before making contact. Her eyes lowered, catching on my neck as her brow raised ever so slightly, "that must have been a massive power surge."

"Is that the vending machine?" Venecia's voice came from the other room, "I think it's on fire."

Amy flew away from me and into the manager's office, taking a fire extinguisher into hand before running into the break room. The lights started to flicker again but only for a few moments before a depressed hum took over the air and we were plunged into darkness. An amber light emanated from my bow tie and I quickly pulled out my dead phone. Tuning out Amy as she deployed the fire extinguisher, my reflection met me. One of the smaller gems on the brooch was no longer grey and faded, but held a bold amber glow. Staring at it in the reflection of my dead phone, I didn't want to look away. Though the color was strong, overwhelming perhaps, something about that made it drawing.

I don't think I had ever heard a more exasperated sigh escape Amy before, "Come on," she said after one last spritz of the fire extinguisher, "we need to evacuate the store."

Cyrus stood, brow furrowed as he looked down to me, extending his hand. Staring up at him through crooked glasses, I felt like I had seen that before too, my mind painting an image before me for just a moment. Blue cloud speckled sky, a tree line behind him, darkly dressed with a white rectangle on his collar, Cyrus looked different, but somehow, still the same. When I blinked, the image left.

Accepting his hand, he pulled me up. As Amy led Venecia out of the back, flashlights in hand, Cyrus let go of me. Starting for the door, following them, his golden hair bounced, even in the dark. Taking a step forward, my mouth open to say something, I didn't know what as my hand extended toward him.

I couldn't step back into the store.

My fingers met with the back of his blazer, taking grip of the fabric, stopping him in the door.

Because if I did, I'd never want to leave.

He stood in pause for a moment as Amy made her way into the store, calling out to customers to head toward the exit. Pulling on his jacket a bit more, I stared at the back of his head. A wish started to burn in my mind, not quite a desire, nor a want. It wasn't strong enough for that, rather, it was a need. No matter what happened, there had been one truth, something that was never wrong.

Nothing could get a rise out of me.

Cyrus turned to look at me over his shoulder, brow raised.

Nothing before him.

I didn't know what to think, not of Netherside, Nox, or what had just happened. But as amber sat, warm in my bow tie, buzzing in my core, as everything I thought I knew had been thrown into question, there was one thing I did know.

I couldn't let go of him.

Not after that.

Looking up to him through disheveled bangs, the red of his eyes glowed in the dark, threatening to ignite something in me.

Not after he made me feel.

Grip tightening, I looked out to the darkened open store through the office door. If I stepped back out there, the beige of hard tags and grey speckled linoleum floors would suffocate it, the embers Cyrus disturbed in me. There was a safety in that, but as I heard his intake turn up with his smile, there was something about the anticipation of the toll of a bell after you've pulled on the string, the moment after the tug but before the ring, in which you await the vibrations of the knell.

"What's up?" He turned to face me fully, causing my grip on his jacket to slide off.

My eyes drifted from the open store behind him, the dimly lit displays and clothing racks. I stared for a moment before I ripped them away, bringing them to the glow of his eyes. The amber of the brooch catching in them as they searched mine, it was enough to make me forget, forget my place in this world, forget my family, my job, myself. There was something I wanted to forget, but of everything I forgot in that moment, it was the one thing I could do nothing but remember.

A fantastical land, a place unknown, what colors could I meet if I went with Cyrus there?

Hand raising to the silk of my bow tie, there was only one way to find out.

"Take me."

Eyes wide, smile frozen on his face, Cyrus stared at me, "What?"

I took a step back, the shouts of my coworkers fading, "I need you to take me."

Looking around, he turned to glance over his shoulder, still smiling, but brows furrowed, "Like, right here, right now?"

"Yes," I looked back to him, the glittering of the glow of his eyes on pause, "it's dark, so they won't notice."

Brows raising even higher, he stood, staring at me, "Are you sure?"

Arms crossing over my chest to put something between us as he stared, I shifted my weight, "What, are you trying to change my mind?"

Mouth open, his word turned into a dawn out croak until he managed to say, "No, I'm just surprised," stepping forward, it was cautious as his eyes dropped to my bow tie, "that's amber isn't it? Like orange, not red, right? Anger and stuff, not uh…" he paused, "not anything else?"

Raising a brow a bit, I studied him as his front began to crack, "I believe so, yes."

Nodding slowly as he straightened, my reply appeared unsatisfactory as his nod seemed more an attempt to convince himself than an expression of understanding. Swallowing, his brow furrowed for a moment as he looked away. Clearing his throat, he looked back to me, the red of his eyes brighter, as if they had caught fire.

Taking a step forward, he made me take a step back, "You're a wild card, you know that?" Taking another step toward me, he backed me into the wall. Little space between us, he pressed himself into me, bringing up his hand. Finger meeting my chin, he tilted my head up, locking my eyes on his as he towered above. Lowering his face down toward mine, he started to close the space even more, hovering but an inch away, "But I guess you've always been that way," resting his forehead on mine I could hear his smile, "I've missed you."

Getting closer, but the slightest of movement would bring us together. Staring at him, he was so close he was blurry as his warmth infected me.

I blinked.

"What are you doing?"

He went tense, I could feel it, his body pressed into mine, "I, I'm uh," he pulled back a bit, eyes searching mine, "I'm taking you?"

Looking between his eyes, pressed into the wall, a brow raised as I studied him, "Is this how you take us back to Netherside?"

"Take us back to…" whatever realization he came to in that moment, it must have been devastating because I watched every stage of grief flash over his face before he flew away from me. Stumbling back, he crashed into the opposite wall. Hands raising to his face, he slid down to the floor.

Staring at him as I pushed myself up from the wall, I straightened my button down, "What's wrong?"

A harsh breath escaped him, a hiss through clenched teeth as he pushed himself back up the wall, his voice muffled through his hands, "Man am I excited for you to gain some emotional intelligence." Taking his hands from his face, he turned from me. Though it was dark, as he ran his hand through his hair, I could see it, the red dusting his face. "It's times like these that I wish I could die."

Stepping forward, he lunged toward me. Burying his forehead in my shoulder, his grip tightened as I crashed into the wall again. Staring forward as the world started to glitter around us, I didn't know what possessed me, but as if another moved my arms, they wrapped around him too. Breath hitched, I could hear it, his smile.

Exploding into light around us, the world disappeared and a moment later, we dropped into nothingness. Grip tightening on him in the fall, I wondered if this balloon would be enough to keep me from hitting the ground.

A couple thumps, screaming of wood on wood, I laid in a heap of myself, glasses crooked, as dust floated through the air. A book fell from above me, soon followed by an avalanche of others.

Coughing, Cyrus laughed, "I'm sorry about that, I swore I had a good grip on you."

Pulling myself up, I slowly regained my bearings. A moment ago, I was in my store, and now… Well, I had no idea where I was now. Surrounded by a study, books sat in a pile at my feet, one falling from my shoulder as I sat up.

Red met me, Cyrus standing there with his hand extended, bending over, "Don't mind the mess, I haven't had a guest in like, twenty years."

The dust in the air caught in the glow of his eyes, like embers between us.

Accepting his hand, he pulled me up with him. The light above flickered red. Glancing up to the light, he ran his free hand through his hair before dismissing it and looking back to me. Smiling for a moment, he let go of my hand. Straightening my button down and bow tie, I looked around as Cyrus turned from me. A crooked messy desk sat at my side, a globe covered in pins atop a pile of books on it. Following Cyrus, I stepped over books on the floor, all but obstructing an intricate rug below them. Shuttered windows on the wall, a faint light poured in through them. Tall piles of books around sent shadows across the room.

The air was warm and somewhat humid, a combination that would usually be smothering as it surrounded me. But comfort was found in it, the way it pressed up against my chest with every breath, almost like the warmth of another, almost like his warmth. Eyes on Cyrus' back as he nearly tripped over a pile of books, I wondered what he had misunderstood moments ago, his warmth still lingering on my skin from when he pressed his body into mine.

Meeting a door, Cyrus pushed on it, but it didn't open. Pushing on it more, it gave a bit, but not much. Laughing, he looked back to me, "Just a second." Returning to fight the door, I just stood, watching him.

"You're a hoarder."

"I prefer the term-" his voice strained as he pushed harder on the door until it gave, shoving whatever had snagged on the other side. Sent stumbling through, he vanished into a cloud of dust, "collector."

Staring at the swirling dust, the light filtering through the window flickered a color. Though it was so brief, I couldn't tell what it was. Careful to not trip over any books myself, I made my way as the dust cleared. Following him

through the door, my mouth was open to criticize him further

when I stopped. The walls in the next room weren't covered

in paper or paint, but they were decorated, every inch, in

photographs. Some were faded, so bleached by time that their

contents were nothing but a haze of what once was. Others

sat vivid against the modest wooden wall, their colors

holding a life of their own. They were taken in the most

mundane of places to the most lavish, and as I walked

around, mindful to not step on the piles of books about, I saw

places that I recognized. Locomotives, theaters, ballrooms,

forests and more, even the Pyramids, they varied wildly. But

no matter how different the background, the subject was

always the same. Stopping, I looked over a photo of a bloody

sunset, the identifiable silhouette of Cyrus Glory in its center.

Glancing over to him as he fought with another door,

I was about to ask something when he opened it. Met with a

wave of silver and gold, through the door ajar, I saw a trophy

case. Approaching as he ratted around about the room, I

noticed several awards I could name. From acting to sports,

achievements only awarded to the most talented and accomplished, they shared a name. When my eyes snagged on the date on one of the plaques, I blinked at it.

"How long have you been alive?"

A smirk found its way to him as he approached a dresser, "I'll forgive you because you don't know," he pulled a drawer open and started to dig through it, "but that's a rude thing to ask."

"My apologies, but," my eyes snagged on a picture of Cyrus in absurdly large bell bottoms, "I do want the answer."

Slamming the drawer closed, he looked like he surprised himself as much as he did me. Eyes wide for a moment, they were soon shaped by the nervous smile that took him, "Six-hundred-and-twenty-three-years." His attention jumped from me as he walked around digging about the room in apparent search for something that was successfully hidden, "Lived in France once upon a time, was cursed at twenty, haven't aged a day since." He picked up a sweater, irritation starting to build in his movements as he threw it back down, "It's a pretty basic immortal story, nothing special."

"Something tells me," I looked back to him after my eyes snagged on an Oscar, "that you are anything but ordinary."

"Oh yeah?" He picked up another sweatshirt, excited for a moment before he threw it back to the floor.

"Yes," I followed him as he scurried across the room, yanking open another chest, "did you know Nox in his first life?" stopping behind him, I crossed my arms over my chest, "You must have, to be this entangled."

Cyrus froze, garment in hand, though his back was to me so I couldn't see his face, "What makes you ask that?"

Walking around, I inspected the wall of trophies, "Oh nothing," my grip tightened on my arm, the image of Nox laying on the ground, the sharpness to his eyes resurrected behind mine, "he just doesn't appear to fancy you."

Slowly turning around to face me, bedazzled jacket in hand, Cyrus stared, brow lowered, eyes heavy on me, "So he did help you."

Bringing my hand up, I ran it through my hair, looking away from him, "He didn't."

Another coat in hand, he froze before throwing it to the ground, eyes low, wide, "What?"

Lowering my hand from my hair, I started toward him, "Yes," stopping at his side, I took the jacket from his hand, folding it, "In fact, he told me it was pointless to struggle." Draping the coat over my arm, I knelt, taking another in hand, "Said that he had repressed my emotions to hide me from you, that now that the powers had been woken, I was doomed to fall to them." I started to fold the next coat, "He told me to destroy him, begged me to end the cycle." Eyes lingering on the sequins on the jacket in my hands, the way the light reflected off them reminded me of the way the moonlight reflected off Cyrus' eyes, "And after seeing all the other incarnations, I considered doing it."

Cyrus took a breath, about to speak, eyes on the ground, shoulders low, but then I went on, cutting him off.

"But," I finished folding the coat, setting them both down nicely on a stack of books, "back in the break room, I saw you. Over and over, every time you've found me, every time you've tried to save me, to save Nox, and well," looking up to him and the way his waves fell forward when he hung his head, I could only look at him for a moment, "who am I, who is Nox, to give up when you never have."

When he turned to look at me through his golden waves, when his wide eyes locked on mine, brows raised, not even the overwhelming clutter around us could obstruct that moment as dust floated through the streaks of sleepy air between us.

"So, you tamed amber on your own?"

Blinking at him, that wasn't what I had expected him to say. Lifting my hand, my finger stopped right above the brooch, not making contact but able to feel the warmth emanating from the light, "Do you mean this?" When he

nodded, I took a step to the side, met with my faint reflection

in a glass case, "You said it was anger, didn't you? It was a

lot, I sent Nox flying. And," lowering my hand, I looked

back to him, "I didn't defeat it on my own," I took a step

forward, "I had you."

Eyes wide as they searched mine, his brow dropped

with such animation that it looked like it hurt as he averted

his gaze, his face dusting red as he turned away from me and

continued to dig through a pile of clothing. Watching him as

he dug through the chest, I wondered what in the world he

could be looking for, though considering the state of this

house, and the fact that there was another door that led to

who knows what, it could have been anywhere.

As he jumped, holding a coat, he lit up. Though a

moment later, the excitement drained from his features as he

sighed, tossing the coat away. Something tugged at the line

of my mouth, something so slight, I almost didn't notice it.

The light filtering through the window flickered yellow.

"Well, that is certainly impressive," he turned a coat around in his hands before tossing it aside, "especially for someone so unfeeling, to care enough about my efforts as to prolong their own suffering."

"At least suffering is something," I looked away, eyes meeting a war-time medal, "I still don't really feel anything but," I looked down to my hands, "when it was stronger, even though it hurt, even though it was bad, when I allowed it to happen, I felt something." Closing my hand, I lowered it, "Nox thought he had the right to take that away from me, so if for no other reason than to spite him, I'll get them back, defeat the colors, and feel again."

Laughing as he picked up another jacket and threw it back down, Cyrus rested his hands on his hips, staring down into the chest of seemingly endless garments, "I see he made a great first impression." Running his hands over his head, I could hear it, the smile in his words, "He's always been good at that."

Leaning up against the wall, I studied him. His tone had shifted, his posture a tad less bold as he paused in his search, "Were you close?"

"Something like that," he closed the trunk, starting toward the next door, "but now I'm sure he hates me."

I followed him as he opened the door with little resistance, "I can't imagine why."

Stopping, he turned to look at me, and there was just something about it, the furrow of his brow, that made me stop too. That sensation took me again, the tugging at the line of my mouth, as I stood, staring at him, the light from the window turning yellow for but a moment. Hand slowly raising to my mouth, I stood in pause.

"Shut up," he turned from me, laughing as he led me through what felt like endless loops of rooms as he spoke on, "A pacifist and born witch, I've known Nox from the day we were both surrendered to the same church as infants." Books stacked high, there were various jackets around, though none of which were the one he was in search of, apparently, as we passed, "We grew up together, at a point I would have considered us as close as two people could get. I was even the first to witness his powers. He was good at keeping them hidden, though," he tripped over some books, nearly wiping out as he crashed into the wall, "one can only hide for so long, I suppose. So, I'm sure you can see where this is going."

Snatching up a coat, he looked at it before throwing it away, starting toward the next door. Struggling with it, he pulled a bit too hard and almost went flying when it gave before storming through it, "Before they hanged him from a tree, he used his last moment to curse me with the gift of immortality. I deserved it, though, so it's neither really here nor there, anymore." Inspecting a coat, he paused before sighing and continuing on, "I thought that was where the story ended, but then one day he found me again, to his great dismay, an incarnation. Same soul, same powers, and thus this cycle began."

Watching him as he disappeared through the dusty threshold, I was starting to see it, the story between the lines as I followed, stepping over the box he had kicked, "And so you've wandered the world ever since in search for his reincarnations?"

"Search is a funny word." He knelt to a pile of clothing on the floor, "I have met every single incarnation, our paths always crossing in one absurd way or another," pulling out a bright orange shirt, he turned it around to see a black number stenciled on the back. Staring at it for a moment, something lit in his eyes as he laughed a little, "whether we liked it or not." Shoving that shirt back in, he continued his search, "Though the nature of our relationship has," he paused, glancing up to me through his wavy locks, "varied," he looked back down to the clothing, "depending on the context, one thing has always held true."

Watching him as he painted past lives behind my eyes, I shifted my weight, "And what is that?"

Lighting up when he pulled yet another black item of clothing from the pile, he looked as if he had finally found what he was looking for until he turned it around and saw something about the front that must have not been what he had wanted. Dropping it in the pile, he ran his hand over his face, "Sorry, um, where were we? Oh, right, yeah," dropping his hand back to the pile, he plucked another item out, "that's how I've spent the last six hundred-and-three years, living countless lives, trying to distract from being trapped in one." He pulled a coat from a pile on the floor, inspecting it, "Only able to convince the world that I'm not immortal for so long, I drift, dying when needed. And it was going pretty well for me, but I guess the last time drew too much attention and Abraxas buried me around it. That, and I landed on The Three's radar."

Watching him as he knelt, digging through the pile, throwing coats that all looked pretty similar to me but must have been dissimilar enough to him that he could tell them apart, I leaned against the wall, "Are they some type of authority?"

"The authority," Cyrus pulled up a coat, the buttons catching the glow of his eyes before he threw it away too, "while there are kings of every realm, The Three float above it all, only intervening when they feel as if not doing so would be more troublesome than the effort of interacting with us, but ants in their crystal ball. And if you really fuck up, they will even put you on trial and lock you in their cosmic prison. I'd avoid them at all costs." Inspecting a coat, it wasn't the right one as he tossed it, "Legend has it they created the universe or whatever but like," he pulled out another coat, throwing it to the side, nearing the end of the pile, "I doubt it."

Meeting the end of the pile, Cyrus sighed, defeated as he knelt there.

Raising a brow, I studied him. He was so peculiar, a movie star who appeared to navigate every role with prowess except his own, "May I ask what you're looking for?"

Sitting up, his brow furrowed as he smiled at me from the floor, "My hoodie."

"Well," I pushed myself up from the wall, looking down at the piles of coats thrown about, "when was the last time you saw it?"

Standing, he paused for a moment, "I was wearing it when I jumped in front of the…" stopping, he stared at me and I watched it, a series of thoughts rip through him just to end with his hand up to his head. Sighing, he ran his hand through his hair, "train." Jumping, he looked up to a clock on the wall, brow dropping, "I know where it is, but," he squinted, digging in his pocket. Fishing out a phone, when the screen lit to life, his eyes went wide, "damnit, okay." Looking back to me, his eyes scanned me up and down as his arms crossed, "Well Igor, do you know how to dance?"

Blinking at him, I had almost missed what he had said, so taken by the way he said it, watching his every emotional shift, his animation, "I do."

The way he lit up, it made that musty house feel bright, "Fantastic."

Taking off like a man on a mission, I watched as he ran from the room. Accompanied by thuds, his voice was muffled as it called back, "Chances are my friend Abraxas has my hoodie, and if my phone is right, she should be at Anton's birthday ball right now with Valor." Racing through the room I was in, what he held was but a blur to me as he darted into another room, "And what better way to introduce you to the kingdom than at a ball?"

Eyes holding on the threshold Cyrus had vanished through, I wondered where all that energy came from, especially since he was old, "Anton is the current king, yes?"

"Yeah," something crashed and Cyrus laughed, "why?"

Eyes not leaving the door he left through, I couldn't look away and miss a chance to see him again. There was something about the way he laughed, the smile I could hear in his words even when I couldn't see him. Another itch came to the line of my mouth, something that wanted to move it, though which way, I couldn't tell. Bringing my sleeve up to brush against my face, I tried to clear the tingle.

"Well," lowering my sleeve, I listened as his footsteps approached, "you wish for me to become king. Isn't it improper for someone like me to crash the current king's birthday ball?"

"Oh," he popped his head into the door, his hair bouncing with the movement, "nah, don't worry about that. Anton was close with Nox and I in life and he knows that he's not really strong enough to sustain Netherside forever. He's just some incubus acting as a placeholder. No one is more excited about your return than him," he vanished back into the room, "second to me, of course."

As I stood there, leaning against the wall, I just hummed in reply.

Anton reminded me of corporate, untrusted.

"Alright," Cyrus came rushing toward me, holding up a suit, tie, and dress pants, "these should fit you," shoving them into my chest, he started toward the door, "get changed and then," he hovered in the door, swinging off of the knob with it on its hinges, "we'll take you home. I'm sure everyone will be thrilled to see you again."

Before I could reply, he closed the door between us.

"Oh, and," his voice muffled through the door, "don't forget but you can't take off your bow tie with the brooch."

Staring at the door, suit in hand, I wondered what I'd feel in that moment if I could feel much of anything at all. Careful as to disturb the brooch as little as possible as I switched out my yellow work button down for the white one Cyrus had given me, my eyes caught on movement at my side. Turning as I buttoned the new shirt up, I was met with my reflection in a glass case. As I pulled the bow tie down over my popped collar, I stared at it. But one color of six, one gem lit to life, it was softer than the color I had seen, a tame pastel orange. Straightening the bow tie, my fingers lingered on the fabric. What other colors were there? How would they feel? How would I tame them? As my hands lowered, so did my eyes. I wasn't quite sure how I had done it before, something nearly innate. But I couldn't let it go that far again. My eyes drifted up to the door Cyrus had closed. I couldn't hurt him like that again.

Pulling the blazer over my shirt and vest, I buttoned the top button. As if dressed for a funeral, it felt as if I were endeavoring the opposite. A new world, a new drive, a new goal. I ran my hand through my hair as I looked over myself one last time. A new life, and it started at that ball.

"Hey," Cyrus' voice came through the door, less muffled than before, as if he were pressed up into it, "you ready?"

"Yes," I looked away from my reflection and turned toward the door as it flew open. About to open my mouth and ask if I looked alright, about to say that I had never been that dressed up before in my life, I'd never get to say those things because that's when my eyes met with Cyrus.

Though formal wear looked out of place on him, it clung to his frame nicely. Highlighting his toned, tall build, his strong shoulders, the blazer sat on him, unbuttoned. Hands in his pockets, his tie echoed the reds of his eyes, bringing out the burning undertones of his golden hair. Bending over to be eye level with me, his tie didn't slip from his vest. Though he too appeared to be about to say something, a preemptive smirk on his face, he didn't say a thing, eyes wide. While we looked like we could have been going to a funeral, I guess we also sort of looked like we could have been attending a wedding as well.

Clearing his throat, he straightened, looking away from me, "I'm happy it fits."

In that moment I felt it again, the twinge on my face, but that time there was an accompanying shift in my chest, a clenching of sorts. What was it, what about his nervousness and poor attempt at covering it invoked that in me? As I looked back to him, I noticed the light filtering in from outside flicker yellow before returning to its natural color.

A hand extended my way, it interrupted my train of thought.

Begrudgingly looking to me from the corner of his eye, the red glowed brighter, reflecting off his wavy long side bangs, "Don't let go this time."

Eyes lowering to his hand, I raised mine to meet his, but hesitated before making contact, "Do you think…" I looked back up to him, retracting my hand just a bit, "I could really become king? I'm not the most," my hand closed, "likable person."

Taking my hand in his, he laced our fingers together. The moment they made contact, his grip tightening on me, the world around us turned to glitter. Pulling me into an embrace, Cyrus' warmth tainted me as his arms grew tighter, the ground disappearing out from under us. As we fell, his head nuzzled into my shoulder, the only thing I heard was his voice.

"They're gonna love you."

Thrown, I didn't have to catch myself this time as Cyrus did. Holding me close, on our feet, I couldn't see much beyond his chest as he held tight for a moment longer. My world stopped spinning, senses taking hold once more as the sound of chatter took my ears. Slowly releasing his grip, he took a half step back. Studying me, I could see it, the glass that took over his eyes as he reached up and fixed my bow tie. With a slight nod, he turned and as his gaze left mine, it followed him.

In the shadow of the Netherside castle, again I found myself standing in that grass. A brow raised as I fought with the blades that wished to grip my shoes, I went stumbling to the side. Crashing into someone, I tripped away from them, an apology on my breath before it was stolen. Staring back at me, a group of three people, they hovered above the ground, ever so slightly, their lengthy hair floating about, as if the air were water. Scoffing as they went on, they navigated forward as if they were swimming, their bedazzled suits catching the light.

"Mermaids," Cyrus said as he stepped to my side, looking down to me as I looked up and over to him, "that's what you were wondering, right?" When I couldn't reply, just stare, he laughed, throwing his arm around my shoulders. Staring to lead us toward the castle, we joined the flow of others heading the same way, "Netherside is home to all sorts of magical shit, I can't wait for you to meet them."

Unable to struggle against his grip, all I could do was look around at the others walking near us. Wings, scales, talons, pointy hats, feathers, and glows, I was but an unimpressive blip in an otherwise interesting world. As my eyes met with others, their colors similarly unnatural to Cyrus', I started to notice something.

"Why is everyone glaring at me?"

His chuckle was more of a cough, his discomfort evident in the way his grip on my shoulder tightened a bit, "They are probably looking at me, not you." As we exited the courtyard, we retraced our steps from the day before. "I don't have a lot of friends in Netherside."

Looking up to him as we stepped into the partly covered outer corridor of the castle, his eyes were forward, notably avoiding others around, "Nox did say you were good at ruining lives."

Whistling, he yanked me around, causing others to look our way as he ruffled up my hair, "Not everyone's lives," he released me, leaving me to straighten my hair, an uncomfortable step away as he smiled, "just yours."

Watching him and his grin through the strands of my disheveled hair as he laughed, I barely noticed when the flame lanterns lining the walls flickered yellow. The flow of nicely dressed individuals turned into a line leading toward the doors we had passed through before to the grand hall attached to the room that changed it all. My brooch weighed on my neck with my next step. Though it had been less than a day since then, it felt as if it had been so much longer. We neared the grand doors, music floating through the air as the couples before us stepped inside. As if the space beyond the threshold were encapsulated in a bubble, the sounds were muffled, the view inside blurry from where I stood.

"So don't be alarmed but," Cyrus looked down to me as we took another step forward, "when we step through that door, the announcer will be able to tell who you are and when your name is said, I'm sure we'll get a big reaction." He wrapped his arm around my shoulders again, "but don't worry, no one will mess with you while I'm around."

Taking one step closer to the ball, the fire next to us on the wall flickered yellow. As the couple before us- two tall figures donning long dark robes that dissipated in the air around them, constantly generating back like smoke pouring from their frames- stepped into the ballroom, they became blurry. Letting go of me, Cyrus patted my back, smiling before he stepped forward. Following him, only a bit of hesitation found me as I stepped forward too. Like stepping through a film, just a water molecule to a semipermeable membrane, when I reached the other side I was met with roaring music and lively dancing. Staring down the grand stairs into a sea of moving bodies, I couldn't locate the orchestra around them. Beings lingered around the edges, talking amongst tables decorated in small food displays and punch bowls.

"Welcoming Cyrus Glory," a voice exploded over the room, and with it, silence followed. Cyrus stood at my side, unfazed by the response, his smile immortal like him, his stance strong, "and his company," the voice paused as I looked around, unable to find its source, "the forty-ninth incarnation of the Great Witch, Nox."

Though silence had already taken over the room, when my name rang out, the air dropped, the movement stopped, and there I stood, atop it all. Looking down and around at all the eyes looking at me, eyes wide, I stood in that moment for a moment too long until Cyrus took my hand, shaking me from it. Looking to him, he gestured to the side with his head, taking a step down the stairs. With my first step down, whispers erupted, dance partners turning away and to each other to converse. Orbs floated above us, grand in size, so big and burning they looked like suns, emanating pure white light above the ball. Though as I approached the whispering masses, their white light flickered purple.

"Nox," someone called from the crowd, "I knew you weren't gone."

Stopping mid-step, I looked up, Cyrus pausing with me as he held my hand.

"Welcome back," another voice called.

Whispers turned into conversation, the weight ignited and became bright when someone yelled "We missed you."

Cheers caught like fire through the crowd, as if it were contagious. Standing there, looking out over the cheers, they surrounded me, and as they swelled, so did something in my chest. The lights flickered yellow, the orbs casting the color over the entire ballroom. Slowly looking over to Cyrus as yellow grew around us, I was about to give into the tug on the line of my mouth when a voice pierced through the cheers.

"How misleading."

Frozen, eyes wide on Cyrus, it took me a moment to look out to the crowd toward the voice that had shattered the moment. Beings parted, scrambling away from the impending individual as Cyrus and I remained, three stairs from the floor. When the front line of beings broke, tripping to the side, two people broke through.

Tall, one spindly, the other more built, they stopped at the bottom of the stairs, not stepping up. The slender one took a step toward me, silver ashy hair of striking length pouring over their shoulders clad in a dark purple silk cape above a purple and black velvet vest. Their chest puffed with their audacity, it was crowned by a lacy jabot, a deep purple gem in a silver brooch pinned to it. Thin silver wired glasses with a thin silver chain hanging from their frames, it draped behind their head and beneath their hair, reflecting some of the light back at me. Tips of elf-like ears separated two long sections of hair to the front, framing in their angular face. Through their glasses, their eyes glowed so purple that it almost drowned out the light reflecting in the glass. Extending their hand, when they smiled I saw them, their fangs.

"How can you claim to be the true incarnate of the greatest witch to ever live," their fingers fell closed, leaving but one extended, pointing at my brooch, "if you have yet to tame the powers and own the name."

"Mind your own, Twining," Cyrus said, taking a step down, letting go of my hand, "He will in due time, and when he does, he'll be the strongest being in all the realms."

"That's debatable," the other said, standing a step behind the first. His well kept slicked back hair and boxy build, as the blue of his eyes dug into me, glowing so brightly it reflected off of the other's light hair he reminded me of a door-to-door window salesman. "That is operating under the assumption that he won't fall to his powers, just as every incarnation has before."

Eyes narrowing on him as the words thrown into the air between us landed, the orbs above flickered orange.

My jaw tightened as I took two steps down, a step below Cyrus, but a step above them. "I assure you, I am up for the challenge." Extending my hand, my brow raised as my gaze landed on purple, "My name is Igor, who do I owe the pleasure?"

The crowd had fallen quiet once again, watching as the spindly individual looked up to me from my hand, head tilted a bit, raised brows tainted by their smirk. Accepting my hand, they were cold, their grip tight, their nails sharp and long, "Twining van Serifino," they bowed their head a bit, "Elected Representative of the Vampiric Order."

I froze in the handshake.

A vampire?

Eyes trailing up from the communion of our hands, they met with Twining.

They let go of me.

My hand remained extended for a moment longer.

They were about to speak, but as I lowered my hand, I cut them off, "Is that supposed to impress me?"

I could sense them, every eye in the ballroom on me. Cyrus tense at my side, eyes wide, he didn't say a thing. Though the urge to look around was great, I didn't bend to it, not looking away from the toxic purple of Twining's eyes. I had dealt with people like this, and vampire or otherwise, they just loved to tell you how to do your job as if they had any clue.

A laugh took Twining as they shifted their weight, looking back to their company, "Very interesting, Maximilianus." Their eyes drifted back to me, though they remained facing the other, "This one has a bite that the others did not. How," they ran their bony fingers through their hair, their sharp jaw splitting the air as they turned from me, "delicious." Back to us, they started into the crowd again, waving as their elegant capes swayed with their every step, "I'll send my ward to fetch you. Please accept my invitation to the Vampiric Castle, I would enjoy speaking again in less public chambers. I find you," They stopped, looking back my way for but a moment, "exciting."

Staring forward as the crowd engulfed them, the air sat in suspension.

Cyrus shoved me, smiling despite his furrowed brows, voice quiet, "You're lucky Twining liked that."

As the attention on me began to weigh, it reminded me of the way customers glared at me when the line started getting too long, "Why?"

Blinking at me, Cyrus sighed, loosening up as he ran his hand through his hair, "Right, you don't know because I haven't told you," lowering his hand, the softness to his smile returned, "vampires, especially ancient ones like Twining, are the most powerful beings, rivaled only by you, Anton, and The Three. Get on their bad side, and well," he looked back out to the crowd, "just trust me, that's not where you want to be. But," he looked down to me, the floating orbs hanging in the air behind him in my view, "it looks like you may not need to worry about that." Taking my hand in his, his grip was steady, warm as he smiled, "Remember what I said?" Dragging me forward, we took off into the crowd, the individuals parting for us, "They're gonna love you."

As cheers met me, support pouring from my surroundings, I looked around, barely keeping up with Cyrus. The lights above flickered yellow again, but this time they held a little longer before returning. Nox's name was called from all around, echoing through the vaulted ceilings, like a lyric to the music as it started up again. The crowd turned into dancers, beings partnering up, moving in synch as Cyrus dragged me through them. Dodging dancers, Cyrus made it look flawless, the pivots of his shoes, the calculation of his movements, but I could see it, his self-possession. He was so controlled that he gave the illusion of being carefree.

Breaking through the line of dancers, we exited the crowd, met with a raised platform that hadn't been there before. Dragging me up a step, Cyrus stopped, looking up. Upon that platform sat a throne, looming and crafted of dark metals. It held a purple sheen, though the gems embedded in it reflected back the white light from above. Sitting on the throne, a large crown floating above his head, Anton's eyes were wide on me as I straightened. His crown appeared to have been crafted by the same artist responsible for the throne, the metal equally dark, the gems without color. Spinning slowly, it rotated in its suspension. An incubus, that's what Cyrus had called him. If memory served, Ross had told me about those once. Beings that survived by feasting off others, he was a strange choice to act as a temporary ruler of a realm that required great power to sustain. As he shifted in his seat, eyes trailing me up, I wondered how he managed it.

"Nox?" Slowly standing, the man of jolly stature towered above us on the platform, "I thought your previous incarnation finally destroyed you."

"I told you. He's the oldest incarnation yet, even older than Nox was. That's never happened before." Cyrus said, throwing his arm around me and yanking me into him, nearly taking me from my feet, "His name is Igor, and he's here for that crown."

Anton stood in pause, the cat-like pupils of his otherwise warm round eyes drifted between us until they landed on me. When they did, the flat line of his mouth curled up, his thinning hair catching the light in an oily sheen as he bowed, "But of course." Straightening from the bow, he looked right at me, though his eyes drifted lower than mine, "As soon as you're at your full ability, I will gladly gift this to you, future king of Netherside."

Cheers roared from behind me again, so loud the ground shook. Slowly stepping around and out of Cyrus' grip, I looked over the dancers as they called out, smiling faces meeting me. The lights flickered yellow as I stared, a swell starting to build in my chest again. It felt similar to before, a rise I wasn't acquainted with. Though they both felt like heat, amber seared, when this color, whatever it was, felt warm.

In that moment, I was swarmed.

My initial reaction was to step back, but that took me right into Cyrus. The lights flickered purple. A small crowd, each individual unique and widely varied, I was met with a sample of Netherside. An individual covered in feathers, one with flowing hair, another with wings, one completely covered in hair, someone with a tail, another covered in scales, one of them didn't have a head on their shoulders, holding it at their side. I stood, eyes wide, looking over all of them. Hand on my shoulder, a light laugh on his voice, Cyrus' tone was soft.

"It's alright, they are just some Order representatives excited to meet you," he leaned in a little closer, "just be yourself."

Looking over to him, brow furrowed a bit as the lights flickered a pale orange, I wondered if he even knew how difficult something like that was for someone as empty as me. But as they asked questions and I did my best to answer, I sensed no judgment, not even a bit of awkwardness in them as they hung on my every word. Even though I couldn't smile like them, even though it was obvious that I was out of my element, they held nothing but respect for me. I was in the middle of explaining what retail was to a curious lizard-person who had never heard of it before when someone yelled out, cutting me off.

"Cyrus," a voice I had heard before pierced the air, causing me to turn and look back over the crowd. Panting as she broke through them, Valor came to the forefront.

Mouth open to say something else, brows furrowed, her bluntly cut hair cut the moment that she stood, frozen in pause. Eyes dropping to the brooch, they widened, watering. Lunging forward, she didn't give me a moment to react before she trapped me in an embrace. As her yellow passed through my vision, I was left standing, staring forward. In the gap she left behind, another stepped forward, in a rush, as if she had been chasing Valor.

Long hair fell around her, nearly reaching the ground as its white tone reminded me of another. Petite, shorter than me, her nearly grey complexion and black dress brought out her large, round dark doe eyes as they locked on me. As they widened, I saw them, hundreds of little white streaks catch the light in her irises'.

"I'm sorry," Valor's voice shook as her arms tightened around me, "I'm so sorry."

Though I didn't ask them to, it felt as if my arms gained the will of another as they raised, hugging her back. Her breath hitched as she buried her head into my shoulder.

"Nox?" The silver haired young lady said, her voice the lightness of a music box playing in the distance, "Is it really you?"

Nodding, it was all I could do.

"I told you I'd bring him back." Cyrus ruffled up my hair, his hand lingering on my head, not allowing me to fix it as my messy bangs hung in my eyes.

"Why did you come back?" Pulling away from the hug, Valor's misty eyes searched mine as the surrounding attention started to drain from me and return to the festivities, the individuals there to question me dispersing and leaving just us, "You said you were done."

"Well," I shooed Cyrus' hand from my head and raked my hair back from my vision, "I can't speak for Nox, as we are different people just bound by his powers, but," looking to Cyrus as he stood at my side, his smile met me, "if there's a chance I can win, I'm not giving up."

Where I had anticipated relief, perhaps even something brighter, I was met with an unchanging expression on Valor's face as she stepped back. Unsure what I could have said wrong, I didn't get to ponder that long as the other young lady stepped up to Valor's side, wrapping her arm around Valor's middle.

"My name is Abraxas," she bowed her head a bit, her long hair spilling over her black dress, "I'm usually to be found in my morgue- I work with the Pulse to cover up paranormal deaths," as her head lifted, her eyes were no longer on me, but on Cyrus, "though I'm behind on work because I had to spend an exuberant amount of time putting that one back together after he jumped in front of a train just to feel something I guess."

Laughing a bit, Cyrus looked away.

Abraxas' eyes held on him, though her words were directed toward me, "I'm sincerely sorry that he found you." Slowly looking my way, her light voice felt so heavy, "You face many toils ahead."

"Well, he has no choice, but I'm going to help him through them all," Cyrus said, stepping between us, smiling as he turned his back to the crowd, the edge of his shoes barely still on the step with me, "So I hope you don't get tired of me."

Looking over Cyrus and his stature, his smile and the way that his wavy middle part framed his face, complementing his cheekbones, something about him made the line of my mouth struggle to stay flat. Bringing my finger up to his tie, it lingered there as my eyes trailed up to his, "You don't have to worry about that," Increasing the pressure, I pushed him, and he didn't fight, hands flying from his pockets as he stumbled back off the step. Tripping, he landed on his tailbone, hands behind him on the ballroom floor as he stared up at me, disheveled hair in his face.

"I was tired of you the moment I met you."

The way he looked at me, eyes wide, almost like confused puppy, that was what did it.

Hand raising to my mouth, I tried to stop it, but as a yellow blossomed in my chest, a laugh took me. The lights above exploded into warm tones, casting yellow over the ballroom, sparks flying from them like glitter as they glowed brighter. It had been so long since I had laughed, I had forgotten the feeling, and for a moment, I was lost in it, tears budding in the corners of my eyes. Hand covering my mouth when I got ahold of myself, I was left, staring down at Cyrus. As my eyes rested on him and the red dusting his face, his breath suspended in his chest, I could feel it, a smile on my face under my hand.

Yellow was like a candle- fire, but contained, warm, but not burning.

Saying something under his breath as he stood, Cyrus was unusually stiff, hand up to his face. As I stared at him, hand staying on my face, I could see it, the red taking his ears as locks of his hair shifted forward. As if he was barely contained, about to burst at the seams, Cyrus brought his other hand up to his face as he shook his head, groaning.

Dropping his hands, he lifted his head, so quickly the movement was nearly a blur to me as his hair bounced, eyes on mine, smile on his red face. About to say something, lit up like the lights above, his momentum was cut when the announcer's voice boomed over the room.

"The Almighty Ghost King, Leader of Limbo, Kasper Kloven, and his Royal Knight Oliver Vestile the Great."

The ballroom quieted, the dancers slowing but not stopping as all eyes met the threshold atop the grand stairs. Cyrus' smile remained, but as I watched a shudder race through him, his brows furrowing as he shrunk, staring up at me from below. Lowering my hand from my face, a bit of my smile remained as well, a brow raised on the zombie before me. I wondered if he knew how much of his heart rested on his sleeve. Eyes raising from him, they met with the threshold as well as two people descended the stairs. They were a way away, but I could see it even from there, the electric blue they radiated. Eyes narrowing on them, trying to see them better as they stepped down into the crowd, individuals making way for them, I wondered why their presence was so disruptive. What was it that the announcer had said? I had been too distracted by yellow, by Cyrus and the red on his face to catch it. Thinking back, that's when my mind snagged.

Eyes widening a bit, my smile faded, the yellow dimming from above.

Ghosts?

The lights above flickered purple.

Though I never got spooked by much of anything, as I stared at the parting crowd before me, I got as close as I could at the time. If ghosts were real, then did that mean all the stories Amy would tell me about the fitting rooms being haunted were true? Was there just some poor soul trapped there watching me? It already felt like I was haunting the place, and I got paid to be there. A shudder took me as the lights turned purple again, holding for a moment longer than before.

Cyrus stumbled up the step to be at my side, voice quiet, leaning in close to me, "He's never come to one of these before," looking over the crowd as they continued to part, it became apparent that they were headed our way as Cyrus looked back to me, "he doesn't like me."

Looking over to Cyrus as he stood, arm pressed up against mine at my side, I couldn't stop it, the tug that started to take my mouth, "Does anyone?"

About to reply, Cyrus stopped, brows dropping as he looked back to me. But when his gaze met mine, he froze. When our eyes locked, I saw my reflection in his, and for the first time in a long time, I saw myself smile. I didn't even look like me, but as Cyrus' eyes glassed, darting between mine, that was okay, because I looked a bit like him. Quickly glancing away, he brought his hand up to the back of his head, a smile taking him too.

Perhaps I stared at him too long, maybe that's why I didn't notice everyone staring at me until someone cleared their throat. Jumping, I looked to my side to see Anton standing there, his crown adding to his stature.

"Almighty Ghost King," Anton's voice boomed over the attendees as they continued to part, the divide in the crowd growing near, "you were finally able to attend one of my balls, I'm flattered."

"Oh, I assure you, I'm not here for you, your highness," the voice that met me, lively and audacious, flattened the room as the final individuals parted.

Stepping through the line of guests, the first thing I saw was his eyes. Silver so sharp it stung everywhere his gaze met, it bought a wave of cold to me as it drifted up my entirety. It belonged to a young man who couldn't have been twenty yet, black shaggy hair, ghostly complexion, black suit and silver tie, the buttons of his blazer were popped, his hands in his pants pockets. Though he appeared formal enough, his stance, the upward zeal to the line of his mouth and raised brow, made him feel like the problem child here to ruin the nice family dinner. And while all of that was striking, the most striking thing about him was what was above him. A crown floating, spinning, as if it were made of an echo of metal, it was solid enough to hold form but not enough to stay solid. It housed a series of gems, each a different, churning color, as if they held life. He took my breath, like his mere presence was a disaster I couldn't will myself to look away from.

Eyes landing on Cyrus, the young man shifted his weight, "I'm here for Nox."

Standing behind him was another young man, fiery orange hair that hung down in a low ponytail at his side. His eyes glowed electric blue, leaving a trail of color behind them as he moved. His black and gold attire was that of a castle assistant, formal and bearing the crown crest. It was too detailed for me to decipher, but at its middle sat a dragon. He was somehow taller than the darkly dressed young man before me, though that nor his eyes were the most drawing thing about him. At his side hung a sword in its sheath, gold plated, gems embedded in the handle, its intricate carvings and notable length demanded my eyes as I was just left to stand there and stare at it.

"Ghost King," Cyrus said, and though it was through a friendly laugh, I could hear it, the nerves underneath, "it's nice to see you."

"If only I could say the same," The Ghost King was calm, cool, intimidatingly so, as his eyes rolled from Cyrus to me. When they met mine, they widened and in that moment, he lit up. "Igor?"

Blinking at him, though his eyes were different, there was something familiar about them. Gaze narrowing on him, it hit me like the car that had hit him. Kasper Kloven, eldest heir to one of the richest families in town, it had been years since he died. I was one of the last to leave his funeral, other than a butler who, legend had it, stayed there for days. Looking him up and down, yellow budded again in my chest. He looked good, like he finally fit in his skin. The last time I had crossed paths with him, he was still having to suffer through being called 'she'.

"Kasper…" I looked him over, taking a step back. "I didn't immediately recognize you, it has been so long."

"You two," Cyrus looked between us as the young man behind Kasper placed his hand on his sheathed sword making it clink, "know each other?"

Raising a brow, Kasper's head tilted, eyes taking me in, "Albeit on an acquaintance level, but yes. We were classmates at the private academy before I got expelled," laughing, he bent over to be eye level with me, "you haven't grown an inch from back then, have you?" Straightening, he ran his hand through his hair, "At least I have an excuse, I died at 18, but you must be, what, like, twenty-four now?"

This young man before me was nothing like the one I had known. Though we in different grade levels and rarely saw one another before he was expelled and then stepped out in front of a car a few years later, the person I remembered was more of a ghost than this actual ghost. But it made sense, if he was free to be himself now.

Kasper bowed his head slightly, his crown following, "Well, how interesting," his sharp eyes locked on mine from the bow, "retail worker witch incarnate, your reputation precedes you." He extended his hand, "May I have this dance?"

A few gasps echoed around us, but Kasper didn't seem to mind. I looked over to Cyrus as he rolled his eyes, and after a moment, he nodded. Brow raised as I looked back to Kasper, my eyes scanned over those staring in the backdrop. It was unsightly to know that hatred even found a home in the land of misfits and magic. It was a good thing Kasper passed so well.

Accepting Kasper's hand, he was cold, a chill that went straight to my bones as he straightened. Part of me had expected my hand to pass through him, given that he was a ghost, but as he smiled at me, starting us down the stairs, he looked just as solid as I was. Leading me away from Anton, the music continued as we stopped in the midst of other dancers. Pulling me close, Kasper took the lead, nearly making me stumble as he took our first step. Correcting

myself, it was hard to look at him, standing so close.

"So," Kasper's voice was soft, quiet enough that only

I could hear, but loud enough to rumble with his undertones,

"what do you think of it all so far?"

"It's," my eyes passed over Oliver, Kasper's knight,

as he watched us, the sharpness of his cool eyes striking even

from the distance as he stood, rigid in stance at the edge of

the dance floor, "interesting." I dragged my eyes back to

Kasper as he stepped us around, "I have only been aware of

my position in this situation for less than a day, I just

returned to Netherside like ten minutes ago." Looking away,

my eyes passed by the fantastical dancing at our sides, "The

last time I was here I believed it to be a dream so, I can't say

that I have any idea what I'm doing at this juncture." My

eyes drifted over Cyrus as he watched, wearing his agitation

like an accessory, "But my company appears to."

"Less than a day? You're kidding." Brows raised, his

eyes dropped to my brooch around my neck, "You're doing

better than the last one already, or so I've heard." Spinning me out, he smiled as he pulled me back in, "It can be a lot, all this. I know I struggled when I first got here, and I can promise the worst is yet to come, but despite that, it will be alright."

All eyes on us, I could feel every one as he guided us about, narrowly avoiding other dancing pairs. His grip tight on me, his chilly boldness, this person was nothing like the young man I had walked by as he protested horror flicks outside of the movie theater. That crown above his head fit him well, though with it, came an additional layer to this interaction. A statement, that's what it felt like, as he pulled me along in time with him, but a statement of what, I wasn't sure.

"It appears your visit today is of note," looking back to him, the silver of his glowing eyes left a trail as he moved, "you came all the way here just to see me?"

Laughing as we stepped in time, Kasper glanced about, "Yeah, well, it's not every day that there's a realistic chance that someone will usurp that exhausting man."

Looking back to me, his brow furrowed though his smile maintained, "You've really walked yourself right into the thick of it, and Anton is the worst. So I thought I'd drop by and make myself allied with you. And," When the music dropped, he dipped me, and had it not been for his strong grip, I would have hit the ground, "if you go nuclear you won't only take your realm down, but mine as well, so I wanted to make it abundantly clear," his eyes locked on mine as he held me there, hostage in the dip, his face hovering but inches from mine as his brow raised turning his smile from calm to combative, "that the moment I sense you're about to crack," the music began to slow, color draining from the world around us as that moment lasted several moments too long, "that I will not hesitate to-" lifting one of his hands from me, he extended it to his side.

Grip open, expectant, something started to materialize in it as the world came to a near standstill around us. As if we had entered a tear in the fabric of time, everything turned grey as the form of a sword landed in his hand, its weight evident in the drop. The same one the Knight had been carrying, its golden ornate handle was the only thing that retained its color, its unsheathed blade so dark it swallowed the light that met it. Grip tightening, Kasper raised the sword closer to me, hovering it a moment from making contact with my neck, "banish you myself."

The lights flickered purple above.

He dropped the sword and it turned to glitter.

Pulling me back up, the music returned to normal, the dancers continuing as if the world hadn't just been disrupted.

Smiling again, Kasper danced us around, a spring to his step, "I don't anticipate it coming to that though, I just wanted to be transparent. This is bigger than just one main character, and usually I wouldn't be one to interfere in the story of another, but my kingdom is my priority, I'm sure you understand." Spinning me around and pulling me in, his arms ended up wrapped around me, my back pressed into his front as his head lingered by my ear, his voice quiet, "In all earnest, this bureaucracy stuff isn't my favorite, please forgive the theatrics. I'd much rather be hanging out with my ghosts, but I am a king so I should like, act like it sometimes I guess."

Spinning me back out, his smile unfading, the tension of his brow melted away as I stared. A statement, a show, that was what that crown above his head, above Anton's, meant. And if I too was to wear one, I would need to also do my best. Stepping into him, I took the lead, nearly tripping him but he caught himself, eyes wide on mine.

"I understand, I have something to prove too." Eyes locking on his, in that moment, one in which my grip tightened on him, one in which I stepped forward and he stepped back, it was slight, but the upward tug on the line of my mouth won out, "If it did ever come to that, then by all means, banish me. But," spinning him out, he managed to make it look like he was expecting it as he looked back to me, arms extended between us, brow raised as I went on, "it won't."

The lights flickered yellow above.

"You sound so sure of yourself." Spinning himself up into me, he reclaimed the lead, stepping me back, "Is that a promise?"

The music stopped abruptly, so sharply even that it made me stumble right into him. Standing far too close, his eyes locked on mine, he didn't appear bothered. Not by the closeness, not by the eyes, not by Cyrus as he held his face in his hands, not by Oliver as his jaw visibly tightened, hand on his sword, not by anything. As I stared at him, trapped in that moment, breath struggling to catch up, I wondered what color was brewing behind the silver of his eyes.

A smile found me, the lights turning yellow again, holding for a bit longer than before, "Yes, I promise."

"Great," Stepping back, he slid his hand down my arm, ending on my hand. "I'll hold you to it." Taking my hand into his, Kasper knelt, bowing his head a bit as his grip tightened on me, "Should you ever find yourself riddled with grief," pulling his hand from mine, he left something cool in my grip, hidden as he looked up to me through clumps of his black bangs, "come visit me." Standing, he slightly bowed as Oliver quickly made his way toward us through the crowd behind Kasper, his air flipping from frightening to friendly, "It was great to see you again, we should catch up sometime. I'd like to ask you some questions about your time at Blazing Star Private High," bending forward, he lowered his volume, smiling through every word as he looked around, "it could just be a conspiracy theory, but you may find it interesting."

As Oliver met Kasper's side, my eyes dropped to the sword in his sheath. They exchanged hushed words, Oliver's brows lowered in obvious concern, or maybe annoyance, whatever it was, Kasper just smiled, laughing it off. Footsteps came racing up behind me, stopping at my side. Glancing over, my eyes were met with Cyrus, his eyes on Kasper.

"It appears we have stayed beyond our welcome," Kasper ruffled up Oliver's hair. A bold move, considering how uptight Oliver appeared, one hand on that sword of his as the other shoved Kasper away. Laughing, Kasper looked between Cyrus and I, "I look forward to seeing what you do, Igor." Shoving Oliver around, Kasper started back toward the door, the crowd parting for them once again, calling out as they left, "And I wouldn't trust Cyrus too much, I have heard nothing but terrible things about him."

When Kasper laughed, thunder rolled above. I didn't even get a chance to look up, because when I did, my vision was bleached with lightning as it struck the ground. When the white faded from my vision, I watched several guests pick themselves up from the dance floor, the ghosts gone. The ground sizzled, lightning trails seared into the marble. Left standing there, staring forward, Kasper's cool touch lingered on my skin. Looking down to my hand as Cyrus mumbled something colorful under his breath at my side, I didn't pay him much mind.

A translucent blue stone sat, shedding fog like dry ice in my palm.

Eyes raising to Anton as he stood before his throne, they met with his crown. Nox wanted me to give up, but this was bigger than Nox, bigger than Cyrus, bigger than me, bigger than everyone in this room. As my eyes returned to my hand, they passed over where Kasper had been, the ground still sizzling. I wasn't going to lose, I couldn't. Kasper was right, if I didn't get stabilized as soon as possible, I was nothing but a liability.

Closing my hand, my eyes closed with it. Pocketing the stone, its cool stained my skin. What was it, yellow. Where did it come from? I needed to conquer it, but in order to do that, I needed to conjure it. Fleeting, it wasn't like amber in the way it festered, easily agitated again long after its initial touch. As if I had never felt yellow at all, it was absent in my chest. What had triggered it?

Opening my eyes, they landed on Cyrus.

What was it that he did again? It was something to do with him.

He was saying something I wasn't paying any attention to as I stood there, staring at him. I'd never hear what it was he had been saying because he stopped when I extended my hand. Staring at me, eyes wide as they jumped between my hand and my gaze, Cyrus stood in pause. Looking around at the whispering audience of ball attendees and Anton, one brow dropped as the other raised when his eyes returned to me.

"Igor, I don't think-"

"Dance with me," cutting him off, I started to sense it again, the stirring of yellow when he blinked at me. Extending my hand closer to him, the line of my mouth threatened to break as I crooked my head a bit, "what, are you a coward?"

The way his brow dropped, the moment he spent glaring at me, it sparked it again, that dull warmth in my chest. A swell, it had started so small, but every moment spent watching Cyrus was a moment of swell more. Taking my hand as he huffed, looking away, Cyrus only managed to keep his smile tamed for a moment longer before it found its way back to his slightly reddened face.

The lights above flickered yellow.

Eyes darting up to them, the color met me for just a second before returning to the white. I was right, Cyrus was the key. Eyes meeting our hands between us, I stared at them. I had to get closer to him. He was the painter, the colors in his hand, and I was but a canvas. But as my grip tightened on his, I wanted to know what picture he'd paint.

Looking back up to him, I pulled Cyrus close. Apparently not expecting that, Cyrus came tumbling into me. Head on my shoulder, arms wrapped around me for support, Cyrus lingered there for a moment before stepping back. His smile and mischievous brows, the strength to his grip, the light in his eyes, his brief lapse of movie star persona had passed. Pulling me in close, he took the lead as he stepped us into the flow of dancers, all eyes on us, even the ones trying to hide that they were watching. Stepping with him, my body knew what to do. As if I had danced this dance hundreds of times before, I knew it without a thought, my body matching up with his.

Movements crisp, his strength, self-possession, he dominated me, rendering me but a prop to his show as he commanded the moment. When he spun me out, the squeaking of the sole of my shoe on the marble silencing the world, our eyes met. Chest raising and falling, brow crooked my way, the fire in his eyes, the strength to his posture, Cyrus may have been hundreds of years old, but the time hadn't dulled him, as bright as I'm sure he was back when his clock stopped. Hair knocked a bit astray, my glasses a little lower, I forgot where we were in that moment, one in which I was taken by him. But then it came roaring back, the eyes, the music, Cyrus' hand holding mine.

A smirk cracked onto my face.

The lights flickered yellow, but this time they stayed that way.

Pulling him back toward me, I spun him into my chest, hands sliding into the lead. Surprised for only a moment, Cyrus' wide eyes narrowed, brow raised as he stepped in closer to me. A dance, often considered a team effort, could be something else. Trying to take the lead again, Cyrus was thwarted by me when I turned us sharply with a spike in the music. Speeding up, the sounds around us began to warp from a waltz to salsa, matching our movements as if they had been intended to pair. Teeth grit beneath his smile, challenging brows dropped, Cyrus' eyes locked on mine, grip tightening on me. A dance could be a testament to how in-tune one was with their partner, sure. But as I tightened my grip on him, a smile finding its way to me as I raised a brow to him, daring him to try to take the lead again, the dance was more of a war.

Yellow swelled above us as I pulled him in closer, his front pressed up into mine with little space left. My step forward was met with his step back. Yellow dripped down the walls. I heard it, my smile in my exhale. When I blinked, I was no longer in the ballroom, though Cyrus was still in my arms. It only lasted a moment, the vision that visited me. Surrounded by trees, illuminated by the glow of a campfire, stars brighter than any I had ever seen above, little flowers below, in another life I had danced with Cyrus. Dressed in all black, a white rectangle in the center of his shirt tube collar around his neck, his hair pulled back modestly, his eyes weren't red then, but the lightest sky blue.

Blinking again, the vision cleared, leaving me to stare at Cyrus and his suit, his red tie matching his glowing eyes, and his wavy locks taking on the yellow from above. When he smiled at me, yellow exploded from above, sparks raining down.

I wished that it could have been just him and I, alone in that moment, above all else.

My next step didn't meet the floor, but stopped short. Looking down, I was met with a yellow glow beneath me, and with our next step, it took us up higher. Floating above the ballroom, as Cyrus regained the lead, he stepped us around further out, no longer on the ground with the rest, the open air our ballroom. Eyes down as we floated higher, yellow left behind like steps in the air below us, all eyes were on me.

"Hey," Cyrus' soft voice broke the moment, earning my gaze back up to him. Closer to the orbs glowing yellow above, we were bathed in their warm light, separated in suspension, in a world of our own above the rest. "My eyes are up here."

Though my one of my brows dropped, my smile twisted up, bringing a feeling of animation to my face I had never known, working muscles I didn't even know I had. Taking the lead back from him, I stepped forward between his legs, making him step back, brows raised, smile remaining. It was hard to tell, as the music swelled, as the yellow grew brighter, as the momentum in my chest built, but in that moment, as I smiled, dancing with Cyrus above all else, I think I was happy.

Music coming to an end, we stopped, standing in the air above the crowd, chests raising and falling with our breathing, eyes locked, mere inches away as yellow hummed around us. As cheers roared from below, Cyrus' arms wrapped around me, my smile not fading, yellow deposited in my blood, racing through me. As if all it would take was the smallest push, I could feel it, hanging on the edge, the color about to fall into its place in my chest, almost awake.

Looking about, Cyrus caught his breath as he looked back to me. Closing the space, he grew near. Leaning his forehead on mine, our bangs mingled between us as I stood, locked up in his grip. Eyes wide, breath hitched, he was too close for me to properly see but I was trapped, staring anyway.

"Look at this," his voice soft, even when subdued it still held his fiery embers, "this is all you." Sliding his hands up my body where they had been resting, he trailed up my every line, setting me on fire as they landed on either side of my face. Leaning back, he held me there, eyes searching mine, the yellow from above reflecting in their red as his soft skin melted into me, "Your powers, no matter what Nox says, aren't dangerous," smiling at me, he ran his thumbs over the sides of my face as his eyes glassed, "they're beautiful."

Staring at him, as my next breath came to me, it got caught in my chest. Eyes stinging, something building in my throat, yellow became so bright that it started to wash everything else out in the swell. Brows furrowed, I didn't understand, as I looked between his eyes, glass budding in mine, because despite the tears that fell down my face, I still smiled.

Yellow sounded like Cyrus' soft laugh, filtered through the shaking of his breath.

Grip on my face loosening, he lowered one hand, wrapping it around my middle. Pulling me in closer to him, his other hand dropped from the side of my face to my chin. Hooking a finger beneath my chin, he tilted my head up. Eyes on mine, they lowered for a moment before looking back up. Pressed into him, I could feel it, a heartbeat racing between us, but his heart didn't work, so did that mean it was mine?

Bringing his thumb up from his hand on my chin, it brushed over my lips.

Eyes lower for another moment before he yanked them away and off to the side, Cyrus' brow furrowed, face growing more red, "I'm sorry, I'm getting ahead of myself, I just," bringing his eyes back to me, his confidence slowly returned as his arm around my middle tightened, "really missed you."

Lips parted to say something, eyes wide as a heat raced over my face, a new color began to form in the pit of my stomach, but as I took a shaking breath to speak, my heart thumped in my chest and the lights above us turned red, drowning the yellow out.

Dropping from the air, the yellow suspending us gone, Cyrus lost his grip on me in the sudden fall. Reaching for him, the ground quickly approaching, my heart stopped.

Arms meeting him as my hair blew into my face, my glasses threatening to fall away, his arms pulled me closer as I wrapped mine around him. One hand on the back of my head, Cyrus threw his weight in the fall, bringing himself lower. Eyes wide as he held my head in his chest, I knew what he was about to do to himself. Black blood flashed in my mind sending a spike through my heart, the lights above us flickering purple.

The last thing I felt before we met the ground was Cyrus' grip as it tightened on me.

No matter how much yellow being in his arms brought into my world, the moment we met the ground, everything went black.

five

Green

White.

Blinking, all I saw was white.

Warmth on my skin faded, leaving me with nothing as I looked around. My first inhale shook as my mind slowed, a momentum coming to a close, the tail end of something fading in my chest. Stepping around, I was alone, the communion of my shoe with the floor not making a sound. As the last bit of warmth dripped away from me, a little still lingered. Bringing my hand up, I was met with yellow. An orb in my palm, it grew in brightness and weight, in warmth and detail, as the line of my mouth twisted up.

"Why?"

Jumping, the orb in my hand flickered purple for the smallest moment as I looked up. Though it hadn't been there before, a tree stood in front of me. Eyes narrowing on it, I wasn't sure if a tree had just spoken to me, but stranger things had happened I suppose.

"Why what?"

Branches rustled in the tree, a couple little green leaves falling. Swinging out of the tree, Nox hung by his legs, upside down from the thickest low branch. An open leather-bound notebook in one hand, a quill in the other, his eyes met mine, "Why are you putting yourself through this?"

Staring at him and his hair as it stood straight off his head, it gave way to his youthful face, one that looked deceivingly young, for how aged his eyes were, "I already told you."

Groaning, Nox fell from the tree, flipping in the air before landing perfectly on his feet, knees bent, "For someone who doesn't care about anything…" straightening, he stood above me, eyes tired, stance considerably coy compared to how he was the last time we met as he closed the notebook, "you're sure stubborn." Looking down, his eyes met with the orb in my hand as he slid the notebook and quill into his belt, "Happiness, huh?" Bending over, he inspected it, "I haven't seen that color in so long, I nearly forgot what it looked like." Straightening, he turned from me, facing the tree, "I understand your resolve, Igor, many incarnations before you have felt the exact same way. You all want to save the world," bringing his hand up to the tree, it rested on the bark, "even I felt that way, at a time, but," lowering his head, he rested it against the tree, "this is not a world worth saving, none of them are."

Closing my hand over the yellow orb in my palm, it warmed me as it shrunk in my grip, "What makes you say that?"

A little chuckle took him, the tension in his shoulders melting as his hand closed into a fist against the tree next to his head, "No matter how much time passes, nothing ever changes. Netherside is wracked with infighting, Limbo is growing too bold, Upside is in ruin, Flipside is full of hate, The Three grow more apathetic by the day- it's just a matter of time before it falls, no matter what you do." dropping his fist, it fell limp, his hand dangling at his side, forehead still pressed up against the tree, "I'm a monster. These powers are too strong. I guess I should just let them eat you up. Maybe you'd lose control somewhere out there, destroy all the realms and everyone could be free of this terrible world."

My smile didn't vanish, though it was small, the warmth of yellow remained in my chest as I stopped at his side. Opening my hand, the light took a new form as my fingers revealed it, a flower resting in my palm. Looking up to Nox from the flower, I extended it to him, "But what if it's okay?" he slowly straightened, eyes drifting up to mine as I went on, "Every line of customers, no matter how long, has to end eventually. I understand your concerns, and they are valid but, I don't know," my gaze drifted down to the flower extended between us, its light yellow glow illuminating his white hair, "while they are strong, these powers, they don't

feel evil."

The way he looked at me, his tired eyes wide,

shadowed by the tree, he was unreadably blank, his voice

soft, "In a world so troubled, what could have possibly

inspired so much happiness in you?"

Looking down to the flower, I extended it his way a

bit more, "Cyrus," when his breath hitched, I looked back up

to him, "he said these powers, your powers, were beautiful."

Brow dropping just a bit, he was nuanced, but I could

see it, the internal war against the colors of his own. It

appeared that he lost as his face started to redden. Turning

from me, he leaned his side against the tree, "You shouldn't

fall for his flattery."

My smile grew as I looked between him and the

flower. A brow raising, I crossed my arms, shifting my

weight as the flower dangled from my fingers, "It appears

that you already have."

Going visibly stiff, Nox didn't reply.

Laughing, I couldn't help it as I stared at his tense shoulders, "It's alright, your secret is safe with me." Looking back down to the flower, I closed my hand over it again, "What will you do," opening my hand again, the yellow orb returned to its shape, small, more pastel than before, "when I manage to conquer all the colors, tame your powers, and take the crown?"

"When?" He turned to look at me over his shoulder, "Don't you mean if?"

Bringing my hand up to my bow tie, yellow found its home in the brooch around my neck, depositing warmth in my veins, sending it over my body until it met my feet. When it did, yellow radiated from my shoes, racing over the abyss, chasing away the white until there was none left. When it met the tree, it exploded into bloom, purple wisteria flowers taking it over. As I lowered my hand, I looked around, smile still on my face as my gaze landed on Nox and his tree, "No."

Eyes lowering from the tree above him, they landed on me, not even the yellow reflecting in them able to bring warmth to his gaze as petals danced in the air between us, "Some colors are easier to tame than others, so don't get all cocky." Walking toward me, his steps chased away the yellow, leaving white footprints behind him on the ground, "You must have gotten this audacity from your wild parents, it's certainly not a trait you got from me." Stopping but a step away, the abyss grew cold, the yellow flickering white for a moment, "Don't say I didn't try to warn you, didn't try to give you an out, didn't try to spare you the painful demise you insist on running toward." Raising his hand, he placed it on my chest. Upon the contact, my body locked up. The pastel yellow that radiated from the brooch on my bow tie caught in his eyes, and in that moment, they looked as if they had glassed over, "Make sure that when your irresponsibility ends the world, they don't blame me."

With a shove, he sent me falling backward, and I was unable to do anything about it. When my back met the ground, everything went black. Though as if I had only blinked, I flew up, a gasp taking me, eyes wide as my ears rang. Staring forward, the world was a bit blurry, but from what I could see, there were too many colors for it to be the abyss. My next breath came to me, calming the racing in my chest. As my brow furrowed, eyes searching the blurry world ahead, I tried to remember what had happened.

Red flashed through my mind.

Cyrus.

Jumping, I was about to call out his name, but then something moved at my side. Eyes lurching down, the light filtering through the window behind me took on a purple tint for a moment before they met him. Golden locks, slouched at my bedside, though he was blurry, I could tell it was him, Cyrus, asleep at my bedside. Bringing up my hand, I was about to reach for him when I stopped. Two colors reflected off my skin. Inspecting my hand as I brought it a bit closer to my bow tie, I was met with pastel orange and yellow. Soft colors, they emanated from the brooch. A slight smile took me, I had now conquered more colors than a handful of previous incarnates.

I was going to prove Nox and his cynicism wrong, no matter what it took.

"Igor, my boy."

My breath caught in my throat as I jumped, lowering my hand and bringing my eyes to the side. Standing in the shadows, turning to face me from the door, a form met me. I didn't need to see him clearly to recognize the blob of clashing colors as Anton. Turning fully, lowering what appeared to be his hand extending toward the door, he started toward us.

"I'm happy you're awake," Stopping behind Cyrus, who didn't even stir, Anton laughed quietly, "Are you alright? That was quite a fall there."

"I am," my eyes lowered to Cyrus, my folded glasses clasped on his hand as his head rested on his arms on the bed next to me, "but I'm sure it hurt him."

"Oh, don't you worry about that," Anton leaned forward into my vision, hovering next to Cyrus, "he'll be fine, he always is. He is immortal, after all."

Gaze drifting from Cyrus to Anton's sharp, cat-like eyes, I wondered if I had ever seen him blink.

When I didn't say anything, Anton straightened, pulling himself back out of my vision, "You're the one I'm worried about. You're not immortal, not yet anyway."

Cyrus stirred, though didn't wake, as if he were having a nightmare.

Though Anton didn't seem to notice as he went on, "Refrain from being so reckless, at least until you claim the crown."

Looking up to his clashing form, I could sense his readiness, as if waiting to spring the next word out, and I did hate playing into it, but I was left without a choice, "Not yet? What will happen when I claim the crown?"

"Cyrus didn't tell you?" barely allowing me to finish, Anton extended his arms, the sides of his patterned blazer flying out with the gesture, "We can't have a mortal king, now can we? Once this crown sits above your head, it will gift you with immortality and the only thing that will be able to harm you would be something burdened with the blessing of blight." Turning, he spun with a flare reminiscent of a silent film actor, too bold to be contained as he stood in pause, "Luckily a power that destructive is rare, only a few poses it. Though," turning, he glanced at me over his shoulder, the skin beneath his combed hair shining in the light even in my blurry view, "you already have met someone capable," turning, he took one bouncing step, "Kasper, the Almighty Ghost King." Anton lowered his voice, "He already threatened you with it, didn't he?"

When I didn't reply, my breath trapped, suspended in my chest, Anton laughed, taking another bouncing step forward.

"Well, I just wanted to come check up on you, you are the talk of the kingdom." Starting back toward the door, the sashay of his shoulders suggested a lightness to his step that wouldn't match the hardiness of his stature, "They are all so excited to see what you'll do. But do be careful who you trust," pulling the door open, a creak took the air, "that brooch upon your neck gives you a power akin to god. If you're not wary…" he started out the door, "someone might just betray you." Closing the door behind him, the creak filled the beat until he stopped, "Oh, and," turning his head, his voice entered the room through the door crack, "someone is here to see you. I've kept them at bay in the front, but Finnegan is known for their," turning, he started to pull the door closed again, his voice echoing down the hall, "tenacity. I can't promise to keep them out for very long."

Closing the door, he left me to sit there and stare at it.

A canary sang, though it was muffled through the walls of wherever I was. Eyes narrowing, vision blurry, I looked around. Where was I? Gaze lowering to Cyrus and my glasses folded in his hand, there was only one way to find out. Leaning forward, the bed creaked a bit beneath me as I reached out for my glasses. Cyrus stirred again, his blonde locks shifting out of his face. Freezing, my fingers hovered a moment away from my glasses. When he was asleep, absent of that movie star persona, he looked gentle. Relaxed brows, the freckles that dusted his face, his hair that looked soft to the touch.

Immortality.

Cyrus called it a curse, but as I sat there, trapped in that moment, faced with the potential of endless ones just like it, I wasn't so sure.

The light filtering in through the window flickered red, for just a moment, startling me. Looking over to it and away from Cyrus, I watched the light dance through the air, occasionally disrupted by the rustling of leaves outside. I had seen red a few times now, briefly, but I didn't know what it was. Though if I recalled, it was the color that disrupted yellow at the ball, sending Cyrus and I plunging to the floor below. Eyes lowering to the sleeping zombie at my side, my

hand raised from where it had been reaching for my glasses.

Hovering right above his head, it felt as if I wasn't allowed to

touch him. Whatever red was, he could make me feel it. And

it almost always happened when…

Lacing my fingers through his hair, I pulled his bangs

from his face.

Heart stopping in my chest, eyes wide as I stared at

him, something shot through me, so sharp that I imagined

being electrocuted would feel quite the same.

He was warm, his hair softer than I expected, fine and

smooth between my fingers.

The light coming through the window became redder,

the color richer than before as it held and painted the

bedspread between us. A warmth finding my face, I had only

ever experienced the sensation with a fever. But, as my

fingers ran though his hair, allowing every fine wavy clump

to spill back down, I didn't mind it.

In fact, I wanted to feel it more.

But, what was it?

Green exploded in the room, causing me to fly away from Cyrus as he jumped awake. Taking over the air, the smoke obscured even Cyrus from me, despite our closeness. Though I could still see it, the red glow of his eyes, even in the smoke. Coughing, Cyrus stood, the chair squealing out behind him. A laugh met me as a shadow approached through the smoke. Though calling it just a laugh was a disservice to its velvety charm. The softness to it, it didn't hinder how lively it was, a combination I had never heard before. But as the shadow started to turn into a form before me, it was a combination that felt like an old friend, a laugh I begged to hear, despite knowing I'd never hear it again. And though the circumstances should have inspired any degree of unease, as they stopped before me, something else made a home in my chest.

As the smoke dissipated, it gave way to piercing green eyes and a smirk that could ignite a revolution in its inherent provocation. Head tilted as fair, lengthy, hair spilled over from where it was tucked behind a pointy ear, elf-like face and elegant frame, decorated in green and black masculine aristocratic Victorian garb, this person before me stole the air from my lungs. As they smiled through an exhale, a fine brow raising, my eyes caught on them, the fangs in their smile. Hands propping onto their hips, though they were short, no taller than five feet, they felt like the biggest presence in the room as they bent over at the middle to be eye level with me as I sat on the bed.

"We meet again, Nox."

A voice like a harp, refined, every sound enunciated with pride through a faint French accent, it was unlike anything I had ever heard before, but at the same time, I felt as if I knew its tones in a way much more intimate than I had ever known another. With them came the aroma of flowers, a sweet sad scent, like the flowers I had passed outside the castle. Eyes wide, locked on theirs, I couldn't say a thing, trapped in their unapologetically audacious, expectant, gaze.

It was then that I realized that I had seen them before, in the briefest passing, as they rode by in the carriage.

Swatting at the smoke, Cyrus stopped coughing as he came back into view. "Finnegan," when he shoved them away, they didn't stumble, but flowed with the movement, every step like a dance, "what are you doing here?"

Eyes lingering on me as Cyrus stepped between us, when they did eventually drift away from me, they moved with a certain self-assurance, a dignity I had never before witnessed, "Oh, Father Glory," stepping up to Cyrus, their lengthy emerald lined satin cape flowed behind them until they stopped, right up against Cyrus. Causing him to step back into the bed, they stepped their leg between his, bringing a fine finger up to the tip of his chin. Tilting his head down, their self-possession was profound as they looked Cyrus dead in the eye, "I have missed you too."

Red eyes searching theirs, Cyrus stood in that moment, not pushing them away. And If I hadn't known any better, I would have thought that the red on his cheeks came from more than just the glow of his eyes.

"Igor, this is Archduke Finnegan van Serifino." Bringing his hand up to Finnegan's shoulder, Cyrus didn't shove them as he had before, but gently guided them a step back from him as he turned to look at me, though his eyes quickly averted down from mine, "An ancient vampire and lifelong friend, they knew Nox in the before times too."

Laughing, it was more of a scoff, made playful by the smirk they wore as they crossed their arms, shifting their weight, "Friend? You wound me, Father Glory." Eyes drifting back to me, Finnegan bent over again a bit to look at me, arms remaining crossed as their animation made their cape shift and catch the light on the internal satin, "I can assure you, the three of us were much more than friends."

Clearing his throat, Cyrus gently pushed Finnegan back again, "With Nox, but not with Igor. They aren't the same person." Looking back to me from Finnegan, Cyrus kept himself between us, "And that was literally over six hundred years ago."

Humming, it sounded like a challenge, something about Finnegan's every move inherently combative, "Funny, because the way you look at me makes it feel like you were beneath me but last night-"

"Alright," Cyrus' voice cracked as he spun around, taking Finnegan's shoulders in his hands, "I don't know what you want, but at this point," walking them backwards toward the door, Finnegan didn't fight as Cyrus pushed them along, "I don't care."

Staring at them from the bed, eyes a bit wider than before as they left my clear sight, I felt as if there was something striking going on, but whatever it was, it went right over my head. Quiet bickering took the air as Cyrus tried to force Finnegan out of the door. As I stood from the bed, their argument speckled with Finnegan's laugh, I found my glasses on the floor. Bending down to pick them up, I slid them on my face as I straightened. But before I could even blink, green smoke exploded right in front of me.

"Twining shared the news with me but," leaning forward out of the smoke, Finnegan appeared directly in front of me, little space between us as they looked up into my eyes, "I wanted to see it for myself." Eyes taking in my every inch, they made me step back, my legs meeting the bed as they continued in their approach. Eyes drifting down to my bow tie, the moment the orange and yellow reflected in the green glow of their eyes, they widened. "Two colors already?"

"Two?" Scrambling footsteps made their way to us through the dissipating smoke as Cyrus ran to Finnegan's side. Chest heaving as his hand flew up to cover his cough, his eyes met the brooch on my neck. Lighting up, I could see it, the smile in his eyes despite his mouth being covered. "I knew this time would be different."

Inspecting me, Finnegan tilted their head, their hair spilling over their shoulder clad in a black velvet vest, decorated in a regal green pattern as it sat above a cream white blouse, the ballooning sleeves becoming on their frail frame, "You think so?" Eyes lingering on mine, Finnegan hummed a bit, and in that moment, I saw it, the smallest nuance, a shift in them. Brow raising, their eyes darted to Cyrus then back to me as the line of their mouth tugged up ever so slightly, "How exciting."

Reaching for me, their hand met my wrist.

I only saw it for a moment, the panic on Cyrus as he lunged for me, before everything turned green.

In a blink, I was floating.

Struggling to stay upright with no ground beneath me to catch my feet, my world spun as green cleared from my view. Eyes wide, the glow from above turned purple as I stared down. The castle in the near distance, the town stretched into the deep recesses of the hazy dark snow globe. So high in the air, I was but a good reach away from the sky, probably able to stretch up and touch it if I tried as another more modest castle sat directly below me. Though I didn't drop, but just floated.

A soft laugh startled me.

The purple in the sky flashed brighter.

Jumping, I went spinning about in the air, suspended as my view met them. Finnegan floated before me, wicked smile on their face, the sparkling ever-night of the Netherside sky reflecting in the emerald brooch that sat, center on their jabot as their hair flared out around them. Arms folded behind them, posture impeccable, they didn't appear the slightest bit bothered.

"It is really something, is it not?" Standing there as if they were simply on the ground, they looked down as I struggled in the air, "Soon it will be all yours." Looking back to me and my undignified floundering, they just smiled, "I cannot wait to see what you will do, I am sure you will be a great king."

Tumbling over in the air, my glasses slid down my nose, my disheveled bangs obscuring some of my vision. But even through the black clumps, I could see it, the way they looked at me, taking in my every inch as I fought to obtain any level of control. And though it would be logically sound to assume that the racing of my heart derived from my current predicament, something in me wondered if it was actualy the weight of Finnegan's gaze.

"But first," Finnegan leaned down toward me, bending at the middle. Bringing one of their arms forward from behind their back, they extended one fine finger toward my face. Flinching away, the sky flashed purple again, causing them to pause, finger hovering but an inch away. Eyes raising to the sky with a grace I didn't think possible, they looked back down to me a moment later, "What, are you scared?" tilting their head to the side a bit, some of their hair spilled over their shoulder as their finger made contact with the bridge of my glasses, "There is nothing to fear," sliding my glasses from my face, when their soft skin made contact with my nose in the process, I steadied, their contact keeping me from tumbling further freely in the air, "it is exciting, we used to do this all the time." Pulling their hand back, they straightened, studying my glasses as I just hovered there, staring at them, barely maintaining my balance, "Fear and excitement are quite similar, they both make you feel the most alive." Folding my glasses, they slid them into the chest pocket of their vest, "The only difference is your attitude, here," raising their hand from my glasses, they brought their middle finger to their thumb, an upward tilt taking the line of their mouth, "allow me to demonstrate."

When they snapped, I only got to see their smile turn into a smirk for a moment because in the next, I dropped.

Falling, the air screamed by me, deafening my ears and choking my breath. Struggling as I felt the pull of gravity grow, I managed to turn over in the fall. As I reached up, blurring eyes meeting the sky, I almost expected to see Cyrus there, reaching back to me. But all I saw as my hair blew in my face, as I fell faster, was the sky as it grew more purple by the moment. Unable to call out for Cyrus, a stinging took my eyes, a yell failing to claw its way from my throat.

Was I

Scared?

Green took over my vision.

Smoke falling away in a beat, Finnegan fell through it as we left it far behind in the sky. Directly above me, they fell with me. Though unlike me, they didn't seem to care. Hair flailing out behind them with their lengthy cape, the purple growing in the sky reflected off the green silk.

"What are you waiting for?" they looked behind me, "the ground is nearing." Looking back, they raised a brow, their smirk revealing the tip of a fang, "You do know you have powers, do you not?"

"Yes," I struggled to speak, the air ripping from me with every breath, "but I don't know how to use them."

Tilting their head, their smirk flattened as we fell, but inches away, "Is that right?"

Nodding as tension took me over, it felt like poison in my muscles, an acid eating away at me, about to burn through my skin. Head turning to the side, my eyes couldn't focus on it, but what appeared to be a center courtyard in the heart of the amethyst structure below quickly approached.

Humming as if we weren't plummeting, Finnegan just smiled at me as I looked back to them, "I do hope you are a fast learner, then." reaching toward me, it appeared effortless, but before they made contact, they paused, "May I?"

Staring up at them, trapped in what felt like an impossibly long fall as purple swelled in the sky behind them, I wasn't exactly sure what they were asking to do, but the way they asked it, it was enough to dull the screaming in my body for a moment.

I nodded.

Their exhale turned up through their smile as their hand met my chest. Sliding their hand over my chest toward my back, they stopped my heart. Closing the space, Finnegan pulled their body into mine, pressing our chests together as they wrapped their arms around me.

The purple in the sky flickered to red for a moment as I wrapped my arms around them too.

Sliding their other hand up to the base of my neck, their fingers laced in my hair. Shivering, my brow furrowed as my face stung, unsure what was going on. Eyes closing as the sensation of their warmth took me, the red from above flashed so bright I could see it through my eyelids. But as I felt their breathing shallow, as their other hand slid down to the small of my back, tracing every line, the sky fought to pick a color, flashing through them so fast that I couldn't tell any of them apart. Each marked by the racing of my heart, a swell took me, bringing a static to the beneath of my skin. Almost an acid in my blood, it was cut with something that took away the bite, but what it replaced it with? I wasn't sure, but as it threatened to tug the line of my mouth up, I wanted

to find out.

Head over my shoulder, Finnegan's face hovered next

to mine, so close that they made me shiver again. Despite the

wind ripping by, somehow, their soft voice was the only

thing I could hear.

"You are falling from the sky, about to die, but." Lips

hovering right above my neck, Finnegan made my grip on

them tighten, "tell me, Igor, do you feel alive?"

Pushing me away from them, they sent me back.

Slowing in the fall as my body flipped in the air, I could see

it, all of it, Netherside. Like a slot machine, colors flashed

through the sky, though as everything slowed, as Netherside

sat, blurry in my vision, I could tell them apart.

Purple, it felt like the drop of my stomach, like my

heart that had already hit the ground despite my body still

being in the fall.

Red, it felt like Finnegan's touch on my skin, the racing in my chest as they closed space between us.

Yellow, it felt like the glass taking my eyes as I rotated slowly in the flip, looking down upon a fantastical world full of feelings.

But then, as I flipped all the way around, facing Finnegan as they fell above me, something else took hold. I wasn't scared, I wasn't happy either, I wasn't exactly sure what red was but that wasn't quite right, there was something else. As Finnegan smiled at me, the combative crook to their brow provocative in essence, their fangs catching the light, there was something daring about the dangerous.

Something…

I smiled, pulling myself into another flip in the air.

Exciting.

Green exploded in the sky above, sending a tint over the entire realm. Arms out at my sides, smile on my face, a rush of energy shot through me. Adrenaline without the cut of anxiety, it didn't matter as time sped up again or that I was about to hit the ground. If I felt this way in the fall, then maybe the crash would be worth it. A cheer escaped me before I realized it was mine, echoing back to me from the impending buildings below.

Finnegan appeared at my side in puff of green smoke, falling next to me without a care, back toward the ground, arms laced behind their head as their legs sat at length, crossed, "It is great, excitement." Gaze drifting up to the green sky above, it matched the glow of their eyes, "Careful, though, the longer you are alive," glancing over to me, they turned in the air, ending up directly above me. Bringing their hand down toward me as the edges of the world met my peripheral vision, the ground closing in, the tip of their finger met the underneath of my chin. Other hand wrapping around my middle, they pulled themselves into me, chests with no space between, too close for me to focus on as their lips hovered above mine, "the harder it is to find."

The walls of the castle courtyard clawed up the sides of my vision.

I was about to hit the ground.

I wished for something, anything, to save me. Because if I died there, I'd never get to experience Netherside in its totality, never get to feel excitement again.

My heart thudded so hard in my chest that I'm sure they felt it too. Vision blurring as tension raced through me, my eyes fought to stay open, but as a pang of static took me, they were forced closed. Though as they closed, as my vision blurred out, as my body anticipated the impact, I saw one last thing. My hair, as it blew forward into my face, turned white.

Eyes flying open, heart racing, the stop was so sudden I nearly fell from my feet. Staring forward, the white of Nox's world burned into my eyes. Hand flying to my face, breath hissing through my clenched teeth, I took a stumbling step back. Slowly lowering my hand, I looked up over it. As I stepped around, surrounded by nothing but eternal white, I realized I was alone. Hand lowering, my vision caught on the colors reflecting off my bow tie. Still just orange and yellow, there wasn't a new one found yet. Dropping my hand to my side, my breathing steadied as it became the only sound to accompany me. If Nox wasn't here, then where was he? Bringing my hand up to my hair, I couldn't remember where I had just been.

Stepping around again, I looked over my shoulder.

Stopping, my eyes met green.

A little orb of light, it danced through the air, circling around me. Stepping about to follow it, it jingled as it bounced through the air, leaving a bit of glitter behind it. Stopping, it hovered directly in front of me, its color bleeding over my front. Staring into it, I had never really thought much of green. It was the color of money and our junior's tags, but as I lifted my hand up to it, I realized it was also the color of life.

The moment before my fingers made contact with it, the orb jumped away. Bouncing about me erratically, it dodged as I reached for it again. A light jingle like a laugh, it took off, bouncing through the air away from me. Chasing after it, the glitter it left behind getting in my face, I didn't stop. Making grand sweeps through the air, the glitter it dropped started to glow green, taking on forms as I ran past them.

"This is the artifact that he left behind, the true king." Cyrus' voice echoed in the abyss, making me look around, "It just sits here, waiting for its owner to come and claim it, to come back and save Netherside from collapsing." Turning, my eyes met with the form the glitter had taken. Red as it caught the light, as it spoke on, I realized it looked like Cyrus, "Isn't that cool?"

Exploding into green glitter again, his voice echoed as it faded.

Looking forward, I almost stumbled as I continued my pursuit of the little green light. Reaching my arm forward, I could feel the static, the electricity on my fingertips, just barely unable to make contact with the green orb. Taking a form a few steps before me, the glitter turned black.

"But of course," another voice bellowed in the abyss as I passed the large, black glittering form, "as soon as you're at your full ability, I will gladly gift this to you, future king of Netherside."

As it exploded into green glitter once again, Anton's voice faded. Chasing me, the cloud of glitter wove about, like a ribbon in the air. Brushing by me, it tingled, much like the static shock one got from hanging up a velvet dress on the metal rack. Taking another form a few steps ahead, the glitter became a richer shade of emerald.

"It is really something, is it not?" The glitter took Finnegan's form as their voice sparked something in my chest, "Soon it will be all yours." Passing by the form, it reached out, their fine fingers brushing against my chest as I ran past, "I cannot wait to see what you will do, I am sure you will be a great king."

When my next step met the ground, the white turned green beneath my shoe.

Exploding, the glitter sped up, racing around me before landing ahead. Taking another form, it turned black again, "You're not immortal, not yet anyway."

Running by it, Anton's voice threatened to make the line of my mouth break.

Exploding again, the glitter flew forward, racing me for a moment before breaking ahead. Taking a form a few strides in front of me, I didn't look at it as I focused on the orb. But a hair away from my fingertips, it didn't matter how fast I ran, no matter how hard I pushed, I couldn't reach it.

"Tell me, Igor," Finnegan's voice met me, the form before glowing green.

My teeth grit, arm stretching out as far as I could go, reaching toward the orb. Running straight toward the form, I didn't stop.

"Do you feel alive?"

Running through the glittering form, my fingertips met the green.

Exploding, it became blinding as green swirled around me, washing away the white. Hair on end, I stopped, not out of breath, not even close, as I stepped about. Eyes widening as the green took forms around me, the line of my mouth pulled up. Surrounded by a scene, castles stretching into the sky, tavern music in the air, fantastical creatures bustling about, though it was all made of glittering forms, I could tell, it was the heart of Netherside. Eyes meeting the ground as my shadow took form, something casted a shadow from above my head. Hand raising, it met with metal. Looking up, my eyes widened as they took in the crown floating there, a slight spin in his suspension. Heart racing, smile on my face, green pulsing around me in time with my chest, every breath I took left me breathless.

But a whisper I heard them again, Finnegan, as a breeze of green glitter danced around me, "How exciting."

A king, me?

I looked down to the glittering silhouettes around.

Could it really be?

Fated to save the world, to live forever, the most powerful being of them all. How could it be me, nothing more than a faded retail worker? The only remarkable thing about me was my efficiency at the register. But somehow, as I stood there, staring around at the fantasy before me, something about the green radiating out from beneath my shoes convinced me.

This was my story.

A sting took my hand. Looking down as I brought my palm up, I was met with green. Staring into the orb in my grasp, I watched as the greens churned, like the leaves rustling on a tree in a summer afternoon, like grassy endless rolling hills, a space where time stopped, where you felt alive. Smiling, I didn't want to look away. What a charming color. It was a feeling that perhaps I had once known, looking at the green gravel at the pet shop. Closing my hand over the orb as a lively world bustled around me, I felt it shrink in my grip. Tamed, I was met with a much smaller orb in my hand when I opened it again. These colors were big, too big to be held in the brooch unless I compacted them in my grip. Lifting the orb up toward my bow tie, my eyes drifted over the greens dancing around me.

When green met with the brooch in my bow tie, fireworks shot into the sky, exploding into green sparks above. The glittering forms about stopped to look into the sky. As if I had woken from a long sleep, energy dripped through me, making me feel lighter, as if any weight I had ever carried had been lifted away. As sparks rained down, I was perhaps the only one not looking up, but around. Meeting a form at my side, it wasn't hard to recognize the silhouette as Finnegan. Looking down from the sky, their glittering hair spilled over their back. Reaching out to me, their fine hand glowed with the pulse of the world around, in beat with my heart.

Much like Cyrus, it was obvious that I had known them many times before.

Bringing my hand up, I accepted theirs.

When we made contact, I blinked.

Blinding white met me, stinging my eyes. Reeling back, my sleeve flew up to my face. Green was gone, replaced by sterile silence, eternal white. Lowering my sleeve, I was alone once more, nothingness my only company.

Stepping about, I looked around.

Stopping, my eyes met his tree.

Standing there, alone in eternity, the tree was still in the lack of breeze, stoic in contrast to what had just been there. Lowering my hand as I turned to fully face it, I couldn't look away.

Every step that took me closer to that tree felt like a step closer to home. Stopping in front of it, wisteria in bloom, its purple flowers hung around me. Staring up at it, my eyes narrowed. Without my glasses, I couldn't be sure. But I thought that I had seen that tree somewhere before, somewhere outside of this abyss. Bringing my hand up to it, my fingertips met something. Looking down, I slid my hand to the side to reveal a carving in the trunk. Squinting, I got closer to the carving, trying to read what it said.

Dizziness took me, the blood dropping from my head. Struggling to remain standing, my ears rang as I fell to a knee, my hand sliding down the body of the tree. Eyes fighting to remain open under the furrowing of my brow, I looked back up to the carving. If it said what I thought it did, I definitely had seen this tree before. But as my eyes blurred out, my view of the tree obscured until everything went black.

Eyes opening, I couldn't feel my body, not for a few moments. Slowly, my vision began to clear, but as feeling trickled back into me, I realized that my vision remained blurry, but not because it wouldn't focus, but because something was so close to me that it couldn't.

Warmth came to life on my lips as I regained feeling.

Stopped, suspended in the air, my predicament came screaming back to me as tension took over my frame.

The warmth left.

Slowly sitting up, Finnegan came into focus as they pulled away from me. Red splashed over their face, the glass in their eyes made my breath hitch. Though, the most stunning of all, was the green glow that bathed them as it emanated from my bow tie, staining their lengths of hair. Weight on my hips, they sat, straddling me as their long hair spilled over their shoulder. Legs dangling at my either side, their hands supporting them on my chest, Finnegan stopped my heart.

Eyes wide on them, we no longer fell, but we weren't on the ground, either. Slowly looking to the side, my eyes met with rounded brick, but a couple feet down. Eyes drifting up, though my vision was blurry, a courtyard, came to my view. A fountain bubbling silver liquid, it sat, surrounded by bushes of the same flowers I had seen around Netherside, but in such impressive mass that my entire surroundings were tainted by their faint purple glow. Eyes catching on my shoulder, they met a green glow. Gaze following down, I found that it outlined my entire body. Hovering, suspended, I laid flat, perpendicular to the ground. I didn't know how it happened, but somehow, I stopped the fall. Finnegan shifted their weight as they sat on my hips, catching my attention. Eyes flying back to them as they leaned down toward me again, my heart tumbled to life in my chest.

Cold met the sides of my face as they slid my glasses back into place. The sky above them matched the green of their eyes as they came into clarity. "That was," getting closer to me, they hovered but a few inches above my face. Their hair spilled to their sides, closing us off from the rest of the world with a curtain as their eyes drifted down to my bow tie, capturing the multicolored glow, "exciting, right?"

Though the sky boasted green, as their eyes drew back up to mine, it started to turn another color.

A door crashed open, "Archduke."

Eyes widening, Finnegan tensed, the smile falling from their face. The green of their eyes flashed brighter, a glowing purple ring coming to life around their irises. Slowly, after searching my eyes for a moment longer, they sat up, bringing their full weight onto my hips. Teeth clenching as I fought to keep my brow even, I didn't have a moment to wonder what sensation Finnegan brought to me because in that moment, the world flashed red, erasing the green, and we fell. Landing square on my back, the air was knocked out of me. Coughing as Finnegan stood from me, the absence of their warmth was so striking it stung.

The door slammed shut, the echoing of footsteps cutting the air, "What in Anton's Netherside are you doing?"

Shaking as I pulled myself up from the cool bricks, one hand up to my mouth to cover my cough, the other supporting me from behind, I looked up. Blood stopping, I stared at Twining as they stood, looming above me.

"You requested an audience with Igor," Finnegan's voice was nearly unrecognizable, drained of its audacity, tamed, as they took a step back to Twining's side, "so I have delivered him."

Eyes lingering on Finnegan as they stood, arms behind them, eyes averted, my heart started to slow as the colors drained from the sky. The purple of the ring around their eyes matched the eerie color of Twining's.

Humming, Twining crossed their arms as they shifted their weight, their lengthy, purple-lined cape shifting with them, "I see," extending a gloved hand my way, Twining looked as if they'd rather take a stake to the heart than have me accept it, "I apologize for my Ward, they get a bit out of hand when not under my watch."

Eyes lowering from them to their hand, I brought mine up from the ground to take it, "Your Ward?"

"Yes," Pulling me to my feet, Twining let go the very moment they could, "Finnegan is the one and only Ward of the elected representative of the Vampiric Order, the only person whom I have ever turned into a vampire. Though," turning to look at Finnegan, Twining's thin brow dropped, "they seem to forget their place, from time to time."

Eyes on the ground, jaw tight, Finnegan said nothing.

The sky flickered orange.

Glancing at the sky, the Vampire's eyes held for a moment before they looked down again. Turning back to me, Twining's cape danced in the purple glow of the flowers that surrounded us, "However, I do suppose they did what was asked of them, I did indeed request your audience." Turning, they gestured with their head for me to follow. "Join me inside, we have much to discuss." Their lengthy hair trailing behind them, the piercing clicks of their stiletto boots marked the moments as they brushed past Finnegan and toward the castle door they had entered through. Throwing the door open, they stormed inside.

Left standing in the courtyard, the sound of the fountain so quiet it was impressive that it was running at all, I looked up and around as I walked forward. A crystal building, made of amethyst, as if it had grown from the ground that way, it caught the eerie glow from above just right. Rounded brick below me, crystal castle towers and walls around, my eyes drifted back over their opaque surfaces and the shadows that passed the other side of them until they returned to Finnegan. Eyes holding on mine for just a moment, they gave a slight nod before turning to catch the door before it swung in. Bowing their head to me, the sight made my stomach drop. It looked wrong.

"Don't mind them," Finnegan's voice barely above a whisper, the smallest tug of a smirk took them as their eyes drifted inside, locking on Twining's back, "much like Father

Glory, they are just a blonde bottom with something to prove."

My shoe caught on the threshold of the door, sending me stumbling.

The clicks of Twining's steps stopped as they paused, sharp back to me. Glancing over their shoulder, when the purple of their eyes met mine, tension screamed over me. Quickly correcting myself as I hurried in my step, I didn't look back to Finnegan as they followed a few steps behind. I hadn't any idea what they just said to me, but the way they said it was really something.

Bringing up my hand, the colors from my brooch met my skin. Orange, yellow, and now green, I had tamed more colors than nearly half of the incarnations before me. Lowering my hand, I fought to maintain control of my expression. Not something I ever had trouble doing before, it was difficult, but the tone of the Vampiric castle compelled me. While Anton's warning was self-incriminatory at best, it could really be applicable to anybody. Eyes locking on

Twining's back, my jaw tightened.

Walking down a hall made of dark crystal, the floor,

walls, and high ceilings were all deep purple. As I looked to

the side, following Twining toward the end of the hall,

Finnegan a few steps behind, the glow of my brooch

reflected in the glass-like structure. Hands finding my

pockets as the bite to the air became too much, my fingers

brushed against something. Cool and smooth, I wasn't sure

what it was. A hitch to my step, I almost stopped when I

remembered it was the stone that Kasper had given me. He

made it sound like it was a way to call for help, to summon

him when I needed assistance. Though, as my hand tightened

on it in my pocket, I knew I needed to save it for when I

really needed it.

Approaching a set of grand doors, black carved wood,

adorned with silver detailing and handles, Twining didn't

show any signs of stopping. Slowing in my step, I watched

their back as they continued on with apparently every intent to just walk straight into the doors. With the next click of their shoe, the door gained a purple glow, and a moment later, the moment before they would have walked right into them, the doors flew open.

Stopping as the gust of air blew by me, the creak of the doors in the aftermath split the moment. Walking again, I followed through the door, entering a darkened cavern. Though I couldn't see a thing, I could just feel it, the sheer volume of air inside.

"I'm sure it has been quite overwhelming for you, as you have only been in Netherside for a matter of moments in the grand scheme," Twining's steps stopped, "so I'd like to thank you for making time to see me."

Stopping, my eyes drifted about the dark, nothing but an ambient amethyst glow meeting them, "You say that as if I were given a choice."

Laughing, it sounded as if Twining sat, "You never have been one for pleasantries, Nox."

In a click, one candle after another came to life on the walls, racing from either side of the door toward the opposite side of the room. Each flame, as they came to life, burned purple. When the flames met in the middle, the entire room blossomed into my sight. Before me stood several thrones, equal in size and adornment, Twining sat in the only one that was different, slightly elevated on a platform above the others. Every other throne sat empty, every one but the one at Twining's right side. Seated next to them in a way that could barely even be considered sitting, Finnegan lounged, legs crossed over one arm rest, elbow propped up on the other, head resting on their palm.

Staring at them, every line of them like intentional art, how did a body so small and frail hold so much power.

The candles around flickered red, for just a moment, before returning to purple.

Rolling their eyes, Twining's gaze landed on me. "I will cut to the chase," sitting back in their chair, their glowing eyes searched me, "My people don't like you."

Eyes unmoving from Twining's, I regretted never listening to Ross' goings on about vampires. Perhaps if I had, I wouldn't have walked right into the stronghold of their castle.

"Is that right?"

Nodding, Twining looked away, crossing one lengthy elegant leg over the other, "A Pulse born king, it is unheard of," eyes snapping back to me, their face remained turned to the side, "unsightly, even. However," running their spidery fingers through their hair, they looked away again, "I find myself bored of the happenings of Netherside as they are, itching for something to change. So, I am able to look past the circumstances of your birth, if it means exciting times are to come. Though, I am not in the majority, and I do foresee it, an uprising of sorts, should you take the throne." Turning toward me again, they leaned their elbow on their right arm rest, propping their chin on their open palm, "Of course I did not only call you here today to tell you this, as I am sure you would easily find it out on your own. I invited you here today because I have a proposition."

Sitting up, Finnegan's legs dangled over the seat of the chair, their feet unable to meet the floor, "Vampires are the black sheep of Netherside, largely due to the slander perpetuated by the current kingship. It makes it difficult for my people to properly enjoy the refuge Nox brought about for us all."

Eyes widening, something a bit prejudice that Cyrus had said lit in the back of my mind.

Twining nodded ever so slightly as they exhaled, "I see you are already acquainted with our struggle," standing, they extended their arms toward the empty thrones, "What we wish to request of you is simple-"

"You want me to change the narrative about vampires once I'm in a position of power," shifting my weight, I looked between Finnegan and Twining, "do forgive me, your highness, but you haven't given me much reason to." Taking a few steps closer, my shoes echoed in the cavern, "Empty threats of hypotheticals don't scare me. Despite every time a customer asserted that I'd lose my job," stopping right below the steps that led to the thrones, I looked up to Twining, "I remain employed, to this day."

Standing there in a moment, Twining's eyes did not move from mine, their expression unreadable.

"Highness?" Twining laughed, though it sounded more like a scoff, "You insult me," turning from me, they looked over their throne, "I am but an elected council member, one of several. We vampires are not a monarchy, but a democracy. We find monarchy to be," they paused, looking back at me, "archaic." Taking a step, they started on a stroll, fingers tracing over each empty throne, "While I am the elected representative in dealings with the crown, I am not in charge of my people. I do, however," starting behind the thrones, each step brought them closer to their own, "hold sway." Passing their throne, they ended up behind

Finnegan's, "Because unlike the other council members, my Ward was elected to a seat too."

Taking some of Twining's hair between their elegant fingers, Finnegan twirled the end around, "If you cooperate with us, Twining and I will oppose any movement against your crown. Wartime efforts must be unanimous, and with both of us standing in opposition, those who voted for us will stand in opposition as well. That should be enough to discourage an internal uprising and promote acceptance of your reign."

Eyes narrowing a bit on Finnegan, I felt inclined to trust them, though I had no reason to. Maybe it was the crook of their brow, the slight upward tug to their mouth, or maybe even the way the green of their eyes made me feel, but as I stood there in tense quarters engaging in diplomatic talks, it was nothing short of exciting.

Green glowed brighter on my bow tie.

"This proposition is unevenly weighted," I took a step up, "you both will stand against your own to save my crown," taking the next step up, I stood on the same level as them, "and in return all I need to do is put in a good word for you? I'm sure you can understand my hesitation."

"Well," Twining stepped around Finnegan's throne, their amethyst cape catching the ambient glow of the candles, "I can assure you that my people having the ability to live along side those of Netherside, free of persecution, is a cause worthy of the sacrifice." Stopping directly in front of me, they extended their hand my way, the haunting of a smile threatening to take their features, "What do you say, your highness?"

Looking up from their hand, my eyes met them, and in that moment, the glow of their eyes appeared to have softened. Finnegan standing a step behind them, leaning over to see me, the unapologetically daring smile on their face lit up the darkness of the cavern. Looking between them, if only Ross could have seen them too. Real life vampires, every bit as cool as I'm sure he thought they were, I could only

wonder what he'd say. If Ross could love them that much,

there was no way they could be inherently bad.

The candles around flickered blue, for just a moment.

Bringing my hand up, it met with Twining's, "You

make a compelling case."

I don't think I'll ever forget it, the way Twining

smiled at me that day.

The door slammed open, and while I startled,

Twining didn't.

"Finnegan," it felt like every other time I heard

someone say their name, they sounded upset about it.

Turning to look at the door, my eyes were met with

red.

Prying himself out of the grasp of two others, Cyrus'

blonde waves fell from their place in the scuffle, hanging

over his face, "Let go of me."

"Kitty, Ragdoll," Finnegan called as they turned to face the door, "stand down."

The two people, a young man with pink mid-length hair and a young woman who donned similar Victorian vampiric dress to the others in all ways except her fishnet stockings and industrial goth platform boots, stepped back, letting go of Cyrus.

Stumbling from their grasp, Cyrus' messy footsteps echoed through the cavern. Straightening with a vengeance, his hair flipped out of his face, his eyes set ablaze. "Are you trying to start a war?"

"A war?" Finnegan took a couple bouncing steps down to the same level as Cyrus, "Always."

Rolling them away from Finnegan, when Cyrus' eyes met mine, his ragged breathing caught in his throat. Gaze jumping down to my hand in Twining's, his brow dropped. Taking my hand from Twining's, I looked back to them.

"My little brother is quite charmed with vampires, you're all he ever talks about." pocketing my hand, I shifted my weight away and toward Cyrus, "I accept your proposition, it's what he would do, if he were here."

A harsh curse under his breath, Cyrus sprung forward. Turning, I only saw him and the red glow that took him for a moment before he came crashing into me. The last thing I saw as I fell from my feet was Finnegan reach out toward me. The last thing I felt before everything turned to glittery static was their hand meet mine.

Red and green collided in the fall.

And though the colors didn't mix, they looked real good next to each other.

Thrown, I went flying until I crashed into metal. A clutter followed as I fell to the ground, the sound of shattering surrounding me. Vision blurring back in, I saw her, for but a moment, as she died in my hands surrounded by glass shards on the ground.

Margo.

My breath hitched.

The lights flickered blue.

When the lights turned white again, when I blinked, she was gone. Left to stare at an overwhelming amount of chrome, my ears rang out until I heard,

"What were you doing?"

Eyes slowly raising, they passed over metal shelving and glass shards on the chrome floor, over colorful puddles and various lab equipment as it sat about me, scattered. Kneeling before me, Cyrus leaned down to catch my eyes. Hair disheveled, out of breath, I hadn't seen him so worked up before.

Coughing, he looked up to me through pained eyes, his hand covering his mouth, "I don't know what they said to you, but you can't trust Twining."

"And why is that?" Finnegan popped their head out from behind him, making Cyrus jump into his next life.

Whirling around to look at them, Cyrus raked his hand through his hair to pull it from his face, "Because they're a vampire."

Standing, it looked more like they floated back to their feet as Finnegan bent over at the middle to be eye-level with Cyrus as he remained on the floor, "I'm a vampire."

"I know," groaning, Cyrus shook as he stood, "but you're different."

"Different?" Finnegan stepped around Cyrus, every weightless movement elegant, "the only difference between Twining and I is how you choose to view us." Stopping before me, Finnegan extended their hand my way, "Do not worry, he did not sign his life away. He simply agreed to reevaluate the way vampires are being viewed in Netherside, and in return we will keep our people cooperative with his reign."

Staring up at them and their extended hand as Cyrus huffed, turning away from us in the background, I remained in that moment. Chrome walls, humming fixtures above, lengthy chrome tables sat about, counters and cabinets lining the perimeter. Not a window to be seen, but one door on either side of the room, it almost looked like a laboratory.

But as I accepted Finnegan's hand and stood, my eyes lingered on the tables. They were far too long and thin, not the usual shape for that surface, in a usual laboratory.

Opening my mouth to ask where we were, I'd never get to, because just as I took my breath in, a door crashed open. I saw it, the moment Cyrus tensed.

"What is-" Abraxas, silver hair pulled up in a messy bun atop her head, two wispy sections flowed on either side of her face, echoing the starry depth of her eyes as she stopped in the doorway. White lab coat brushing forward in the gust of air that came with her hurry, black scrubs sat beneath it on her fine frame. What appeared to be urgency melted into annoyance as her eyes met Cyrus.

"Hello."

It only took a moment for his tension to drain, covered by that stupid smile of his as Cyrus brought up one hand in a wave, "Hey."

"The infamous Abraxas," Finnegan let go of me and started toward her, their cape trailing behind, "it has been ages, decades even."

As if she would have preferred a vandal, the way her eyes dragged between Finnegan and Cyrus said it all. Sighing, she didn't even acknowledge the vampire, brushing past them and toward me. Stopping a step away, she spared me but a glance before looking down. Following her gaze, I too was met with the mess I had made upon impact. Turning a bit, I glanced back at the wall I had crashed into. Shelves knocked from the walls, their contents on the floor, even the counter was dented some. With a wave of her hand, the broken glass about took on a silver glow.

"Whatever it is that you're up to, I don't have time for it," turning away from me, as she left, the shards pulled together on the floor, rebuilding themselves until they formed beakers and test tubes, "I am very busy, still having to deal with the fallout of Nolan's little stunt on Halloween. Jackass killed five kids, just left them there, in a summoning circle, at the high school, people saw. It's been a disaster."

Watching as the array of equipment rebuilt itself, the liquid floating up from the floor back into its various containers, I didn't look up as Cyrus spoke, but it was obvious from the hesitation in his first word that he was flying by the seat of his pants, "I want my clothes back."

When her steps stopped, I looked up to Abraxas. Slowly turning, I think I saw all the rage of a boil in her eyes, though the rest of her was still, "Your clothes?" turning all the way around, she started toward Cyrus, "You brought chaos into my morgue," he backtracked as she continued her pursuit, "for your, clothes?"

Backing up into the wall, Cyrus' smile didn't fade as he nodded.

Looking between his eyes, the moment of tension Abraxas created felt as brittle as the thin glass about. A groan left her as she turned from him so sharply that her coat smacked him on the way. With another wave of her hand, a cupboard across the room opened and in a blur of black, something came shooting out of it. Absolutely taking Cyrus out, a mass of black fabric hit his face. Struggling with it, Cyrus stumbled until he ripped the fabric from his head. Studying it as it laid, muddled in his arms, he lit up.

"Thank you."

As Abraxas knelt over to pick up some of the reassembled equipment near me, her exhale was hard, "Yeah yeah," sliding a scale back onto the counter behind me, she went on as she reached for a beaker, "it took you a while to come after them, I was surprised."

"Yes, well," Cyrus' voice muffed, earning my gaze, "I've been a bit preoccupied."

Standing there, eyes wide, I watched as Cyrus struggled to pull his button down up over his head like a goblin. Heat began to bud on my face as the cool white of the lights above shifted, turning warmer. Toned, but not religiously so, his torso sat, decorated in scars. Though as my eyes trailed up his eternally youthful skin, tracing his every line, indicative of his muscles and history as he struggled, they met with something dark. It almost looked like a burn, but completely black, as if he had been stained by ink. Over his heart, it took up most of that side of his chest, reaching toward his shoulder.

I perhaps would have stared at him forever, had I not heard Finnegan's breath hitch at my side. Looking over to them, I only saw it for the briefest of moments before they corrected themselves, but it appeared to be concern. Though it was quickly replaced with something else as a red dusting took their face. Looking to me, brow raised, they just looked back to Cyrus again.

"You have to unbutton it, darling," Walking up to him, Finnegan took Cyrus' shirt in their hands, "why are you rabid."

Watching as Cyrus didn't struggle, allowing Finnegan to unbutton his shirt, I couldn't look away. Red and green, the way their eyes' glow reflected in one another, I liked it. Something soft came about Cyrus, something I never saw in his features when he looked at me. But as he stood there, watching Finnegan unbutton every button with a dexterous care, there was a tenderness evident in the slowness of his breathing. Something that, as I stared, I wanted to come to know myself. Looking Finnegan over, Cyrus' eyes raised. When his gaze met mine, his widened. Face lighting up as Finnegan unbuttoned the last one, he turned away. Standing there, back to me, tension took Cyrus' frame, bringing definition to his muscles as one hand raised to the back of his head.

"Between kidnapping Igor, the ball, figuring out where Finnegan took him, and helping Igor tame the colors, it's been almost non-stop." Bending over, he took up a black shirt. "I didn't expect to just run into the next incarnation like that and have him in Netherside already."

As he slid his arms into the long sleeves, pulling the black button-down shirt over his back, I heard Abraxas stop in her tidying.

"I trust you took the severance protocol into consideration, despite the unexpected nature of your meeting."

When Cyrus froze, hands up to his collar after buttoning his shirt, back still to us, I felt the air grow cold.

Slowly turning to look at him from the last piece of equipment she picked up from the floor, Abraxas took a step toward him, "Cyrus."

Turning around, brows furrowed but smile remaining, the red of his eyes dimmed as he brought up his hands in caution, "I, uh-"

Slamming the book in her hand on the chrome table at her side, Abraxas made us all jump, trapped in the tension. A hissing escaped her clenched teeth as the room grew even colder, making her breath visible. Standing there like a man before a firing squad, Cyrus' black shirt had a rounded clergy collar, a white rectangular card visible at the middle beneath his chin as it held the rest up, stiff. Looking like a catholic priest, he was lucky he was immortal because from the way Abraxas looked at him, if he hadn't been, he would have been a step away from meeting his god.

"You couldn't have possibly just snatched him from Flipside with no consideration to the ramifications," taking a step toward Cyrus, he took one back, "there's no way you'd just do that, just pluck a Pulse and run away with him. Because if you had, then that means there's a mess to clean up, and you know whose job it is to deal with that?" Stopping when she had him pinned to the wall again, her bun looked as if it would come undone at any moment, barely kept in place atop her head by a thin hair tie, "mine."

Cyrus must have been born guilty for it to look that natural on him.

Snapping, Abraxas made a television mounted to the far wall come to life. Holding Cyrus there, her eye contact did not break as the television turned on. Flipping through channels on its own, names, dates, and news anchors got but a moment on the screen, though a moment long enough for me to put together that they were missing person stories being covered by the news. As the dates flew by, too fast for me to keep track of, the flipping channels didn't stop. Speeding up, it must have flipped though tens more channels before it stopped. Turning to static, the television's white noise was the only sound, for a moment.

Slowly looking over her shoulder, Abraxas' eyes captured the static of the screen. Turning back to Cyrus, she studied him before stepping away. Eyes jumping between Abraxas and the television, though the rest of him remained stiff, when his eyes met mine, Cyrus' brow furrowed. Pocketing her hands, Abraxas started away from him.

"I apologize, it appears you did do your job." Continuing to tidy the space, she left Cyrus, stiff against the wall, "I usually keep a tighter eye on situations like this, but due to the former demon king, my team has been busy trying to make a quintuple homicide with no motive make sense to the Pulse public." Eyes jumping to Cyrus, they made him tense, "And this one isn't known for following the rules."

Looking back to her, his demeanor flipped with the provocative drop of his brow, "That's right," pushing himself up off the wall, his golden locks bounced with his step, "you just assumed that I fucked up, you're so full of yourself, Abraxas." Stopping at my side, he leaned into me, throwing his arm over my shoulder, "I'm not incompetent, I know what I'm doing."

Sighing, she just rolled her eyes as she continued to clean, though I thought I saw it, a little bit of a smile take her.

"Well now that that's settled," he started to pull me along, "Igor and I will be going."

Looking up to him, no space between us, my breath sat, suspended in my chest. Black hugging his features, his clergy collar on display in the opening of the v-neck of the hoodie, though he looked good in a suit and tie, this looked better. Staring to usher me toward one of the doors, he was probably saying something, but as he laughed, that superstar spark to him, I didn't hear a thing. His warmth melting into my side, his grip tight on my shoulder, I wondered what it was like, to be made of colors so bright. How close to him would I have to get for them to bleed into me?

The lights flickered red, cutting off whatever he had been saying.

Looking down, Cyrus stared at me.

The slight upward tug that took the line of his mouth as his eyes searched mine, it let on that the smile he wore most of the time wasn't real.

Clearing their throat, Finnegan stole the show as they strolled up to Cyrus and I, "Oh do let me tag along," they stopped right in front of us, all but pinning Cyrus and I to the door, "You can tell me all about it," reaching forward, they trapped Cyrus as their hand met the knob at his side, "how you took care of everything."

I felt Cyrus tense, brow twitching down a bit, though his smile didn't fade, his fiery eyes holding on the vampire. As Finnegan leaned in closer, their eyes hooded just a bit, there was something about the way they looked at Cyrus that caused a jolt in my blood.

"I'm sure it's a riveting tale," Clicking the knob to the side a few times, it sounded like a dial as Finnegan went on, "Since you're just so," eyes dropping just a bit, but a few inches between them, Finnegan held the moment hostage as they looked Cyrus back up, "competent."

Cyrus swallowed.

The door clicked open.

Looking behind me from the corner of my eye, I was met with an abyss as a gust of air blew my hair around. Silver, a sea of churning glitter met me, filling the frame as it caught on the light.

A frail palm met my chest.

Looking forward, I only saw Finnegan for a moment before their hand took grip of my shirt.

Pushing me back, my shoe slipped over the threshold of the door.

Glancing to my side as I fell into the silver, my eyes met with Cyrus. Hand up to Finnegan's as it grasped onto his shirt too, there was something about the annoyance that painted him, something that made it almost look like something else- though whatever it was, I wasn't sure.

All I knew, as we were devoured by the silver, dropping into a free fall, was that it felt like red.

The glitter before me washed Finnegan away, though their hand remained, grip unfaltering. Glitter taking on the colors of my brooch, Cyrus' arm remained around me. And though I was falling, over and over again I found myself falling, it was starting to feel like flying.

That was

Until my back hit the ground.

Air knocked from me, the cough that took me stung as my glasses landed, crooked on my face. A breeze blew past me, the first thing I felt as my eyes closed, the silver draining away. Blades of grass tickled my face as my hearing rang back in, the shriek of pain fading from my spine. Eyes opening as I laid, flat on my back, a warmth met my front. Staring at the canopy of evergreen trees, the faded stars speckled above, they weighed so little that it took me a moment to realize that Finnegan was on top of me. Coughing at my side, Cyrus was about to say something but suddenly stopped.

Pulling themselves up, one knee between my legs, the other between Cyrus', Finnegan's lengths hair spilled over their shoulder, brushing against the side of my face as they hovered above me. One hand on my chest, their other on Cyrus', they looked between us, slowly, with a type of intent I couldn't fathom. But something about it, something about laying beneath them, about Cyrus laying at my side, about the warmth of both of them simultaneously on my skin, it made my breath catch.

Blinking, when my eyes opened, for a moment, just a moment, we were no longer there. No, we were far away from there, in a different forest somewhere, surrounded by trees taller than any I had ever seen, wildflowers about us as we laid in the grass. A fire burning behind them, a small shack to the right, as I stared up at Finnegan, Cyrus still at my side, I couldn't look away. I knew the lengths of their hair, I knew the snaggle tooth of their suppressed grin, I knew the way they looked when they wanted something but wouldn't say it, I knew what their features looked like, illuminated by nothing more than candlelight.

I knew I knew them, perhaps not now, but in another life.

Looking to my side, I saw Cyrus, eyes blue, freckles more prominent, gaze glassy as he smiled, looking up at Finnegan. Unhindered, happy, he looked as if he had never so much as had a bad dream before.

When I blinked, my world returned around me.

And though Cyrus still looked up at Finnegan, a begrudging red dusting to his face, the irked twinge to his brow and angry twist to his smile were a far departure from the young man I had seen before. Though he hadn't aged a day, he had aged an eon, somehow.

Shoving Finnegan off us, Cyrus sat up, a sharp breath more like a click as it hissed through his teeth, "How about you go run back to your master."

Humming, it turned into a small laugh as Finnegan raised to their feet with the grace of air, weightless, "Excuse you, I have every right to be here." Extending a hand my way, the combative tilt of Finnegan's head, their nuance screamed as I accepted their hand. "I find Igor exciting," their eyes tracing my every line until their gaze met mine, they tightened their grip on my hand, "and it appears," pulling me to my feet, they pulled me in, but an inch away from their face, "that Igor finds me exciting, too."

The light from the moon above turned green, tainting the color of everything it reached.

"What?" Before Cyrus had finished his word, I was yanked around. Gaze studying mine, it dropped to my brooch. I watched them, the three colors I had tamed reflect in his eyes as they widened, a smile coming to follow. And unlike the smile he usually wore, I could tell this one was real. Hand on my either arm, his eyes jumped back up to mine and as I watched the swell grow in him, the moonlight started to grow yellow.

"You're doing so good," pulling me into an embrace, I could feel it, the tremble in his grip as it tightened, "I knew you could do it."

"Just three more," Finnegan popped out around Cyrus to catch my eye, "and you will be king."

Stepping back from the hug, he kept his hands on me, holding me tight, "How do you feel?"

Staring at him, I took a breath, but as it caught on the way in, eyes unmoving from his, I stalled. I had been asked that question many times, but never before could I have answered honestly.

"I," after not having spoken for so long, my voice cracked, causing me to clear my throat. Hand up to my mouth, balled into a loose fist, my eyes averted from Cyrus. I felt something, I definitely felt something. I felt it as his warmth spilled through my clothing, as Finnegan tilted their head, but I had no idea what it was. "I'm not sure," smiling a little as I looked between them, though it was cold, wherever we were, it felt warmer with them, "but not bad."

Brow furrowing despite his smile, Cyrus nodded a bit. It was slow at first, as if to convince himself, but as his smile grew, brow raising, it appeared he had been successful, "Awesome," leaning his forehead against mine, he pulled me into a looser hug, "we can work with that."

The moonlight turned red.

I heard it, the smile in his exhale.

Red flickered, faintly, between us, lighting his features for just a moment before it disappeared.

"Not to," Finnegan stepped around us with a youthful leisure even my younger brother would envy, "interrupt, but," pulling Cyrus back away from me, they sent him stumbling and left me wondering where in that small body they hid that strength, "to interrupt. We have a situation on our hands, do we not," turning to look at Cyrus, they tucked some of their hair behind their ear, "Father Glory?"

Stiffening, backed up against one of the trees, Cyrus' eyes darted to me. "Yes, well," looking away, as he shifted his weight, my attention caught behind him on a row of headstones. Not far from work or home, we must have been next to the cemetery it all started in. "Igor, tell me," looking back my way, his hesitation was unlike him, "before we met, did you often go missing?"

"What?" Looking back his way from the graves, the air started to grow cold, "of course not, I have a full-time job."

"That is interesting because," popping up at my side, Finnegan pulled something from their pocket. Round, silver, they clicked the lid of their pocket watch open to look at two different clock faces, one where you'd expect, the other on the underside of the lid, "you have been gone for a week, and no one has noticed."

"A week?" Looking back to Cyrus, he just looked away from me, "but it's been a day, two tops."

"Correct, but that is Netherside time," Finnegan turned the pocket watch to face me, "there is not a consistently accurate conversion between the two, but to put it simply, every moment in Netherside is many moments, Flipside."

"So," the drawl to Cyrus' voice chilled me, "while yes, it hasn't been very long for you, it has been quite long here, especially for no one to have reported you missing yet."

Staring at him, my breath caught in my throat.

Had no one noticed?

The warm tones bled from the moonlight, leaving it to grow cool.

How had no one noticed?

A flake of snow drifted between Cyrus and I.

Eyes widening as snow fell through his vision, Cyrus looked up to the sky. Staring at it for a moment, his jaw tightened. Gaze dropping to me, he became unreadable. A shaking breath left him as an unknown resolve took visible hold. Pushing himself up from the tree as snow started to fall in more abundance, it stuck enough that by the time he reached me, his steps crunched. Taking my hand in his, he pulled me with him.

Stumbling as I started along with him, I was about to ask what he was doing, but then I saw it, how tight his jaw was. Finnegan at my other side, their hands in their pockets, they didn't say a thing as they gazed into the sky. As the snowfall became heavier, blanketing our surroundings, the silence became insulated, and in turn, even louder.

Passing my store, the yellow of the sign radiated into the overcast sky.

Amy and Venecia didn't think it was weird that I stopped showing up to work?

The moonlight flickered blue.

Cyrus' grip on my hand tightened.

Was I not actually as valuable to the team as I had thought I was?

The snowfall grew heavier.

Finnegan took a breath that shook on the way in at my side.

As we entered my neighborhood, following the path I had unwillingly taken Cyrus on before, the snow became difficult to walk through.

Stopping in front of my family's home, I stared at it.

Mum, wasn't she worried?

The moonlight flickered blue again, but this time, it held for a moment longer.

My breath clouded before me.

I could no-call-no-show six times in a row, without a word to my family, and it inspired no alarm?

My breath caught on the way in.

No

Actually

It made sense.

My shoulders relaxed with my exhale as my eyes drifted down.

It wasn't that they didn't notice.

A small smile took me as the moonlight swelled blue, painting the white canvas of the surrounding snow.

Did they just not care?

Neither Finnegan or Cyrus would look at me.

I looked up to my family's house through my bangs, "Why are we here?"

Taking a breath in, Cyrus hesitated before speaking, "Usually when something like this happens, Abraxas' team handles it. They fake your death so you're able to freely leave this world, your family can eventually move on, and your assets aren't tied up in a missing person's case."

"We do it all the time, when we turn new vampires," Finnegan took a step forward, their cape trailing behind them in the snow, "it is a problem if you just get kidnapped. And

Father Glory here definitely just kidnapped you, with no regard for the fallout."

"I was fully expecting to hear your name pop up on her TV, to have Abraxas rip me a new one and swoop in to fix my mess like usual, but, I would have never expected that they just didn't…" Cyrus paused, and though he took a breath to say more, no more came.

"I think what Father Glory is trying to express," turning, Finnegan's light skin reflected the snow mounting around us, their air spilling elegantly like the flakes that slid down the strands, "is that there may still be some loose ends you need to tend to, regardless." Turning back toward my family's house, they raised a hand to the sky, catching some falling flakes, "We would not want you to become our king and have some weird hang-up from your past resurface in ten years and cause a scene." Turning, their hand became visible to me. "Even if your family does not care about your absence, we do not want to take any chances."

The flakes did not melt in their grip.

My eyes jumped to the house.

No.

The moon flashed orange.

There was no way.

Taking a step forward, the first was slow, but every one after that carried me faster up the path. Breaths coming ragged and sharp, the struggle through the snow didn't faze me. Not even as the visibility became nearly zero did I stop, the snow storm turning into a blizzard in a moment.

Neither Cyrus or Finnegan followed.

I knew I had been absent, cold even. Stumbling, I fought my way through the piles of snow. I knew I had closed the door in Ross' face more than he had even been allowed to walk through it. I stood at the front door. Reaching for it, the knob stung my hand in the cold.

It was locked.

Panting, I stared at it.

I knew I was nothing more than a shadow in their world.

Taking off around the house, I ran under the overhang of the roof to avoid the snow.

I knew I couldn't tell you a thing about my father, having never had a single meaningful conversation with the man.

Hand on the siding of the house, my cough tore my throat, bringing iron to rise in my mouth but I pushed on.

I knew my mum hid things from us, things I may have been able to piece together if I had ever cared enough.

Running around the side of the house, the deck before me was no longer visible beneath the snow, nothing more than a raised platform of white as the blizzard raged on.

I knew everything was fake, their smiles, their conversations, every interaction hey had ever had with me.

Always walking on eggshells, on edge because of my attitude.

Fighting through the snow up onto the deck, my shoe caught on the way up. Falling forward, I crashed into the snow. Though my impact was cushioned by the snow, it still hurt. Laying there for a moment, panting fogging my crooked glasses, snow fell on top of me from the sides of my indent. Stinging screaming up my palms, the snow scratched my wrists as I pushed myself up. When my eyes met with the glass patio door, my breath hitched. Staring forward, frozen, half picked up from the snow, I was met with the family dinner table.

A Christmas tree decorated in silver and blues up in the corner of the living room, the communion of the walls with the ceiling and every seam of the fireplace lined with tinsel, they had even lined the chandelier above the table in garland, hanging ornaments from it at varying heights to catch the light. Warm, the fire roaring, presents beneath the tree, only three stockings up on the mantel, it was a far departure from the desolate cold of the outside. Slowly standing, snow falling from my shoulders, I couldn't look away from them, my family, as they sat at the dinner table. My one step toward the door crunched beneath me in the snow. Long runner hanging off either side, the center was christened with a wreath boasting several lit candles. A dinner spread my mum must have tended to all day, one my father probably tried to help with but was more in the way, one Ross would someday come to really appreciate, dotted the table between them atop the fancy china we never used.

My father's back sat to me, mum at the head of the table, and Ross slightly off center across the way, facing me, though I couldn't hear them, I could see that they were laughing. My eyes drifted to my seat, one I had rarely even sat in, as it waited for me, empty at the other end of the table. Though there was no place set for me, instead a display of decorative trees and glittery deer statures found there home on the table before the chair.

Hand raising to the window as the snow raged on, blowing my hair sideways, it stole the feeling from my fingertips. Able to see into the warmth inside through the shadow of my reflection on the window, obstructing the obliterating white of the snow outside, my eyes met Ross. Bandaged and bruised, he must have gotten into another fight standing up for someone. Though that didn't hinder it, his silly smile as he said something else that made my family laugh.

He was always good at that.

Maybe that's why he'd never leave me alone, because I was the one person he couldn't make laugh.

Hand tightening into a fist against the window, I watched as they ate, laughing as if there wasn't a thing wrong in the world. As if their eldest son didn't just leave for work one day a week ago and never come home. Something welled in my throat, but before it could take hold, my jaw tightened.

The moonlight turned orange, lighting the snow ablaze in amber, as if I stood at the foot of a ranging volcano.

I knew I was uncomfortable to be around, that I was unreachable, unavailable, disinterested, distant. I knew that, I always knew that, I just never knew what to do about it. But despite that, I thought, I had convinced myself, that even though I was that way, that somewhere, somehow, they still loved me.

But there they sat, perhaps even happier now that my oppressive presence was gone.

My forehead met the glass of the door. Brows quivering as the lump in my throat grew, my breath hissed through my teeth as the orange grew stronger, drowning the other color out.

I knew they would have been happier if I had never been born, I just didn't want to believe it.

The line of my mouth cracked up.

But that was alright.

It was better this way.

Eyes raising back to them, to my brother, my father and my mum, if that's what was best for them, at least one of us had any sense of decency.

Lowering my hand from the window, I looked at it.

I didn't know how to use my powers, not really. But I had an inkling, an idea, a feeling even. Whenever something happened, whenever I unlocked a color, there had always been something there. It was what made the sign fall, what took Cyrus and I into the sky at the ball, what had saved Finnegan and I from the fall.

A wish, that was all.

I had wished that the woman would get out of my store, wished to be alone with Cyrus, wished to be saved, and it all came true. Cyrus had never told me the details of Nox's powers, and I had been too occupied to ever ask. But as I looked back up to my family, I just knew.

If I wished that I would disappear from their lives, it would come true.

Hand meeting the doorknob, my grip was strong despite how numb my fingers had become.

Jaw tightening, I closed my eyes as the sharp wind blew by. If I was the most powerful thing to ever be, then I wished that they couldn't see me.

A tingle took over my body, bringing a twinge of discomfort to my every inch that wasn't numb. As if my entire body had fallen asleep, pins and needles pricked me, making my grip on the door tighten. Holding my breath, I stood that way for a moment as the sensation screamed over me.

Pulling the door open, the breaking of the seal didn't manage to stop my heart.

But the silence that followed did.

Slowly opening my eyes, they met with my family, unbothered, not even having noticed the back door opening a few feet away. Exhaling, my breath didn't cloud. Perhaps I was too cold. Hesitation took hold of me as I pulled the door open, just enough to slip inside. The warmth from across the threshold seeped out, killed by the cold before it could meet me. When Ross laughed again, my eyes jumped to him.

"And then I was like, 'I know you're married to the principal, Dr. Colburn, but like, are you sure there should be a plant in there?' And they were like, 'trust me'." He fiddled with his poorly tied tie, alluding to his nerves despite his goofy smile maintaining, "But, like, I don't trust them."

When my parents laughed, I just stood and stared. I had never heard them laugh like that. As if they didn't have to act, as if they were comfortable, a family. The snow outside stopped, but did not hit the ground, suspended, trapped in the air. As my eyes dropped to the floor, I stepped inside the door.

"Don't give Dr. Colburn too hard of a time," Mum said as she held her cup in her hand, her red velvet dress with white fur trim catching the Christmas lights in her movement.

"We were once good friends, you know," my father lifted his arms, his heavy tattooing visible below his rolled-up sleeves as he laced his hands behind his head, "and they may not look it now, but back then, they were the last person you wanted to mess with."

"Yeah yeah," Ross leaned back in his chair, apparently barely able to sit still, "whatever, you make it sound like they were some assassin or something."

They both laughed, but neither of my parents replied.

Closing the door behind me, I couldn't look up. It appeared that I had been correct, all it took was a wish and my will became reality. Of course Cyrus would keep that from me, if I had known at the start that I could have just wished this all away and gone back to how things were, and I would have. But not now, I couldn't now, not after hearing the way my family laughed without me. Because even if I did wish it all away, wished to be back at that table with them, wished to forget Cyrus and Finnegan and Netherside and all the colors I had come to know, even if I wished to forget hearing the way my family laughed without me, I knew I never would forget, not really.

Walking from the dining room, past the table as their topic shifted to the principal of the private high school Ross attended, I didn't pay the details any mind. When I had attended, there was a different principal, but one day he just went missing. I suppose this must have been the new one. But it didn't matter, nothing mattered. Stopping by the fire, not even the warmth of the flames could touch me. Three stockings hung above the flames, which was curious, because last I checked, four of us lived here. Looking up to the mantel, my eyes met with the line of family photos. Birthdays and vacations, as I stood there, taking a framed photo into hand, my disinterested face staring back at me from the past, a breath left me. Looking down the line of photos, as I saw nothing more than the same, I knew they wouldn't miss me.

There was nothing to miss.

As I listened to them laugh again after Ross said something about dirt in a printer and the choir teacher, my grip tightened. Staring at my faint reflection in the glass of the photo, I looked like a completely different person. Brow furrowed, it shaped my eyes and darkened their brown in contrast to the color my face now had, as if I had been a corpse reanimated, I looked nearly dead as I stood next to Ross at a tourist attraction in California I had been dragged to a few years ago. If only I could have gone back, been the brother Ross deserved, the son my parents wanted, would they have laughed with me like that too?

I'd never get to know.

Because as I stood there, in the center of a world of suspended snow, there was only one place left for me to go.

Closing my eye, my breath left me.

I didn't want to think it, to pull the full thought through my mind.

But I had to.

It was only a matter of time.

I wasn't worried about them, they would be fine.

No hearts would be broken today, none but mine.

"I wish," my breath shook, voice barely escaping me as tears welled in the corners of my eyes, "I wish that," teeth clenching, my grip tightened on the photo, my family's laughter stinging a bit more each time, "I wish to be erased from the memory of Flipside, as if I had never been here at all."

The air went cold as my heart dropped.

Eyes opening, I was met with blue reflecting in the glass of the photo. My irises glowed with the color, so bright that it burned a hole in my vision as I dropped the photo.

When it hit the ground, it sounded just like it, the glass that shattered when Margo died.

Staring at the photo through glass shards, my image faded away.

Eyes jumping back up to the mantel, they met with another picture.

One at a time, each photo down the line on the mantel, my likeness disappeared, leaving a hole behind. I vanished from every one of Ross' birthdays, from my graduation from the private academy, from the trip my parents took us on for their anniversary. When I vanished from the last photo on the mantel, fading out of the day Ross was born, blue exploded. Though unlike the other colors, nothing moved, not even the air, as the tint took over everything, strangling the remainder of the color from my surroundings, leaving nothing but blue.

When the fire went out, it didn't create smoke.

The conversation at the table stopped.

Taking a step back, my head slowly turned to the side.

Silence sat as my eyes met with my father's. Staring forward, mouth open, stopped halfway through a word, he was as dim as the surroundings. Mum sat, hand frozen in a gesture, and though her smile remained, I could see it, something fade in her eyes. Ross' back to me, I couldn't see his face, but I could tell, he was stiff.

As they slowly came out of the moment, the house felt a bit colder than before.

Clearing her throat, mum, picked up her cup. My father sat back a bit, looking down to his plate. Taking a step back, I couldn't breathe.

Did it work?

Was that all it took, a wish, and I was gone?

Any moment now things would go back to how they were, all the same either way, because I hadn't mattered, not really. The kindest thing I could do was leave, that way they could just be happy without me. Frame tense, eyes to the floor, I waited, waited for my mum to laugh and talk about the garden, for my father to ask Ross about his music, for Ross to tell our parents what he learned about vampires today, but when nothing came, not a single word, I looked back up.

Turning, Ross looked down at his side. Eyes following his gaze, the blue of one of his irises so bright it glowed in contrast with the grey of the world, that's what did it, what stopped everything.

"Who was this place set for?"

An empty place at the table that I hadn't seen before, obstructed by the decorations, set with obvious care, it wasn't at my usual chair as it sat at Ross' side. Staring at the place, it was rare, to see mum hesitate like that. But as she sat there, mouth open but no words to speak, I watched it for the first time, glass, as it shone over her eyes.

"I," she looked back to Ross, "I don't know."

Looking back to the place that sat, so close at his side it must have been for someone he loved, his brow dropped, eyes studying it. Hand shaking, my vision blurred, tunneling at the edges as my intake trembled down my throat. Meeting my mouth as ice shot through me, my stomach hit the ground. They had set a place for me, they had been expecting me, they had wanted me there.

The conversation did not pick up again.

Backing up, my eyes jumped between the members of my family.

What had I done.

Blue bled off the Christmas tree, spilling down Ross from his eyes as tears took him, though his smile remained. Blue crawled off every now incomplete photo, from the one of my mum's eyes that held the color, off my father's faded button down, to the floor. Racing toward me, it tainted everything, about to crash into me.

But I didn't want to feel it.

Barreling out of the room, I ran into the wall in the hall but kept going. Crashing into my bedroom door, I struggled with it, my hands too cold to open the knob. Getting a grip, I pulled the door open as a chilled gust of air crashed into me. Running into the room, I turned and saw it for only a moment, the wave of blue about to hit me. Slamming the door, I closed myself off from it. Teeth grit as I panted, stumbling back from the door, I stared at it.

The light on my desk flickered on, glowing orange, the only other color in my world.

Why were they acting like everything was fine?

I backed up as the blue crashed into my door again, shaking the house.

Why hadn't they reported me missing.

I stepped into my desk, knocking the lamp from it.

Why weren't they out looking.

When the lamp met with the floor, the moment the bulb shattered, extinguishing the orange, the door flew open.

Why did they care.

Watching as the wave came spilling in, sloshing over everything, I stumbled away from my desk.

They had no reason to care.

Backing to into my dresser, my hand knocked something from the surface.

Why did I care.

When the empty fish tank from my nightstand hit the ground, the glass shattered.

It was all because I cared.

Blue crashed into me.

Underwater, blue overwhelmed me, stinging my senses, rendering my body unable to move, left to the weight of the current as the water filled my room to the ceiling.

Vision blurring as my lungs screamed, what air I had escaping me, though all I could feel was blue, in the dimming of my view, I saw red and green too.

My eyes closed.

"Margo!"

Nothing more than a hazy echo at first, when I heard it again, my eyes opened.

"Margo!"

Standing in my room, feet on the floor, hair suspended around me in the water, I didn't struggle to breathe despite being drowned. Standing at my sides, a glowing hand each on my shoulders, Cyrus and Finnegan brought green and red, albeit dim, back into my world. Looking between them, neither were looking at me.

Eyes trailing forward, my heart stopped.

There I stood, nine years old, in the doorway. A bright red shirt and black shorts, my rainbow backpack grasped in one little hand, my glasses in my other, I was so young, so small. Smiling from ear to ear, my blazing orange hair a mess, I came running into the room.

"Margo, guess what?" Dropping my backpack, I immediately tripped over it as I ran toward my dresser but that didn't stop me, "mum is going to have a baby, I'm going to be a big brother!"

Breath hitched, eyes wide, I watched him, my younger self, as he leaned up to the fish tank. There she swam, back and forth, around the plants and about the bubbles, Margo, my orange fish, apathetic to my presence, but the apple of my eye all the same.

I heard Cyrus' sharp intake, but I couldn't look at him, unable to rip my eyes away from her.

"I'm going to do everything with him," digging something out of my pocket, my unruly hair bounced with the movement as I pulled out a crumpled paper, "Look," unfolding it, I held up a poorly constructed scribble of me with a baby standing at my side, "I'm going to be the best big brother, I'm so excited." Bringing up his little hand to the glass of the tank, he watched Margo swim by through his splayed fingers.

I needed to move.

I needed to pull him back.

I needed to stop what was about to happen.

But

I couldn't move.

I couldn't pull him back.

I couldn't stop what was about to happen.

Not as he smiled at her, "I already love him so much and I haven't even met him." Leaning his little forehead up against the tank, he closed his eyes, "But don't you worry, Margo. Even after he's here, I'll still love you too. I'm so happy, wish I could hug you."

Red.

A spark from his little palm, it flashed in the dulled world around me, striking straight through the tank.

The moment the glass shattered, it held, suspended in a breath before it fell.

Water rushed by him, knocking a younger me to the floor with it. Red pooled in the puddle around him from small cuts on his arms as he sat there, eyes wide, staring forward. Slowly looking down, that's when he saw her, Margo, on the floor.

Cyrus' grip tightened on my shoulder.

"Margo," reaching for her, his shaking bloodied hands hesitated before taking her up into his grip, "Margo, no, I, I'm sorry, I-" voice cracking so hard it cut him off, tears started to take him as she struggled in his hands. "Margo, please-"

That must have been when he noticed the cut across her side.

He stopped breathing.

The house started to shake, a pressure growing with his eyes.

Margo stopped moving.

My mum's voice came from down the hall, footsteps racing toward us.

I watched as the first tear fell from his face, plummeting the room into a chill with it as it dropped.

As the door flew open, blue exploded, throwing my mum back into the hall. Knocking everything away, blown into the walls, my room was destroyed around us in that moment. Calling Margo's name as she sat, motionless in his hands, his cries turned into yells, his yells into screaming, cracking sobs. Blue crawled on the ground away from him, slithering over every surface. Meeting at the top of the room, when the blue tendrils combined, they exploded into every color, sparks raining over the surroundings.

Standing there as different colored electricity cracked in the water on the floor, I couldn't even blink. This wasn't how I remembered it. This wasn't what happened. Margo died and I never felt again, that was all. Her tank cracked, I couldn't save her, and I decided that was the last time I'd feel a single thing. That had to be it, that had to be all, there was no greater story.

I cared too much so I decided to not care at all until it was no longer a choice.

Right?

The door creaked open, fighting against the whirling winds in the room. Mum pulled herself through the threshold, nearly nine months pregnant, disheveled and cut, she struggled as her knuckles on the frame turned white. Orange hair flying around her as her eyes met her child, she froze when she saw what was happening. Doubled over, sobbing, I held Margo in my arms at the center of it all, my screams warping in the storm.

Staring at my mum, I had expected her to look afraid, concerned, or even confused. But as her eyes jumped around the room at the colors, none of those things painted her. No, mum looked mad.

Shoving herself into the storm, I had never heard her yell like that before, "Nox."

Though the world around me raged, in that moment, for me, everything stopped.

She knew?

Throwing herself into the thick of the hurricane toward me, mum struggled with every step, her voice somehow echoing in the small room, as if it were secretly much larger, "Nox, what are you doing!"

A flash of white took the room, chilling the air even further.

When it faded from my eyes, I heard Cyrus stop breathing.

An arm wrapped around my mum as a gust of air tried to take her out. Standing there, clothing blowing in the whipping winds, Nox's eyes met the younger me as I crumpled before them. Colors reflecting off the white of his hair as he steadied my mum, holding her close at his side, he just stared at little me.

"No," his voice, it was softer than I had ever heard it, but still somehow clear in the chaos, "what happened?"

"I don't know," mum raked her hand through her hair, so much younger than I would have expected, though this was so long ago, it did make sense, "it was so sudden."

Teeth grit as glass took over Nox's eyes, I watched it, as his brow furrowed, knocking tears loose, orange flash in his iris. Throwing himself into the fray, he took my mother with him. "Igor," the way he yelled my name, the crack in his voice as his grip tightened on my mum, something about it lit in the back of my mind, "Igor, it'll be alright, just hang on."

Reaching me, Nox let go of my mum, all but throwing her at me. Collapsing to her knees, she wrapped her arms around me. The moment she made contact, blue started to bleed over her, an infectious glow that tainted her every tone. Teeth grit, she buried her head into me, grip unrelenting, despite the tremble that took her.

"Igor, sweetheart, I'm here, you're going to be okay."

Standing above us, Nox stared for a moment, but then he shook his head. Hand ripping back to his eyes, he wiped his tears, and as his arm lowered with a vengeance, he looked up into the storm.

"I don't know why you chose him, but I won't let you hurt Igor," stepping around as colors roared by him, Nox extended his arms, "not him, not Sierra's son."

Eyes lowering to a younger me as I writhed on the ground, my mum holding me, my yells choking me, my heart stopped. I was only nine years old, how could I feel that much?

Wait, nine?

How many years did Cyrus say the last incarnation got?

My eyes raised to Nox.

Ten.

Colors screamed around, speeding up as they grew nearer, the ground rumbling, the world distorting. The colors crashed into one another as they careened closer in the wind, creating a warping ball of black. Watching it, Nox stepped around, keeping himself between us and it until it got closer.

"What are you doing?" My mum looked up to him, still holding me as I sobbed on the floor.

"I'm going to save him." He jumped, trying to grab the orb but missed.

"What?" My mum pulled me into her, "How-"

"You just have to trust me, Sierra." Looking back over his shoulder, his eyes held on my mum for a moment before he smiled at her, gaze raising to trail the ball as it swung back around, "it's the least I can do for you."

Racing toward me, the ball's destination was destined by every incarnation before.

It was my time to die.

So why

Jumping in the way, Nox blocked the ball. Colors exploded, throwing him back but he slid to a stop right before crashing into us. He almost fell to his knees as black disappeared around us. A harsh breath escaped through his clenched teeth, but I heard it turn up at the end, as if he were smiling. Turning, he shook as he looked down to me. A gaping black gouge in his core, it oozed oil, the rainbow sheen leaking down his front. My mum stared, eyes wide and teary, unable to speak a word as Nox's trembling hand reached toward my head. Fingers meeting my hair, he ruffled it, and despite the storm, despite his wound, despite the tears in his eyes, he smiled at me.

"I'll protect you."

When he lifted his hand from my head, little colorful lights swam in his grip. Red, blue, green, yellow, orange, and purple, my feelings were rendered to nothing more than marbles in his palm. Watching them, their colors danced in the glass in his eyes. Closing his hand over them, the moment before he crushed them in his grip, he looked up to my mum, one more time.

"Thank you."

When his hand closed, white exploded, bleaching everything. It was as if the air had been sucked out of the room, leaving numbing, sterile, silence. When my surroundings returned, Nox was gone. Sitting there on my knees, a younger me was motionless, breathless, stiff. My mum knelt there, eyes wide, teary, frozen. The silence was so loud it hurt, the stillness shocking compared to the chaos. Slowly sitting up from the floor, a younger me stared into his hands at Margo as she laid there, dead.

Though as my eyes met his, I saw nothing in him.

Absolutely nothing.

And I think that's why my mum's breath hitched.

Because she saw nothing too.

The scene before us exploded, phantoms turning to blue glitter. Taking a step back as blue surrounded me, I was stopped. Turning my head to the sides as blue grew into an orb before me, I was met with Cyrus and Finnegan, both holding me there with one of their hands.

Though neither of them would look at me.

Turning forward again, I only saw it for a moment, the blue orb before it hit me.

Taken to my knees, I fell from their grip, hitting the floor.

I may have yelled but I couldn't hear it, not over the sound of every time I closed the door between Ross and I. I couldn't feel anything, nothing more than the weight of what I had done. The empty place, set just for me, the hole in every family photo, the way my mum looked at Nox, the way she held me. There was more to this story, more than I'd ever know, because no matter how much she may have loved me, to my mum I was now a stranger.

As two hands met my back, the blow lessened, for a moment. But then images flooded my mind, yells of others faded in my ears. They flashed by so quickly, I could barely see them. A church, a harp, flowing white fabric and stained glass dancing in the light, a tree, a noose blowing in the wind, a raged crowd and flying stones, there was fire, so much fire. Footsteps as they echoed against wood, a hand meeting a lever, being held back by another, it felt as if two tragedies intertwined in my mind, the same event in different eyes, but then it all stopped with the metal creak of the hinge of a door.

When my eyes closed, white took me over.

Gasping, everything stopped.

The sudden shock of stillness stung.

Shaking, I lifted my head up from the floor. Sitting up from my knees, someone crashed into me. Kneeling there, eyes wide on the white abyss, I didn't need to see him to know it was Nox.

His arms tightened around me, his intake shaking, "I'm sorry."

Staring forward, everything was still.

But then, the white blurred in my eyes, and when the first tear fell, the abyss turned blue.

Wrapping my arms around Nox, my forehead fell into his shoulder, shoving my glasses up and out of place.

I wanted to fight it, to cover it in orange. But as blue took its hold, I knew, with every shaking breath and every stifled sob, that the only way out, was through.

Where had I been my whole life? I was there, but not really. I missed out on so much, every family trip, every holiday, birthday and special occasion. I worked and I worked and I worked just to have something, but it was really nothing. And no matter what I did, there was no going back. I didn't have a chance to fix it, I'd never get to go to another one of Ross' birthdays, never be able to write my mum a heartfelt note on Mother's Day, never get to ask my father about the stories behind his tattoos, never invite a coworker out for a drink sometime. I missed my every chance.

And now there were no more, because I was no more.

As my grip tightened on Nox, blue screaming through me, ripping a hole that would probably never really heal, I knew it was the right thing.

It had to be.

They had to be happier without me.

Footsteps echoed around, and I didn't have to look up to sense them, the other incarnations, as they came to a stop, surrounding us.

"I tried to save you," Nox pulled me closer, "I'm so sorry, I failed."

Shaking my head, that's all I could do.

Time didn't feel real there, but as my body ached, exhausted from the self perpetuating pangs of sobs that had tore through me, it must have been a long while before I fell quiet.

And the whole time, they stood there in silent support, the ones who had come before me.

Pulling back from the embrace, Nox's hands steadied me, remaining on my arms. Eyes searching mine, I could see blue swimming in the glass of his. Gaze drifting about, it floated over the others as they stood, eyes low on the ground.

They stood in a circle of a crowd, all forty-eight of them, all of them facing me, all of them but one. Eyes meeting him, the incarnation before me, he stood, his back mostly turned, arms crossed over his chest. So young, only ten years old, the bitterness to his exhale when our eyes met stung as he ripped his gaze away, turning his back completely.

Looking down, a glowing orb floated between us, dripping, as if it were made of humid smoke, too heavy for the air. Its blue was softer than what I had seen before, a color far less loud. As if it no longer demanded attention once addressed, it was still there, but a little bit less. Reaching up to it, I took it into my hand. A light chill, it wasn't as heavy as I had expected it to be.

"Thank you," looking up to Nox from the light, I watched him tense, "it's because of you that I made it this long. I'm, sure it was hard, carrying all the colors on your own."

"It's my fault you have them at all," looking away from me, the softness of his voice brought a warmth to the chill bellowing in my hand between us, "I'm sorry I've been so mean to you, I wanted to do anything I could to dissuade you, to spare you. The more colors you have, the worse it will hurt when they turn on you."

Watching as the smoke poured through the space between my fingers, it rolled off his knees as he knelt before me. The last time I had met blue, it had left me empty. I had thought it was a choice, that I had come to know how much feeling really hurt so I never wanted to again until it was no longer a choice. But now, as I sat there, staring into the blue orb in my hand, as the color passed through me, having been honored and allowed, it left something behind this time, something more than nothing.

A silver lining.

"If."

Nox looked up to me, eyes glassy beneath the tremble of his brow, "What?"

"If they turn on me," I lifted blue up toward the brooch on my bow tie, "I know you fear them, but the more colors I see," when the orb met my bow tie, the abyss turned blue again, but it was a much softer shade, one that you'd expect to find dotting a field of wild flowers in spring after a long winter, "the more I want to meet."

Watching as blue came to life on my brooch in the tears in Nox's eyes, a shaking breath escaped him. The others that stood around whispered amongst themselves, looking up to the blue taking the eternal sky above.

Bringing my hand up to my brooch, my fingertips hovered before it, "thank you for holding onto these for me, but I'm here to take them off your hands."

Shaking his head, Nox leaned forward into me, face buried in my shoulder. The other incarnations went quiet as I sat there, eyes wide, a bit tense. I was about to say something, but then Nox laughed. "Well," I could hear his smile through his breath, "I wish you luck with the last two then. You're in for it."

"What," I looked down to his head, his flippy white hair reflecting the blue of our surroundings at the tips, "why?"

"You'll see."

The other incarnations laughed.

When I blinked, everything went black.

Though as the abyss disappeared, Nox's warmth did linger, making the nothing I was left with a little bit more something.

"Just one more time," Cyrus' voice echoed in my mind, "please, Nox. Just come back, one more time. That's all I need, come back, and I'll save you." His warmth took me, as if in the darkness, I was met with his embrace, "you've granted everyone else's wish, it's time that I finally grant yours."

Waking like a start, a jump to a dead engine, I flew up. Breath catching on the way in, eyes wide, I stared forward but my surroundings were nothing more than a blur. Hand finding its way to my face as I tried to tame the tremble beneath my skin, my body ached.

Despite just waking, I was tired, so, so tired.

As colors came spinning into my mind, an amber drawl, a tense yellow ball, a dramatic green fall, and the blue of losing it all, a groan escaped me. I meant what I had told Nox, that the more colors I saw, the more I wanted to meet.

But damn.

Lowering my hand, the light from my brooch caught on my palm. Each color was something on its own, but seeing their glow bleed together like that made something else entirely. It wasn't complete yet, I had just two more to go. As I stood from the bed, I wondered what they were.

Stumbling into the side table, I heard the scratch of metal against wood. Reaching down, my hand met my glasses. Sliding them back into place, the same room I had woken in before came into view. Though I had barely spent any time there, as the last time I was kidnapped by Finnegan. There was a front door, the one I had watched Anton leave though. But there was another. Dragging my unwilling body along with me, the exhaustion became more evident with every step. But I had to ignore it, I only had two more colors left.

Reaching the door, I discovered an attached bathroom. Entering, I found a set of nicely folded clothing on the stone countertop. Taking a shower helped some with the tiredness in my muscles, though as I dressed in the formal attire provided afterward, it did still take me a bit longer than usual to will my fingers to button my shirt.

Walking by stone walls and beneath a domed ceiling, stained glass decorated the light that came in from above. Hands finding the pockets of the suit I was provided, I wondered where Cyrus had put my uniform. Stopping at the door of the room, I glanced back into it.

I was alone.

But as I turned back toward the door, the weight of the brooch on my bow tie reminded me that I wasn't, not really.

Opening the door, it creaked, bringing to rise some tension in me. But as I stood in the threshold, I knew that there was no reason to be tense about opening doors anymore. No matter how loud it was, Ross was never going to hear me again, never come scrambling out of his room to unload every word about vampires he could possibly get out in my direction in the short walk from my room to the front door.

A shaking breath left me as I closed the door.

Walking down a stone hall, the flames of small candles intermittently placed along the wall turned blue as I passed.

Though I had spent very little time in this castle, it felt familiar, like I knew where each turn would take me. A tug in my chest, it led me, though I hadn't any idea where. Especially when I was faced with a wall. Staring at it, it was just a section of stone wall like any other. Glancing down each way at the line of candles mounted to stone, the flames from whence I came all blue, the one I had yet to pass still burning normally, I was left to look back at the candle mounted to the wall right before me. Something inspiring budded in my muscles, an inclination of sorts, willing me to raise my arm. Hand meeting the metal neck of the candle stick, my fingers wrapped around it. Pulling down, the neck slid to the side, clicking something in the wall.

The flame turned green.

Shaking, the rumble in the floor made it through my shoes as a panel of wall pulled forward. Sliding to the side, dust knocked loose from the ceiling, clouding the air as a dark passage opened before me. Staring at the mouth of a shadowed, spiraling stairwell, a smile found me. Glancing around, there was no one else about. Heart starting to race, I took my first step into the shadow. As my shoe met the first stair, a candle mounted to the round column in the middle lit to life, casting green light into the space. Each step, faster than the last, I started to run up the spiral staircase. Rumbling took the ground again, knocking more dust loose from above as every candle I passed lit green. When the door below closed, all I was left with was green lighting nothing more but the next couple steps ahead, everything beyond that remaining a darkened mystery.

Perhaps that's why I almost didn't see it in time, the closed door at the end of the passage.

Stumbling back, hand clawing at the wall to keep myself from tumbling down the spiral column of stairs, the fire flickered purple, for just a moment, before returning to green. Panting as I regained my footing, I inspected the door. Not closed all the way, a crack remained open, a faint glow coming from the other side.

I was reaching for the handle, about to touch it when I heard,

"Just two more."

and stopped.

Leaning back from the door as Cyrus' muffled exhale made its way through the wood, my eyes met the crack where it hadn't closed properly. Kneeling, I peeked through it. My breath caught when my eyes met them. Standing on a rooftop balcony, backs to me, Cyrus and Finnegan looked out to a sight I couldn't see from there. Hand up, Finnegan's fine fingers met the sky, so low they could touch it.

Humming, they swirled their fingers through the darkened glitter of above, causing some to rain down over them with the faintest jingle of a bell, "Once he takes the crown, maybe I will not be able to touch the sky anymore."

Leaning his elbows over on the railing, Cyrus buried his face in his hands, "I hope so. Our snow globe can't get any smaller or it'll swallow us all up. With how powerful he is, he should be able to maintain the realm and then some. Maybe we'll even get to see what has been lost to the haze again, if there is anything left beyond it."

Lowering their hand, they leaned against the railing too, inspecting the glitter on their fingers, "Do you think he can handle it?" They lifted their hand up, the glitter catching on the little ambient light there was in Netherside, "When he unlocks all the colors, he will likely be more powerful than The Three. That is a lot for one person."

"He'll be okay," Cyrus straightened, looking out, but perhaps even further than that, "all he has to do is unlock the colors, I'll handle the rest. This won't go like the last time."

Finnegan didn't reply, not in a beat of time that felt natural, as if something unsaid took its place. I shifted a little to better rest my weight on my knee, but in doing so, my shoe scraped against a small rock on the ground, making a bit of a sound. Locking up, my eyes jumped back to the crack. Finnegan turned their head, just a bit, but didn't turn fully around.

I was sure they had heard me until they looked back out again.

"You are getting a bit ahead of yourself there, Father Glory," Turning toward Cyrus, Finnegan slid closer to him, a playful drawl taking their tone, "He has to meet red and purple first. And while we have discussed how to handle the latter, it is the former that interests me more." Sliding into Cyrus' side, they leaned down to catch his eyes, their hair spilling over them to dangle over the railing, "I bet I can inspire it in him before you can."

Tense, Cyrus didn't immediately reply as he slowly looked down to Finnegan. And while the sharp crook of his brow would suggest an edge, his wayward smirk took his words up, "Oh yeah?"

Humming, Finnegan stepped back from Cyrus, their lengthy silk and velvet cape swayed with the movement, "I am a vampire, it is in my blood."

Laughing, Cyrus turned around to face them, back against the railing, "You're real sure of yourself."

Shrinking down a bit, while I knew it was unlikely for them to be able to see me through the crack, having Cyrus fully face me made me feel like he could.

"What," taking a step toward Cyrus, they closed the space, pressing his back into the railing, "like it is difficult?"

Eyes low on Finnegan, a warmth took Cyrus as he stood, no space between them. Fine finger meeting Cyrus' chin, Finnegan angled his head down. Standing on the tips of their shoes, Finnegan brought themselves up, bringing their faces close together. Eyes wide as I knelt there, my heart started to pick up, and though something in me felt as if I should look away, I couldn't.

The flames lighting the secret passage turned red.

Crashing into him, Finnegan stepped between Cyrus' legs as their lips met.

As Finnegan brought their hand up to the side of Cyrus' face, other arm wrapping around the small his back, the kiss escalating, I stopped breathing.

While, objectively, I knew this was something that people did, I had never had any interest in it.

Well, not until now, apparently.

Hand raising to cover my mouth, brows furrowing as a heat came to my face, my exhale that escaped through my fingers fogged my glasses.

As Finnegan moved in closer with a tilt of their head, Cyrus' arms wrapped around them, taking some of their cloak in his shaking grasp. Hand sliding up the side of Cyrus' face, Finnegan laced their fingers in his hair and a moment later, they tightened their grip.

A sound escaped Cyrus, sending my heart into my throat, lighting my every inch ablaze.

The sky outside turned red.

Losing my balance as I knelt there, I fell into the door.

When it creaked open, the air dropped.

Jumping away from Finnegan, I only saw the startle on Cyrus' face for a moment before he fell backwards over the railing of the balcony. Eyes wide, I sprung from the ground, blood gone cold. Hand reaching for him, he fell faster than I could catch him as I ran into the balcony railing, knocking the air from my core. Frozen as Cyrus vanished from my vision, my gaze dropped.

Plummeting, Cyrus didn't appear to struggle as he neared the ground.

A hand covered my eyes.

Though I didn't see it happen, the sound he made upon impact would haunt me.

It was… wet.

"Careful there," Finnegan pressed their front into my back as they stood behind me, hand over my eyes, shoving my glasses up, "he will be fine, but you are not immortal," leaning even closer, their breath met the side of my neck, "not yet."

Stiff, I swallowed, unable to move as heat washed over me. I had never felt this sensation before, but as a cold sweat began to prick my skin, the dissonance between the chill and the burn made my every muscle tense.

"I heard what Anton told you, I know that you know. I just do not know why you have not brought it up yet."

Turning me around, they slid their hand from my face, down to my jaw, then let it linger there for a moment longer as they pressed my back into the railing. Staring at them, glasses crooked, I'm sure I had taken note of it before, the way the long strands of their fine hair flowed with their every intake, the way the tips of their fangs peeked through their smile, but as if I was seeing them for the first time, these things burned into my eyes.

"It, it- uh," my voice cracked, making me tense. Fixing my glasses, I ripped my eyes away from them, "It appears that Cyrus has a complicated relationship with the concept so," looking back to them as I lowered my hand from my glasses, it took my everything to retain eye contact, "I figured it was a bridge that I'd cross when necessary."

Humming, Finnegan studied me, the budding of a reply on the precipice of their soft lips. Though I would never be graced by it, because just as they were about to speak, a red cloud of glitter exploded next to us. Taking over the air, the red stole Finnegan from my eyes and a moment later, their grip was yanked away from me, the quite sound of a sharp choke meeting my ears.

"Good morning, Igor," Cyrus' voice made its way through the cloud, "I'm sorry this batty bastard can't keep their hands to themselves."

As the cloud cleared, Finnegan returned to my sight, held by the back of their cape like a kitten by the nape of their neck- powerless and deflated. Opening my mouth, I was about to reply, eyes drifting toward Cyrus, but my word died in my throat.

Cyrus' gored body stood, one arm extended at his side as he dropped Finnegan to their feet. Taking a step back, I met the railing, blood spiking cold. Ribs protruding, legs obviously broken, he was mangled, exactly how you'd expect one to look after falling from that height. But as my words turned into an inaudible sputter, the most concerning thing about the situation was his head.

It was missing.

"What?" Cyrus' voice came from a bit lower. Eyes tracing down his body as the red cloud completely cleared, they met his. Head sitting in his other hand, black blood seeping through his fingers from the base of his severed neck, Cyrus appeared genuinely confused with the crook of his brow until it hit him with the urgency of an epiphany not all that different from the speed at which he met the ground.

"Oh," lifting his head up, he returned it to its rightful place above his boyishly charmed shoulders, "sorry."

Eyes unable to even blink as I stared, the flesh at the base of his neck and his severed head reached for the opposing side, marrying and pulling together with the fervor of a rushing slug. Teeth grit as my brow dropped, the blood from my head was quick to follow. Vision tunneling, there was only a darkness around the edges for a moment before it all went black.

I felt them, both of them, as their hands met my back. On my knees, one hand up to my face, cupped over my mouth, the other balling into a fist against the ground, I had never felt so cold before in my life. Finnegan and Cyrus spoke, but I couldn't understand either of them, their words wobbly and far away. Eyes closing, they refused to stay open under my quivering brow.

What was wrong with me?

I was so tired.

A hand met mine on the ground, encasing it in warmth. Pulling my fist up with them, Finnegan took my hand in both of theirs. Looking up through disheveled bangs over my glasses, my vision started to come back, though a bit fuzzy. Kneeling before me, their cape and long hair spilling to the stone beneath them, they brought my hand up to their lips. Closing their eyes, they kissed the back of my hand.

Eyes wide, glasses crooked, I couldn't breathe, not as their soft lips pulled back from my skin, leaving a gentle warmth behind.

The sky gained a warm tint.

"Igor," opening their eyes, they lingered on my hand for a moment before raising to mine, "when was the last time you ate?"

I blinked at them.

The last time I ate? Staring at Finnegan as their eyes held on mine, softening more with each moment, I had no idea. It must have been during my lunch break on the last full shift I had worked at the store before I even met Cyrus.

Eyes rolling up from me to Cyrus as he stood above, one hand on my back, the softness drained from Finnegan, wholly replaced with a type of annoyance that had been aged like fine wine. "Father Glory."

I felt it, the moment Cyrus went tense, his grip tightening on me a bit.

Slowly standing with the grace of the air itself, Finnegan kept my hand in theirs, "Please forgive me, but the assumption I am left to form here is that through the entirety of the company you have kept with Igor, you have not offered him any food. And that is such a poor reflection on your character, one can only hope that it is untrue."

"I…" taking a step back, Cyrus looked down to me as his hands met with his hair, "I'm sorry, I was just so worried about his powers killing him and I've been immortal for so long I totally forgot that food is like, a thing."

Sighing, it turned up with their smile as they looked down to me, "It is no wonder you are unwell, between that and the unruly show Father Glory just put on," grip tightening on my hand, they shot a glare back up to Cyrus, but it wasn't as sharp as it could have been, their smirk turning it a bit playful, "allow me to take you out to dinner."

Pulling me into them, they yanked me out from under Cyrus' grip and into their arms. As green exploded around us, starting to take me away with it, I was almost lost to the emerald alone, but that's when another hand met my back and in that green, I saw a flicker of red.

Dropping into nothing but the marrying of red and green, it was starting to feel less like a tumble, perhaps more like a fall.

Feet meeting the ground on the other side of the glitter, the blood dropped from my head once again, sending my world into a spin. Two sets of arms steadied me, keeping me from dropping to my knees. A scoff was the first thing I heard through the ringing in my ears, but it didn't sound particularly mad. My eyes struggled to open so I didn't see the expression Finnegan wore as their grip remained on my hand, but from the sound of their words, I would have bet that they were smiling.

"Just when I thought I would get Igor all to myself."

Cyrus' hand remained on my shoulder, tightening, "As if."

With a click of their tongue, Finnegan started to pull me forward, "Worth a try."

Stumbling in my first few steps, my eyes managed to open. Vision blurry for a moment, the shapes of the stone sidewalk beneath me had only barely formed in my eyes when we stopped.

Leaning into my side, Finnegan's soft hair brushed up against my cheek, making me go stiff, "If you ever get tired of being a third wheel, Father Glory, you are free to leave."

Laughing, Cyrus snaked his hand across my back and around my far shoulder, pulling me into his chest, "Careful there, don't get too friendly or your Master will be mad."

World pulling into focus, I slowly looked up to my right. Finnegan stood, looking up and behind me, the glow of their hooded emerald eyes catching on their white eyelashes as their brows turned the peace of their elfish face to poison, "Twining could not care less with whom I keep company."

"Is that right?" Cyrus stole my gaze, up at my left. One brow raised above his scarlet eyes, his sunshine waves framed his face as it sat, shadowed and turned down toward Finnegan. I had never noticed it before, but as I stood there, pulled in close to his chest. He had more muscle than I would have guessed. And as every inch of me that was pressed into him began to heat up, overly aware of his every breath, his warmth, every shift of his chest as he said something else snarky to Finnegan that I didn't hear, my heart started to race.

When Finnegan continued to antagonize Cyrus, both pulling me as close to their sides as they could, I looked between them. Between Finnegan's silky hair and the way it caught the ambient warm glow from above, between Cyrus and the way the low lighting brought out his freckles, between Finnegan and their animation, between Cyrus and the fire in his eyes, between Finnegan and their soft lips, between Cyrus and his chiseled jaw, with every dart of my eyes, heat came to rise in me until it made my body ache.

Eyes jumping forward to a door before me, my glasses fogged with my shaking exhale in the cool air.

What the fuck was going on.

Shoved a bit by someone passing by, we went stumbling to the side. A muddled mumble escaped the rugged being, covered in scales, their thick tail dragged on the ground behind them as they shoved the door open with similar belligerence. Standing in that moment as the door swung shut with the ringing of a bell, the chill of the air passing by sobered me enough to notice my surroundings. Back in the central square of Netherside, Cyrus and I had previously walked past the door we now stood before. Looking to the large window at the side of the door, my eyes met with floating pots and pans, with possessed spoons stirring the contents above flames that just burned in the air. Looking up to the sign as we straightened, its wooden carved charm caught me as it swung with a squeak on its rusty chains affixing it to a pole protruding from the stone wall above the wooden door.

The Cranky Witch

Both Cyrus and Finnegan jumped at my sides, but only one arm shot across my vision. A hand met the door, pulling it open before me with a creak, ringing the bell on the way out. As Finnegan slowly lowered their defeated extended arm, they looked up and over to Cyrus as he stood, holding the door open.

Looking between them, the unspoken was so loud, I couldn't even hear what it was saying. As Cyrus winked at me, bowing a bit, heat came to rise in me again.

"Yes yes, very chivalrous, Father Glory." Pushing me along, Finnegan led us through the door.

The way Cyrus' exhale turned into a bit of a laugh as we passed him only served to increase the rate of my heart. It was something of a swell, unlike one I had felt before. A warmth, the type that infected all it touched, it spread through me with a jolt. Entering the Cranky Witch, my eyes only got to drift by Cyrus, unable to take in his every line, before I stopped in my tracks. Floating dangerously close, an inch away from colliding with my head, a purple bubbling potion bottle left a trail of fog behind it as it floated across the room. A mild hum of conversation rested in the air, the tables around filled to capacity inside the woodland tavern before me. Orbs of variously colored light drifted about, bathing the space in atmospheric hues as beings diverse in type all converged, laughing at the tables and bar. Something one would expect to only find in the confines of a scrappy fantasy game, I half expected a vendor's menu box to open before my eyes with the various eats and restoration potions available to buy with the in-game currency.

"Welcome-" though her first word was full of life, as Valor appeared from around a corner behind the bar, three plates of drinks and food floating around her, when her eyes met us, her tone died with her smile, "in."

"Aw, don't be like that," Cyrus stepped up to my side, "is that any way to treat a customer?"

Walking up to her side of the bar, Valor simply waved her hand and drinks floated from the platter to the patrons around, "Yeah, customers who cause problems like you, Cyrus."

As if a bomb had dropped, the atmosphere flatlined, the hum of conversation silencing. Creaks filled the air as the beings around slowly turned in their rustic wooden chairs. All eyes on him, Cyrus stood, stiff. Clearing his throat, it turned into a nervous chuckle as his eyes darted back to Valor. Raising a brow, the echoes of a smirk on her face, she just continued to send drinks to patrons as she brushed by us.

Voice low, it was barely loud enough for us three to hear as she passed, "Fuck around and find out, I suppose."

Brows dropping with a scoff, Cyrus took ahold of my arm and started to pull me along with him. Eyes on the ground, jaw tight, his grip wasn't as he led us toward an empty table. Eyes on his hand as it sat, wrapped almost completely around my forearm, where he touched burned. But I didn't hate it, no, it was actually the opposite. Unable to look away from the way his skin turned white over his knuckles, the shadows of his veins crawling up his toned forearm, all I could think about was the way he took the fabric of Finnegan's cape into his needy grasp as they kissed.

As if it were burned into my memory, every intricacy of that sight overwhelmed me.

My shoe caught.

Stumbling forward, I was met with warmth. Eyes wide, glasses pushed up crooked in an embrace, I could feel how toned Cyrus was as he held me. As he took a breath in, resting his head atop mine, his voice was soft, though I could still feel every vibration in his chest against mine.

"Sorry, I should have warned you that Valor is a cheapskate and her floors suck." He brought his hand up to the back of my head and in that moment, pressed into him, my mind was taken by the most intrusive thought I had perhaps ever had in my life.

On his knees before me, the glow of stained glass framed him in my view.

Flying away from him, I took two stumbling steps back until I accidently bumped into someone else. Jumping away from the bird person I had bothered, I couldn't even get an apology out as my heart raced, a flushed fluster washing over my face. Glasses crooked, I looked back up Cyrus, only able to see him a bit in my fuzzy vision. And though he was blurry, I think he looked confused for just a moment before his unbothered smile returned like usual.

Reaching for one of the chairs, Cyrus stopped when another hand met it first. Smiling as they pulled out the chair, Finnegan's combative smirk turned soft as they looked from Cyrus to me. Looking between them, I fixed my undoubtedly dumb posture and straightened my glasses. Eyes down, jaw tight as I approached the table, I had an idea of what was trying to take me over. But I couldn't let it, I wouldn't.

As I thanked Finnegan and sat down, the hum of conversation started to return around the tavern. Sitting down with a vengeance, Cyrus popped his elbow on the table, perching his chin on his open palm, eyes averted. Sitting with much more grace, Finnegan leaned back in their chair, crossing one leg over the other, arms gently folded against their chest.

Bringing my hand up to the back of my head, I ruffled my hair, trying to chase the feeling of his fingers away. I wasn't an idiot; I was an entire adult. I was aware that these types of feelings objectively existed, they just never had for me. My coworkers occasionally recounted their intimate adventures, though I didn't ever pay it much mind, so even though I knew what this was, I didn't know what to do about it other than sit there, staring at the table in front of me. What could I even do about it? Like, we were in public, and I didn't even know how to begin to broach that topic with one person, let alone two, even if we weren't.

"Was it worth it?" Finnegan's eyes rolled over to Cyrus as a potion bottle of water landed on the table before them.

Taking the next potion bottle as it landed, Cyrus took a grumpy drink instead of replying.

Watching as one more landed before me, I took it in hand. Its sobering cold was a welcome relief against the heat burning underneath my skin, helping to get me out of my head, "Was what worth it?"

Lowering the bottle from their fine lips, Finnegan's eyes caught on mine from slightly over the glass that took on their purple hue, "Sleeping with just about everyone in Netherside."

Choking on his drink, Cyrus set his bottle down with a bit too much force, "Not everyone."

"Ah, yes, that is right," Finnegan's eyes held on me for a moment more before drifting away with the daintiness of a light breeze, "not everyone," right before their lips met

the bottle again, I heard them mutter one last word, "yet."

One would think they hated each other, by the way

they shot back and forth as I sat there, staring. But as I took

my first drink of water in days, I didn't think that was quite

what was going on. Whatever it was, I couldn't look away.

Not as each sharp exchange was twisted up by the tug on

Cyrus' mouth or as Finnegan eagerly awaited Cyrus' replies

with palpable anticipation and engagement.

And though I was in the most fantastical place I had

ever been, the plates of food floating around me, the glowing

orbs above, the mythical creatures seated about, none of it

could court my attention like those two.

When Finnegan laughed, their hair slid over their

shoulder, like a spill of liquid silver. It looked soft, thick, like

if they were to be on top of you, it would fall to the ground

around, cutting you off from the rest of the world leaving

nothing but their exciting emerald eyes and fine lips, their

pointy ears and fangs that peeked out ever so slightly when

they smiled. The way they sat on me as I hovered right above the ground at the vampiric castle resurrected, the way their weight shifted on my hips haunted my skin as if they had never left. The feeling they had invoked in me in that moment, it brought an ache.

Every candle lit red, the orbs about turning too, until the entire tavern was crimson and warm. Their banter cutting off in the moment, Cyrus and Finnegan slowly looked my way as the red hue overtook everything. Eyes wide, my face burning, I quickly brought my glass potion bottle up to take another drink.

This was bad.

Staring down at the plate of food Cyrus had ordered for me, it didn't look like any food I had ever seen.

"It looks odd but," Cyrus handed me a fork, "trust me."

Accepting the fork made of braided thin metal, it barely felt like anything in my hand. It felt like the plate stared back up at me, though it thankfully didn't have any eyes. Perhaps a type of meat, I didn't lack the wherewithal to ask what it was as I took a piece onto my fork. I had never really cared either way about food, it was more annoying than anything. But as I sat there, tasting for what felt like the first time, I couldn't believe how good it was. Taking another bite, it was everything I could do to remain composed and not act like I hadn't eaten in days.

"I cannot remember the last time I ate something." Finnegan took another drink of their water, sitting back in their chair.

"Yeah," Cyrus took a bite of his food, "you vampires just eat each other."

Shrugging a little, Finnegan looked away, "You did not complain the last time I ate y-"

"Igor?"

Almost choking on my food as I went stiff, a voice I knew but couldn't place felt like a physical blow to my back as it came from behind me. Eyes wide on Cyrus for a moment, I had barely paid any attention to what they had been talking about before, but whatever it was must have struck something because it appeared that had they not been interrupted, Cyrus would have turned red enough to melt. Quick footsteps landed at the side of the table, drawing my attention.

Eyes meeting him as others ran up to his sides, a long flowing black robe dressing his frail, fine features, I almost didn't recognize him with his light hair styled out of his face like that. Standing before I knew my body even moved, eyes locked on his, they had always been so dark under the florescent lights of our store, I had no idea how sparkly they really were.

"Salem?"

Eyes searching mine, shorter than me, Salem Willow stood, alive. But I knew he wasn't, I saw it on the news, the day he died. I went to his funeral, I stood and watched everyone lie about caring about him like they always did. I was even there when they lowered his casket into the ground, one of the last to leave the cemetery, despite the rain.

"What are you doing here?" the hints of his Russian accent came through on his every word and as I stared at him, I realized he had spoken so seldom and softly at work that I didn't even know he was Russian before this very moment.

"Me?" looking him up and down, his black hooded robe reaching the ground, he looked more alive than he ever had, the color to his skin and absence of the dark circles beneath his eyes making him look like an entirely new person, "I thought you died."

"I did," eyes snagging on my brooch, his held there before jumping back up to mine, "did you?"

"No, I-"

"Wait, no way," a voice cut me off, one so boyish and warm I didn't expect it when my eyes landed on its owner, "I remember you. You're the Igor my brother was talking about?'"

Eyes having to trail up because he was so tall, only one member of the group of five standing next to my table, he was by far the biggest. One look at that blonde, spiky haired jock was all it took to take me back to my store. I remembered him too, loitering about, staring at Salem. I was one step from banishing him from the store when one of our machines nearly caused an electrical fire. But that wasn't the only place I had seen him and his red and white Juniper High Devil's letterman jacket, no, he had died with Salem, the only remaining darling of his affluent family, Hugo Kloven.

"Do you know him?" a young man at Salem's other side said, donning a long white lab coat over boring business casual attire. A short black afro, rectangular glasses, and eyes so green they held a bite against his dark skin, I nearly missed what he had said at all as I stared at him. He was one of the most gorgeous people I had ever seen in my entire life.

Heart spiking in my chest, it didn't slow as it raced when my eyes jumped away from him.

"Yeah," Salem looked over his shoulder to the others behind him, "we were coworkers." Looking back to me, his concern started to grow, "Did something bad happen to you after I left?"

The jock looked down to me, his bushy brows lowering over deep red eyes as he bent down a bit to be level with me. Under his obvious observation, I was suddenly thankful that the coat I was wearing was not only buttoned, but also down to my knees. He was so tall, I hadn't noticed them before, but as he crooked his head, looking me over, two black, round goat-like horns sat among the golden mess of hair atop his head. "No, remember? Kasper talked about him. Said he was the next incarnation of Nox."

The way Salem's eyes widened on me stole my breath away.

"Good day, Demon King." Finnegan stepped up to my side, leaning against the table behind us, "What brings you and your posse about these parts?"

I slowly looked back toward Hugo as he straightened, eyes leaving mine. Swallowing, my gaze lingered on his horns for a moment longer. Demon King? From what I knew of Hugo, that sounded about right. Profound anger issues, they only ever did him good on the football field until he died suddenly in a rumored ritual. Eyes drifting over to the other two of the party who hadn't spoken, they snagged on one. Darkly dressed, a hood reminiscent of a reaper pulled over their head, their face was mostly obscured as they held a scythe at their side, hanging back. There were no survivors, and though the case remained inconclusive, there were rumors about who killed them all. It appeared that this must have been what Abraxas had been so busy with.

"Doing errands for my brother," Hugo looked between Finnegan and Cyrus as he stepped up to my other side, "Funny, running into you." His eyes returned to mine, "Talking with Igor was on my to-do list."

Popping up out of what felt like nowhere, a young man of light tone with flippy blonde hair that clashed with the darkness of his clothing made me stumble back into the table. "How cool, you're like a witch, right?" Holding stuffed cat that had been obviously well-loved in his folded arms against his chest, he tilted his head to look at me better, "They say you're supposed to be the next king of Netherside."

"Edgar," pulling the ball of startling sunshine back, the young man in the lab coat who I could barely even look at sighed, "I apologize for my brother." Shoving Edgar behind him despite the protests, the young man stepped up to me, "My name is Jack, I'm the head of the Paranormal Research department in Limbo." Gesturing behind him, though he sounded a bit flat, I could hear it, the smile in his voice, "and this is Phantasmal. You seem to already be acquainted with a couple of us, but we are a high school club close with King Kasper and were tasked with inviting you to Limbo. I believe he wanted to hold audience with you in private." Turning back to me, when Jack's eyes caught on the way I was starting at him, he stood with that for a moment before clearing his throat and turning back toward the others to take his spot, "Would now be a good time?"

Cyrus was about to say something, his head already shaking, when I cut him off.

"Yes."

Everyone stared at me.

Why did everyone stare at me.

Did I sound too desperate to be anywhere but here?

Laughing a little, I shifted my weight, trying my best to not act weird, "I'd love to visit Limbo."

"Fantastic," Jack pulled up his sleeve to look at a watch on his wrist, "the invite only specified you, but it shouldn't take too long, from my understanding."

Jack was about to continue when both Cyrus and Finnegan wrapped their arms around me on my either side, snaking around my middle, fingers lacing over one of my hips each.

"He doesn't go anywhere without us."

Mouth open, whatever I was going to say was choked out of me by their touch. Tension so striking, it seared my face shot through me. Teeth gritting, brow struggling to not quiver as I felt the flush over my skin, I closed my eyes for a moment. Though my intention was to ground myself, my mind painted the darkened canvas of my closed eyes with intrusive images, ones so vivid they could have been flashbacks.

Cyrus beneath me, disheveled, hair a mess around his reddened face, shirtless in the grass, his features shadowed by the fire cackling nearby. It was so real, I could smell the flowers, feel him squirming as I moved, the sweat on his shaking palms as they met my back, fingers digging into my skin.

Eyes flying open, my heart jumped so far into my throat that it made my voice crack as I ripped myself away from them, "No," stumbling forward, I took two tripping steps around to face them but when my eyes met Cyrus, I had to look away. "I can go alone."

"But-"

"It will be alright," cutting Cyrus off, I started to turn from him toward Phantasmal, but I was snagged by a hand on my wrist.

Looking over my shoulder, eyes meeting Finnegan's, I didn't even have to close mine this time to be overtaken by a vision of them. On top on me, hair spilling between us, they lowered toward me. Eyes on the brilliant starry sky behind them, it was unlike any sky I had ever seen as the anticipation that tore through me in that moment made my every muscle tense. Kissing my neck, they sent a shiver through me. One hand sliding up my bare torso, it trapped my wrists above my head. Their bare chest against mine, the next thing I felt as they moved into me knocked me back into the present.

Several lanterns on the walls shattered, red sparks flying.

Yanking my wrist from their grasp, for the first time I think I saw concern flash over Finnegan.

"Are you alright?" they slowly lowered their hand, looking back up to me from it, "Your face is red."

So tense it hurt, I had no choice. If I wasn't locked up, if my every inch wasn't restrained, if I gave into red, there was no telling what I'd do. No, that wasn't quite right. I knew exactly what I wanted to do, and they were both standing there before me. I wanted to shove Cyrus into the wall, I wanted Finnegan's hands in my hair, I wanted things I couldn't even admit to myself that I wanted, things I wanted to do to them, things I wanted them to do to me, thoughts I had never even known someone could have.

I needed to get away from them, I needed to think, before one of those obscene thoughts made it out of my mouth.

I couldn't even risk a reply as I just nodded, looking away from Finnegan.

Eyes a bit wide as they jumped between the three of us, Salem just stood there for a moment. But a moment appeared to be all it took for him to come to a conclusion because the surprise in his eyes transmuted into something else, something knowing, something I hoped he'd keep to himself.

Putting his hand on my shoulder, he looked back to Edgar. "We'll send him back as soon as we are done, don't you worry."

Before Cyrus could argue, the shadows of everyone around broke free of our shoes. Staring at the ground, the candles and orbs of the tavern violently turned purple for just a second before I dropped into darkness. Cyrus' voice was muffled in the black, but he called my name. Falling, why was it always falling? There was enough magical nonsense in Netherside, one would think that someone would have come up with a more comfortable mode of transportation at this point. Completely unable to see, as Salem's arm wrapped around my shoulders, what felt like hundreds of strings caught on me, a puppet tangled as the fall slowed.

Darkness stripped away, dropping me to my feet. Balance thrown, despite Salem's attempt to steady me, my knees gave out and took me down. Landing on the ground, it only took a moment for a cool, grounding wet to make it through my pants and to my knees. Arms wrapped around my middle as I hunched over, the roaring ache that wanted to possess me was debilitating. I had never wanted anything, let alone anyone. Desire, arguably the opposite of apathy, I had no idea how to cope as a harsh breath escaped me.

Opening my eyes, they were met with well-kept, bright, lively grass. Raising my head as someone stepped up to my side, my breath suspended in my chest. A storybook castle, one that would be guarded by a dragon, stood before me. At the heart of a whimsical statue and hedge garden, a grand fountain sparkled at the base of a main courtyard before tall, wooden doors. Twilit, I looked around to what appeared to be an endless urban park, well maintained grass bushes, trees, and winding paths beneath a rosy sunset sky.

"Welcome to the Boggle Realm," Salem said at my side, extending a hand down my way, "King Kasper is usually here, despite having a grander castle in the Almighty Realm."

Looking up to him, the cool air of a perpetual summer evening helped slow the burning within me. Staring at him above me, he was thin, exceedingly, sickly so, but for some reason, something about his robe looked as if he had something on his back, widening his profile beneath the fabric.

It was wild, that he was right here before me, hand extended my way. Though, somehow, at the same time, I wasn't surprised. He was too strong a presence to die with death.

Accepting his hand, I could still feel red clawing at me, but without Cyrus or Finnegan around, it started to retreat just enough that I could move. But as I stood, I could tell that it was but one untamed thought away from coming back.

"So," Salem looked to me, the others a step or so behind us as he started toward the castle, gesturing for me to follow, "Nox, huh?"

Trying to stay in step with him, my attention was caught by faint forms floating around. Transparent, exactly what I thought ghosts would look like, the apparitions of animals chased each other around the park, playing.

"Yes," my eyes held on a ghost of a squirrel for a moment before they returned to Salem, "an incarnation, anyway."

"I was right," looking up toward the castle, Salem's smile lit up the twilight, an expression I had never seen him wear. "I went to work at your store because I heard it was haunted. And while it was no question that strange things always happened there, I had an inkling that it wasn't ghosts," looking to me, his smile made me look away, "but you. And I was right. Though, I would have never guessed that Nox was even real, or that you had anything to do with him."

Hugo leaned over in at my other side, startling me as he walked along with his hands in his letterman jacket's pockets, "Didn't you say there was a whole cult that worshiped Nox or something?"

"What?" I looked from him to Salem as we started on a winding stone path up toward the castle.

"Yeah," Salem's eyes held on Hugo for a beat longer than was called for, "Jinx. They wanted to put him back together, claimed he was fragmented."

"Wait," Hugo straightened, the dumb look on his boyish face indicative of the three braincells I'm sure he possessed, "how would that work if Igor is his incarnation?"

"An excellent question," Jack made me startle as he leaned in from Hugo's other side, "One I'd love to find the answer to. If you'd consider working with me, that is, your highness."

"Fragmented, a cult?" my eyes lowered to the stones beneath my shoes, but strides away from the castle, "Cyrus hasn't said anything about any of that."

"Not surprising," Salem laughed as we approached the doors, hopping up each step with a spring, "From my understanding, he has a reputation for being sketchy."

Watching as Salem pulled open an unbelievably large door as if were nothing, the creak of the midlevel hinges spilling the air, I could just stare at him. The Salem I knew couldn't even lift a bin of security tags.

"What happened to you?"

Blinking at me, his smile faded, just a bit, as he gestured for me to enter. Walking up the last couple steps and into the threshold, I turned to watch the others enter until Salem followed the reaper in, letting go of the door.

"Well," when the door closed, we were trapped in darkness for a beat until a few clicks echoed and the room illuminated by electric blue flames along the walls, "a lot, there could be a whole novel. I'm sure it was on the news, how we died. But afterward, after a brief period of haunting the school, we were welcomed into Limbo, sorted into factions, and now we continue our investigations."

Walking through a hauntingly empty grand room, two large, marble staircases wrapped from either side, crossing paths as they wove into the air above. The only shoes that made sound against the stone floor were mine as we passed suits of armor and statues, tapestries and vases.

"Factions?" My eyes drifted past an open hall to the side, briefly catching on what looked to be a sheet ghost floating down it.

"Yes," Jack took a few steps ahead to then turn around and walk backward as we neared another set of large doors, "there are a few factions here in Limbo. We have the Boggle, usually animals or other simple specters," gesturing to Edgar, he went on, "then we have the Shadow People, who act as security and peacekeepers," gesturing to the one who hadn't spoken, Jack didn't really look at them, "the reapers who guide souls to where they need to be," next he gestured to Hugo, "the demons, who, well-"

Hugo laughed, looking down to me, "We're the bad guys, it's okay, you can say it."

Jack didn't appear to like that, but instead of arguing, gestured to himself, "And Earthbound, we have no abilities or function of note."

"There are also the angels," Salem said, reaching for the next set of doors as we approached, "but we don't have any of those in our club."

Stopping at the doors, I looked them over, standing with what had been said, but then my eyes met Salem, "What are you?"

Tensing, his smile didn't fade as the others walked into the room, "A demon, like Hugo."

Passing by, my eyes lingered on him. I didn't know Salem very well, but something about that didn't sit right.

"I'd love to explain it all more in depth to you sometime," Jack fell back to walk immediately at my side, so close his pine cologne overtook me, "I heard that you're still new, and it is a lot to take in, so there's no rush, but," bending to be level with me, his hands in his lab coat pockets, his shockingly green eyes searched mine with a bit too much care, "I cannot wait to study you."

Heart starting to uptick, my jaw tightened. The way the green of his eyes reflected off the depth of the darkness of his skin, his sharp defined hairline that was visible between the bounce of his afro with every step, the friendliness of his smile, despite the bluntness of his glasses, it was all too much.

Nothing of note? I'd disagree.

Ripping my eyes away before red could take hold again, I looked to the ground in another vast, darkened room. Did ghosts have a thing with lights, why was every room so dark.

"Don't suffocate him with unnecessary exposition," Kasper's voice came from the darkness, "he will learn in due time." Footsteps approached in the darkness and with each one, blue candles lit about, illuminating the room.

Looking around as the chandelier above lit too, I wondered if the dramatics ever got old.

Standing before a throne, Kasper waved at me. Leaning against the throne behind Kasper, arms crossed over his chest, dressed in black and gold royal garb, sword hanging off his hip, Knight Oliver's orange hair at length, it flowed a bit, like tamed flames. In a black hoodie and skinny jeans, crown absent from his head, hair tastefully messy, Kasper looked nothing like the king I had danced with at the ball. I was expecting formalities, not that, as I stared at him, breath caught. A weathered deck in one hand, propped up on the toe of his black and white skater shoes, he dropped it to the ground. Jumping down from the raised platform his throne sat upon, he landed on the skateboard with no effort. When his shoes made contact with the deck, the board gained a light blue glow. Eyes widening as he skated closer, I took a step back.

Oh no.

Hands in his hoodie pocket, he made it look easy as he rolled toward us, "Thank you for bringing Igor here," riding around us in a circle, all he had to do was slightly lean and he wove around Phantasmal with shocking precision, his board leaving a blue light trail behind him, "Now get out," ruffling Hugo's hair as he passed him, it was then that I realized just how much time had passed since Kasper died. Hugo was only a child at his brother's funeral.

Laughing as Hugo fixed his hair, he stumbled away from Kasper as he skated around them, corralling them toward the door, "Yeah, yeah, we'll leave you two to your fancy upper king talks." Waving at me, Hugo's smile didn't look like it belonged to a bad guy. "It was nice to meet you again, Igor!"

Turning to look my way as they started through the door, Salem smiled at me too, "Let's hang out soon."

As Jack nodded to me, exiting, he made me look away. But in the process of averting my eyes, right before the door closed behind them, I swore I saw Salem take Hugo's hand, matching rings catching on the candlelight.

After staring at the door for a moment, Kasper turned and started skating back my way. "They all seemed to really like you." Smiling at me, the tuft of fluffy bangs over his forehead dancing with his every move, he closed in as he went on, "Thanks for making the time to come here. I didn't mean to rush you, but when I caught word of how close you already were to unlocking all the colors," jumping off his board, he took a couple bouncing steps and landed right in front of me, but a couple inches away, "I kinda panicked."

Stiff, eyes wide, I couldn't look away from him. Like a moon reflecting light, while it wasn't as blinding as the sun, there was a comfort to it, a confidence. I hadn't noticed before, how his eyes smiled even when he wasn't, how his fair skin looked against the black of his hair, or how well his clothing clung to his frame. So close to me, I could even smell his cologne, like a black tea it made heat come to rise in me again.

What the fuck.

Why.

Stumbling back, hand up to my mouth as I turned away from him, my grip was tight, brow trembling in the drop.

Why was everyone hot all of the sudden.

"Are you," leaning around me to catch my eye, Kasper studied me, "okay?"

"Yeah, uhm," Straightening, tense as all hell, I did my best to smile, "what, what was it you wanted to talk to me about?"

Staring at me as he straightened too, hands in his hoodie pocket, he hummed as he shifted his weight. "Well," turning from me, he stepped on his board, sending it up into the air. Catching it without a hitch, he left me there to stare at his back as he walked toward his throne with a life to his every step that I hadn't even seen in anyone who was actually alive, "I know we briefly spoke at the ball but, I wanted to make sure you knew that I'm on your side."

The ball pulling into focus in my mind, I was overcome with the way Kasper pulled me into him as we danced, the dip that lasted too long and got too close. I hadn't noticed at the time, didn't even care that he was so attractive, no space between us. Ripping my eyes away from his back, I couldn't do this, couldn't be distracted as I followed him, "Is there a particular reason?"

He let go of his skateboard and it hovered down to the side of the throne, leaning up against it on its own, "Yeah," Sitting down in his throne, he pulled his legs up onto it, crossing them. "I'm genuinely concerned that Anton isn't going to go down without a fight, even though the crown is rightfully yours."

Stopping a couple steps away, I couldn't look up to him, "I wouldn't be surprised. He imparted the most ominous of warnings to me the other day, saying to be careful because anyone may want to steal my brooch."

Snorting, Kasper leaned back in his throne, looking to Oliver, "Yeah, Oli told me that Anton has a history of being the fucking worst so I wanted to try to come up with a plan, should he be up to something. Rumor has it," he paused, looking back to me to stare into my eyes for a moment, "Anton was the priest who hanged Nox in life, and I'm not going to let him do it again."

Eyes widening, the candles around flickered orange for a moment, sparing me from red for a moment.

Glancing around at the orange flames, Kasper looked back to me, "I know, gross, right?" he leaned forward, getting a bit too close, "Has the immortal or the vampire said anything to you about what will happen if someone takes your brooch?"

Heart thumping against my chest as their mention resurrected red in my blood, it came with a bite this time as my intake caught, "They, uh," eyes darting down to the side, brow fighting to remain neutral, my brain went back places it shouldn't. "Not, uhm, not really, no." Bringing my hand up, I raked it through my hair as I tried to keep my tone even, "Cy-Cyrus-" the moment his name rolled off my tongue, an image of him saying my name in unspeakable composure beneath me invaded my mind.

Turning away from Kasper, hand flying to my mouth, eyes so wide they hurt, every candle in the room turned red.

Jesus fucking Christ.

Clearing my throat as I begged my body to stop, the heat on my face stung, "Cyrus said that if I took it off, my powers would go out of control and destroy everything."

A weird beat passed before Kasper slowly said, "Right."

"And Fin-Fin-Finnegan," tensing more with each stutter, I closed my eyes but all I saw was a blessed view of them from my knees, "they- uhm, they…"

Shaking I was so tense, I couldn't even talk, face burning, the sting of sweat taking me as my heart raced so fast I could feel it in my reddening ears.

"Say, Igor," Kasper's tone slowly shifted, something playful about it as he went on, "You've unlocked orange, yellow, green, and blue, so far yeah?"

I nodded, hand so tight over my mouth that I could barely even breathe.

"So all that remains is red and purple?"

Nodding again, tears started to bud in my eyes as I was nothing more than a victim to the anxious ache taking me. A faint laugh came from behind me, a quiet exchanging of words following that I couldn't understand. But as I watched Oliver exit the room from the corner of my vision, shooting me a bit of an amused glance on the way, I didn't have the capacity to care.

When the door closed, Kasper spoke, "Cyrus is real hot, isn't he?"

Tensing, eyes wide, I couldn't move as I heard the wheels of Kasper's skateboard approach.

"You know, I read the only book in the entirety of limbo that I could find on Nox, and it said that with each incarnation, the powers grow." Skating around me, he made me stumble away to keep my back to him so he wouldn't see how embarrassed I was, "And since your powers are emotionally based like mine, I'm sure what you're going through is intense."

Walking away from him, I didn't know what to do, I just didn't want him to see how stupid I'm sure I looked.

Skating after me, it sounded like a waving stroll as his wheels ebbed and flowed with every turn, "What was just annoyance forty incarnates ago has grown to rage, a simple startle turned paralyzing fear." Cutting me off when I tried to turn, he cornered me against the wall of the throne room, "What may have been but a crush," Stopping in front of me, he flipped his skateboard up. Eyes on the ground, I couldn't look up at his as he closed the space, standing directly before me, my back to the wall, "has devolved into a desperate desire."

The flames around roared as Kasper extended his finger to the tip of my jaw, tilting it up and making me look at him. Unable to look away from his silver eyes despite the tears budding in mine below quivering brow, face so red it hurt- where I expected to see judgment, mockery even, I was met with something softer, kinder, as Kasper smiled at me.

"Sounds like a nightmare, honestly," taking back his hand, he straightened, "it's really important that we talk about what to do about Anton before you unlock all of them, but there's no way you can focus until you've tamed this color."

Flames calming about, they still burned red, but my next breath was a little easier to take, "I don't," looking away, it was everything I could do to keep my voice even, "I don't know how."

Raising a brow as he dropped his board back to the ground, he looked up to me, "How?"

Nodding, I crossed my arms over my chest to put something between us, "At this point I understand that the only way to tame the colors are to honor them, running away only makes them worse," I glanced back to him for a moment, "obviously, but," looking away again, I shrunk in my coat a bit, "the others, they were just about me, but this…"

Hopping on his board, Kasper shifted his weight on it, "Have you told Cyrus how you feel?"

"It's a little more," running my hands up over my face, I had to force every word out as I shoved my glasses out of place, "complicated, than that."

Kicking off, he skated around, hands in his pants pockets as he left a blue, glowing, trail behind him, "How so?"

"It's, well," A vision took me, one of two sets of arms wrapped around me, an embrace, warmer than any other as, from the corners of my vision, I was met with blonde wavy locks and lengths of silver hair as they each buried their heads into my shoulders. Smiling a little under my hand as it sat to my face, though I felt the burn, I beneath it was something simply warm, "it's not-"

"Not Cyrus?" Kasper circled around me, stepping about on his board in some godlike display to remain facing me as he did, "Then does that mean it's Finnegan?"

"No," pulling my glasses from my face where they sat, amiss, I folded them in one hand and pinched the bridge of my nose with the other, my arms partly crossed over my chest, "I mean in a way, I-"

Stopping in front of me, Kasper leaned over to be eye level from his board, making me step back into the wall, "Which one is it, Cyrus or Finnegan?"

Staring at him, the only thing in focus in my world, I shrunk into my jacket a bit, "Yes."

Blinking at me, he stood there, unmoving, "What?"

Eyes slowly drifting away as a wave of heat came to my face, I shrunk a little more, "Yes…"

Brows lowering a little as his head slid into a tilt, his confusion was evident until suddenly, it hit him.

Straightening, eyes wide, his brows shot up. Blank for only a moment longer, a smile twisted his lips, "Is that right?"

Nodding as I slid down a bit more, I couldn't even reply.

Humming, he pushed off on his board, skating away, "That's not entirely surprising," glancing at me from over his shoulder, he smiled, "legend has it the three of you were an item in the before times. It has just been hundreds of years since an incarnation came of age. And since that's the case, I'm sure both of them would be more than happy to hear how you feel."

Leaning up against the wall, shrunk down in my coat, eyes averted and brow low, the burning of my skin only grew, "they've been so busy fighting the entire time, I'm worried if I tell them, then that will make it worse."

"Fighting?" doing a jump on his board, his clean landing guided him back my way, "No, that's just the way

Cyrus and Finnegan are. No matter what it looks like, they are in love."

"Lo-" The word caught in my throat, choking me, "Love?"

Stopping in front of me, he balanced on one end of his board, the other up in the air, "More than any two beings ever have been." His laugh was soft, more like a smile come to life as he looked away, "Though, maybe that's not exactly right. Perhaps you love them the most."

Love.

The flames around grew hotter, spiking the air.

Looking about as the fire flickered, my eyes widened. I loved them, I always loved them. Flashing before my eyes, what felt like tens of lifetimes, tens of meetings, passed in but a moment. Cyrus and Finnegan, no matter when, where, or who I was, they were there. Crossing paths at a market, Cyrus stopping dead in his tracks before stumbling to me. Encountering one another in a garden, Finnegan turning so fast that their hair flared out just to see me. Over and over, one way or another, they always found me. Over and over, one way or another, they always loved me. Whether it was in the way Cyrus tried to make me laugh as a child, or the way he looked at me now, it was different, but always love.

And though what I was experiencing was overwhelmingly physical, that wasn't all that was there. The charming persistence Cyrus had when we first met, the innate way he just knew it was me. The complexities of Finnegan's intentions, the ungodly grasp they hold over every situation. The way they banter, and how it would be a lot less words to just shut up and kiss already. The promise of forever, an eternity to watch them shine.

An eternity of them being mine.

"Well," Kasper gestured toward the door and with the movement, a blue glow took over the threshold. "I shouldn't keep you. You still have the stone I gave you, yeah?" When I nodded, he smiled as the door creaked open, "Great, just throw it on the ground and it will open a portal to me when you're ready to talk." hopping off his board, his voice lowered as he approached me, "You can come back once you're thinking with the right head."

Staring at him, I had no idea what he meant as the footsteps approaching stopped.

But when I saw the smirk crack on his face as he turned away, it hit me. Kasper's laugh only lessened the embarrassed sting a bit as a groan escaped me, eyes dropping.

I didn't even look at the person who had approached as I stepped up from the wall, "But I don't know how to tell them."

"Oh don't worry about that," starting away from me and back toward his throne Kasper waved, "when you're with them, you'll just know."

About to reply, it died in my throat as someone laughed at my side. Eyes wide, I slowly looked over. I had never heard him laugh like that before, and as Salem stood there, looking away, it sounded like it could purify any blight. Gesturing toward the door with his head, his hands in the pockets of his long, dark robe, he turned.

Looking back to Kasper, I was met with an empty throne room. Blinking, he was nowhere to seen. Straightening, uncomfortable in the burning of my own skin, I only stood for a beat longer before following Salem. I'd just know, what did that even mean.

Reaching Salem's side as we started through the doorway, he looked up to me as he spoke, "Your brooch," his eyes drifted down, "it holds your powers?" When I nodded, he smiled as he looked forward, "Pardon my eavesdropping, but King Kasper said you only had two more colors to tame, right?"

"Yes," I stared at him for a moment before looking forward myself, eyes meeting the grand front door.

"That's interesting. There are two more slots on your brooch, so that makes sense, but what do you think the middle gem is for?"

Bringing my fingers up to the brooch on my bowtie, the colorful lights marrying on the skin of my hand, the tip of my finger hovered over the center gem. Shaped like a star, it sat, dull, in the middle, if I remembered right. "I suppose it could be decorative."

Nodding a little as we approached the front doors, leaving the dimly candle lit castle behind, he brought his hand up to it, "I read everything I could find on Nox in life, and legend has it, there are seven colors, not six."

My step hitched.

Seven?

Turning to look at me, we stood in that moment.

Smile faded, he studied me.

My mouth open to say something, it never made it out.

Looking back to the door, his tone lowered, "It was a note I found in a declassified Jinx record, though it had been heavily tampered with so, take that with a grain of salt." Smiling, he started to put pressure on the door, "If Kasper says there are six then there are probably six, he knows a lot more than he'll ever let on, so I'd trust him." Pushing the door open, he started through it, "I was just curious."

Before I could reply, Edgar's voice came from outside, "That was fast."

"Yes, well," Salem shot a glance my way as he stepped out the door, "Igor has some," his eyes took all of me in as he descended the first step, "urgent business to take care of. Edgar, would you send him back please?"

Looking away, heat started to come to rise in me again. Stepping through the door, I was met with Phantasmal as they stood at the foot of the steps. Jack at Hugo's side,

Edgar and the reaper nearby, Salem stopped in front of them.

They were so young. Despite looking happy, Salem more

lively than he ever looked when alive, there was something

about them. Something that, despite the overbearing of red,

made the candle burning the wall at my side turn blue.

Raising his hand in a wave, I only saw Salem for a

moment more before my shadow grew beneath me and a

heartbeat later, I fell.

Though as I dropped into darkness, hundreds of ropes

like a web beneath my weight, I didn't fight.

I couldn't.

Not anymore.

It was no use, after all.

Because as I tripped out the other side of the shadow,

barely landing on my feet in Cyrus' cabin, when my eyes met

them, that's all I could do.

Fall.

Halfway through a word, Cyrus stopped, arms frozen in some sort of expressive display as he and Finnegan turned to look at me. Vampire draped over Cyrus' ornate sofa like they were posing for a painting, Cyrus standing next to a haphazardly stacked pile of books, the obstructed light from the curtained window behind it turned red as it stretched across the floor between us. My shadow retuning to its original size, it waved before snapping into place.

"Igor," starting toward me, Cyrus' panic was palpable until his eyes met mine, freezing him in his step.

"Are you," though their movements were usually delicate, as Finnegan scrambled to their feet, running to Cyrus' side, it appeared they forgot themselves, "alright?"

Straightening, the insulating silence of his cabin, cut off from the rest of the world, it felt timeless around us, private. Face surely red, hair a bit disheveled, I'm sure they could see it with the cadence of my chest, my shortness of breath as the fire they lit in me devoured any air I took in. Starting toward them without a word, with each step a memory came back. Another precious moment from lives long past, Finnegan pinning me to a wall, Cyrus beneath me in the confessional. Long nights, simple mornings, domestic laughs, I was to be the last.

There would be no incarnation after me.

That way I could love them both, for eternity.

Stopping right in front of them, my eyes drifted between them. Red and green, comedy and calm, passion and possession, there were no words to describe what I wanted to do.

When my breath hitched, I couldn't help but smile, because I found a few.

Kasper was right, I just knew.

"Take me."

Eyes wide, smile frozen on his face, Cyrus stared at me, "What?"

Taking a step forward toward them, I caused them to both step back, "I need you to take me."

Looking to Finnegan, Cyrus took a moment to look back to me, "Where?"

"Here is fine," I looked back to him, the glittering of the glow of his eyes on pause, "it's just the three of us, right?"

Brows raising even higher, he stood, staring at me, though Cyrus didn't speak.

Blinking at me for a bit longer, Finnegan shook the moment, the knowing gleam back in their emerald eyes as they glowed a little brighter, "Is that right?"

Arms crossing over my chest, I shifted my weight, "What, are you trying to change my mind?"

Mouth open, Cyrus' word turned into a drawn out croak until he managed to say, "No, I'm just surprised," stepping forward, it was cautious as his eyes dropped to my lips, "You're a wild card, you know that?"

Uncrossing my arms, my eyes scaled him up and his well-fitted black hoodie, clergy collar and defined Adam's apple, sharp jaw, wavy locks, and reddening face to land on his. The line of my mouth twisted up, red undoing me, taking over every inch as the tension melted into something else, "Actually, no, I have changed my mind."

Eyes wide, neither of them had a moment to react before my hands met both of their chests. Sending them stumbling into the wall, some books fell from the stack at our side. Taking grip of the fabric, I pressed them there, hardly any space between the three of us, our combined heat like home on my skin.

"I'm going to take you." Eyeing them up, I tilted my head, my bangs drifting to the side as I slid my hands down their fronts, "If that's alright, of course."

Looking to each other, Finnegan and Cyrus shared a silent moment, eyes wide, faces both dusted in red. I could feel it, their shallow breathing, the heat rising in them even through the fabric of their shirts. Looking back to me at the same time, I could see it on their faces, the submission to red as they nodded.

I watched red come to life in my bowtie that night as the light bathed Finnegan and Cyrus in its fever. Reflecting off tears as they budded in Cyrus' eyes, he laid beneath me as they broke free and streamed down his face. Smiling, it stifled his shaking exhale as he reached up. Hand meeting the back of my head, he took grip. Yanking me down, when our lips met, my hands planted on either side of his head on his bed, it took my eyes a moment to close. Kissing him back, I could feel it in his every movement, a hope come to life.

He had always believed in me, knew I could do it from the moment we met. And I wasn't going to let him down. As I pulled back from the kiss, I only got to see Cyrus, hair a mess, fluster obvious, for a moment before a dainty hand met the beneath of my chin. Tilting my head up, Finnegan's emerald eyes burned, illuminating the smile. Shoving me back off Cyrus, their gentle touch turned dominant as my back hit the bed. Hair bouncing in my face, Finnegan on top of me, I couldn't see them as they leaned down, but I could feel their warmth hovering, but a moment away from meeting my lips.

"I have missed you."

Kissing me, while it should have felt new, I could tell, we had kissed many, many times before as I knew the nuance of their every move. Cyrus pulling in at my side, he kissed my neck, causing me to tense.

Smiling as Finnegan pulled back, the communion of red and green illuminating the chamber, I brought my hands up to both of them, resting on their chests. Though their hearts had long since stopped, I hoped they could feel the racing of mine.

White meeting my eyes, it stilled the red roaring through me, soberingly sterile. Standing in Nox's abyss, silence laced the air, though along with it, came a sweet aroma. Stepping around, I was met with his tree, the wisteria still hanging in bloom as its vines overtook the branches. Eyes drifting down to the trunk, the faint carvings visible from even there, I knew where I had seen that tree before.

A warmth caught my attention. Looking down to my hand, a red glow bled through my fingers. Opening my hand, I was met with another orb. Its heat inspired an anxious sting in my palm, one that begged for action, a need above all else.

A breeze distracted me, ruffling the leaves of the tree.

Looking up from the orb in my hand, I started toward the tree. Living behind Blazing Star Private High, it was the crowning plant in the Gardening Club's student garden. It wasn't too uncommon an occurrence to pass it by and see Kasper staring up at it before he was expelled. Rumors ran rampant about the tree, but only one of which ever courted my attention. Legend had it that the tree could grant wishes.

Ruffling startled me.

"Look at you," a couple leaves fell from the tree as Nox swung down, hanging by his knees from a branch. Hair standing straight up, eyes on me, he made it look effortless as he just swung from the tree, "only one more to go." Swaying a bit, he made leaves fall between us with every move, "Of course it's purple, which not a single incarnation has tamed, so y'know, but congrats all the same."

Standing there, staring at him as he hung, just a couple feet away from me, there was something different about him. Was that an attempt at being friendly? Despite being my damn near reflection, he was difficult for me to read.

"I'm not worried," turning a bit, I raised my hand, the red orb coming up with it, "red was perhaps the worst experience of my life, so no matter what it is, purple can't beat that."

"Worst experience of your life?" pulling himself up, Nox shifted in the tree. Dropping, he landed on his feet, "What, your first time didn't meet your expectations or something?"

Closing my hand over the orb, I felt it shrink in my grasp. "No," refusing to look at him, I took a step away, "while I had no expectations to meet in the first place, I'm sure if I had," bringing red up to my bowtie, I felt it catch like a flame, lighting my blood as it took its place in my brooch, "Finnegan and Cyrus would have exceeded them."

The abyss turned red in a blink, as if that was all it took, a moment for the color to conquer.

Laughing as he approached, it was hard to tell if the red dusting Nox's face came from our surroundings or from within, "Well, I'm happy to see you appreciate what you have." Stopping in front of me, his eyes searched mine, "Please take care of them, they both deserve it."

Lowering my hand, the combination of the glowing colors from my brooch beaming onto it as I did, my eyes found their way back to Nox. "I will, though," pocketing my hands, I shifted my weight away from him, "I do hope they like me for me, not just because I'm an incarnation of you."

"Oh," turning away, he started back toward the tree, the floor turning white beneath his every step, "I don't think that should concern you. Sure, the connection is there, my soul within yours that is forever bound to both of theirs, but," hand meeting his tree, he stared up into it, just as Kasper used to, "there is much more to you than the parasitic sliver of my soul."

Approaching the tree, every step brought me closer to standing at his side. As my shoes left the ground, in the path behind me sprouted flowers, the silence that drifted between us felt heavy as I stopped at his side. Glancing back to the trail of flowers behind me, there was only one color missing from their petals. Looking up into the tree, watching the flowers dance in the breeze, the red abyss around us, there was a warmth that hadn't been there before.

"I don't have the only one, do I?"

Humming, Nox looked to me.

"The fragment of your soul that I possess, it's not the only one, is it?"

"Ah," Nox shifted his weight away from me, crossing his arms over his chest as he looked back up to the tree, "yes, there are many, too many." Spinning on his heel to face me, his back landed against the tree. A pause took him as he leaned there, "I was hanged from a tree just like this one. When I died, not only did I curse those who killed me, but the very tree too, apparently. Though it was unbeknownst to anyone, even me, until it was cut down and its wood was used to create things. Suddenly every day objects could grant wishes, a wooden pen casing that makes what's written with it come true, a bow that creates music that forces anyone who hears it to tell the truth, a chess board that can sway the tide of war, there are so many I don't even know what they all are or even what they all do. The me that lives within each object is but a sliver of my soul, his own individual me, none of them are connected." Looking up to me, he ran his hand through his messy bangs, giving me a brief glimpse at his whole face, "I didn't mention it because it isn't really relevant to you at this time, I didn't think Cyrus would either. Who told you?"

Blinking at him, I felt as if I had heard that story before, some bedtime fairytale. "His name is Salem, he's a demon from Limbo who is close with the Ghost King. He said he read about a cult that claimed you were fragmented and wanted to put you back together."

The laugh that took him, it was sweeter than the blossoms in the breeze, "He isn't wrong, though they did their best, Jinx was never successful. They figured if they could find all the objects and bring them together, they could help me move on before my power grew too exponentially and destroyed everything. They got real close, but," looking away, the wind blew his hair around, "when the head of Jinx realized where the biggest sliver of my soul lived, she didn't want to risk anything happening to its home. It was really something," looking back to me, his eyes trailed my stature up before landing on mine, "the day the head of Jinx stepped down in defeat, claiming she could never find the last piece of the puzzle, full well knowing it was living in her own son."

Eyes widening on his, I only saw the hint of glass take his before they darted away from me.

"My mum?" taking a step back, the red around us started to fade.

Nodding, his jaw tightened as he regained composure, "Sierra dedicated her entire life to saving me, just for my curse to choose you as the doomed next incarnation." A small smile taking him, he brought his hand up and ran it over his face, "But I suppose she doesn't have to be troubled by that any longer, huh?"

The abyss turned blue.

She knew, she always knew.

The way she fought against my powers as a child flashed in my mind. Despite being pregnant with Ross, the way she clawed her way to me, took me in her arms, protected me, the way she spoke with Nox, the smile she always wore, the little I even knew about her…

My mum.

Bringing my hand up too, it met with my mouth as my eyes fell away and my teeth grit. How could I have ever thought she didn't care. She didn't care now, but that was only because she couldn't, because I stole it from her.

Clearing his throat, Nox pushed himself up off the tree, "While there is much to tell you, I want to not overwhelm. It is true, this story is much bigger than just you." Stepping by me, his shoulder brushed against mine, "But there will be no happy ending for anybody if you don't get out of this novel alive."

Turning around, as my eyes met him, they met with something else, too. Standing in front of a wooden bookshelf that hadn't been there before, the flowers from my shoeprints stood at its base. Easily twenty, likely more, spines of novels stared back at me as Nox reached for one.

"When you conquer the colors and take the crown, then I'll let you read them, the stories that have led us here." He pulled one novel out, "I think there are only a few more chapters left to be written in yours." Flipping through the pages, he stopped on one, eyes drifting over the page at a steady pace as he spoke on, "It's still being written, as we speak." Reaching over toward the shelf without looking away from the open book in his hand, he took another out and this time, held it toward me.

Accepting the book, though its weight was nothing to sneeze at, it felt friendly in my grip. It didn't immediately earn my eyes though, as I smiled at Nox. He had just said "when" I conquered the colors, not "if."

Turning the book over, my eyes met the front cover. Staring, my mouth sat open in a reply that would never come. The title- it was an unusual word, though I had heard it somewhere before, just once.

Phantasmal

Opening the novel, the flames on the cover felt warm in my hands. Eyes darting over the words, flipping through the pages, I was met with what appeared to be a first person recounting of the events that led up to the bloody scene at the high school that Abraxas was occupied with.

"Salem, he's in that one." Nox stepped up to my side, looking down to the book, a smile taking him as he hovered a bit close, "Not that I'm supposed to have favorite characters as the author, but if I were, he would definitely be one. Though," he straightened, "that's even hard to say, because I fancy Loux too, and Algernon is really interesting- oh, and not to forget Colin, he may have my favorite arc of them all."

"The author?" I looked up to him from a passage about Salem straight up stepping on Hugo's head.

Humming, he smiled as he started back toward the shelf, "I've written them all, in a manner of speaking." Holding up the book in his hands, he turned it toward me. As he went on, I was left to stand there and watch every word he said appear on the half-written page, "Yours is unfinished. We're right after the quiet before the storm, about to hit the dark night of the soul." Turning the book back around, he closed it, "The rest should write itself, it always does."

Eyes on the back of the book he had just shown me, the one in my hand become heavier.

"It's all a story?" Staring at him, my eyes raised from the book in his grip, "You're in control of everything?" When he didn't reply, when the weight started to mount, when I was left to wonder what was being written on the page before him in that moment, my breath became a rock in my core, until a light lit in my mind, "If you're the author, then just write a happy ending."

The little chuckle that took him, it caught the moment as he gazed down at the book in his hands, "Throw that book you have there at my head."

"What?" I stepped back, looking between him and the book I held, "No, why would I do that?"

"See?" Shrugging, Nox turned back toward the bookshelf, "If it were as simple as me writing it and you doing it, we wouldn't be in our predicament. Characters are a pain like that," he slid the book onto the shelf, shooting me a look over his shoulder, "having a will of their own."

Standing there, tension draining from me, I was left, without any breath in my chest to speak.

"Where does the author end and the narrator begin?" he ran his fingertips over the spines of the novels on the shelf, "They are all very much their own people, with their own motivations and autonomy, but without me there would be no story. Did I will them to be, or did they will me?" fingers lingering on one book, I stepped closer to him to see the name on the spine.

The 15th of Finality

"I'm not quite sure." Nox dropped his hand.

Standing next to him, eyes scanning over as many spines as I could, I took in only some of their names.

The Graveyard Shift

Ghost King

Remnant Rebel

Perilloux Paradox

Perilloux Parallax

Perilloux Prefix

The 13th of Games

The Perilloux Palace

Dear Mr. President

Operation 15

Eros Erroneous

A Warning to All Writers

You Jinxed Us

Hell's Bells and Buckets of Blood

A Rose By Any Dumb Name

Algernon's Anomaly

As I was reading over the spines of several books that all had the same title, I blinked, and the bookshelf disappeared. Jumping, I looked down to my now empty hands.

"But I digress," turning to face me, Nox smiled, "this novel is in your hands, just as every one on that shelf was in the hands of the narrators who have come before you in this great big story. Now," Looking to his wrist, as if there were a watch there when there definitely wasn't, he took a deep breath, "looks like it's about time for your dark night of the soul. You better be getting back."

Blinking at him, though what he had just said felt impossible, something about the way he said it was enough. A lonely author with a story that had gotten out of his hands, it must have been what Nox had been up to all of this time, alone in this abyss. He was the most powerful being to ever be, it would make sense that even the words he writes come to life, taking on their own will. A breath escaping me, it left me without words, but that was alright, because I didn't feel like there were any needed. A happy ending was always my goal, nothing had changed. Nothing more than wanting to not only end this story, but make it a good one, knowing that he'd be here reading it.

"I'm so proud of you," Bringing his hand up, it met my shoulder. I may have jumped a little, but when his warmth met me, it was hard not to relax, "You only have one color left."

Staring at him and the way the colors of my brooch lit the silver of his hair, I barely had enough breath to speak, "Are you sure?"

Tilting his head a little, he took his hand back, "About what?"

Bringing my hand up, my fingers hovered right above the brooch, "Salem said something else, too. That there weren't six colors, but seven."

Eyes widening, just a bit, Nox stood with that for a moment. "Oh," turning from me, he laced his fingers behind his head, "Yes, I only knew six colors in life. Orange of rage, yellow of joy, green of excitement, blue of sorrow, red of love, and purple, of well," looking back to me, he smiled, though it didn't make it to his eyes, "you'll find out."

Turning back around, he started toward the tree, "Should there be a seventh, we were never acquainted, that I'm aware of."

As the ghost of the book's weight haunted my skin, I looked down to my hands. "What is the last emotion and why won't anyone tell me?" Looking back up, my eyes narrowed on his, "What did you say just now, dark night of the what?"

Stepping up to me, the bounce to Nox's step faded with each one, "I believe in you," stopping right in front of me, Nox's eyes sat, averted beneath his stiffly low brow, "please conquer purple," looking back to me, glass in his eyes, he only managed to look at me for a moment, "then come back to see me."

Before I could say a word, I blinked, and everything went black.

Nox must have been so lonely.

Eyes opening, at first it was slow, my mind hazy, unable to remember much of anything in that moment. Tired, why was I so tired? Had I not just slept? Taking a breath, the dust of castle room that I was starting to become accustomed to met me. Though the ceiling was blurry, I knew it was stone. Bringing my hand up to run down my face, it never made it, as it bumped into someone else. Freezing, eyes wide, it must have been then, when my senses returned to me.

Gaze slowly lowering, it pulled into focus, close enough for me to see, a vampire and an immortal, both asleep on me. Locked up, staring, my eyes jumped between them, each resting their head on my bare collarbones, one arm each draped over my middle. Covers pulled up over us, it was the type of warm that could convince you to never get out of bed. Like an avalanche, my ability to think returned to me, and with each thought, just as a snowball grew as it careened down the mountain, they became exponentially more severe until I was left with:

Where were their clothes?

And

Where were mine?

The door opened.

Jumping more than I ever have in my entire life, I inspired the same in the two people sleeping on me. A boisterous, booming laugh cut short when Anton's eyes met us. Frozen, standing in the threshold, holding the door wide open for himself and Kasper, it was the first time I had witnessed an emotion take the man with any legitimacy. Jumping to reach for the blanket, the striking insecurity I saw flash over Finnegan made nothing else matter in that moment. Yanking the covers up over Finnegan, I pulled them into my side. Frame tense, grip on the covers whitening their knuckles, Finnegan cursed beneath their breath as they leaned into me.

The flames that sat about the room turned orange as my eyes shot back to Anton.

Cyrus at my other side, covers pooling in his lap, the muscles shifted over his scarred and darkened torso as he leaned back on one hand, "I know you're a king and all, but like, knock please, your highness."

A blunder of an apology left Anton as he whirled around like a top about to spin out.

Kasper stood for a moment longer, eyes drifting between the three of us, wider than usual as the hauntings of a smile took his face. Turning, he raised his arms in a shrug, "My bad," shoving Anton out the door, his voice echoed into the hall, "I come seeking your audience, Igor. I'll be waiting for you, but no rush." Stopping, he glanced back as the door started to close between us, his smirk only visible for a moment, "Congrats on red."

The door closed.

I stared at it.

A harsh breath escaping them, Finnegan pulled themselves up from my side. Eyes meeting them, they averted back down to the bed the moment they met with their bare skin.

"I beg your pardon," they reached down off the side of the bed, pulling their cape back up, "thank you for your consideration." Draping their long cape over themselves, they stood, making the bed creak. Without another word, they gathered a few items of clothing from the floor and started toward the bathroom across the room. With each step, their necklace bounced against their chest, the green glowing orb trapped in an intricate cage pendant faintly pulsing like a racing heart.

Staring at the door as it closed behind them, the bed felt empty in their absence.

"Are they," I looked back to Cyrus voice low, "alright?"

A sigh took him as he laid back down, hands laced behind his head, "Finnegan has always had a complicated relationship with their body," looking to me through disheveled golden locks, the red of his eyes became a bit brighter when they met mine, "so it means a lot that they trusted you with it." Yawning, he sat up, reaching for his shirt off the side of the bed, "They'll be okay," pulling his shirt over his head, his hair fluffed. As he stood to put on the rest of his clothing, I looked away, "but when we move into the king's quarters, we'll want to get a lock on that door."

Eyes jumping to him as he turned to look at me, a warmth spread over my face. When we moved in to the king's quarters? When we, Cyrus, Finnegan, and I, moved into the king's quarters? When the three of us, when we, when…

Forever blossomed in his eyes as Cyrus winked at me.

Kneeling down, he nearly closed the space between us as I still sat on the bed, "What," voice barely above a whisper, I could still hear the smile in it has he hovered, an inch away from my ear, his warm exhale rolling down my bare chest, "didn't think that far ahead?"

When he kissed my neck, my entire body seized, hands grasping fistfuls of the covers at my sides. Teeth grit, the lamps on the walls lit red, painting the entire room in desire. Pulling back, he stopped right in front of my face, red bathing him, bringing out the warmth in his every inch. Eyes drifting down from his to that line that tugged up on his lips, an image flashed to life in my mind. Though, unlike before, the intrusive memory was mine.

He took a breath.

Before he could say another stupid thing, I kissed him.

Staring at myself in the mirror, in another set of vaguely formal clothing that just seemed to materialize out of the ether for me in the bathroom every morning, I straightened my bowtie. A dull star gem in the middle, it sat, surrounded by smaller, tear shaped gems, all of which were lit, all except one. The circuit almost complete, I just needed purple and every color would be mine.

Walking out of the bathroom, I may have opened the door a bit too quietly. Pulling back from a kiss, Cyrus against the wall, Finnegan pinning him there, I would have been jealous, had I not had them both calling my name the night before. Clearing my throat, I tried to clear my head as well. I had things to do, other than those two.

Scrambling to my sides as I approached the door, they both fell in step.

"What does the ghost want?" Finnegan took my hand in theirs, lacing their fingers through mine. "You held company yesterday, did you not?"

Staring forward, their warmth sent a spike through my blood, threatening to crack my voice as I spoke, "We did, but the conversation didn't get very far because I was," eyes drifting down to them as their hair swayed with their every step at my side, I quickly looked away, "distracted."

Cyrus snorted, though he did seem like he tried to hide it.

Walking down the hall, the castle started to feel more familiar in a friendly way. I had been here before, I could tell. But now the stones beneath my shoes became less hard with each step. Home, it was the only one I had now.

One of the lamps on the wall turned blue as we passed.

"Hey," Cyrus' low voice startled me out of my head as we approached the Netherside throne room doors.

Looking up to him as he walked with his hands laced behind his head, his eyes were up and away from me as we came to a stop and he went on.

"The Almighty makes me anxious."

I turned to face him, my back to the doors, "Why do you say that?"

Humming, he shifted his weight, still not looking at me as his eyes drifted down, "I just have a bad feeling."

"His brother and the company he keeps." Finnegan slowly slid their fingers from mine, leaving me to savor every last moment of contact, "While it would be hypocritical of me to judge, given what I am, but something sits unwell with me about Salem Willow."

Nodding, Cyrus turned away, "Yeah, him, the Demon King, and what was the other one," turning back, he ran his fingers through his hair, hand resting atop his head, his locks caught up, "the Earthbound, especially the Earthbound. I wouldn't trust any of them."

"Funny," I shifted away from them and a little closer to the door, "King Kasper said the same thing about you."

Cyrus lowered his hand, a huff escaping him.

"They are hiding something, I can smell it." Finnegan looked to the door, arms crossing over their fine chest, "It reminds me of back then, the Great War, the last time any of us saw a Dark Angel before they fell in the genocide."

"A sign of the times," Cyrus said, almost too quiet for me to hear as his eyes met Finnegan beyond me.

Brow raised, Finnegan just looked at him for a moment longer before looking back up to me with a smile, "You are about to be a king, Igor. You must start to be conscious of the intentions of those around you, and we can offer our input, but ultimately it will be up to your own intuition and judgment."

Looking between them, Cyrus and his stubborn disposition, Finnegan and their niceties, and all I could do was nod. Not audacious enough to believe I knew it all, but perhaps a bit inflated by my impressively quick ascension to the throne, I reached for the handle of the door.

"I have faith in you," Cyrus' voice followed me as stepped into the throne room, "but if you need me, say my name, and I'll be there."

Turning as I closed the door behind me, the way Cyrus looked at me, there was something about it, something ever so slight, a shift, a sheen, something that, had I been less caught up in myself, would have made me pause instead of close the door between us.

A laugh met me from behind.

I jumped, and for a moment, the surrounding candles flickered a color, though too quickly for me to see which.

Turning, my eyes dragged over the vastness of the room, far vaster without the company of others dancing and mingling. Standing next to an empty throne, skateboard under his arm, Kasper turned to face me. Anton nowhere to be seen, I started his way. Footsteps quiet, an apprehension bubbled up more with every one until I was but a couple away from him, though unable to look him in the eye.

"Seems like you-"

"Please," I didn't like cutting people off, but as heat came to rise in me, I spoke before I could talk myself out of it, "spare me."

Blinking, Kasper laughed a moment later. Dropping his board down the step to the throne, he jumped onto it, "That's fair, I'd probably ask the same." Without having to push off, his board started to glow blue as he rolled my way, circling, "So, where did we leave off?"

Stepping around to watch him as he glided around me like a vulture, I wondered if there was anyone anywhere in Netherside I could trust. Don't trust Cyrus, don't trust Kasper, don't trust Hugo, don't trust Anton, don't trust Salem, don't trust Jack, don't trust the vampires. Was Nox my only true ally? He had an agenda of his own too, I'm sure everyone did. I could trust my coworkers, I even made the potentially fatal mistake of trusting my managers, too. But here, this was different. It wasn't an us against them, the staff against the customers, no, it was me against the world. Though, of all of those people, there was only one who had given me any real reason to not trust them, the only one who had hurt Nox.

"Where's Anton?"

Jumping from his board, he let it roll away as he landed in front of me, "He said he had a meeting or something."

Eyes drifting to the darkened throne behind Kasper, I wanted to know what it was like to sit in it. "You wanted to discuss a plan, should anyone try to stop me from taking the crown."

"Ah, yeah, right," his board rolled back to him and just before it were to crash into his shin, he stepped on it, causing it to pop up into his hand, "I had gotten so distracted by the latter part of our conversation that I forgot where we were." Shifting his weight in his black pants, rolled up a bit above skater shoes, his dark hoodie was becoming on him as the faint glow of his eyes brought a spark to the dimly lit chamber, "The reason I asked about what they had told you about the brooch, and what would happen if it were to be removed, was because I think that's what Anton is intending to do, take it from you." Eyes lowering to it, the colors mingled with the blue glow of his eyes, "It appears that Cyrus didn't tell you, which is suspicious in it of itself, but supposedly, if the brooch is removed, the person who takes it will be bestowed with your powers. Assuming they can handle them, anyway." Looking down, he ran his free hand through his hair, leaving it to rest on his head, "Anton is likely waiting for you to reawaken every color so that when he takes the brooch, he will take all of your powers, too and be able to continue as king." Dropping his hand from his hair, he looked up to me as a clump fell into his face, "I'm not exactly sure how that pairs with the information you gave last time, about your powers destroying you without it, because one would assume if they took your powers, they couldn't hurt you, so like, I don't know if it's even true, but it is important for you to be aware of any and all possibilities."

"Take my powers?" I took a step back, my heart starting to slip down into my stomach, "If they did that, would they take my emotions again too? I can't," bringing my cold hand up to my face, a pit started to grow inside my ribs, a pit I had never felt before, "I can't go back to nothing again."

Shrugging, a sigh took him, "I'm sorry Igor, I don't know. Jack and I dug through every library in Limbo and that's all we could figure out. Nox has always been a mystery." He paused, eyes scanning the floor, "But it was weird, not as hard to find as you'd think. The page was bookmarked, the text recently disturbed, hardly any dust on it. Someone else knows about this, too."

Breathing picking up, my limbs started to grow cold.

Maybe Kasper saw it, my color start to drain because he smiled, brow furrowing,

"But don't worry, I'm not going to let that happen. I would like it if myself, my knight, and Phantasmal could receive invitations to your coronation. That way, no matter who makes a move, you'll have ample security." Holding his skateboard up under his arm, he extended his other hand,

"Would you like to accompany me back to my castle? We would be able to speak about the details in more private quarters there."

Eyes drifting down to his extended hand, I stared at it. Stable, with purpose, he didn't shake or falter. But if that was a good or bad thing, I didn't know. Was he confident because he was trustworthy, or was he overly polished because he wasn't. A day ago, I hadn't questioned Kasper's intentions even once, but now, as I stood there, surrounded by uncertainty and insecurity, something had changed.

But what.

The candles flickered, though again, too fast for me to comprehend the color.

If I took his hand, he'd take me away from Cyrus and Finnegan again, back to his turf and away from mine. Did he want to get me alone? Did he want my brooch? Or was he just also wary of Anton? Heart starting to pick up, this felt different than red. With every uptick of my pulse came a bit more acid in my throat, a heightened awareness of the size of the room and all the air weighing down on me inside it.

Something felt wrong.

Taking a step back, with each breath, my next left me more breathless. Jerking my head around, I looked behind me, a prickling in my back making me feel like I was being watched. Whispers catching in the corners of my ears, I stepped about. I couldn't make out what they said, but I could feel them on my skin, poking and prodding me. Eyes flying up toward the darkened vaulted ceiling, the rafters obscured by shadows, I saw the slightest bit of movement.

"Are you alright?"

Turning back to Kasper, the ringing in my ears like the scream of a bow sliding from its strings on a violin, my breath refused to come to me. Mouth open to reply, though I had no idea what I was going to say, I'd never have to figure it out, because it was then, in that moment, that I heard it above the whispers and ringing.

Cyrus' yell.

Green smoke exploded between us, wiping Kasper from my view.

Pink, blue, red, orange, yellow, clouds of smoke surrounded me, thickening the air. Like chalk, the colors stained as they flew around. Stepping about, sleeve up to my mouth, glasses dusted in a muddle of colors, I couldn't breathe without coughing. Hands met me, yanking me in the haze. Grips rough, their nails dug into my shoulders, my arms and sides. Fighting against the grips, their onslaught was relentless, allowing me no escape no matter which way I pulled. Whispers engulfing me, enveloping one another, overlapping into an inaudible roar, they came from everywhere and nowhere at once as I failed to pull myself away from any of the hands scaling me. Teeth grit in the struggle, weakness threatened to take me but then, with a click, purple snapped in the air, causing the hands to falter. Pulling myself away, I went stumbling, one shoe catching on the other.

Purple.

It was purple.

But

what was purple?

Tumbling to the ground, the stone hard against my shoulder, I couldn't even turn over before someone was on top of me. Obscured by the haze, nothing more than a shadowed form, their pink glowing eyes pierced the veil between us. Cold sweat screaming over me, the adrenaline that ripped my veins numbed me as my eyes were taken captive by theirs. Prey to a predator, they stirred something primal in me, an instinctual dread, something more human than any feeling I had ever met.

Purple was nothing like the others, there was no drip into my blood, no buildup.

All at once, purple was a flood.

Paralyzed, I knew I needed to act, needed to run or fight back, needed to do anything at all, but my body betrayed me. Every attempt to move, to force myself up, I felt purple, like a weight on my limbs, lead in my blood, weighing me down, draining everything from me. Shoe meeting my chest, they shoved me down, forcing the air from my lungs. The flames on the walls turned purple, creating an ambient glowing frame to capture the moment as colors continued to explode all around.

Chest heaving, every intake tainted by the smoke, another figure came into my view, then another, and another, their glowing eyes of various colors surrounding me. Leaning forward, the figure atop me bled through the smoke, a glowing light dangling from their neck matching the rose of their eyes. Increasing their weight on my chest, the smoke cleared enough for me to make out a black strappy platform boot as it dug into me.

"Pathetic," a Long Island zing clipping her words, as she leaned forward, her face broke through the smoke, "you want to be king but look at you, you can't even move."

I had seen her before, but as her fishnet covered arm reach toward my neck, her lengthy fingers crowned with pointed black nails extending, I couldn't remember where. That was, until her black lips parted, twisting up to reveal her fangs.

A vampire.

Her finger hooked over my bowtie.

I needed to move.

She started to pull.

I needed to fight.

Her nail scratched against my skin.

I needed to do something.

A yellow glowing light trapped in a small circular cage dangled between us from a chain around her neck.

But I couldn't.

The silk of my bowtie started to groan under the strain.

She was right.

Piercing eyes like stars in the murky darkened air above, they looked down on me as their numbers increased.

Pathetic.

Eyes closing as she leaned down, her face but inches away from mine, I turned my head to the side when I felt her exhale on my skin. Mouth opening, I could hear it, as her intake turned up with her smile. She was so cold, it radiated, making my hair stand on end as her lips brushed against my neck.

Tense, tears falling from my closed eyes, chest aching, ribs giving beneath her, bowtie moments from being torn from my neck, it didn't matter how far I had come, what I had done, who I had tried to become.

Purple was about to be the death of me.

Footsteps caused her to tense, pausing.

Labored breath suspended in my chest, vision blurry as my eyes opened, all I could see was someone's shoes as they stopped next to my head. Smoke rolling low like clouds on the floor, it barely overcame the toes of their formal boots. Lengthy tips of a cape wafting the smoke as they shifted their weight, something about them stopped everything, even the relentless purple.

"That's enough," they leaned down over me, and that was when relief finally came, for above me stood Finnegan. Dropping to a knee at my side, their lengthy hair spilling like a curtain between us and the chaos, they were all I could see. The green of their eyes radiating, the smoke in the air took on their hue as they searched mine. Bringing up their hand, their cape flared out around them on the stone floor shifted. Hand closing, one dainty finger remained extended as the soft pad of its tip met the between of my eyes.

A moment passed, shared in a silence that brought a still to the panic, as we stared at one another.

The flames around lost their striking purple, fading into a warmer color, and with the next beat of my heart, the room became red.

I loved Finnegan so much.

I didn't know what I'd ever do without them.

The line of their mouth turned up, a brow dropping as their head crooked and suddenly, I was staring up at a stranger. "We wouldn't want him to spoil before we even get a taste, now," increasing the pressure of their finger on my forehead, their voice fell into a whisper, "sleep."

My ears rang out into a deep roar, blood dropping, numbness washed over my entire body, taking my last bit of life with it. So cold it stung somewhere beneath the numb, somewhere deeper, I tried to fight back against the spell.

No.

The fire turned blue.

It can't be.

My eyes wouldn't stay open.

Finnegan, they…

My vision blurred.

Purple.

My eyes closed.

So much purple.

It was then, in that moment, as purple became all I knew, that
I came to realize what it was.

FEAR

A creak brought me back.

Slumped over, the first sensation that met me was a sharp, bitter cold against my face. But as my rattling breath brought life back to my lungs, struggling against the cotton feeling that stuffed up my chest, that same sharp feeling met me all over.

Another creak.

Eyes fighting to open, my limbs heavy, my mind was waking but my body resisted.

I managed to exhale.

Fingers regaining sensation, they twitched as I fought to wake.

Head hung low, leaning against something thin and cold, my when my body finally gave, shaking into life, another creak came with the movement.

A dull one, a groan of metal and wood, it came from above me.

Pulling my head up, my strength broke, dropping it back, but it didn't fall far before it was met with metal. Breath shaking as my eyes dragged themselves open, my vision violently blurred. Nausea striking me, my hand tried to fly to my mouth, but my entire arm was stopped.

Creak.

Pulling my head up, eyes stinging as they closed again, I couldn't hold it up and my forehead came crashing into more metal. Teeth grit, it took my everything to keep my stomach as the blood dropped from my head. Eyes opening again, they fought to focus.

As everything came blurring in, I saw it, the metal.

Encasing my arms and legs in strips, fit to my body, it wrapped around my middle, climbing up over my head, completely trapping me. A human shaped cage, as I lifted my head, looking up, I was met with a chain attaching it to a darkened ceiling. I had seen something like this before, and if I had only listened to Ross when he was going on about it, showing me the page in whatever book he had been reading, maybe I'd be able to remember what it was.

Swaying, it creaked.

Dizziness gripped me as I regained command over my muscles, struggling, but the more I moved, the more I swayed, the more it creaked, the more the metal dug into my skin, the more disoriented I became.

What happened.

How did I get here?

I couldn't remember, not as I dangled several feet above a shadowed, glassy stone floor in a room too dark to see anything else.

Cyrus.

I needed Cyrus.

As my body became my own once more, I stiffened, fingers wrapping around the cage trapping my arms. Pressing my back into the cage surrounding me, I braced myself, despite the stinging of the metal as it bit into me. Taking a deep breath, even though my racing heart burnt the air once it got into my lungs, I had enough left to yell,

"Cyrus!"

Where I had expected to be met with an echo, I was crushed by suffocating insulation.

No one would be able to hear me, no matter how loud I yelled, not even Cyrus.

A laugh turned my blood cold.

It didn't echo either.

"My darling, why are you yelling?" Finnegan's footsteps clicked, marking the moments as they grew closer in the darkness, "Cyrus is right here."

Purple fire exploded around the parameter of the room, searing the air and heating up the metal surrounding me. Hissing as it stung against my skin, it didn't matter, my struggle, there was nowhere for me to go. Eyes barely able to stay open through the pain, they met Finnegan as they stood on the ground below, illuminated in violet, but then, I saw Cyrus.

Head hung low, arms cuffed out, ankles cuffed down, a bracket around his ribs and neck kept his limp body up against a circular, wooden structure standing upright at Finnegan's side. As Finnegan raised their dainty hand up to it, taking it into their grip briefly before spinning it, the click of the wheel Cyrus was bolted to turned into the sound of pages flipping in my ears and when Finnegan's eyes returned to mine, it pulled into focus in my mind, the cover of the book Ross had been reading.

Medieval torture.

Laughing, Finnegan watched as Cyrus' limp head dropped forward and back as his entire body spun on the wheel, "You have really lost your edge, Nox." They grabbed onto the wheel, causing it to stop with a sudden jerk that jolted his limp body.

But then, Cyrus woke.

Throwing his head up, the struggle was instantaneous as his wavy hair fell into his face. A cloth tied around his mouth, gagging him, came into view as it muffled his yells. It was impossible to tell that Cyrus was hundreds of years old, the vinegar to his struggle held such bite,

that was

until his hair shifted out of his face with his next struggle

and he saw

Finnegan.

I had never watched someone die before that moment, not like that.

Paralyzed, chest heaving, teeth clenched over the dark cloth, I could feel Cyrus' heart flatline from all the way in the air.

With a click of their tongue, Finnegan shifted their weight, their elegant cape trailing behind, "Both of you have, really." Yanking down on the wheel again, this time with much more force, Finnegan sent Cyrus spinning. His muffled protests resembled profanity as Finnegan took a few gliding steps away, as if they were at a ball, "One would think that with time would come wits, but," stopping, their back toward both of us, Finnegan reached into their cape. Turning, their cape flailing out like a flash, something shot through the air, catching the purple light for a fraction of a moment before a deep thud of wood met us.

Cyrus fell silent, the clicks of the wheel that filled the air becoming slower.

Eyes screaming over to him, they stopped short, caught on a blade reflecting the ambient purple glow. Vibrating, the dagger grew still as the wheel slowed to a stop, embedded deep in the wood, but inches way from Cyrus' chest. I struggled in the cage, but as every contact with the bars burned me through my clothing, seizing my body, I couldn't even unclench my jaw to yell as my muscles shook with the pain.

The wheel clicked one last time before it stopped, trapping Cyrus upside down.

"Somehow, you two are still as daft as the day you died." Turning to face us fully, Finnegan's eyes began to glow brighter, the green conflicting with the purple as the line of their mouth twisted up, darkening their features, "But that is alright," reaching into their cape again, they pulled their hand out, and between each finger, a small dagger caught the light, "it made you easier to fool."

The green of their eyes became brighter.

Contagious, the same glow took over the wheel around Cyrus and a moment later, it started to spin again. His struggle did nothing, his words muffled, as Finnegan reeled their arm back, blades reflecting the purple light. Like a shot, Finnegan threw another dagger, but this one didn't meet us with a wooden thud, no, but a moist squelch.

Then came the yell.

Black blood blossoming on his shirt around the dagger embedded in his chest as he spun, Cyrus' voice cracked, the metal brackets groaning in his recoil. My body moved before my mind could process the pain of the metal cage burning into me. Unable to get any leverage with my limbs restrained, my muscles trembled as the cage creaked, swaying with my fight. Blood bled down my arms from my hands as the skin burned away, but despite how fruitless my efforts were, I didn't stop.

It didn't matter how hopeless.

Finnegan threw another dagger, hitting Cyrus in the arm.

How much it hurt.

Another caught the light before landing on Cyrus' leg.

I had to get to him, I had to save Cyrus.

Three more daggers met him at once, landing in his chest. Coughing up black blood, it dropped down his fine jawline as he spun.

As my blood dripped from my wrist, as it fell through the air, it changed color, and upon impact with the glass ground beneath me, it splattered purple onto Finnegan's face, cutting off their laugh. Humming, they turned, looking up to me.

"Careful, my love," raising their hand, it took on a green glow and a moment later, my body took on the same glow and locked up, "you are not immortal, nor will you ever be," turning back to Cyrus, they twirled a dagger through their fine fingers like a pen, "because the moment you tame fear, when the final color is won and the circuit is complete, I will be taking that brooch, the powers that live inside," they threw another dagger and it met its mark in Cyrus' stomach, "and the crown along with it."

Body still, unable to will even the smallest muscle to move, Finnegan's green held me a hostage within myself.

Eyes wide, view trembling, glass took them over as I watched Finnegan start toward Cyrus.

This whole time.

From the moment they appeared before me, falling through the sky, their hands on me, their hair splayed out on the bed beneath me, it was all for this? The flickering colors of the brooch reflected in the kaleidoscope of my eyes. All for these stupid powers I didn't want, for a crown I didn't ask for.

I thought.

The way Finnegan made me feel when their bratty smile lit on their face.

The way they bantered with Cyrus.

Their edge.

Their tack.

Their green.

I loved them.

Over and over again, no matter where or when.

Reaching up to the wheel, they grasped it, stopping it and violently throwing Cyrus.

I thought they had loved me too.

Ripping a dagger from Cyrus' abdomen, a slosh of blood followed it, splashing black over their front as Finnegan took a step back. Bitter iron took the air, acidic as it burned my every intake. Tears falling down my face, it was all I could feel as I stared at Cyrus. Blood staining his blonde wavy locks, the glow of his red eyes dimming, I knew he couldn't die.

But.

My tears dropped to the glass floor below.

He could feel it.

It was all he knew.

Pain.

He sobbed, teeth clenched over the cloth gagging

him.

So much pain.

Eyes drifting up to me from the ground as Cyrus

choked on his gasp, Finnegan brought the blade up. Parting

their elegant lips, fangs came into view as they opened their

mouth. Tongue meeting the blade, they licked his blood from

it, slowly, savoring every moment, just as I had come to

know their tongue the night before.

I would have lost my stomach, if I could have.

"What," they lowered the knife, "are you going to just

sit there behind the curtain and watch? Igor needs your help."

Bringing their arm out to the side, they rested the tip of the

dagger against Cyrus' chest. "You saved him before, kept

him from meeting his end in the vampiric courtyard, but now

you take your sweet time? While we both know Cyrus cannot

be mortally wounded," they slowly started to apply pressure to the dagger, "the same is not true for his mind."

Breaking the skin, they shoved the dagger between Cyrus' ribs.

Coughing up more blood, it choked Cyrus.

Heart dropping, eyes unable to rip away from Cyrus as his tears mixed with the blood dripping down his jaw, I couldn't move, I couldn't breathe, I couldn't do anything. As purple clawed at the corners of my vision, I had to fight it. I couldn't give in, now that I knew Finnegan's intentions. Purple could save me, save Cyrus, but if Finnegan took my brooch, there was no telling what they'd do. A carefully set trap, I had walked right into it.

My heart pounded, just once, but it was so hard it felt as if it were trying to rip itself from my chest. With it came a wave, something cold, as it raced through my blood. Separating me from my skin, dizziness took me. A weight pulled down on my eyes, trying to force them closed. As a fuzzy prickling came to life on my skin, I knew I had felt this somewhere before.

Finnegan ripped the dagger out from Cyrus again, making him yell out, his restrained body writhing.

Fighting to keep my eyes open, to stay in my body, I couldn't let him take over. I could feel him, screaming, but an inch beneath the surface. But if I let Nox out, he'd fall into the trap. Cyrus would be okay, he had to be okay, he was always okay. No matter what, no matter when, no matter where, through all the years and every time we met, his smile was always the same.

Stabbing Cyrus again, Finnegan began to laugh.

My body started to shake, despite Finnegan's spell. I could hear Nox, calling to me, beckoning me inward to his endless white abyss. But as my teeth grit, tears dropping from my eyes, I fought him. But it was hard, so hard, because I could see it, the light in Cyrus' eyes about to go out.

My heart thudded again, Nox's fingers tight around it, trying to rip it from its place. Purple began to flicker on the metal cage before me, mingling with the other colors glowing from my brooch. The green trapping me began to falter as I fought against him, trying to keep him contained. As I shifted a bit, barely able to move at all, a clump of my hair fell forward and as it passed through my vision I could see it, the tips of my black hair beginning to turn white.

Stabbing Cyrus again, Finnegan's eyes darted up to me for a moment before returning to Cyrus. Leaning in, they slowly twisted the blade in Cyrus' chest. He would have screamed, if it wasn't for the gag stopping him as his blood bled down the hilt of the dagger, down Finnegan's hand, to drip from the tip of their elbow.

With every beat of my quickening heart, purple bled into my vision, tainting everything around me, the black of my hair fading to white. The green holding me hostage broke, allowing me to move again. Struggling in the cage, the searing metal meeting me, my teeth grit to muffle my yell as

I shook my head, my glasses threatening to fall from my face. Vision blurring as I looked up, teeth grit, hair disheveled in my face, I barely had it, a grip on myself, one slip away from falling within, from waking in that white abyss.

Though I had it, that grip, no matter how small.

But,

when Cyrus looked up to me,

and I saw it, that immortal spark in his eyes

go out,

that did it.

That's when Nox must have heard it,

My wish.

No mater the ramification, I wished to save Cyrus.

Body numbing, the black of my hair in my face bled away as weakness won out, separating me from myself. Eyes about to close, resigning to him, I couldn't fool Nox any longer. Our wishes were one and the same. Body falling limp, I was one blink away from being gone when a door opened, making the air in the room flatline.

The roaring of purple flames came to a halt, the fire around us suspended, frozen. Finnegan's eyes widened on me, stiffness taking them for a moment before they slowly turned around. Cyrus, though his head hung low, body defeated and bleeding, his eyes followed Finnegan's gaze. White fading from my hair, dizziness dispelled, I snapped back into myself with a jolt, as if my body felt like it were plummeting as I fell asleep. Eyes flying up to the door across the room, a click of a footstep split the moment.

"My my, what is all this?" When Twining stepped forward, illuminated by the purple fire that matched the eerie glow of their eyes, everything stopped.

Gaze landing on Finnegan, both of their expressions were telling of a conversation between them, despite no audible words being exchanged. Continuing forward, Twining stopped a couple steps behind Finnegan and a few before me. Shifting their weight as they looked around the room, their cape trailed behind them as they crossed their arms. A small laugh took them as they glanced back at Finnegan. As Finnegan stood there, eyes wider than I had ever seen them, what appeared to be hints of genuine concern painted them, though why was beyond me.

"I see," turning back toward me, Twining looked me up and down, "well of course that isn't working. No matter what you do, he loves you far too much to ever fear you." Bringing up their arm, they pointed back at the door, eyes not leaving mine, "Leave the rest to me, Finnegan, you are dismissed."

"No-" Finnegan's word cut short, their panic extinguished as a purple glowing ring took over the green of their eyes. Locked up, a struggle took them, as if they had been possessed. Hand tight on the dagger they had,

embedded in Cyrus' chest, they were stiff, teeth grit, brow

furrowed as they fought against themself.

Cyrus stared at them, dim red eyes catching the green

and purple of Finnegan's in them, gag keeping him quiet.

Shaking his head, whatever he tried to say was muffled. As if

Finnegan didn't actively have a dagger shoved between his

ribs, Cyrus looked concerned for them.

"I said," turning back toward Finnegan, Twining's

back faced me, "you are dismissed, Finnegan."

The metal clang sliced the air as Finnegan stumbled

back from Cyrus, pulling the dagger from his chest before

dropping it. Hands up to their head, smearing Cyrus' blood

into their silvery hair, the war Finnegan fought was an

invisible mystery to me, but their efforts were obvious until

suddenly, they froze.

A moment passed, one in which I saw glass take over

their eyes. Slowly lowering their hands as they straightened, poised as ever, Finnegan didn't say a thing, face with little expression. Gaze on me, it lingered for a moment before it drifted back to Twining. With a slight bow, they turned. Posture stiff, with every step away their cape swayed, their steps in time with each beat of my heart. As they reached the door, their hand meeting the knob, they turned to look back at me once more and in that moment, I could all but hear it, what their eyes said.

But that's when I looked away, teeth grit.

How dare they appear apologetic, after their betrayal.

As they opened the door, they ripped their eyes away from me, and as they stepped through, I saw it for just a moment, their shoulders tremble.

When the door closed, all was still, stalled, until Twining let out a long sigh, "My apologies," they raised a hand my way, the sharp tips of their lengthy claw-like nails catching in the light, "What even is this, how barbaric."

The cage around me gained a purple hue and a moment and a metal click later, it opened.

Falling, purple flashed before my eyes but I fought it.

Meeting the ground, my legs screamed as splitting pain seared through my bones with the crack. Falling to my knees, in a heap of myself on the glass tiles, my body shook, forehead to the ground. Unable to feel my feet, my gasp between the tears tasted like acid. Broken, both of my legs, they had to have been broken. A laugh took the air. Trembling as I picked my head up from the ground, glasses crooked and cracked, I looked up to Twining through my disheveled hair.

"You have profound power at your disposal and yet," Twining bent over to look at me, brow raising with the upward tug of their smirk, head slowly tilting, "you appear to have no idea how to use them, wholly unable to even fight back." Straightening, they glanced back toward Cyrus, "It must be intentional, but why-"

When they stopped, eyes locked on Cyrus who stared back with the venom of an immortal scorned, I watched something light to life in Twining. It started as a chuckle, but with each one, it cracked into a laugh as Twining started toward Cyrus.

"Oh, I understand now. Creative, resourceful even," stopping right in front of Cyrus, they looked him and his bloodied body over, "though, you know that would have never worked, right?"

The urgency that took Cyrus, it was unlike anything I had ever seen. Struggling with his restraints, he whipped his head around, his words muffled.

"Get away from him," my words tasted bloody as I pulled myself up from the floor, unable to feel my legs as I sat up.

"Do not worry," Twining turned from Cyrus, though stayed standing before him as they looked at me, "I could not care less about him, it is you that I am-"

"Run!" Cyrus' word stopped my world.

Eyes jumping back to him, he had freed himself of his gag, leaving it hanging around his neck. Tears in his eyes, they roared red again despite everything he had endured.

"Don't hold back," coughing up blood, it barely hindered him as Cyrus struggled against his restraints, the metal starting to gain a red glow, "get out, this isn't a part of our-"

Twining hissed through their teeth.

A flash.

That's all it was.

A flash of movement and they had their hand in Cyrus' mouth.

His eyes so wide they could have fallen out as tears budded in the corners, Cyrus' shock as Twining held onto his tongue burned into me. A smirk poisoned Twining's exhale, turning it up as they tightened their grip. Before Cyrus could react to their talon-like nails digging into his tongue, another flash of movement ended the moment.

They yanked their arm back.

Blood splashed across my face, getting into my eyes over my glasses. Hand up to my face to wipe away the blood, it smeared, stinging my eyes as iron took my next breath that would never come to me in completion, because when I heard his yell, it hitched. Flying open, my screaming eyes struggled to focus through the clouding. Blood seeping through his clenched teeth, tears pouring down his face, Cyrus choked. Eyes on mine, I saw the light go out, everything dull within him as he went under, head dropping.

The sound of his blood bellowing to the floor deafened me.

Purple pulsed through me. Purple begged me. But as I sat there, numb, eyes wide, unable to even breathe, I couldn't give in. While horrific, Cyrus would be okay, he had to be okay.

"I am impressed," Twining turned to face me, bloodied hand grasping a mass of muscle. Throwing it to the ground, it bounced, rolling away in a moist heap. Twitching as it came to a stop a few feet away, the moment I realized it was Cyrus' tongue, my hand flew to my mouth to keep my stomach down. Eyes closed, barely able to breathe from under my hand, a moment away from being sick, purple clawed at me.

Denying colors only made it worse, I knew that.

But I had to.

"If that did not scare you," Their voice so much closer to me than I had anticipated. I opened my eyes to see Twining kneeling immediately before me. "What will?"

Trying to pull myself back from them, I couldn't move my legs and my arms shook, making me fall but I caught myself. Laughing a little, they crawled after me like a predator, their purple eyes reflecting the colors of my brooch. My back met a wall. Forcing themselves through my legs, they pinned me up against the wall. Hand meeting my hair, they tightened their grip in it, ripping some out. Hissing through my teeth, eyes locked on theirs, I was trapped, cornered, but I couldn't give in. If I didn't have purple, they couldn't take the brooch from me, not without destroying themselves too.

The fire flickered amber around.

Glancing about, they chuckled, "Ah, are you mad? Well," leaning in, they yanked my head to the side, baring my neck, "let's change that."

Lowering their head, they kissed my neck. Trying to shove them off me, they were too strong and I was too weak as tears fell down the side of my face, teeth clenched so hard they creaked. I felt them laugh, their breath against my neck. Kissing me again, they didn't pull back this time, and a moment later, a screaming pain shot down my spine, freezing my blood. Biting into me harder, they made me yell out as I felt blood trickle down my neck, pooling at my collarbone.

"What do you care about most?"

Twining's voice echoed in my mind as I felt my blood drop. Strength draining from me, my arms slipped down from them, falling to the side. Dizziness taking me, my entire body cold, my head dropped to the side, eyes falling closed as my ears rang.

Images raced behind my eyes, barely asleep, barely awake, as my life flashed before me. Inconsequential, uninspiring, nothing of note, not one thing mattered to me. Day by day, image after image, nothing caught, nothing snagged, nothing stood out, that was, until it all stopped.

"Igor!" Another voice came to life in my mind as it sat, suspended in a haze, "Welcome home!"

An image started to pull into focus, not clear enough to be a dream, but not hazy enough to be a ghost. Messy, fiery orange hair, met my view as someone crashed into me, wrapping their arms around my middle. Not hugging them back, just staring at their head, this was a scene I had found myself unwillingly cast in endless times.

"Ross," my own voice echoed in my mind, devoid of tone, how I used to sound, "please let go."

Squeezing me a little tighter, Ross whined before stepping back from the hug. Smiling up at me with his eyes just like our mother's, his had always been brighter, blue like wildflowers, green like grass.

"Guess what I read today," Ross scrambled to reach for a book that was sitting on the dresser next to the front door as we stood in the entry way of my parents' house. I tried to step around him toward my room, but he stopped me, holding up the book, "look at this," he pointed to a picture printed on the page, some scanned image of a discolored, rotting paper, "they found this in a castle in France, and when they translated it, they realized it was a letter written by a vampire."

Not replying, just staring down at him, that was the only way I knew how to interact with him back then.

Turning the book back around his eyes scanned over the page, "The vampire was writing to another vampire and in the letter they talked about what happens when they drink someone's blood." Flipping the page, his smile never seemed to fade, "They said that they can see into the mind of their victim, rifling through their memories as long as they keep drinking their blood." Looking up to me with so much life, his hair bounced, "Isn't that rad?"

Silence sat between us as he looked between my eyes.

Laughing a little, he closed his book and looked away, "I'm sorry," stepping to the side, though he had calmed a little, his smile remained, "you're probably tired after work."

Stepping around him, I didn't say a thing. Didn't even glance at him, nothing. If I had, maybe I would have seen the way he watched me as I left, the way his smile flattened.

Twining's hum echoed through my mind as the vision started to fade, Ross' image maintaining through the obscurity, *"Ah yes, that's right, your little brother. You did say he was charmed with us."* Biting me harder, Twining brought me back to my body for a moment until I was plunged back into my mind. The vision scrambled, but then rebuilt itself, showing my parents' house from the outside as I walked home from work. *"Oh, what a lovely part of town. I fancy myself a visit, may even bring back a new ward upon my return."*

No.

They pulled their fangs from my neck.

Not Ross.

Standing from me, they looked down upon me.

They couldn't.

Glaring up at them, back against the wall, a heap of myself on the floor, I was unable to move. Vision blurring on them as they brought their sleeve up, before it wiped their mouth, their tongue flicked out, licking up my blood from their lips.

If I had only listened to Cyrus, if I hadn't trusted Finnegan, I wouldn't be here.

Twining started to turn from me, their cape drifting behind them.

Finnegan.

Eyes falling from focus, a deep ache started to come to in my legs.

I had to stop them.

I couldn't will my body to move.

I had to protect Ross.

Weakness winning, my head dropped.

The last thing I saw before everything went black was the tips of my bangs as they turned white.

I didn't have a choice.

Eyes opening, they were met with white, so much white. Looking up, standing in Nox's abyss, I wasn't alone. Standing before me, jaw tight, eyes glassy beneath his fluffy white hair, Nox stared back at me from below a darkly furrowed brow.

I needed to keep the brooch safe, because if I didn't, if it fell into the wrong hands, the world would end.

Nox extended his shaking hand toward me.

But.

If something happened to Ross, my world would end.

Bringing my hand up, I accepted his.

The moment we made contact, purple exploded, a storm so strong it destroyed the abyss, Nox's image before me getting lost to it as his hair whipped around.

I wished to protect Ross, above all else.

As everything disappeared around me, I heard it, Nox's voice for just a moment.

"Your wish, is my command."

In that passing beat, as purple became my everything, I was nothing.

But, in that nothing, I found something.

Mind falling away from me, it landed somewhere else, somewhere long ago and far away.

Sitting in a tree, a leg dangling over the branch, their back up against the trunk, the body I was in stared into a sky so clear and blue, it was unlike one I had ever seen. Their only company that of rustling leaves and distant birds, it was like I was a hostage within another, simply watching as they braided flower crowns.

A stick snapping below caught their attention. Pulling their leg up carefully onto the branch, they perched there, looking down and around. Placing the flower crown on their head, it knocked some of their hair loose, and as the tip passed my vision, I realized it was white.

Nox.

In a heavily forested area, a little wooden cabin sat, nestled in the trees a bit away. The remains of a firepit below, I had seen this place through Nox's eyes before. When some rustling came from below, he looked that way, heart picking up, but that's when it stopped, because that must have been it, the first time he saw them.

Finnegan van Serafino.

When was it?

Wading through tall walls of wildflowers, their hair shorter and flippy, they donned a loose-fitting tunic, cinched at the waist with a green chord that matched their eyes. As ageless as the Finnegan I had come to know, the only difference was the length of their hair as they broke through the line of flowers and stepped toward the firepit. With each step, it bounced against their chest, that necklace they always wore. Even when they wore nothing else, that glowing green orb trapped in an intricate metal cage remained around their neck.

Staring at them, Nox must have been as taken as I was the first time I saw them because it took him far too long to come back to himself. Leaning back behind the trunk of the tree he sat in, he watched as Finnegan circled the fire pit. I could feel it, despite being but a guest in his body, the warmth on his face as he watched Finnegan kneel down and extend their hand over the coals.

Blinking, Nox took a breath as he ran his hand over his face. Jumping from the tree, he fell with grace, landing without a thud. The moment his feet met the ground, flowers bloomed around his shoes. Straightening, he tilted his head a bit, staring at Finnegan's back.

Clearing his throat, it seemed to startle him that Finnegan wasn't startled by it. Slowly turning to look up at him, Finnegan sat in a moment.

"Oh, hello there." Fair skin and pointy ears, a smile took their frail features as they stood.

Taking a step back, Nox's expressions were so telling and exaggerated, I could feel them as he wore his fluster on his sleeve, the flowers around him on the ground all turning red, "Are you lost?"

"No," Turning to face Nox fully, Finnegan folded their arms behind their back, swaying to a beat only they could hear as they looked around, "Legend has it that a mischievous spirit lives out here, protecting the forest." Eyes locking on Nox, their brow raised, "I wanted to meet them."

"Oh yeah?" Nox couldn't breathe, I could feel it as his heart began to race, "And why would you go looking for a thing like that?"

"Well," the way Finnegan's eyes trailed up Nox, tracing his every line, lingering here and there for a moment too long, though this must have been six-hundred years ago, I felt their hungry gaze as if I too were under it, "they say he is quite charming."

Stiff, Nox just stared at them for like seven seconds too long before saying, "I think you are in the wrong forest, this is the Woods of Repentance, where witches are taken to be executed by the village holy man." Turning a bit, Nox ripped his eyes away as red splashed over his face, "You better get out of here before he finds you, you'll burn until there is nothing left."

"No," bending at the middle a bit, their eyes locked on Nox's, "I am exactly where I intended to be." Extending their hand toward Nox, when they smiled, their fangs came into view, their green eyes beginning to glow, "It is truly a pleasure to finally make your acquaintance, Nox."

Was it then, as they laughed at Nox's surprise?

Opening the door to the wooden cabin, Nox stepped in first to see Valor, Abraxas, and Cyrus sitting inside around a small wooden table, a cauldron brewing something exciting between them. Standing, Cyrus and his well-kept hair and clergy collar, looked as if he were about to say something of concern, his brow furrowed and hand extended toward Nox, but then he stopped when Finnegan stepped inside.

I had never watched someone fall in love at first sight before.

Or was it when Cyrus ran up to them to introduce himself, red in the face?

When exactly was it that Finnegan decided to betray us?

Could it have been the long nights they spent together, looking up at the stars and sharing stories about the shapes they made? Or maybe it was when Finnegan found themselves tangled up in bed with Cyrus and Nox every night? Had it been planned since before then? Or was it something that came after. Was it when they became a part of their little family, three witches, priest, and a vampire? Did it come to them through the years they lived like that in that little cabin, hidden from the nearby village? Maybe at some point in the garden Nox kept, or perhaps at one of Cyrus' services, or even as they assisted Valor in potion brewing, or when they would salvage bones with Abraxas?

Or maybe it was later.

Memories continued to flood me, one after another, and though none of them belonged to me, they all had one thing in common.

Finnegan.

Was it as we met, time and time again, one life time after another; falling in love in every one just as we had in the first?

Had they always been out for my powers, just waiting for an incarnation to get close enough to enact their plan?

"Your necklace," Nox's voice met me, pulling another memory into focus, "did you make it too?"

"No," Finnegan's image came to me, sitting by a fire, working on something with their frail fingers atop a small rock slab, "it was a gift from my Master, Twining." Holding up something small and metal, a chain dangling from it, they inspected it in the moonlight, their flippy silvery hair a bit longer, pulled back in a messy bun, "It is called a blithe, something unique to my kind." Lowering the round metal object, they started to place small stones in it with a thin metal tool, "it is the keeper of not only my abilities, but my eternal life as well. Should I ever be mortally harmed while separated from it, or should it be destroyed, that would bring me to my end." Looking up to Nox as he sat next to them in the grass, the brilliant stars above, the fire crackling before them, a bit of their hair fell into their face as they winked at him, "that is a well-guarded vampiric secret, however, so please do keep that to yourself."

Staring at them for a moment, Nox just nodded as he watched them work away.

"Here," Finnegan looked over the object a bit more before extending it to Nox, "this should help."

Accepting the object, the moment it met Nox, the gems in it lit to life with every color of the rainbow. Staring at the brooch that I had come to know, the night around them became painted in the rainbow glow. A chain dangling from it fell through Nox's fingers, catching the moonlight.

Sitting in that moment, Finnegan smiled as they got closer to admire the lights, "Made from the same metal as my blithe, it should help contain and regulate your powers as well." Gently raising their hand, they took the necklace from Nox and when it left his hand, the colors went out, leaving it nothing but dull gems in a metal casing. "Though unlike mine, this is not the source of your powers, they are innate to your kind. So, should you ever be separated from it, the control it grants will be lost, rendering you unstable if you have come to rely on it, and it may even retain a significant portion of your powers, so do take care to not let it fall into the wrong hands." Shifting to kneel before Nox, they tilted their head, the love in their eyes so palpable it made my heart jump seeing it. "Now, close your eyes."

Sitting in the grass, legs up at his either side, hand laced in the grass behind him, Nox rolled his eyes away, a smile finding him as he did as told. When his eyes closed, so did mine. A rustling met his ears and a moment later, a cool chain met the back of his neck. But before he opened his eyes, something so warm met his lips, he melted into the kiss. Pulling Finnegan into him, Nox sat up to wrap both of his arms around them.

Pulling back, holding Finnegan close between his legs, the colorful glow of the brooch between them, Nox kissed them again.

Did they ever love me?

Foreheads resting against one another, Nox opened his eyes, looking down. Able to see both his brooch and Finnegan's blithe, he admired the way the colorful glows mingled together. Taking one of his hands from Finnegan's back, he brought it between them. Palm meeting Finnegan's blithe, it was heavier than he expected. Holding it, he could feel the green light pulse, just a little faster than that of a usual heartbeat. Staring at it, the blithe in his hand, Nox smiled.

Then, he blinked.

Eyes violently blurring open, my gaze was met with purple.

Standing, chest heaving, so out of breath my ears rang and numbness raced over my skin as acid burned up my throat, I was back in my body. Hand before me, it shook, but in its grasp sat a blithe, replacing Finnegan's in my vision. The glow faint, racing haphazardly like a panicked heartbeat, it sat in a cage pendant exactly like Finnegan's, though instead of green, it was purple. Vision struggling to maintain clarity, my eyes drifted beyond my hand, down the chain attached to the pendant and to the neck it looped around.

Gored beyond recognition, Twining knelt before me, the only hint of them their lengthy hair as it sat, stained and disheveled in stringy clumps over their face. Clothing tattered and torn, skin ripped, face swollen, the whites of their rolled-back eyes red with blood, they would have been limp on the ground if I hadn't been holding them up by their necklace.

My surroundings came into screaming clarity.

Standing in the midst of ruin, the glass walls dripped in blood, the air so stale with iron it felt heavy. Slowly looking around, I saw blithes, crushed, all about, their lights out, as they laid near bodies dressed in vampiric garb. Tens, definitely even more, they were motionless, in heaps, crushed against the walls, torn apart.

Cyrus.

Looking around with enough fever to snap my own neck, I froze when I saw him. Limp, still restrained to the wheel, his head hung low, he didn't appear any more injured than he had been before Nox took over. Relief almost met me, as my gaze lowered, but then a dismembered arm caught my eye. Staring at it as the fingers twitched, my eyes widened. Looking down to myself, that's when everything stopped.

No white remained on my clothing, it had been stained black with blood.

Skin covered in it, hair dripping with it, glasses smudged with it, but none of it was mine.

My first breath upon waking trembled on the way in.

A massacre.

A choking laugh made ice shoot through me, causing my eyes to lurch down.

"I underestimated you, Nox." Twining's voice was but breath with shape as their limp head rolled to one side, their eyes barely maintaining focus as they drifted in and out of it, "A delectable final meal."

Teeth gritting as my grip tightened on their blithe, I yanked them up. I didn't want this. Any of this. Not the gore, not the harm, not the blood, none of it. But they made Nox do it, put him in a position that the only way out was a massacre.

Purple had still yet to light on my brooch, the other colors reflecting in the blood dripping from Twining's hairline.

"Oh," Their limp head rolled around more, their neck must have been broken, "I see, you are back, Igor." Their face, though skin ripped and gaping, still managed to smirk. A shot of movement blinded me, so quick that I was yanked down by my bowtie before I could even blink. "I refuse to go down alone."

The fabric groaned, my bowtie about to snap.

Purple shot through me.

Hand meeting theirs on my bowtie, my other yanked up on their blithe. Struggling against them as they pulled me down, I fought to stay on my feet. Arm shaking, purple shot through me again, from my pounding heart into my right hand as it gripped their blithe.

Yanking on it with the power of purple, a metal clink split the moment.

Falling from me, Twining lost their strength, their weight almost taking me down as their hand slid from my bowtie. Pulling my bowtie back, I shoved them to the bloodied floor in front of me. Staring down at them, my chest heaved, body screaming everywhere they touched. Laughing as they laid, a disfigured limp heap at my feet, blood started to gurgle up their throat, turning their breath into a choke. Standing there, vision trembling, blurring in and out, I had to end this.

But how.

Slowly looking to their blithe in my hand, as the faint purple glow dimmed, I stared at it.

What was it that Finnegan had said? That to end a vampire, one would either need to destroy their blithe, or kill them when they were separated from it? That was surprisingly simple, it was no wonder they wanted Nox to keep it a secret.

Grip tightening on the blithe, I had a choice to make.

The line of my mouth turned up.

I closed my hand over the blithe, lowering it.

Eyes drifting to Twining, I took a step toward them.

Their eyes tracked me, the only part of them able to move.

Stopping right next to them, smile growing, I could feel it, purple bleeding into me.

And this time, I had no reason to fight.

Purple exploded around me, bringing shocking light to the room, baring every detail of the atrocity that had come to be by my very hands. The flames roared up the walls, screaming to the ceiling, overtaking the corpses around. I could see it, my purple reflecting in Twining's eyes, outshining their own inherent glow. Raising my shoe, scuffed and covered in dried, cracking blood, I only made eye contact with them for a moment.

But in that moment, I smiled.

Bringing my foot down into their head, I shoved their face into the filth, putting all my weight on it. Just destroying their blithe would be too kind after what they had done. Leaning down, voice lowering as I pressed into them, I could feel it, every color on my brooch heat up, glowing brighter.

"Why," Twining's strained whisper bubbled through the blood pouring from their mouth, "does nothing scare you?"

A chuckle took me as the colorful light of my brooch became blinding, "Retail."

The fleshy resistance, the bend until the give, the squelch, much like stomping in a pumpkin, when my foot met the ground through their skull, the glass cracked. An explosion of light, colors so bright they turned white, shook the castle. As they faded, leaving nothing but a numb buzz to the air, I was left to stare down at what was once Twining's head.

Slowly pulling my foot up, brain matter sliding from the toe of my shoe, I took an unsteady stumbling step backward. Stepping on a body, it crunched beneath my weight. Panting, eyes wide, my ears started to ring.

A chill took my hand as I tripped away from that body and over another. Looking down at my grasp, I was met with Twining's blithe. The color had gone out, leaving nothing more than an empty cage pendant on a broken chain.

The cracking of glass stopped my heart.

Racing beneath my feet, the cracks shot across the floor from Twining's remains, quickly reaching the walls. As they grew, more offshoots arising from every inch the cracks took, purple flashed through me. The creaking of glass surrounding me, growing exponentially louder with every moment, I ran toward Cyrus. Tripping over bodies and dismembered parts, I came tumbling into his chest. Shaking him, he didn't wake, his bloodied clothing crunchy and dry. Hands meeting the metal restraints holding him to the wheel, I struggled with them.

My heart thudded in my chest, with it came screaming adrenaline.

Purple shot from my hand, shattering the cuffs holding Cyrus to the wheel. Falling forward, his deadweight hit me but didn't take me down. The cracks groaned like ice, the vibrations of their journey toward the ceiling met my shoes as I threw Cyrus' arm over my shoulder. Dragging him, he was heavy, or maybe I was weak, but as I started toward the door, we nearly fell with every corpse I had to step over.

Hand meeting the doorframe, I braced myself before I fell. Twining's dulled blithe in my hand against the glass doorframe, the broken chain dangled, chiming against the glass. Shoving against the door with my shoulder, it gave, falling open. As we stumbled through it, my gaze caught on something amongst the carnage. Blue, two glowing eyes, hiding behind a pile of bodies, Nox must have missed a vampire in his rampage.

Dragging Cyrus through the door, we entered a hall. Standing there, staring down it, it was so long and dark, there was no way we'd get out in time. A crack split the air, the entire castle rumbling. Looking behind me, I saw chunks of the castle fall, crashing into heaps of bodies, destroying them further. As another shake took the castle, I turned to look at the wall. If it fell, Cyrus would survive, but I wouldn't. The cycle would start again, the powers would get stronger, and even the world could end.

I had to get out.

Stumbling up to the wall as another quake shook me, my free hand met it, bringing Twining's dead blithe up with it. Shoving it into my pocket, I brought my hand back up to the wall. Trying to breathe as my muscles burned, pushed past the point of exhaustion, shaking more with every movement, I closed my eyes. Feeling the cool glass wall against my palm, I made a wish.

This time when cracking met my ears, it was music.

Shattering from where I touched, the wall eroded away, turning into glittering sand before us. Too dark to see out clearly, the fresh air insinuated that it was the outside, but that was all. Another quake shook the castle, nearly knocking me from my feet, but instead I dragged us, stumbling forward and out through the hole.

Falling.

Why was it always falling?

Arms wrapping around Cyrus in the drop, as we free fell through the open air, I couldn't help but be reminded of how we first met, but this time, I was going to be the one to protect him. Looking to the side as air screamed by my ears, my hair whipping in the wind, I caught a glimpse of the quickly approaching vampiric courtyard below. Purple spiked in me, but as I closed my eyes, I had to fight it. I couldn't be scared yet, I had to save us. Then I could be scared, only once we were safe.

Tensing as my teeth clenched, tightening my grip around Cyrus, I wished for us to land safely.

Green lit to life in my chest, exploding through my veins.

Coming to a jerking halt, slow enough to not kill me, but fast enough for me to think that it had for a moment, we were left, suspended. Eyes opening, they were met with the churning galaxies above as green rolled in the undertones. Slowly looking to the side, my eyes met the ground, just inches below.

Shattering deafened me, breaking my concentration and dropping me to the ground. Cyrus' dead weight above, he knocked the air out of me. The ground rumbled, stones sent bouncing on the bricks next to my head. Pulling myself up onto my side, propped by my arm, I watched as the Vampiric castle caved in on itself, purple flames melting the glass that managed to survive the cracks as large chunks fell off and into the hellish center. Towers toppling, walls crumbling, the roar of shatters stung my ears.

But then, above it all, another sound rang true.

"Igor!"

Breath hitching, eyes wide, that was the last voice I had expected to hear. Picking myself up, I pulled Cyrus along with me as I turned to face them. Standing, back to the collapsing castle, I was met with a handful of vampires as they ran toward me. Bloodied and tattered, there was hardly more than ten. There were a couple I had seen before, the fishnet vampire who attacked me and another I had seen in her company at the vampiric castle. In the back and walking with a limp, I recognized the bule glow of his eyes. He had been Twining's right hand at the ball, he was likely the vampire who survived Nox. What was his name? Maximili-something, I couldn't even remember, but I shouldn't have spared him.

The group parted as someone made their way through.

When my eyes met them, my jaw tightened.

Panting as they looked us over, Finnegan's glassy eyes reflected the fire behind me.

"Igor, I-"

Whatever bullshit they were about to say would forever remain unsaid when I cut them off, my hand shooting forward, snatching their blithe in my fist. Staring at me, soot smudged on their face, their hair messy and hands bearing Cyrus' dried blood as they raised up to mine, their eyes shook as they slowly looked down to my hand.

Frozen, they didn't even breathe as their eyes widened.

Grip tightening on their blithe, I watched alarm splash over the vampires behind them, but none dared move. Staring into the green of the blithe, pulsing in the caged pendant, it was not only their green, but it was the green of staying up late laughing, the green of good news, the green of spontaneity and youth, it was the green that kept your heart beating, the green of what made life worth living. It was excitement, and though I was new to colors, green was easily my favorite.

Hand quivering around the cage, I could feel the pulse steady, not race like Twining's did when faced with the same fate. Slowly looking up to me, the tears budding in Finnegan's eyes broke free, streaming down their face.

Their castle crumbling behind me, their whole word was ending, and for some reason, they looked at me.

Brow dropping, my breath hissed through my clenched teeth as my heart plummeted into the acid of my stomach. How dare they look at me like that. Yanking them forward by their blithe, my head ended up next to theirs, my voice low.

"The moment I take the crown will be the moment yours become numbered. Leave Netherside, take the remaining vampires with you, and never, ever, come back. Because if you do, I will personally execute every last one of you."

Shoving them away, I had a choice, their fate in my grip.

Tighten or loosen it, Finnegan's life hung in the balance.

But as their eyes met mine, the green catching in their tears as their hair flew forward, I knew there wasn't ever a choice, not really.

They betrayed me, but that didn't make me love them any less.

I loosened my grip on their blithe, allowing them to stumble back into the group behind them. Met with open arms, the vampires braced Finnegan, steadying them.

"Banishment?" the vampire with the ridiculous name I couldn't remember said as he stood, arm around Finnegan, blue eyes blazing, "You bluff."

"You think so?"

Lowering my shaking hand as I shifted Cyrus' weight, pulling his arm back over my shoulders more, it found my pocket. Fingers meeting with the metal necklace inside, I pulled it out, closed in my fist. Reeling my arm back, the galaxies above turned amber as I threw it as hard as I could. Hitting Finnegan in the chest, they flinched back, but caught it before it fell. As their wincing eyes opened, they lingered on me for a moment before dropped down to what they had in their hands.

I only watched for a moment before turning my back, but a moment was all it took to see the realization ignite in their emerald eyes.

"No-" I hadn't heard Finnegan's voice crack like that before, had never heard what it sounded like when their composure shattered, their pride thrown to the wind. A struggle behind me, I could hear the scuffing of shoes as they yelled, demanding to be let go, to be allowed in the crumbling castle as it burned, to save Twining.

But as I took my first weakened step away, dragging Cyrus with me, we all knew it was too late for that.

"Igor!" this time as they yelled my name, it was clear to me in the venom of every letter, only one of us still held the other in their heart.

Stopping, I glanced over my shoulder. Being held back by every vampire in the group, Finnegan struggled, their disheveled hair a mess, their eyes roaring green as tears fell from them beneath their darked brows that twisted their sweet face, obscuring its charm. What I saw born within them in that moment as they cursed at their company, trying to rip themselves free, it was the type of color that ruined you, the type of color that if I ever let it get near, would absolutely be the death of me.

As glass threatened to take me, I didn't have anything to say to them.

Vision blurring, my body suddenly became cold. Heartbeat taking over my ears, I didn't hear the things Finnegan yelled at me, but the poison in them was clear as purple clawed at the sides of my vision. I had fought it for too long and had no more strength to fight it any longer. Trying to step away, my shoe caught on Cyrus, my knee giving out on me. As I fell backward, blood dropping from my head, skin becoming numb and fuzzy, my eyes met the sky as it grew dark with the rancid smoke of burning corpses. As my eyes closed, I anticipated the impact with the ground, but it never came.

I just fell further.

As if I had been caught by tens of strings, they softened my fall in the darkness. I had felt this somewhere before, but as I was thrown up again, I couldn't remember where. Stumbling to my feet, my eyes opened as I caught myself from falling. Blinded my blurry light, my ears rang with scattered voices. Swaying, holding Cyrus at my side, my legs started to scream.

Purple took hold with each beat of my heart as I looked up.

Barely able to focus, my eyes caught it for a moment, the sign to Valor's pub, the Cranky Witch. Eyes dropping before me, I was met with the door.

I fought to take a step forward.

With the next beat of my heart, purple grew.

What had I done.

Falling into the door, I shoved it open with my shoulder.

Nox killed them.

Stumbling through the threshold, the bustling conversations flatlined.

Nearly every single vampire.

Barely able to hold my head up, my eyes met a room staring back at me.

Dead.

Kasper, Oliver, and Hugo stood by the bar, Valor right across from them, frozen mid-conversation.

Taking a step forward, dragging Cyrus with me, I watched the moment alarm seized Kasper.

I had killed them.

Falling forward, my legs gave out.

I had…

Crashing into the floor, Cyrus' limp body fell away from me.

Oh god.

I ~~killed~~ someone.

I ~~killed~~ Twining

I

I killed

I

killed

Like an assault, images took over my mind, sensory overwhelming me. The way Cyrus yelled, the smirk Finnegan wore, the sound of the knife sliding into his flesh, the creak creak creak creak creak of the cage, the way the metal seared into me, the give of Twining's head under my shoe, all at once, everything, I finally grasped everything.

Purple exploded, shattering glass, shaking the walls, blowing everyone back away from me. Clinging to Cyrus, I lost myself. Yelling to stay away, to not touch him, to not touch me, as hands met us. Shoving someone away, I sent them crashing across the pub, I didn't even look up to see who. Mind flatlined, purple starting to take hold in my brooch, it clogged my every thought, spiking my pulse, eating away at me. Yelling, that's all I could do, holding Cyrus close, as the potions on the back wall exploded, sending glass and liquid everywhere.

Yanked from him with so much force, I fought like a caged animal, no pride, no dignity, as tears overtook my eyes, but I was overpowered. Purple, there was only purple, so much purple, as I watched Cyrus get pulled from the bit of my vision that was clear. Whipping my head around to whoever held me back, defusing my every attempt to rip myself away, I was met with Hugo.

If I had been able to think in that moment, I would have wondered why he looked so sad.

"Igor," a voice came from in front of me, and though it was concerned, it inspired nothing but more panic in me as I flinched away, fighting with Hugo. "What happened?"

"Sire, you cannot reason with him, he is lost to a panic," another voice came from in front of me but before I could whip my head around to see who it belonged to me, a hand met my eyes, plunging me into darkness.

Ears ringing out, so deep and loud I could hear nothing else, my body went cold, weak, as if I were dropped into the deep ocean. Falling limp back into Hugo, it was instantaneous, going under. As every sensation faded away from me, the last thing I felt was the way Finnegan's lips felt when they met mine for the last time.

And the last thing I saw in my mind's fading eye was the green of theirs.

My favorite color.

n i n e

Other End

Staring down at purple as it sat in the palm of my hand, it was silent, in the abyss of white.

The last color, it was finally mine.

Standing before me, eyes on the ground, Nox didn't say a word. As I glanced up to him through a clump of my bangs and over my glasses, it was easy to understand why. Finnegan didn't only betray Cyrus and I, but Nox too and to save us, he had to do what he had to do.

Like a snap of static, purple stung my hand, demanding my attention. Jumping, I looked back down to the orb, a harsh breath escaping me as the zing faded from my skin. Inspecting it, the orb in my palm like electricity, it stormed within itself.

After a moment longer, I closed it in my hand. Squeezing it, it reminded me of how Twining's blithe felt in my palm. Opening my hand, I was met with a smaller, calmer orb. Slowly bringing it up toward my brooch as it sat, affixed to the bowtie around my neck, it didn't feel real.

The other end.

But moments ago, I was assaulted by amber in my store, knocking out the power and destroying the vending machine.

I was at the ball, enlightened by yellow as I danced Cyrus into the air.

I was falling through the sky, enthralled by the green of Finnegan's eyes.

I was on my knees, shattered by blue as I erased myself, becoming a stranger to all I knew.

I was beside myself, unable to quell the ache of red as I took Cyrus and Finnegan to bed.

I was trapped, paralyzed by purple as the vampires pushed me to my absolute limit.

And now, here I stood on the other end of it all.

It was a place none had stood before, a place no one believed I'd find. Well, except Cyrus. A small smile found me, my eyes closing as purple met with the brooch.

Cyrus always knew.

As purple joined the others, completing the circuit of colors, I felt it shriek through my veins with a thud of my heart. Eyes opening, they struggled under the weight of the feeling. Surrounded by purple, the abyss was set unease. A harsh breath escaping me, the feeling began to drain, dulling into the backdrop with the other colors in my brooch.

Straightening as I looked around, I found myself waiting for something to happen.

But nothing did.

Anticlimactic, I had expected some sort of fanfare, I suppose.

Smiling a bit as I shrugged it off, maybe anticlimactic was okay after the time I'd had.

Shifting my weight, my eyes drifted back to Nox.

A deep breath took him as he looked back to me, eyes taking in all of me, from my shoes up. Eyes landing on mine, he only was able to maintain the contact for a moment before he looked away. As silence sat between us, the unsaid screamed. We both knew what he had done to the vampires, but it appeared that neither of us were ready to talk about it.

Not that there was much to be said.

"Thank you."

Humming in question as I studied him, he looked as if he were more alive than the first time we met, warmth to the undertones of his skin, a clarity to his eyes that wasn't there before.

Nox brought his hand up to the back of his head, eyes still averted, "Incarnation after incarnation, all my powers have wanted to do is die. But somehow," he looked up to me through clumps of his fluffy hair, "you convinced them to live."

Bringing my hand up to the brooch, my fingertips lingered a moment before making contact, "Convinced is too kind a word."

Chuckling, Nox lowered his hand, and though it was small, a smile did remain on his face. About to say something else, he jumped, looking up into the abyss. Before I could ask him what was wrong, his eyes jumped down to me, the faintest echo of something meeting my ears.

"Cyrus needs you."

When I blinked, Nox was gone, surrounded by black, but then, when my eyes opened, they were met with the familiar blur of the stone castle ceiling. Ears ringing back in, when they gathered themselves, the first thing they heard was Cyrus yelling my name.

Flying up from the bed I laid in, purple took the candles lining the walls as I looked around. Staring back at me, sitting up in bed at my side, glass in his beautiful crimson eyes, Cyrus was a mess. He must have just woken from a nightmare. Panic cracking into tears, his brow dropped with the line of his mouth as he crashed into me. Sitting there, staring forward, trapped in his embrace, I didn't know what to do as Cyrus absolutely shattered. Bringing up my arms around him, I could feel every shake of his sobs as he buried his head in my shoulder. Heart snagging as I rested my head against his, the flames around turned blue.

"It's okay," I brought my hand up to the back of his head, "we're safe."

Holding me tighter than ever before, I could feel every erratic breath, every muscle in his hands as they clutched at my shirt. Covered in dried, cracking blood, clothing ripped and tattered, holes where he had been stabbed, his blonde hair was stained darker in patches where his blood had splattered. The door to our room flew open, and though they were a bit blurry in my vision without my glasses, I could tell who it was.

As they stood in the threshold, Kasper, Oliver, Hugo, and Valor didn't say a thing.

"Where are they?" When Cyrus' sobs turned into words, it took me a moment to decipher them so in my brief hesitation, he said, "Finnegan."

Candles flickering orange for but a moment before returning to blue. I held him a little tighter, "If they know what's best for them, no longer in Netherside."

His breath hitched, leaning back from our embrace, "What?"

Not looking away from him and the way the rainbow glow of my brooch reflected in the tears in his eyes, I did everything I could to keep my voice steady, "What they did is unforgivable," the others slowly entered the room in my blurry vision behind him, "Once I become king, I will make it official, that no vampire is welcome in Netherside."

Eyes widening, though I had watched Cyrus face ultimate betrayal, endure torture, I hadn't seen such despair on him before that moment.

"Not that there are many left," Kasper's voice was soft, but it still made Cyrus jump as he turned around to see the others.

"It's all the realms can talk about," Hugo leaned up against the wall behind Kasper, "they're calling it the Great Vampiric Massacre."

I felt it when Cyrus stopped breathing, "Massacre?"

Slowly letting go of him, I stood from the bed, leaving him there to stare up at me as I turned away. Taking my glasses from the side table, I slid them into place on my face. Though they were bent out of shape, somehow the cracked lens had been repaired.

"It wasn't you though, was it?" Valor's voice was unusually tame as I heard the click of her shoes start to approach, "It must have been Nox."

I didn't say a thing.

I didn't remember much of what happened. I shook Nox's hand and the next thing I knew, I was holding Twining's bloodied blithe in the company of corpses. Where I went, what I did, what I saw, while Nox was in control, I no longer knew. Staring at the opposite wall, I had a choice to make, one that would define me.

"Igor," the bed creaked as Cyrus stood, "what happened?"

His footsteps started toward me, but a couple later, stopped short.

Remaining quiet, my eyes drifted down.

"It appears that whomever is responsible for the massacre knew how to kill a vampire, not knowledge commonly held," Oliver's voice chilled the room as he approached, his steps on a mission, without falter as they led him right up next to me, "they are still recovering the corpses, but, one of note was found," Inspecting me, I didn't look at him and his braided, screaming orange hair as it fell over his shoulder. It reminded me of Ross. Kneeling, he brought his hand up to my leg, "that of Twining, the Elected Representative of the Vampiric Order."

I heard Cyrus' sharp intake.

Stepping away from him and his touch that burned through my pant leg, I wasn't sure if it was because it was hot or cold. Staring up at me, his unusually controlled face was absent of expression before he straightened, folding his arms behind him. Glancing away, the haunting blue of his eyes left a trail behind them.

"When you found your way back to us, you were both horrifically wounded. While Cyrus healed with time, Valor and I did our best with your mortal body. Your legs were of particular concern to me, I have not any idea how it was that you walked through that door with your femurs snapped in such a way." Glancing back my way, his eyes caught mine, then drifted down to my neck, "How are you feeling? I am more than happy to tend to any pain."

"Igor, please," Cyrus took another step toward me but still didn't meet me, "you have to tell me what happened."

Turning to face everyone, Hugo as he looked at the floor, leaning against the wall behind Kasper, arms crossed over his chest, Valor as her piercing eyes did not leave me, unblinking, Kasper as he stood, hands up to his hair, brow furrowed as something must have dawned on him, Oliver as he averted his eyes, jaw tight, and Cyrus as he stood but two steps away from me, one hand extended my way, I stood in that moment for a moment longer.

"It was exactly as Finnegan had said," Bringing my hand up, it fell short of meeting my brooch, "the vampires waited until I had one last color to unlock to kidnap us and try to force me into it so that the moment I completed the circuit, they could remove the brooch, take my powers, and the crown." As I watched Cyrus' eyes fall to my brooch, I saw the moment purple met them, "After Finnegan failed to scare me by torturing you, Twining took over and after you lost consciousness, they-"

I stopped, eyes widening, the candles around turned purple as my hand flew to the side of my neck. As a realization dawned on me, my heart hit the floor, but then Valor spoke before I could.

"You weren't turned," eyes finding her as she went on, she just looked away, "I saw the bite, but vampires bite people all the time without turning them, so don't worry, they didn't turn you. You still have a heartbeat."

Heart starting to steady, hand sliding down from my neck, I was able to breathe again. As my hand fell from my neck, I could feel it, two small scars, slightly raised, at the base.

A shaking breath escaped me as the candles faded back to their normal flames around.

"They threatened to hurt my little brother, put you through so much agony, they weren't going to let us go, they were going to kill me. Traitors, all of them, so yes," I lowered my hand. As I looked down to it, the weight of Finnegan's blithe resurrecting upon my skin, I made my decision, "with the power of purple, I killed every vampire there, and with the power of the crown, I will see to it that the ones I spared will never be welcomed back."

When the air hit the floor, the candles flickered a color, but it was too quick for me to catch.

Hand raising to his mouth, Cyrus stood, frozen. The way he looked at me, it wasn't fear that I saw in his glassy eyes. I didn't know what it was, but it felt as if weren't for his hand over his mouth, he would have said something.

I'd always wonder what it would have been.

"What," I turned from him and started toward the bathroom across the room, "are you disappointed I didn't kill Finnegan, too?" Stopping at the bathroom door, I stared forward at it, "I did consider it. But," hand meeting the doorknob, I closed my eyes, "I couldn't bring myself to it. Perhaps somewhere in me doesn't want to believe it, that they could make me feel the way they do and betray us like that, no matter how true." Opening the door, I stepped inside, "Though, if I ever see them again, if they ever come near you or this place, that'll be it, that will be their end."

Closing the door behind me, my vision of the bathroom didn't stay clear for very long. Hands finding my face, they pushed my glasses up as my intake shook. Back against the door, I slid down it until I was left sitting on the floor. One hand slid over my mouth to keep myself quiet, it probably didn't matter, though, because I'm sure the candles in the other room all turned blue.

This was to be my kingly legacy, who I had to be.

The position to which Finnegan had sentenced me.

Standing behind the curtain, eyes low, the suit Anton had me wear felt stiff. I could hear them, the footsteps of the many who wanted to bear witness to my coronation as they filled in the ballroom before the throne. Stepping up to the curtain, the loafers on my feet had yet to be broken in, the leather creaking with my weight. Hand meeting the luxurious velvet of the curtain, I pulled it back, just a bit. Peeking out, my breath hitched at the sheer number of beings as they took their seats, an endless line of others still entering through the door atop the stairs. The orbs above glowed a soft white, floating in the air, illuminating the space with the help of the candles lining the walls. Watching as someone of note was announced when they entered, it reminded me of when I first stepped foot in this ballroom, when my presence in Netherside was announced. It wasn't that long ago, but so much had changed.

Eyes drifting down to the front row, they found Kasper as he sat between Oliver and Hugo. Looking down, my eyes drifted over Valor, Abraxas, Salem, and the rest of Phantasmal as they made up the remainder of the row. Talking amongst themselves, something about it felt off. Maybe it was Kasper. He wasn't smiling.

Eyes drifting to Hugo as he leaned over to hear something Salem had to say, out of place in his letterman jacket in such a formal setting, he also appeared subdued, troubled. Perhaps they were worried, perhaps I should have been too. But as my eyes met Anton's back as he stood next to the throne, talking with some of the castle staff, I wasn't. If what everyone had been telling me was true, I was the most powerful being in the realms now, despite not feeling like it. And if Anton lacked the wherewithal to not mess with me, even after what I had done to the vampires, then he too would meet a similar fate. Whether it was by my hand or Kasper's blade, Anton wasn't going to get away with anything today. He had hurt Nox once, never again.

Eyes falling away from him, they were met with a singular empty seat at the middle end of the front row.

Staring at it, I may have stood there forever, but then a hand met my shoulder from behind. Jumping, the orbs above turned purple, silencing the entire ballroom as I flew around. Standing there, hands up and eyes wide, Cyrus stared back at me.

A slight smile cracking onto his tired face, his voice was soft, "Sorry."

A harsh breath took me as I turned to fully face him, the orbs turning white once again. Conversation resumed behind the curtain as I dropped it, cutting us off from the rest of the kingdom. Cleaned up, the only evidence of the day before in the form of a new set of scars to his body, it was hard to tell that Cyrus had been tortured to unconsciousness just hours ago. Though I could see it in his eyes, the immortal sparkle they usually held was dulled. In a stiff suit that looked silly on him, it was the same he had been wearing when I saw him the first time, through a curtain of dust, as he sat beath me in the open casket.

My zombie.

The ringing of a bell flitted through my ears, the graveyard shift that started it all.

"Look at you," he shifted his weight, smile meeting the other end of his mouth, "I knew you could do it."

Admiring the way the glow from my brooch painted him in a rainbow, I looked away before I stared too long. "It doesn't feel real."

"Yeah," he stepped up to me, raising his hands, "though this was always the plan, it's really something now that it's time." Fingers meeting my bowtie, he adjusted it with great care, "Igor, promise me that no matter what happens today, you'll remember that I love you."

Brow crooking as I leaned back a bit, I looked between his eyes, "Is that supposed to be ominous?"

Eyes jumping to mine, he stared at me for a moment before laughing, "No, I'm sorry." Slowly letting go of the bowtie, it was like he wanted to savor the feeling, "I'm just nervous. We've never gotten this far, it's uncharted waters. And until that crown is on your head, you're still mortal and something could happen to you." Hand meeting the side of my face, I could feel it, deep in his muscles, a tremble, "I can't let anything happen to you."

Leaning into his hand, his movie star persona failing him before my eyes, I could just smile at him. A brat, a bit too much bite, and too blonde for his own good, Cyrus Glory was my everything. Bringing my hand up to his as he held me, I stepped in a bit closer. Eyes drifting around to make sure we were alone, they returned to his.

"Take me."

Eyes wide, smile frozen on his face, Cyrus stared at me, until his smile flattened with the roll of his eyes and he decided to play along, "What?"

Chuckling, I stepped in a bit closer, bringing our chests together, "I need you to take me."

Lowering his arms, he wrapped them around me, unable to keep the annoyed act going as the line of his mouth cracked up a bit, "Like, right here, right now?"

"Yes," I rested my forehead up against his, "it's dark, so they won't notice."

Moving in a little closer, he stopped, but an inch from our lips meeting, "Are you sure?"

Eyes closed, I tightened my grip on him, "What, are you trying to change my mind?"

Snorting a bit, his exhale turned up, "You're ridiculous," closing the space, he kissed me, though it was different than the other times. Softer, sweeter, it slowed the racing of my heart as he pulled back, "I love you."

Resting my head on his shoulder in the embrace, I wished that I could have somehow gotten closer to him, despite being as close as two people could physically be, short of one thing, I suppose. "I love you too."

"I always have," he brought his hand up to the back of my head, "and I always will, no matter what, when, or where, in this life and every other, since time immemorial."

This felt like a goodbye.

Pulling back from the hug, my eyes searched his. Opening my mouth, I was going to ask something, though I wasn't even sure quite what myself when Anton's booming voice cut me off.

"Netherside, we are gathered here today for a historic moment. Today is the day that Nox will finally take his rightful place as your king."

Staring at Cyrus as he stared back at me, tears threatening to take his eyes as he smiled, cheers exploded from the other side of the curtain. Bringing his hands up to my shoulders, he turned me around and I was too weak to fight. Leading me toward the curtain, he leaned in behind me, head next to my ear as he lowered his voice.

"I'm so proud of you," stopping right by the curtain, his grip tightened, "now, let's bring this incarnation cycle to an end, finally grant Nox's wish, together."

As he pushed me through the curtain, stumbling forward, I realized something.

Though it had been mentioned a number of times, now that I thought about it, I didn't actually know Nox's wish.

Frozen, I stared forward as an entire ballroom of beings stared back at me.

Cheers roared, shaking the room, surrounding me as the light orbs above grew brighter. One shot a beam down, trapping me in its spotlight as I straightened, gathering myself after my stumble. Glancing back to the curtain as it fell closed, Cyrus was gone.

Anton's rough hand met my back, causing me to jump. Looking up to him as he stood at my side, decorated in royal drapery, crown missing from above his head, his wrinkles smiled with him. I wondered if he smiled like that when he hanged Nox. The cheers calming, the electricity in the air didn't as Anton led me a few steps forward, stopping before the throne. On the tail end of clapping, Kasper nodded at me from the front row, Oliver's sword hanging at his side between their chairs.

"It feels like it was but yesterday that I met Nox, nothing more than an abandoned babe at my Church's orphanage Flipside some six-hundred years ago. And somehow, I knew," Anton lifted his hand, smiling down at me, glass taking his darkened eyes, "I just knew when I held him in my arms that there was something special about him, even then. And now," gesturing to my brooch, he stepped to the side, "after fighting for centuries, he has returned to us, having conquered his profoundly powerful disposition, the savior of Netherside for endless time to come."

As cheers exploded again, I found myself taken in the moment. The other end, I had made it out, I just needed the crown and it would all be over. Though, as my eyes drifted to Anton, it struck me odd, what he was saying. A weirdly fond sentiment for him to hold, all things considered.

"He has done what no other incarnation before has been capable, more than earned his place at this throne, allow me to formally introduce you to your new king, the forty-ninth incarnation of Nox: Igor."

When the applause roared, it was so loud it drowned everything else out. Looking around, I couldn't help but wonder what my coworkers would have thought, if they could have seen me now. Seen the smile I couldn't fight, the red I'm sure dusted my face as my eyes dropped to the platform before me. The orbs above turned yellow, bringing a warmth to the ceremony. Eyes drifting to the side, they caught on the metal of the throne, and in it, I saw a reflection. Though it was where mine was supposed to be, it wasn't of me, but of Nox. Smiling at me, he looked out to the crowd too. There was a reason I was able to succeed where the others had failed. I wasn't doing it alone.

Looking forward again, my eyes caught on movement in my peripheral. Stepping through the curtain, crown in his hands, was Cyrus. Walking toward me across the platform, before the throne and every witness, he smiled at me. Stepping to turn toward him, I was briefly distracted by Anton stepping back. Taking himself out of the spotlight, a few strides away at the side of the throne, I wondered when he'd try to make a move. Cordial, jovial even, he was too nice, too excited to lose his seat of power. He had to be planning something, Kasper wouldn't be worried for nothing. And if the rumor was true and he really did hang Nox, what would stop him from trying again?

When Cyrus stopped before me, he earned my eyes.

Standing there on a platform above a room of onlookers, in our best suits, this was reminiscent of another ceremony. The lights above slid from yellow into red as my pulse spiked. Taking him in, the implication of immortality met me.

Forever.

Savoring every beat of my heart, I knew this was the last time I'd ever feel it race.

Though this felt like an ending, as light bled in through the stained-glass windows, painting Cyrus in colors, bits of dust catching in the streaks between us like stars in the moment, I knew it was also a beginning.

Stepping right up to me, his eyes searched mine before glass took them.

Voice barely above a whisper, it cracked, "Are you ready?"

Taking one last moment to feel my heartbeat in my chest against my ribs, I nodded.

As he raised the crown up above us, it left my vision because all I was interested in looking at was Cyrus and the way the glow from my brooch illuminated him in my every feeling.

I think, as I tried to fight the glass that threatened to take my eyes, that while no one had ever told me Nox's wish, I knew.

It was my wish, too.

The only thing that made this all make sense, the piece to the puzzle that made the greater picture complete.

It was his dying wish, and it was about to come true.

Closing my eyes, I could feel Cyrus about to lower the crown atop my head.

But then, as my last look at him burned into my eyelids, the last thing I'd see as a mortal, he stopped.

I heard it, the way his exhale turned up.

When my eyes opened, my heart flatlined.

Why was he smirking like that?

Pulling the crown back from my head, he dropped it upon his own. Landing there, it sat, crooked. Before I could even react, his hand shot forward, latching onto my bowtie.

The air hit the ground.

Panic broke out in the crowd.

Kasper stood.

My hands flew up to Cyrus', struggling against him as he tried to pull the brooch from my bowtie. Barely able to fight him, my strength drained from me. Eyes wide, brain taken by static, I was ready to end anyone in this room who so much as looked at me funny, anyone but him.

I heard Kasper's sword unsheathe, the zing of metal splitting the air.

Thunder roared, rattling the ballroom over the hum of panic.

Electricity made my hair stand on end.

Eyes screaming red, his smirk warping the charming features of his face, Cyrus' touch burned mine as his fingers dug in behind the brooch. Kasper's sword slashed up through my vision, raising into the air. Glowing electric blue, snapping with his power, its light overtook that of my brooch.

As the sword dropped above Cyrus, I didn't have the breath to tell Kasper to stop.

The brooch ripped from my bowtie.

An explosion of air blasted from it, colors riding the wave as it threw everyone and everything away from us. As white overtook my word, everything went numb, everything except the feeling of Cyrus' hand beneath mine, struggling to rip my brooch away.

"Get off of me!" A child's voice, one I had never heard before but somehow knew better than my own, echoed out in the recesses of my mind, pulling an image into focus.

"No," Cyrus' voice cracked as he held onto someone, purple raging around them.

Doubled over on the ground, face pressed into the floor, hands up to the brooch as it sat, pinned to his shirt, I saw him, the forty-eighth incarnation of Nox, my immediate predecessor. Cyrus fighting to hold onto him, waves of purple trying to keep them apart, Valor, Abraxas, and Anton all stood back near the walls of the castle ballroom, frozen.

"Please!" tears streaming down his face, forty-eight shoved Cyrus away, trying to yank the brooch off, "I can't do this anymore!"

"You have to!" Cyrus, forced his way through purple, hand fighting to meet the child's back.

"Cyrus," as the child's eyes opened, a kaleidoscope of colors fighting in his irises, his voice warped, and as his next words bellowed into my mind, the voice I heard was not that of the child, but of Nox himself, "I wish to die."

Cyrus stopped fighting.

Forty-eight ripped the brooch off and a moment later, everything went into screaming white.

The image shattered as sensation came racing back to me, his yells echoing into feedback in my ears.

But then, as the white abyss came into focus around me, as Cyrus stepped back from me, brooch in grip, as my hand slowly lowered from my bowtie, as my expression fell flat, everything came to a numb,

screaming

halt.

Eyes wide for only a moment longer, they lost their

animation.

Nothing.

Absolutely nothing.

No orange, no yellow, no green, no blue, no red, and not

even purple.

Gone.

They were gone.

Cyrus had taken them.

The abyss snapped cold.

"Traitor." Nox appeared behind Cyrus with a blink of my eye, and a moment later, wrapped his arm around Cyrus' neck.

Unfazed, Cyrus didn't even struggle, "Traitor?" with a flash of red, Nox was sent flying back. Coming to a violent tumbling roll on the ground, Nox didn't get up. With a scoff, Cyrus glanced back at him, "I'm just granting your wish." Turning back to me, he brought the brooch up to the knot of his tie. But then, he paused, not pinning it in place as he eyed me up, "What? Isn't this what you wanted too? Remember," stepping up to me, he closed the space, "what was it that you had said," he inspected the brooch and my stolen colors as their light flickered, unstable, "oh right, that you'd gladly return the brooch." Stepping around me, he maneuvered the brooch around between his fingers like a coin, "As much as I would have loved to take it from you then, it had to be complete otherwise it would have been of no use. I had to wait and hope you could do it, tame the powers, contain them, so that when the time came," Stopping in front of me, he looked over the brooch my way, "I could steal them."

Empty, his words did nothing but echo through me.

Cyrus was a traitor? It had been his plan all along, to help me tame Nox's powers so he could take them for himself? Everything, every moment, was a façade, fake, a means to this end? Though those things should have mattered, should have stirred up something, anything, within me, they didn't. Even the nagging in the back of my mind that I knew he had said something incorrect, I just couldn't remember what, was nothing in that moment. As if he had reached his hand into my chest, taken hold of everything I had become and ripped it clean out, there was nothing left, not even a flicker of feeling. As my eyes drifted back to Nox as he laid on the ground, unmoving, I didn't care.

I couldn't care.

This was what happened when I cared.

People got hurt.

About to pin the brooch to his tie, Cyrus' red eyes looked dim to me now as they locked on mine, the entire world desaturated, even the colors of my brooch lost their vibrance.

When the brooch met the fabric of the knot, the abyss turned red. A gust of air trying to knock me from my feet, I stumbled back, but didn't really fight much to stay standing. Barely able to even feel my body, mostly limp, I would have fallen if not for something stopping me from behind.

Yelling, it was warped as Cyrus was taken to his knees. Ground shaking with his impact, he looked as if he were about to be crushed by something I couldn't see. A violent tremble took him, his head pressed into the floor, tears taking him as he gasped for air, barely able to keep himself from screaming.

Ripping him apart, it was obvious.

My powers, they were going to destroy him.

But, as they crushed him, as they beat at and slashed him, trying to take him apart, trying to do to him what they had threatened to do to me, it was then that it dawned on me.

They couldn't.

He was immortal, even if they destroyed him, he'd regenerate, over and over, for all eternity.

And though the realization should have moved me, should have mattered at all, it didn't.

Wind whipping around, blowing his hair as colors sparked in the air, Cyrus was the center of gravity in the abyss. Eyes jumping to mine, colors swam in them, a rainbow in his irises as a smile tore across his face. Picking himself up, it was a fight, but a fight he won. When he took a step, colors raced from the communion of his shoe with the ground, bleeding like watercolor as they muddled with each other. A laugh taking him, it started small but grew, echoing through the abyss as he turned to face Nox.

Flashes of stinging light blinded me, like a barrage of paparazzi cameras, they came from every direction. Before the bleaching faded from my eyes, I heard a yell, though it didn't belong to Cyrus. Blinking, hand up to my eyes, my vision started to clear. A huddle of a struggle, Cyrus was barely visible beneath the swarm of incarnations. Others appearing near me, the younger ones ran my way. Taking a step back, I ran into it again, whatever was behind me. Slowly turning, my eyes met him, forty-eight, as he hid, peaking out around me.

Throwing one off him, another incarnation pounced on Cyrus, all of them grasping for the brooch. Nox started to pick himself up from the ground in the backdrop, his tremble obvious to me even from the distance. Surrounding me, arms up, the younger incarnations faced Cyrus, each one with their own brooch, a color or two to their names, only capable of feeling so much. But it was something, it was enough.

More than me.

Bringing my hand up to my bowtie, my fingers met the place my brooch once was.

I needed to do something, right? I needed to fight with them, I needed to stop Cyrus, I needed to take back the brooch, I needed to save the day.

But why?

Why did it matter anyway?

A flash of red light blinded me.

Another yell came from the huddle, but as it grew in intensity, cracking, one of the incarnations went stumbling away. Hand up to his chest, a red mark spread over him, eating him away. Falling to his knees, before he met fully with the ground, he eroded, turning to ash and disappearing before my eyes.

Through the opening in the swarm, I saw it, the way Cyrus smiled, hand glowing red before him. Shoving others away, his red infected every one, sending them, yelling as they fell to the ground, turning to ash before they could.

Red.

I watched as he took out another incarnation.

Why was it red?

He destroyed another.

This wasn't an act of love.

He defeated the last one.

It couldn't be.

Tension ran through the incarnations around me, but they didn't budge, standing their ground. Pulling himself to his feet, Nox swayed, hand to his head as Cyrus turned to face me. Staring toward me, Cyrus' steps were slow, labored, though he definitely tried to hide it, he was obviously weighed down, barely able to move beneath my colors.

When Nox's eyes raised, they met mine, and in that moment, I witnessed hell light to life in them. Running toward Cyrus, the floor turned orange beneath Nox's shoes with every step.

Stopping, Cyrus raised a brow, "Oh, you finally decided to get up," raising his arm at his side, he didn't even turn around. The ground began to rumble, alerting the children around me but I wasn't fazed. Breaking from the floor, it grew with the rustling of leaves and creaking of wood, a tree, right in Nox's path. As he ran by it, a branch shot up behind him, something dangling from it. Catching him around his neck, it yanked him up into the air, feet barely on the floor. The tree finished growing, looming above as Nox struggled, hands up to the noose around his neck.

"Nostalgic, isn't it?" Turning to face Nox, Cyrus shifted his weight, looking up to him, "only one way to kill a witch."

Running from me, the children swarmed Cyrus. Ten, eleven, twelve years old, they didn't even hesitate. With a laugh, Cyrus swiped his arm over them, staining them all in red in one swoop and before it had even come to the other side of the swing, the children turned to dust. Watching through the clouds of red glitter as they fell between us to the ground, my eyes met Cyrus' as their glow reflected off the particles in the air.

Forty-eight grasped onto the back of my shirt.

"Igor," Nox's voice strained through his struggle, his pained eyes barely open. He looked as if he were about to yell at me for help, to try to call me into action, but I think that was the first time he had gotten a good look at me, because he stopped when his eyes met mine.

He must have seen it, how empty they were.

"Don't you worry," Cyrus started toward the tree, a leisure to his step, as he shook out his hand, "I'll take care of him next." Stopping at the tree, my stolen colors whirling around him, he didn't turn to look at me, "and the kid, too."

"Why are you doing this?" Nox could barely speak, not enough of his weight off the ground to kill him, but enough to pull the rope tight around his neck as he clawed at it.

"Why?" Cyrus laughed, bringing his hand up to the tree, "You begged me to kill you the last time, don't you remember? You begged and begged and begged, saying you couldn't do it anymore. No matter how hard I worked, how many times I found you, how many loves we shared, it was never enough for you, no, all you want to do is die. So fine," his hand met the tree, causing it to grow, "die."

As the tree shot up, it dragged Nox's feet from the ground.

"I've held you as you died, forty-eight times in my arms. I've promised to find you, to save you, to do anything for you, even though you did this to me, even though you knew," voice raising, it cracked as he stepped back from the tree, "I was the one who wanted to die, not you!"

Choking, Nox fought with the rope but no matter what color flashed through the abyss, raving around us, they all failed him.

Laugh breaking into a sob, Cyrus swayed before falling to his knees before Nox.

Shoved forward, I looked back to see forty-eight, without expression, staring up at me. The emptiness in his eyes a reflection of mine, his grip tightened on my shirt. Nox was dying, I could feel it, the abyss starting to shake, a rumble deep in the ground. But what was I to do?

It wasn't like it would matter. It didn't matter how many colors I met, what I gave away, I ended up right where I started: nothing. We would die in this abyss, finally granting Nox's wish. The cycle would end, Cyrus would become king, and Netherside would go on without us, perhaps even better off.

No one would miss me, no one would even care. I no longer existed outside of Netherside, and the two people here

I thought loved me, in the end, were using me. Nothing to fight for, nothing to save, no reason to move. Forty-eight understood that, Nox knew it, everyone had been saying it from the moment I met Cyrus; I was a lost cause. The only person who said otherwise, the light that inspired me to fight for mine, knew he was going to kill me the moment he met me. Every step of the way, it fell into place, the dots retroactively connecting in my mind. The Three's threats, Valor's concerns, Twining's observation about my ineptitude, how it seemed intentional how unequipped I was to use my powers, it all made sense.

There wasn't a single person who cared about me.

I wasn't worthy of it, apparently.

The abyss flashed a color, so quickly I couldn't tell what it was, but it made the air grow cold.

Nox's eyes opened, meeting me as his struggle started to weaken.

I saw it, a moment of realization flash over his fading features.

"Maddox," Nox's voice was barely audible, but when he uttered that name, forty-eight tensed behind me. Loosening one of his hands from the rope around his neck, Cyrus crumbling beneath him, he extended it toward me. Without any air left to speak, all he could do was mouth the words, "save him."

A flash of red from his hand, it shot by me, crashing behind us, shaking the ground.

Looking up, tears in his angry eyes, Cyrus turned to me, his features illuminated by red. Glancing behind me and past Maddox, I was met with a red, glowing splatter on the ground. Similar to portals I had seen before, its churning, glittering hum had a pull to it. Hand dropping, Nox went limp, but his eyes remained on mine, barely open.

Snorting, Cyrus was falling apart, face twisted in a smile, eyes bleeding black tears, colors warping around him.

They were too much because I was too much, those feelings were the cause of all this. If only Nox would have let me die when it was my time, maybe I wouldn't have had to experience this, wouldn't have had to see Cyrus this way.

The abyss flashed a color again, but again too quickly for me to know what.

Pulling himself up to his feet, Cyrus nearly fell, moving like the zombie I had originally thought he was, "What, you're going to try to escape? And go where, do what? This is the end of the line, Igor." Taking a dragging step toward me, the colors became a muddy mess beneath his shoes on the white floor. Voice starting to warp, head crooked too far to the side, his unblinking eyes zeroed in on mine, "I don't want to kill you, you did nothing wrong, it's not your fault, none of this is your fault, it was never your fault, but," taking another scraping step toward me, he had nearly closed the space but I didn't budge, "he wanted to make you immortal and there was no fucking way I was going to let him curse you with that."

Grabbing me by my shirt, Cyrus' touch stung, sending shrieking pain through my veins, locking me up, but I didn't fight. Twisted, an abomination, this wasn't the young man I dug up that night on the graveyard shift. He wasn't the zombie who stared up at me with the animation of a cartoon character, not the charmer that rolled with every punch, not the bold, determined, unfazed flirt that dragged me into this, who took the blows with me, who looked up to me red in the face, golden wavy hair splayed out beneath him on the bed. I knew he was an actor, playing every role but his own, but I would have never imagined, despite every single warning I got, that his true role was that of the villain.

"Die in my arms," his voice cracked, despite his wicked smile, "one last time."

Looking between his teary, kaleidoscope eyes as the colors within them raged in war, I knew this was it.

The other end.

My eyes closed, the last sight of Cyrus burning into them. Just as every incarnation before me, Cyrus would be the last thing I saw.

A yell pierced the moment.

Yanked away from me, when Cyrus' hand lost its grip on my shirt, I went stumbling back. Eyes flying open, they met Maddox, his little hands up to the brooch on Cyrus' chest, fighting a losing war against him.

"Run!" the child looked back at me, words clipped by the struggle, "Go through the portal, escape!"

Standing there, frozen, I stared at him, my shoe one step away from the portal. "What are you doing?"

Yelling out as Cyrus burned him, his flippy hair bounced in the fight, but he didn't let go, a fire lit in him that wasn't reflected in the absent colors of his brooch, "While I don't care about anything," Cyrus' hand met Maddox's chest, staining him in red as tears took my predecessor's eyes, "Nox does, and he wants to save you."

Exploding into glittering ash, the last thing I saw was his smile.

Nox's head dropped.

I felt it, the moment he died, like something inside me went out.

The abyss rumbled, the ground cracking as the eternal light above flickered. Eyes jumping up to him, I saw it, the last tear that fell before Nox too exploded into ash. As it rained down, glittering in every color there was, his tear hit the ground and when it did, it turned red.

An explosion threw me, the ground shattering beneath my shoes. Falling back into the portal, my eyes met Cyrus as he picked himself up, the world crumbling around him. I only saw him for a moment before I was overtaken by red, but a moment was enough.

Because in that moment, I didn't see what he had become, but in that moment I was in forty-eight others, all at once. Cyrus' mouth saying something I couldn't hear, my mind struggled to put the words together. Vision blurring out, I only managed to gather the words 'wish' and 'forget'. As I fell into nothingness, red consuming me, I could only wonder when it would be my turn to see him for the last time on the other end.

ten
Witch's Curse

I never liked Cyrus Glory and Cyrus Glory never liked me.

Whether it was sucking up to the head priest at our church orphanage, showing off all the scripture he had memorized, or somehow already being a zealous bastard by the age of seven, preaching like he had been ordained, I did my best to stay away from him. I did my best to stay away from everyone, really, because I had a secret, one that was kept between me and the trees.

A secret that would surely be the death of me.

Sitting among the wildflowers and stones of the forest outside my village, I listened to the birds as dots of sun danced over me through the tree cover in the breeze. My bangs passed through my vision as I laid on the ground, looking up. Hair unnaturally white, it was a strike against me the moment I was born. To whom, though, no one ever did know. I just showed up one day on Anton's doorstep. Ostracized for taking me in, he didn't seem to care about my hair.

Cyrus, on the other hand, never stopped mocking it.

Word in the village was that his mother was a working lady who couldn't afford to keep him and lose business. If there was any validity to that, I'd never know. But it was a good story to account for his, apparent, good looks. Blonde hair as gold and robust as his wasn't common in northern France in the mid 1600's, though was widely sought after. What always got me about him, though, were his stupid eyes. Sometimes when he was outside, they'd catch the sun just right and they'd turn from a cloudy grey to a radiant but subdued blue.

Groaning as I ran my hands over my face, I never knew why Cyrus occupied so much of my mind.

Sitting up, when my hands met the grass at my sides, flowers sprouted from the ground. Looking down to them, they were all red. Huffing as I stood and stretched, I ignored them as they blew about in the breeze. They could shut up.

Hand running over each tree as I passed, I could feel it, the pulse they sent out to each other, the way every plant connected. I started to run. This was the only place I could go to be alone, the only place I was free. People avoided the forest, rumors of witches lurking among the trees. Funny, they weren't wrong, but not quite right, either.

Colorful lights exploding from me, like sparks in the air, they turned into glitter as I ran through them. Jumping over a rock, yellow helped me, taking me into the air, high enough to reach the leaves of the trees. Landing, flowers bloomed in my shoe prints.

I couldn't remember the first time I used my powers, they had just always been there. Gentle, simple magics, definitely not something to fear, but if anyone ever found out, it would be one way to the gallows. They couldn't understand, they wouldn't.

Green turned into a bat, flying along with me as I ran, yellow into a fawn at my side, blue into a bunny bouncing by my feet, purple into a cat at my other side, orange into a dog, it chased the cat. Laughing as I looked around, surrounded by the only friends I had, my gift never failed to make me smile. Red turned into a person, but a silhouette, as they glittered in the sun, running so close to me I could feel their warmth. While the others changed, red always took the same form, but it did age along with me, always a tiny bit taller no matter how much I grew.

Running around a tree, the red form chased me, but I was too fast. Laughing as I dodged their hand, birds flew from a nearby tree, a butterfly flitting about. Pulling myself up into a branch, I avoided them once again, laughing from above.

I loved the forest, all the plants, animals, and bugs. They didn't judge me, they just let me be and I did what I could to help them. It was a peaceful place, a quiet place, a much-needed reprieve from-

"Nox?"

My heart hit the dirt as my magical forms exploded into sparkling dust. Eyes lurching down, they met him as he stepped through the red dust, Cyrus.

Red glittering among his freckles, the way the light caught on his face as he looked up to me almost made him seem embarrassed.

Frozen, blood cold, I sat on the branch of my favorite tree, staring down at him as he stared at me.

Bringing up his hands to catch the last bit of the dust, I watched my life end in his eyes, but then he said, "That was beautiful." Looking around at all the flowers left in my path, the glitter settling around them, he paused before jumping, looking back up to me with the brightest smile I had ever seen, "you're a witch?"

I didn't say anything, I couldn't even breathe.

He had never looked at me that way before.

"I won't tell anyone," he started toward the tree, inspecting it for a foothold probably, "I promise." Coming all the way around the tree, his search fruitless, he looked back to me, "how did you get up there?"

Blinking at him, I remember thinking that was the dumbest thing he had ever said. Though, as his visits to the forest with me became more frequent, the numbest of dumbest things he had ever said only grew. And as the years passed by, as we started to sit a little closer at the fire while I used my gift to illustrate my stories, as he always remained a bit taller than me no matter how much I grew, time did the things it is known to do and before either of us even knew, we had fallen in love.

When I asked him why he didn't turn me in the day he had followed me into the forest, "beautiful", is what he always said. That "something so beautiful couldn't be evil" and that someday he "hoped that others would feel the same".

Sitting up in my tree, my leg dangling off the branch, I stared at my paper before me. I always got stuck at this part in my stories, that bit at the end when the hero had to figure it out. I really should have put more thought into them beforehand, the books I'd write. I had a whole stack of them, squirreled away in the forest. Stories of ghosts and kings, of conquering the world and jumping through time, they were rough, but I was going to do them justice, someday. Glancing away from my thin, animal-skin parchment, I looked down to Cyrus. Leaned against the trunk of the tree he could never manage to climb up into, he held a book of scripture in his hands. For someone who took their religion so seriously, he still loved me. Flipping to the next page as the setting summer sun painted him in warmth, he really was an anomaly, especially when I had him on the ground beneath me.

A witch and a priest, we were an abomination if we were to ever be seen.

When we turned fifteen, Cyrus was ordained. I sat there and watched the ceremony, in my best religious garb, trying to keep a straight face. He had always been an actor. While I preferred to tell stories, he put on a show. Flawless, you'd have no idea that I had him pressed up against a tree out back just moment before. Signing his life away to the church, he took a knee before Anton, the head priest, as he draped a stole over him. Crimson red, it suited Cyrus well.

An instant hit, we always knew it was inevitable. Charismatic, trustworthy, and genuine, effortlessly handsome to boot, it wasn't something all that common back then. People moved to our little village, just to attend his services as word trickled along with the merchants. Spending most of his free time in the orphanage, I think Cyrus secretly wanted kids, but he'd never admit it to me because he knew if we were together, that would never be.

I started actually trying to make something of my writings, always yearning to entertain with my stories. Though I was nervous to try to integrate too much into the village because as I got older, my powers got stronger, managing to act up and surprise even me from time to time. So, on the outskirts I remained, watching Cyrus as he stood in the spotlight. His eyes caught mine, holding for a moment of tension too long before returning to the merchant he was speaking with in the town square.

Everybody loved him, but I loved him the most.

It was a day like any other, the day I was sitting beneath a tree near the church in the center of town, the day everything changed. Writing in a parchment notebook, I was dipping my quill into the ink sitting at my side when it happened.

"What are you writing about?"

Looking up from my sentence, my eyes met with a girl not much older than me. Short, bluntly cut hair, her eyes bright brown, they were almost yellow. In a tattered tunic covered in flour, I had seen her before at the bakery. Humming in question, I lowered my quill from the page.

"In your books, I see you writing in them more than not."

Eyes darting down to my book then back up to her, I sunk in my shirt a bit. "Oh, well, just stories."

"Stories?" She sat down on her knees in front of me, "I can't read, but will you tell me?"

Eyes wide, I just sort of stared at her. People didn't usually talk to me because of my hair, but here she was, making eye contact and everything. Mouth open, I caught myself sputtering but then I said, "Of course," without thinking.

Her expectant eyes above her goofy smile as she placed her hands on her lap was too much so I looked away.

Clearing my throat, I pondered which story to tell her.

There were so many, it was all I ever thought about as I sat on the sidelines. There was the one about the two boys who got haunted and had to work together to make it through, or the one about the boy who died and becomes the ghost king, or even the one about his brother who is possessed by a demon. Maybe the one about the boy trying to break free of his captors, or the one where they conquer the world. I'd have to change them, no matter what story I told, because every character loved like me, and that would just as easily get me hanged.

Oh, my eyes drifted back to her, I knew which one to tell.

"Once upon a time," I set my book down at my side, closing it, "there was a boy who couldn't feel a thing."

Eyes wide, she barely blinked, staring me down, "Nothing?"

Looking away, I swallowed, trying to keep my nerves down, "Nothing at all." Shifting, I pulled myself up to my feet, "this boy went through his every day, completely numb. He didn't know why, but it didn't matter to him. He was content, working at a wares shop in his town."

"What happened to his feelings?"

When that question didn't come from the girl, but another voice, I jumped out of my skin. Looking up, I was met with a couple of townspeople who had stopped, both just looking at me.

"Oh, well," I looked away from them and to the horizon instead, "he could feel once, he felt very much in fact, more than the usual person. But then one day an evil witch stole his feelings away."

Gasping, the girl sat back, "No."

Fighting the line of my mouth as it tried to tug up, I went on, "But the boy didn't remember this, all he knew was that one day he could feel and the next, he never did again. That was, until he met a bo-" clearing my throat, I caught myself, "he met a girl who told him… *she* knew of that evil witch and she wanted to help the boy get his feelings back."

"Aw," another voice startled me, drawing my attention to my other side to find a couple ladies stopped to listen.

"So," the girl on the ground before me smiled, "what happened next?"

As a couple more people joined the growing group, my next breath didn't want to come to me. Never before having been in this much undivided attention, my heart started to race. "At first the boy didn't know what to think about it, numbness was all he had really known. But the… girl, was persistent, going as far as to follow him to work. Which he probably would have disliked, if he had been capable."

Laughter broke out around me and I was just left to stand there.

Was this what it was like to be Cyrus?

"The boy started to notice that the more time he spent around the girl, the more he began to feel and slowly, one feeling at a time, they started to come back to him. It started with anger when someone was rude to him at his shop, then happiness when he danced with the girl at a gathering, next came excitement when he made a new friend, and then came sadness when he had to say goodbye to a loved one." Getting carried away, I didn't realize until I stopped to take a breath that a crowd had started to form. Straightening, I looked around, not looking at any one person long, trying to not think about how many there were, "Through it all, the girl was by his side, helping him through each feeling he took back from the evil witch. They became close, so much so, that when love came, it bound them together." Cooing came from the crowd, more people stopping because of how loud it was, "But then," I could feel it, them hanging on my every word, sitting in the moment of suspension with me, and that's when it won out, my smile, "came fear."

"Oh no," the girl sat up on her knees.

Smiling at her, my eyes lingered for a moment before looking back out and around, "the friend he had made, betrayed him, hurting him in a way no one else could." Stepping around, arms joining me in a gesture, I could feel them, every eye following me, "Thinking that was the end, that he had finally met every emotion there was and he was safe to settle down with the girl, the boy was then hurt again, but this time it was by," my eyes met the girl in the front, her animation making my heart soar as I said, "the girl."

A roar of concern came from the crowd, and it took my everything to not laugh.

Their attention, their engagement, it made me feel alive in a way I never had.

"Stealing the boy's feelings again, she had waited until he found them all to take them for herself."

"What," the girl dug her hands into the dirt in front of her, "didn't she love him?"

"She did," I knelt down to her, smiling, "very much so."

"Then why?"

Messing up her hair as I stood back up, I looked out to the crowd, "She thought they would hurt him, and even though they hurt her, she would endure anything for him."

"But," the girl threw a handful of dirt down, making a small cloud, "that isn't what he wanted, right?"

"Of course not, though there wasn't much he could do about it, succumbing to the crushing numbness he had only just managed to escape. He had faced many toils, but she was not one he ever expected." Silence sat, power in the beat as I took a moment to look around, until my eyes landed on the girl, "However," when she lit up, I smiled, "there was something she didn't know, something she unintentionally did. He had thought he had met every feeling, but there was one more, one that she had introduced him to." Standing

straight in the center of attention, there were more people

than I could easily count, it must have been damn near the

entire village, "He knew anger, happiness, excitement,

sadness, love, and fear, but she had brought despair into his

world."

When the crowd didn't like that, in the way that you

like it because it's a good story, but you don't because it's

sad, I stood in that for a moment.

"Does this story have a happy ending?" the crowd

parted as a voice came out over it, allowing Cyrus to walk

right to the front.

Smiling at me in that way that he did, I couldn't

return the sentiment because while I was the only one who

could see him, everyone could see me.

"I don't know," I bent down, picking up my

parchment book, "I haven't finished it yet. I'm not quite sure

how he'll use despair to pull himself through it or how he'll reconcile with the girl." Flipping to the last page I had written before being interrupted, my eyes rested on the last word, "But I think it will. Though he is left with nothing but despair, despair is not nothing. And one thing, anything, is better than nothing."

"Will you tell us when you finish it?" the girl stood, running up to me, "I want to know how the story ends."

"Please give him a happy ending," someone from the crowd said.

Clapping, a few cheers here and there, I dropped my notebook in shock. Looking over everyone who had only ever overlooked me, for the first time I was seen, and they liked what they saw.

Smiling at me, looking me up and down, Cyrus shifted his weight in his clergy garb that clung to his form in just the right way, "Tell us another."

About to say no, flustered beyond my capacity, I didn't get to because before I did, the girl echoed the sentiment. A few out in the crowd sat down, others asked for more, and I was left, notebook on the ground at my feet, unable to breathe.

That was, until Cyrus winked at me.

Taken by the moment, lost to my smile, I didn't even have to pick up my notebook, I knew these stories better than I knew myself. The lost ghost boys fighting a prophecy, the boy with a heart of gold struggling against a demon, the unlikely underdog hero who becomes the ghost king, the children of corruption who just wanted to be the good guys, the villain who wishes to save the world by ending it, these people weren't real, but they were to me, and in that little bit of time, they were to the townspeople, too. When Cyrus stood before a crowd, he became someone else, when I did, I became myself.

As I gestured my arms up as I described the climax of my ghost king story, as if I had a sword about to swing down into the head of the demon king, I wished that I could put on the full show like I would for Cyrus alone in the woods.

But.

I knew I couldn't.

They wouldn't understand.

Swinging my arms down, describing the way the blade met with the demon king's neck, a blue glow met my eyes. The form of a sword in my hands, made of eerie blue light, it crashed into the ground before the girl, but she didn't jump away, her jaw just dropped.

Letting go of it, I fell away as it dissipated.

Another glow caught my eye, making me turn around. Red ribbons like the fire I described in the demon realm danced around, other colors sparking in the air, making a whole show. As I stared at them, glass took my eyes.

Oh no.

I slowly turned around to look at the crowd.

No.

The way they looked at me, it said it all.

No no no no no no no

Cyrus stared, a rare moment in which his persona fell.

I backed up into a tree.

"A witch," someone in the crowd said, "Nox is a witch."

And just like that, they turned on me, yelling that word from all directions like it was dirty. Someone tried to rush me, shoving past Cyrus, but that's when he snapped back and got to me first. Yanking me around, he twisted my arms behind my back, bending me over. Shoving me to my knees as I struggled, my yell was muffled by one of his hands covering my mouth. Eyes wide, tears taking them as I stared forward at the hate before me, I was trapped, on my knees, for everyone to see.

I had gone and done it, got too comfortable, let it slip.

And now Anton was going to kill me.

"I have a plan," Cyrus whispered in my ear, barely audible over the yelling from the crowd, "play along."

Freezing in my struggle, it only took a moment for me to realize what he was doing. He was a holy man, this was his job, just another show. Fighting against him again, I didn't want anyone to think we were in good company, because even though I had just sentenced myself to death, I didn't want Cyrus associated as a conspirator.

"What is going on," Anton's voice like the crack of a bell silenced everyone. Bold steps carrying him forward, the crowd scrambling over itself to get out of his way, he stopped before us. Looking between Cyrus and I, stiff holy garb catching the light as his chest expanded with his deep breath, he had given us that look plenty growing up under his care, but never in such serious times.

"What are you two doing, causing a ruckus."

"It's Nox," a random man called from the crowd, "he's a witch."

"We just saw it," a lady yelled, "his magics."

Standing in silence as the crowd yelled over itself trying to recount what had happened, his eyes didn't leave mine.

"See," another voice came over the others, "he's not even denying it."

Anton's eyes held on me a moment longer before they drifted up to Cyrus, "Is this true?"

Shoving me down more, Cyrus was center stage in perhaps the most important performance of our lives, "Yes, Father. I saw it too, illusions, he even conjured a weapon."

Humming, Anton looked back down to me, "I see, there's been a witch under my nose this entire time and I didn't smell it? You must be skilled at hiding it, but you're at the end of the line, son." Turning from us, he raised his hand toward the town's square, "Cyrus, take him to the gallows."

"Father," Cyrus' voice made Anton stop and turn around as he went on, "I want to do it."

"But," Anton turned fully, "you grew up together."

"Precisely," shoving me into the dirt, he pressed my face into it, but I could tell, in his grip that surely looked tighter than it was, that he was shaking. Though I was sure it wasn't nerves, he didn't get nervous, no, it was more likely the guilt of the way his hands were treating me. "We have been friends for years, and he's been a witch this whole time. He is an affront to god. I want to do it, and I want it to be personal."

I felt a chill take the air, dirt lacing my shaking intake. I didn't know what his plan was, I could only hope that he knew what he was doing.

"I see," Anton turned away from us, "I will allow it."

"Thank you, Father." Cyrus ripped me up from the ground, roughing me into submission as he forced me to my feet and my head down, "Stay quiet, traitor."

Eyes wide on the ground as he shoved me through the parting crowd, townspeople who had just cheered for me spitting at me, I knew that no matter what was about to happen, if I were to survive, then I would never be allowed another moment like I just had, and that, it itself, was a lot like dying.

Dragged through the center of town, the crowd followed, calling after us, every obscenity in our language flying through the air, I didn't struggle against Cyrus any longer. I couldn't. Passing the gallows, my eyes caught on the noose, blowing about in the breeze, a grim display, a warning to those like me. When his eyes found what mine were looking at, Cyrus shoved my head back down, taking a fistful of my hair.

"I'm taking you to the forest," his voice was but a whisper, "to the burn pit. Can you create an illusion of fire?"

Looking up to him through my disheveled hair from the corner of my eye, I started to piece what he asked together, "I think so, but," I looked forward toward the tree line, the burn pit barely beyond it, "while we could try to fake that, we can't fake bones. There would be something left behind."

"But that's the thing about heaven's holy fire," I could hear the smile in his whisper as we approached the burn pit, "it leaves no trace, sending you straight to hell where you belong." Stopping above it, a hole three or so feet deep, nearly ten wide, the remnants of rubbish sat around, "Now," he leaned in, right next to my head as he forced me straight up, chin above my shoulder, "scream, your life depends on it."

Shoving me over the edge into the pit, I landed hard among metal and weak splintered wood. Hissing through my teeth in the dust that was brought up, my body shook as I turned myself over. Laying in the company of what else the town had thrown away, elbows on the ground behind me, I looked up to Cyrus as the town filled in behind him. Pushing her way to the front, the girl who had spoken to me first nearly made it into the pit with me before Father Anton grabbed her, holding her back. Tears in her eyes, she didn't fight.

A righteous fury to Cyrus' eyes, I saw that zealot in him I had once hated until I realized that too was an act. Reaching down to the side of his coat, he pulled it back to show his bible as it sat, leather bound to his belt. Sliding it from its straps, he flipped it open without even looking at the page, but no one else could see that because I was the only one facing him, the only one to see his eyes and they refused to leave me.

"Foul witch, you have taken advantage of us long enough, no more will you live among us, bringing your devilish curses into the lives of the good people of this town. Never again will you set foot on our god-given earth, an affront to all that is good and holy." Holding out his book, he brought his other hand up to his heart, hovering an inch before his chest, "Now," he dropped a finger, "with god on my side," he dropped another, "and the power vested in me," another finger dropped, "I, Father Cyrus, send you back from whence you came," he dropped one more finger, "to suffer for all eternity in the pits of hell."

When he dropped his last finger, he threw his arm to the side, and in that moment, I knew it was my cue. I wished for fire, so much fire, more fire than anyone had ever seen before. Flames exploding from me, they roared, overtaking the pit in its entirety, reaching tens of feet into the sky, so high that every town around must have been able to see. Yelling as the flames obscured me, I was no actor, but I did my best.

Eyes wide as his hair flared in the heated wind, when everyone else ran away, Cyrus remained. And as the flames grew, their red hue took over his eyes and I was left to lay there, staring up at them, thinking that red looked so much better than blue. Tasting blood as my yell broke, tears welling in the corners of my eyes. Flames raging even higher and hotter, they didn't hurt me as I pulled myself up. Clawing my way out of the pit, my arms shook as I pulled myself up over the back of it. The wall of flames separating me from the town, I looked back through them to see the last of the people as they ran away.

When my eyes met Cyrus' as he closed his bible, he smiled at me, though I could see it, the glass reflecting in his eyes.

Turning, I ran, and as I did, as I went further and further into the forest, barely dodging trees and catching myself as I stumbled over rocks, the flowers that bloomed in my wake wilted.

And with that, he, or rather, we, became Father Cyrus Glory.

I'd never forget the way he cried that night, panting so hard he was nearly sick after he came barreling through the woods looking for me after the town was asleep. The way he held me, the way he assured me it was going to be okay, despite him being the inconsolable one. I remember sitting there, back against a tree, Cyrus kneeling between my legs, and staring up at the stars beyond him.

Far enough into the woods that no one would find me, I used my gift to build a little house. It took a while, and a lot of almost dropping an entire tree on myself, but I managed it. I must have been a witch, but I wasn't what they always told us they were. Were there any like that, did they have a valid reason to fear those like me? Or was it simply that we were different?

A dead man, I had too much time to myself to ponder. Days spent alone in the woods, nights up waiting for when Cyrus could sneak away to see me in the cabin, I did manage to write a lot but that was just about all. Abusing his sway with the orphanage children, Cyrus utilized their loud mouths to spread spooky rumors about the forest and soon enough, even visitors knew to stay away. Though sometimes the warnings would inspire someone with something to prove to venture past the tree line. Unlucky for them, the forest was indeed haunted by a spirit with too much time on his hands, so it didn't take long for them to run away, screaming back into town.

It must have been months that I spent out there alone before the night Cyrus came crashing into the door, expecting it to have been unlocked or something. Feeling the vibrations from his impact all the way on the roof, I sat up. Hearing his hushed curses, I laughed a little as I looked over the ledge.

"Using the lord's name in vain, are we, Father?"

Jumping out of his skin, Cyrus looked up to me. In the moment before he spoke, I admired him and the man he was growing up into.

"There's another," panting, he brought his hand up to the wall, slumping over as he coughed, "another witch." Ripping his head up, his eyes caught the moonlight through his disheveled, wavy blonde hair, "We have to save her."

Staring down at him, just when I thought I couldn't possibly love him any more, he always managed.

"Alright," Cyrus straightened his religious garb, looking out into the woods toward the town, a deep breath taking him, "when I give the signal, do what you did before with the fire and when no one can see you, run up to the pit and bring her back to the cabin." Looking back to me, Cyrus furrowed his brows, "Sorry, I'm not trying to be bossy."

Laughing as I turned to him, our eyes met, "Don't worry," bringing my hand up to his chest, I gently pushed him back into the tree. Closing the space, I watched him turn red as a rose before I kissed him. Pulling back, resting my forehead on his, I couldn't help but smile, "you couldn't boss me around even if you tried."

Groaning as he pushed me away, I could see it before he turned, he was smiling too. Watching as he left me alone in the forest, I didn't know what we were getting ourselves into. As I hid, high in a tree, waiting for his signal, how could I have known. At the end of his speech, when he threw his arm to the side, I wished for fire. Flames screaming into the sky, higher than before, Cyrus stood before them, his hair flying back in the gust. Righteous, he was unfazed, god on his side as others ran.

Jumping from the tree, I landed with the help of green. Flowers blooming in my steps, I walked up to the ledge of the pit. Staring up at me, tears in her eyes, was the girl who had asked me about my stories. Smiling as I extended my hand, she didn't even hesitate before jumping to take it. Pulling her out of the pit, I kept my arm around her as we ran back into the woods.

That was how I saved her, Valor.

Word spread through the land of a particular holy man, one blessed by god with the ability to be rid of any blight. Father Cyrus Glory, with every witch he eradicated, gone without a trace, sent right back to hell, he became more well known. Soon churches from the surrounding towns brought their witches for him to expel, and with every one, our company grew. Our act was perfect, down to a science.

Standing on the other side of the fire, looking through the flames at Cyrus as he stood, arms out at his sides, smile on his face, red reflecting in his eyes, before I knew it, years had gone by and we, in what felt like the blink of an eye,

turned twenty.

Bringing the newest abomination back to the cabin

that night, it was a bit quieter than it had been. Finnegan

having smuggled another batch of accused witches out of the

country, they had yet to return. Though, as I opened the door

for her, the moonlight catching on her hair that was white

like mine, there was someone still home. Despite trying to

convince her to leave now that she could control her powers

better to start a life somewhere new, she never would.

"Nox!" Valor came running up to us, but before she

could say another word, she stopped, dead in her tracks. Eyes

meeting the young woman with me, her mouth fell open as

she took a step back.

Raising a brow as I watched her, it took me a couple

seconds too long to figure out what I was watching as

Valor's face turned red. Eyes drifting down to the young lady

of petite build, white hair and silver eyes, I saw the same red

dusting take her too. A smile tugged up on my mouth.

"Valor, this is Abraxas," shoving Abraxas forward in the nicest way possible, I stepped back toward the door, "she was sent here on a transport from Germany, so she doesn't speak French- good luck."

Stepping out the door as Valor called after me, I laughed as I closed it between us.

Back against the door, a smile on my face, I listened to Valor desperately try to apologize in her horrible German. A breath escaped me. Ever since this forest became my home, I had met many others like me. Though they were all called witches, very few actually were. Some were simple human, just different, but others were like me, just not quite. People who could change their form, people who could read minds, see the future even, there were those who could see the dead and those who basically were dead but not, like Finnegan, though they drank blood so that was a bit off-putting but who was I to judge. Stepping away from the cabin, hands finding the pockets of my tunic, I walked, aimlessly among the trees. Though Finnegan's outside connections were the only reason we were able to get those Cyrus 'executed' back out into the world, their long stints of absence was hard on both Cyrus and I. Though they had only found their way into our hearts but a couple years ago, it felt as if they had always been there.

They had told me something, about their kind. That while they looked young, they were actually quite old, and would continue on that way, eternally. They would live forever, save tragedy befalling their blithe.

What would that be like, to never die?

To live for all eternity with Cyrus and Finnegan.

Though I knew that wasn't what Cyrus would want. Passively suicidal from the day we met, though still here for some reason, the day he died would surely be the happiest day of his life. When Finnegan offered to do to us what had been done to them, pausing our bodies where we were for all eternity, I was going to agree, but Cyrus didn't even let Finnegan finish their sentence before he rebuked it. Finnegan never asked again, but I could tell, something about it weighed on them. I tried not to think on it, the day in which Finnegan would be the last one left.

A rustling in a nearby bush sent ice through my veins. In a flash of purple, I landed in the tree above. Scanning the ground, I held my breath. Running around a tree, his shoe caught on a rock and he went stumbling forward, nearly into the tree I was sitting in. Panting, a smile on his face, he looked up to me, his hair bouncing with the movement.

When his eyes met mine, catching the moonlight just right, I could have killed Cyrus, he had scared me so bad. Laughing, he ran his hand through his hair as he straightened. I let out a harsh breath as I rolled my eyes away from him. Jumping down from the tree, I pressed him into the trunk of another.

He was lucky he was hot.

I thought this was it, my happily ever after. Someday Cyrus would grow up, outlive Anton and take over the church, using his sway to expand our operation by looking the other way. Maybe I'd find a way to share my stories with the world, ask Finnegan to leave them places during their travels. Maybe someday the three of us could run away somewhere, create a place where the misfits would be welcome. What a wonderful place that would be.

It was a quiet October day, one that I had spent writing, or rather, trying to write. Sitting alone in the cabin, Abraxas and Valor out in the forest somewhere, I just stared at my parchment, quill in hand. Ink dripped from the tip, splattering on the page. Sighing as I set the quill down, I ran my hand through my hair. Of all the stories I had written, this was the one that gave me the most trouble. It had been years, but for some reason, I just didn't know how it should end, the story of the boy who could feel nothing.

Dropping my head to my desk, I laced my fingers through the back of my hair.

The colors of the pendant Finnegan had made me glowing in the poorly lit cabin, my eyes held on it as it sat on the desk next to my face, chain around my neck. As my powers grew stronger with age, my pendant was the only way I could utilize them with any refinement. I had no idea what I'd do without it, but at the same time, I feared become too dependent on it, should something ever happen to it. I told Cyrus that it regulated my powers as they grew, could contain them if separated from me but could never fully own them, and that I couldn't take it off or they'd go out of control, but he didn't really seem like he was listening at the time, a bit distracted by writing his next sermon, so I wouldn't be surprised if it would later come up that he misunderstood something.

Smiling a little, I closed my eyes.

Mind absconding, I drifted in and out until I was stirred by the smell of smoke. Slowly lifting my head, my hands still laced over the back, at first I thought my eyes were just cloudy but then I sat up with a start. Standing from my chair, it screamed against the floor as smoke surrounded me. Coughing, hand up to my mouth, I looked around and that's when I saw them, the flames eating at the walls from

the outside.

Running, I bolted toward the nearest room. There

weren't many, add ons I had managed over the years, but in

that moment those four extra rooms made that cabin feel like

a mansion. Trying to call out for the others who could be in

the cabin, I couldn't even get Valor's name out as I opened

one of the doors. The smoke was thick, stinging my eyes, but

even though it I could tell no one was there. Tripping over

my own feet, I ran into the door of the next room. Throwing

it open I scanned the room through the smoke. No one was

there, either. Checking the next, my body grew weak, and by

the time I opened the fourth door, I was seeing spots. When I

was met with another empty room, I went stumbling

backward. Where was everyone?

Tripping across the main room, running past my desk,

my eyes caught on my parchment. Stopping, as the smoke

grew heavier, the structure creaking, I ran back to my desk.

Grabbing my parchment notebook, I ran back toward the

front door. Trying to open it, it wouldn't budge. Slamming into it a couple times, coughing so hard my ears rang, it was then that I realized.

It must have been blocked from the outside.

Bringing my hand up to it, body beginning to go numb, soot staining the tips of my white hair with black, I closed my eyes.

I wished to be free.

Lighting up, purple sent cracks through the wood until it shattered beneath my touch. Shoving through the broken pieces, I went falling out of the house. Pant leg snagging on some of the shattered wood, it took me to the ground. Head hitting first, my ears rang and vision went out. As everything came veering back in, I tried to sit up, coughing up blood. Eyes opening, though they were blurry, they could make out what remained of the door. Nothing was blocking it, so why? My eyes struggled to take it all in, but then I saw it.

A lock.

Having fell from my hands, my parchment notebook sat on the ground before me, fire consuming it.

Hearing ringing back in, I was swarmed by yells. Sitting up all the way, I slowly turned around and what I saw killed me before they even could. The entire town surrounded my cabin, torches in hand, cheering as it burned. Something shoved over my head, I was plunged into burlap darkness. Jumped, hands on me I didn't know, they forced me to the ground, overpowering me. Tied behind my back, the rope they used ripped against my wrists in the fight. Yanked to my feet, I tied to drop back down, did everything I could to try to break free, the ropes rubbing my wrists raw. But as blood dripped down my fingertips, they were too strong, there were too many of them. And though, as they dragged me out of the forest, I wanted to wish for them to die, wanted to wish for them to burn, I knew I couldn't.

Even if I did, I knew my powers wouldn't listen.

Because, just like me, they never wanted to hurt anybody.

Shaking breath escaping me, I stopped fighting. If I was about to die, I needed to die with dignity. I needed to die in a way that would outlive me, so that when the others heard, when the news made it to other countries, when those we saved heard the story, they'd know that I was never broken and that they could remain unbroken, too. Straightening, head held high despite the sack over it, I knew each step was a step closer to the gallows.

Hatred yelled out around me, I could feel the heat from the torches.

Everyone in the town was here, a spectacle, really. I could only hope that Cyrus, Abraxas, and Valor could use the scene as a cover to run, I could only hope they'd meet up with Finnegan in Germany like we had planned if something like this were to ever come to be. Because if they caught one of us, they caught all of us, not just me.

The ground leveled beneath my shoes, indicating that we entered the town. The type of cheers that took over the air were not the same kind I got when I told them my stories. As they led me along, their hands rough on my sides, blood dripping down my fingers, I wondered how they found me. As I was forced up a set of wooden steps, I wondered if they had us completely figured out, of if someone had somehow seen me. There was only one path to the cabin not riddled with traps, but it was long, winding, not the path we took out of the forest. Had they disarmed the traps? As the soles of my shoes met with the wooden stage of the gallows, there were too many questions but not a single sound answer.

It didn't make sense.

Stepping onto the trap door, I felt it shift, rickety beneath my shoes.

Well, there was one way.

My jaw tightened as someone lowered the noose over my head, tightening it around my neck.

But there was no way.

The bag was ripped from my head. Roaring yells crashed into me as my hair fell into place, eyes squinting as I reeled back. Vision adjusting to the twilight, smoke bellowed into the sky, turning the rising moon red with the haze. Straightening, I looked out over the town I wanted nothing more than to be a part of, over the people I just wanted to charm with stories, over friends I may have made, had I not been born this way.

Alone at the gallows, I stood beneath a beautiful tree, my rope tied to one of its branches. Wisteria vines wrapped around it, they mingled with the leaves above, its purple flowers dangling down around me. Petals around my shoes, they danced across the wood of the gallows with the breeze. If I was alone, that probably meant the others hadn't been caught, that they must have gotten away. Relief met me as I looked back out over the town, standing tall. The executioner was absent from their wooden lever before me as it sat, unmanned. Staring at the lever to the trap door beneath my shoes, all it would take was one pull and that was it.

The crowd started to part, falling silent as they made way. Splitting down the middle on either side of the lever, it was obvious who was approaching through the sea of people. I always had a feeling that Anton was going to be the one to kill me.

When the front of the crowd parted, my eyes met his, but Anton wasn't alone.

Standing upon the gallows, noose around my neck, petals blowing by my shoes, I had yet to die, but that was the last time my heart beat.

There was a way they would have been able to find the cabin, only one way.

But I thought there was no way that could be true.

Until Cyrus' hand met the lever.

"That was an impressive game you were playing, Nox," Anton said, hand meeting Cyrus' shoulder, "We may have never caught on, had it not been for Cyrus telling me."

My eyes fell to my love as he stood, nonchalant, as if my life wasn't literally at his fingertips, "You…"

I couldn't breathe, I couldn't move, not as he raised a brow at me, the line of his mouth curling up with it as he gave one, simple, nod.

That wasn't Cyrus, no, that was Father Glory.

A yell came from behind the crowd, and though I felt as if I knew it, I had never heard it sound like that. A struggle, everyone turned to look, and that's when I saw them. Finnegan trying to fight their way through the back of the crowd, their flippy white hair catching the warmth of the twilight sky as it bounced with every shove.

"Cyrus, how could you-" when they yelled, when their voice broke, they were a totally different person, a far departure from the flawlessly composed person I knew,

"Nox-"

Another stepped up to the crowd, taller than Finnegan, though they gave off a similar air with their silvery hair and glowing purple eyes. Looking at me for a moment, their thin brows dropped as they rolled their eyes. Fine lips parting, I could see it as they said something inaudible to me, the same fangs that Finnegan had.

The moment their mouth closed, Finnegan froze.

I could see it even from up there, the purple ring that took over Finnegan's irises, surrounding their emerald green. Struggling with themselves, that was the first, and only time I ever saw it, tears fall from Finnegan's eyes. Shaking as they tried to claw themselves forward, their muscles forced them to slow. Despite their drive, I watched them stop, straightening. Unmoving, their eyes locked on mine, and even though their body calmed, I could see it, they wanted to scream. Turning from me, they walked back out of the crowd, stopping at the other person's side.

Why.

Shaking breath leaving me as my eyes started to glass, I didn't understand. A laugh ripped my attention back, my eyes landing on Cyrus.

His grip tightened on the lever.

Staring down at him, one of the loves of my life, as he smirked up at me, every moment of our lives together passed by me. Had it all been faked, from the day he met me at the tree? Every day he came to visit until it turned into nights that he stayed, every story we shared, every inch of skin that we bared. Was it all a lie, did we actually save a single life? Looking out over the town, I was ready to fight every person in it, every person, except one. And as he started to pull on the lever, it came to me.

"Do you remember the story," I looked down to the gallows before me, "the story about the boy who couldn't feel a thing?" Slowly looking up, I was again the center of attention as clouds began to form in the sky, "I know it now, how that story ends."

I saw it, a moment in Cyrus, as his grip loosened on the lever as the wind started to pick up, a rumble taking the sky.

"You had asked me back then, Father Glory, if the story had a happy ending, and I spent a long time, years even, trying to write one. However, now I know why I could never write it. This story can't end happy. But," I looked out to Finnegan as my voice cracked, a bitterness begging to come to rise in me as the sky darkened, "I wish it could have." Looking back to Cyrus, my brow lowered as my voice raised, glass washing over my eyes, "I wish that we could have found that place we talked about, a place where everyone was safe. I wish I could have told my stories, bringing my characters to life." As my tears broke free, a color started to light to life on my brooch as it hung around my neck, a color that had never been there before, as my voice broke with my heart, "And I wish-"

Cyrus pulled the lever.

Dropping, the noose cut me off.

Black exploded from me, my yell carried by it so loud, I'm sure the towns around heard it as my last word echoed against the distant hills with a roar of thunder. Leveling the crowd, it sent everyone tumbling back, everyone except Cyrus as he held onto the lever. Hair blown back, surrounded by raging black, fighting against the wind as I met the end of my rope, the last thing I saw was my reflection in Cyrus' eyes. Though there was no fire, somehow, they were red.

And just like that, I was dead.

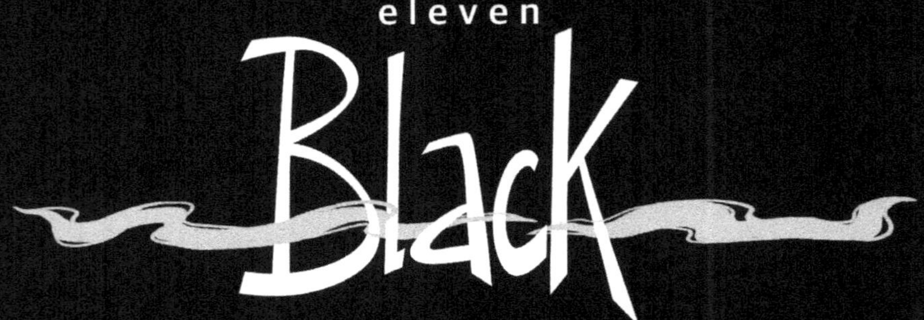

A chill took me, bringing me back to myself. Head

hung low, back up against something hard, it took my eyes a

moment to focus. Bringing my head up, my stiff neck fought

the movement. Met with rows of headstones, they sat, dimly

aglow by the beginnings of an early morning twilight. Frost

on the dead grass around me, my hands brushed into the wet

chill as I pushed myself up. Sore, body aching, my back

creaked as I straightened. A striking cold came to rise on my

skin, causing me to seize under the sting, arms, wrapping

around my chest. Trembling, a harsh breath escaped my clenched teeth as I tried to breathe through the freezing burn. Looking up behind me through pained eyes, I was met with a tree.

What was I doing here?

Looking back down to myself, I was met with the yellow of my work uniform shirt and lines of my pressed pants, nametag, and nine years of service pin catching the morning light. Bringing my hand, damp with melting frost, up to my face, I pushed my glasses out of place as a breath took me. That's right, I wandered into the graveyard on my walk home from work.

Pulling myself up to my feet, hand braced on the tree, it was hard to stand. So cold my body fought every move, the pain beneath the numb outer layers of my skin reached to my bones. Despite just waking, I was tired, so tired, as if I had been on an entire adventure. Straightening, I looked up into the tree above me, the fading stars peeking through the evergreen canopy. An urgency in my muscles, it was as if I had just left something unfinished, a momentum that had been cut short. But as I ran my hand through my hair, I turning toward the graveyard, I couldn't remember.

I must have had an interesting dream, it was too bad that I couldn't write it down, it probably would have made for a good story.

God, it was so cold.

I was lucky I woke before I froze to death out here.

Starting toward the graveyard, I pocketed my hands as my shivering exhalate clouded in front of me. With each step the frosted grass cracked beneath my weight. On the tip of my brain, I tried to remember my dream. It wasn't like it mattered, I didn't care, but it nagged me, which was probably the closest thing to care I was capable of feeling. Heart in time with my slow steps, it never raced, never dropped, just continued on, like a metronome. Eyes drifting up to the heavenly clouds in the sky, even the sunrise was dull.

A bit of frost broke free from the tree above me and landed on my bare skin, causing me to tense. Bringing my hand to the back of my neck, it passed over something. Pausing in my step, my hand lingered on the side of my neck. What felt like two raised bumps near the base, they were faint, but enough that my palm picked them up. Trying to look at my own neck, I quickly realized the obvious. Letting out a breath, I didn't care, it didn't matter.

Walking along headstones, going no particular way, I wondered what had compelled me the night before, bringing me to the company of the dead.

It wasn't like anything important ever happened at the graveyard.

When I blinked, something flashed in my mind.

Eyes flying open, I stared forward at the grass.

Too fast for me to comprehend, I didn't know what I had just seen, but as I stood there, I did know something about it was red.

Another shivering breath left me, clouding my vision and the winter chill deposited further into my skin. Crossing my arms over my chest in a pathetic attempt to stay warm, my shoulders tensed.

Why was I still out here?

As the cloud cleared from my vision, my eyes caught on a fancy headstone at my side.

Standing there in that moment, my gaze rested on the name.

Salem Willow.

Turning to face it, I stood with it for a moment before my eyes drifted right to the other names.

Jack Payne, Edgar Candyl, Ash Lore.

Eyes drifting back to the left, they met two more names.

Hugo and Kasper Kloven.

A fake potted plant caught my eye, sitting at the base of Hugo's headstone. A bird of paradise in bloom, as a drop of dew rolled from its plastic leaf, I felt as if I had seen it before. Eyes drifting up to Hugo's name, I knew I had heard it before. On the news, sure, when they all died at the high school it was a national headline. But this felt different. Eyes returning to Salem's headstone, it felt like I had heard his voice say it. Actually, as my eyes met Jack's headstone, I felt like I had met him, though I knew that I hadn't. And it wasn't in the I-saw-him-somewhere-in-passing way, but in like the I-know-what-his-cologne-smells-like way.

Something shifted in my chest as pine took my senses.

Stepping back, when my eyes met Hugo and Kasper's headstones, I stopped when I felt something cold in my pocket brush up against my leg.

I lowered my hand toward my pocket.

A ring of a bell floated through the air.

I froze.

Another ring bounced off the headstones.

Eyes raising to the side, they met with someone.

A darkened silhouette upon the sunrise, they stood, leaning against a headstone a few down the way.

The bell rang again.

They call it the graveyard shift.

Eyes drifting down, they caught on a glint of silver near the base of the headstone.

It was a common turn of phrase for a time worked through the night.

Feet taking me toward them before I felt my body move, I wasn't compelled, I didn't care, still as I had ever been.

But

whatever caused me to take those steps was greater than a compulsion.

It was possession.

Legend had it that, once upon a time, it wasn't unheard of to be buried alive, so to combat this, the peoples of old would tie a string to the wrist of the deceased, feed it six feet up, and attach it to a bell so that, in the event they woke up, the person working the graveyard shift would hear the ringing and exhume them.

With each step, as the sun started to break over the horizon, the person came into clarity before me until I was left, standing one step away, before them and the headstone.

An occupying thought, though snobs will say the phrase was coined much later and held no such connection.

As I opened my mouth, another ring took the morning air.

The sun broke over the hills, bathing us in light.

Slowly looking up from the grass between us, as his head rose to face me, I saw it for only a fleeting moment, but for the first time since the day he was born, Ross, my little brother, wasn't smiling. But the moment it appeared to occur to him that he was in the company of another, that changed, a smile taking his shadowed features. It was hard to tell, as his eyes met mine, if the bags beneath his were just a trick of the light or not.

Unfazed in a cemetery in the middle of the night, he had always been like that.

Mum called it bravery.

The chill stung my throat with my intake, "What are you doing here?"

A pause took him, a moment passing between us with the winter wind until he finally said, "I don't know," looking between my eyes, his smile on his face, it didn't show in his as the sun shed light on how pale he was, "how about you?"

Standing there, staring at him as a bitter breeze blew right through me, it took me a moment to even open my mouth again, but no words came.

I was here because I took the scenic route home after work, right? If that was the case, why did my words catch in my throat? Bringing my hand up to my neck, it stopped on the way up when my fingers brushed into my bowtie. Worn and old, the fabric had been with me on the front lines of retail for years. But, for some reason, its rough fabric against my fingertips felt wrong.

A ring took the moment.

"It's weird, isn't it?" Ross looked down to his side, eyes meeting with something near the base of the headstone he was leaning up against, "this bell. I was just walking around when I heard it, seems like it called out to you, too."

Staring at a little silver bell as it hung off a rounded pole sticking out of the ground next to the headstone, it rang again, a thin snapped silver thread tied to it blowing with it in the wind. I had never seen that bell before, but why did I feel like I had? Why, when my fingers lowered from my bowtie, did the cool sensation of its metal resurrect on my skin. Eyes catching on the grave below, the grass was grown in, despite being mostly dead from the cold. Quite some time had passed since whoever they were had been laid to rest. And nothing about that was strange, nothing at all, but as I took a step back, looking over the ground, something was.

 As a relentlessly cold wind gust past us, taking some of me with it, I looked back up to Ross. In nothing more than a hoodie, he didn't even flinch at the cold, eyes on the fading stars above as a tuft of his messy orange hair blew across his forehead. "I think someone I know died," his eyes slowly lowered to me, and though they were usually bright, the blue and green of his irises were so dull you could barely tell them apart, "but I can't remember." Pushing himself up from the headstone he leaned on, he swayed a bit before straightening, "that's absurd, though. How would I just forget a whole person?" taking a step toward me, his eyes dropped, "I can't remember, but I can't forget either. I just-" his knee buckled, sending him forward. Catching him as he crashed into me, we both fell to our knees. Arms wrapped around him, his limp head resting on my shoulder, he was so cold, too cold, how long had he been out there?

Staring down at his back as my arms wrapped tighter around it, he didn't even shiver, "Ross."

His ribcage barely expanded with his weak breath, "How do you know my name?"

"What do you mean," I shifted, eyes drifting away from him, "I'm your-"

Eyes snagging, mouth open, my last word died on my tongue the moment my gaze met the headstone he had been leaning on.

Ross went limp in my grip.

The wind stopped.

No.

My heart pounded so hard it caused me to seize up, grip tightening on Ross as I held him in my arms.

It wasn't a dream.

Eyes closing with the next pound of my heart, the haze that had held me turned to ash, clearing my mind of the frozen fog as every letter carved into me as it was carved into stone.

It had been him, always him, from the moment I dug him up to the moment he killed Nox, everything, every smile, every bounce of his golden locks, it was all a part of his plan, all a means to this end. Everyone warned me, over and over again, through when I looked into his eyes, I only saw one thing: eternity.

But.

Cyrus Glory had betrayed me.

Invisible pressure collapsed on me, shoving my knees into the dirt as I clung to Ross, unconscious in my arms.

Colorful light so bright I could see it through my closed eyes met me. Barely able to open them, I was briefly blinded, a curse riding my exhale, until they adjusted. Circling like vultures, orbs, they hovered around us, bobbing in the air as their colorful light cast our shadows in every direction all at once.

As I looked between them, they didn't make sense. Cyrus had stolen them, my colors, how could they be here? I became numb, the moment he took the brooch. But then, as I stood there, staring up, my eyes widened. Something Nox had said came to light in my mind, something I barely remembered Finnegan saying, too.

Amber passed by, and as I felt its sharp warmth on my skin, my teeth grit. As yellow chased it, it softened its edge in my blood. But as blue slowly followed, my eyes began to sting. When green crossed in front of me, my heart began to race. As red strolled behind, the racing of my heart jumped, bringing heat to my face despite the tears forming in my eyes, but then purple darted by and with it, everything flatlined. Speeding up around me, they left no room for escape, but I wasn't going to run.

No.

Not as I knelt there, eyes locked on the name before me, watching as the circling colors illuminated every letter. Because as amber crashed into yellow, blue crashed into green, and purple overtook red, I didn't have anything to run from. As the three muddied orbs combined, spinning around us in the air as if I had a gravity, I watched the colors fight against one another in the growing light. But as each one went out, overtaken by the darkness, I realized I knew something Cyrus hadn't the whole time.

What I felt the moment he took my brooch, it wasn't an absence of color.

He hadn't taken my feelings, they were just overwhelmed by another.

It was the very first one I met.

The color not even Nox knew about.

Number seven.

As the orb came to a stop between me and the headstone, hovering in the air, it was still, a cool calm to it as I stared into it.

Black.

Blowing my hair around with the gust it created, I could see my reflection in it.

Cyrus thought he had taken all my powers from me, taken Nox, taken everything, but he was wrong. Raising one of my hands from Ross' back, I reached toward the orb. Nox died for me, Cyrus used me, Finnegan betrayed me, Ross forgot me, and this was all I had left to gain, black. Fingers pausing, a moment from making contact, I could feel how cold the color was without even touching it. I had wrestled anger, danced with happiness, charmed excitement, survived sadness, courted love, tamed fear. And even after all that, after losing it all, I was still here.

Cyrus took everything away from me, but from nothing, something was born.

A gift, Cyrus had given me grief.

But as my finger met with the orb, as I allowed black to flow into me, I knew it was more than that. As an explosion of light shot off from us, a shockwave that threw Ross and I away from each other, I didn't see just black. No, as my back met with a headstone, as the air was knocked from me, as it took over my veins, as it seeped into my muscles, as it slowed my heart and humbled my nerves, I saw every color in grief. I saw the happiness that turned sad, I saw the fear that turned mad, I saw the love that burned most of all, I saw it, the color Nox saw the moment of the fall.

My eyes opened.

The sun turned black.

And I saw it, the way the colors changed, the way red turned to revenge.

Head dropping, back screaming from the impact with the hard headstone, I sat in the brittle grass, taking in the feeling. Hair hanging in my face, my glasses sat, broken on the ground. Air knocked from me, it left a vacuum in my core.

For a moment, all was still, as the clouds above broke and rain started to fall.

Slowly lifting my head, I took a breath.

I opened my eyes.

Black settled in my chest.

The rain stopped in time, trapped, suspended in the air.

A rolling gust of colors exploded from me, bringing back vibrancy to my surroundings. A numb stillness, the world was silent as I stood, sliding my back up the headstone. Straightening, I swayed a bit as I tossed my hair out of my face. Looking around at the drops of rain that sat, floating in the air about, my eyes caught on one right in front of me. Hand trembling as I brought it up, I extended my finger. Tapping the water droplet, it turned yellow upon the contact. Shaking, it jolted before my face, floating in the air. Shooting straight up from me, I watched the drop gather more drops on the way, growing as its piercing ring was the only sound in the world. Exploding above me, it was silent, but it looked like a firework as sparks rained down from it, turning everything yellow for a moment.

A smile found me.

Looking back down, I reached for the next closest drop and when I tapped it, it turned red. Shooting up, it gathered more water until it exploded too, turning the graveyard red. Stepping around, every drop I made contact with shot up, flashing a different color, exploding in silence. Staining the sky, my colors outshined the sunrise.

Staring up as colors splashed over me, each explosion in time with a beat of my heart, feeling started to return to my body, the cold that had taken me melting away. Smiling as yellow rained down again, I stepped around. Nothing like

when I tamed purple, this felt real, like I had actually done it.

Though, as I stepped back, glancing toward Cyrus'

headstone, I realized that, unlike the other colors, I didn't

have to win over black.

Why was that?

My eyes met Ross, ending my train of thought.

Taking my first step his way, flowers bloomed beneath my

shoe, the petals black. As I closed the space between us, I ran

through the suspended rain, and with each contact, every

droplet shot up into the sky, silently exploding in vibrant

colors above. Stopping before him as my powers lit the world

in rainbows, I took to my knees on the grave. The only sound

that of my shaking intake, we were the only two people in

this world, this paused moment in time where the rain sat

suspended in the air. Head hung low, back against Cyrus'

headstone, he was motionless, color drained from him. A red

firework exploded above us as a little smile found me.

Though, as I leaned forward, taking him into an embrace,

blue overtook the red. Holding him close, his limp head fell onto my shoulder. Arms wrapping around him, my eyes closed. He was cold, so cold, he must have been out there for far too long. As I let out a shaking breath, I made a wish.

That no matter what, somehow, someway, we would meet again, someday.

Blue sparks rained down around us, staining the grass in the color. I could feel it, the cold begin to leave him, his pulse pick up as I lowered my head to his shoulder.

"Thank you." My voice shook, barely a whisper as tears started to bud in my closed eyes, "You've always treated me so well when I gave you nothing in return," bringing my hand up to the back of his head, my grip tightened on him as my voice cracked, "I wasn't a good big brother, and now I'll never have the chance, I can't stay here." Stifling a sob as I buried my head into his shoulder, I held him for one last moment, "I'm sorry."

Blue exploded, taking over everything when I pulled away. Leaning him back against the headstone again, watching as his hair fell back over his face, I saw them for a moment, the tears falling from his closed eyes before the name on the headstone behind him caught my gaze.

Jaw tightening as my heart ached more with every beat, I stood.

I'd have to end it, the story of the boy who could feel nothing. Bringing my hand up to my bowtie, without the brooch it felt too light. Nox already wrote the ending, but, I was going to do it differently. Hand dropping from my bowtie, my eyes averted. It wasn't like he was alive to stop me.

Looking up to the colors as they swam in the sky, I thought on what Cyrus had said about the brooch, on what Finnegan had told Nox, on what Kasper said about the book, and it all made sense. Finnegan told Nox that if his brooch was removed, it would possibly retain some of his powers, and it appeared that Cyrus didn't remember what Nox had told him about it. Nox even knew Cyrus hadn't been listening

way back when, and Cyrus admitted to it too. He must have

been the one who had previously read the text Kasper and

Jack found that suggested my powers were tied to the brooch

and was thinking that when he took it, my powers would

completely transfer to him and spare my demise. I was so

overtaken by black, by grief, that my colors appeared stolen,

but I was just overwhelmed, short circuited. What Cyrus had

must have been but a trace of my powers, there was no way

for him to know the difference.

But…

That was only part of it.

Cyrus claimed that if I took off the brooch, my

powers would not only kill me, but destroy everything else,

too. He said that he had seen it happen to incarnations before

me, Nox even made it sound like that was true when he

begged me to end it all. Was that a lie, too? Here I was,

without the brooch, but with my powers, every color, even

black, and I wasn't dead. It would only make sense if he had actually taken all of my powers, but he hadn't, they were here with me. I had my powers before the brooch, of course I'd have them without it, too. Watching as colorful shadows shot across the frozen grass with each explosion, I wondered what even was true.

Was there something I was missing?

As my eyes scanned above me, something began to look off. The colors danced in the sky, but as I watched them a bit closer, I noticed that they looked restrained, as if they weren't dancing at all, but trying to come back down instead. Though, with every dive downward, they kept running into something I couldn't see. Brow furrowing as I stepped back, looking around, I stepped into several more drops of suspended rain, sending them shooting above. Was there something separating us from the rest of the world? When the ascending rain drops reached the sky, they each exploded into purple.

I heard it, a terrible tear, a sound I had heard somewhere before as the air plummeted with a bitter chill.

Smoke rolled by my shoes, thick and heavy, from behind. Whirling around, my eyes met Ross as he laid back against Cyrus' headstone, the smoke parting around it before rolling over his legs. As the stillness around us started to swell, my eyes slowly raised up behind the headstone. A rip in the world itself, a purple vortex floated in the air of the graveyard and as the weight of the air began to weigh on my shoulders, smoke bellowed from the rip before me and from it a dark form was born.

"Igor," the world shook as a voice came from the slowly clearing smoke, so deep and muddy it was as if it congealed the air.

"Your time has come," another voice said, one that rang in my ears as a form floated away from the first.

"We meant what we said to that imprudent immortal," a third voice said, and though I understood it, something about it sounded backwards, as if it were echoing back into itself as another form broke off from the second.

"It's a pleasure," I straightened, looking them up as the smoke cleared between us, "I've heard a lot about you."

Met with three tall, hooded figures, they floated a couple feet above the ground, Cyrus' headstone between them and I, I knew where I had heard those voices before. Darkness where their faces would have been, a deep shadow seeped out of the holes of their robes, dissipating into smoke as it drifted in the air. Turning to face them fully, my heart steadied by black, The Three didn't scare me.

The form in the middle floated forward, "I hope all good things."

"Naturally."

I heard what may have been a laugh, I wasn't sure, as the form floated around the headstone and right up to me. Taking a few steps back until I was stopped by another headstone, my eyes darted to Ross for just a moment before returning to the form before me. The other two floated around either side of Ross and stopped next to the one I faced.

Staring up into the darkness beneath their hoods, within it, I could see stars.

Starting to raise their cloaked arm up toward the sky, smoke poured from the opening between us along the way, "You must know why we are here."

Recalling what they had said to Cyrus, pieces fell into place, things I didn't have the context at the time to understand finding meaning one dot at a time until a picture pulled into clarity in my mind. My breath caught in my throat, though, that didn't stop my brow from raising.

"To banish me?"

"That's right," the form on the left said, bringing their cloaked arm up, too, "we will end what Cyrus began."

"I'm too invested in the stories this time just to let you destroy it all, the readers haven't even met my favorite character, Quill, yet," the one on the right raised their arm toward the sky, "you were an interesting character while you lasted, but this is where your novel must come to an end."

Looking between them, hand atop the cool headstone behind me, my grip tightened, "What do you mean? I've conquered all the colors, done what no other incarnation could, I don't even have the brooch and I'm fine. I'm not going to destroy anything," I paused, eyes lowering, "other than Cyrus."

"As entertaining as that would be," the one in the front tilted their hooded head, "you don't really believe you've conquered Nox's powers, do you?"

Before I could even breathe, the figure dropped their arm toward me, blinding me with their smoke until a grip met my neck. Yanking me up, I choked on my own weight. Gallows flashed behind my eyes as I clawed at their grip, but my hands went through.

Through pained eyes, I watched the figure to the left tilt their head, "While we do commend you for getting this far, albeit with Nox's help, even if Cyrus hadn't banished him, even if Cyrus was here to help with the blow, even if you still had the brooch, you wouldn't have stood a chance against them all."

The third tilted their head too, "We intervened in your reawakening because we wanted to watch and make sure you didn't destroy anything other than yourself, because now that you have all the colors, without your brooch to regulate them, you're in for it, my friend."

"Goodbye Igor, the final incarnation of Nox," the figure pulled me up close to the darkness beneath their hood as I struggled to no avail, "After hundreds of years of granting the wishes of others, rest in peace my friend, as we finally grant yours."

The two other figures dropped their arms and with them, the invisible force keeping the colors above at bay fell too, the rain resuming in its fall. Thrown into the air, toward them, I only saw my colors for a moment, eyes wide on the sky, as they fell like shooting stars toward me. Suspended in the air, the moment before they took me out, was the moment I saw what they did, the incarnations before me, right before they died. And it was then, as the colors collided with me, that I knew I was right.

I was the only one who actually knew Nox's wish.

When they struck me, with them came every thought, every feeling, every memory of those who came before me, and with each one, it became more evident, what was actually happening. I lived forty-nine lives in that moment, stories that came to an eternal end at Cyrus' hand as they tried to save Nox, tried to try to save me. They were gone now, every last one of them, even Nox was dead.

Really dead.

I could feel it, black start to consume me as my body seized, suspended in the air above the graveyard. It started at my finger tip, the one that had touched it first. Searing over my skin, I was on fire, but as colors blinded me, as they screamed through my veins and consumed me, my body hurt so much that it didn't hurt at all. With each beat of my heart I could feel it, like the deafening ring after a bomb, a swell inside pounding on my ribs, begging to break out.

This was the power Cyrus warned me about, what would happen without the brooch, what was waiting for me, had Nox not extended his hand to help. This was what would end the world, what had killed every incarnation before me, and would kill the next after me, if I wasn't the last.

But I needed to be the last.

I had to be.

If I died now, Nox's wish would die with me, remaining obscured until the next one was met with the same fate, realizing it when it was too late.

Black bled over me, taking every inch, closing in, turning my limbs to ash.

If I died now all the work my Mum did would go to waste.

Consuming my torso, black eroded me away, my colors exploding around me in the sky.

If I died now…

Black met my heart, stopping it.

Everything froze, the world going still.

Blurring beneath the profound cold that took me, my eyes closed.

If I died now, then…

Eyes opening, I was met with white, so much white. Looking up, my breath hitched. Stepping around, as my eyes scanned the abyss, my heart started to sink. It felt different.

Empty.

I was alone.

If I died now, the ending of the story of the boy who felt nothing would never be happy.

Hand burning, it caught my attention. Opening my palm, I was met with a glow that felt like home. Orange, yellow, green, blue, red, purple, they sat like marbles against my skin. Their glow the only colors in that desolate abyss, all I could do was stare at them, no longer having a brooch for them to call home.

Gravitating toward each other, they combined until the orb in my palm became dark and dense, weighing my hand down. Black rested there, staring back up at me, my refection captured in its shiny onyx. Cyrus took my colors away from me as I had come to know them, but as I picked up the black orb between my finger tips, I came to know them once more through another. Holding it up, it sat in stark contrast with the white abyss. As I stared into it, I saw them, the colors inside, floating around my reflection.

They were too much, without the brooch, I knew that. If I was going to survive them, I had to get it back. But without them, there was no way that was going to happen. Dropping the dark orb back into my hand, I knew one thing to be true. Closing my hand over it, my grip tightened.

Sometimes the only way out, was through.

Bringing it up to my chest, when my hand met my heart, it beat.

Eyes closing, I smiled.

I was going to grant Nox's wish or die trying.

Eyes opening, I was met with the sky. Falling, what was it with falling. Hair blowing into my eyes as I plummeted, a smile cracked onto my face. An explosion of green threw the rain away, clearing the sky and tainting the sunrise. When the gust hit the ground, it rumbled the earth, blowing away dead flowers from graves and knocking the bell from its hook. I heard it as I came to a stop, suspended in the air, the last ring of the bell before it landed in a puddle on the ground.

Air clearing between us as I hovered about ten feet above the ground, hair flowing as green radiated from me, my eyes met them. All three of them, knocked to the dirt, and though I couldn't see their eyes beneath their darkened hoods, I could tell they were staring at me.

A laugh bubbling up in my chest, it only took a couple moments for it to boil over. World warping around me, the pressure in the air grew, and with every laugh, I felt it, myself slipping away more. This was dangerous, Cyrus was right.

"Look at you," standing in the air, I bent toward them, my voice growing less stable with every word, "*The Three* my ass, I bet those cloaks of yours are filled with nothing but hot air." Straightening, I threw my arm to the side and with it came a gust of air so strong, it ripped through the forest, leveling trees. Staring as the creaking of breaking wood faded from my ears, my pause only lasted a moment before a laugh took me again. "You, banish me?" Slowly dragging my eyes back toward them as my head crooked, there was an audacity to me I hadn't had before, a confidence that came with the power screaming through me, "Right."

And though somewhere I must have known, as tears took my eyes and my smile warped my features, as my hair flowed with the colors roaring around me and my voice grew uncharacteristically animated, that part of me, the part that knew I was losing my grip, didn't give a shit.

After a life of passivity, of the customer is always right, and taking a backseat in my own journey, the pen was in my hand, and I was going to write the end of this story.

When I threw my head back, a gust of air shot above me, blowing away the clouds with so much force they retreated over the horizons. Eyes trailing a satellite as it was shifted in its orbit, a panicked, blinking star above, my exhale electrified the air. One of The Three said something stupid that I didn't hear as the roar of power rushed through my ears. A plant about to go nuclear I could feel it, the precipice of power I was hanging over, it was paralyzing. I couldn't think, and when I didn't think about it, it was fine, but I had something I needed to do, a wish I needed to grant. And while I had every power in the universe at my disposal, I didn't know jackshit about how to use them. Eyes closing as my hand met my head, fingers lacing in my hair, I tried to beat off the intoxication that had taken me just enough to conjure my next step.

I just had to find my way back to Cyrus.

Then I could lose it.

I had read something somewhere about absolute power corrupting or whatever, but this was fine, I'd be fine.

I just needed to think.

Something cold caught my attention in my pocket.

Eyes flying open, my smile cracked onto my face.

Head dropping, with the movement the world shook, quaking enough to knock The Three back down. Looking between them, I snorted, trying not to laugh. I held so much power, I could take out The Three, level that godforsaken graveyard that started it all, erase Cyrus' name from the headstone and desecrate his resting place. If I did that, I'd probably become the king of everything, not just Netherside. Hand raising toward them, head slowly tilting to the side, as my hair slid across my forehead, a wish began to come to rise in me. It was a wish for destruction, for power and glory, one of drunken courage and insatiable greed, but then, that's when my eyes caught on something.

Unconscious against Cyrus' headstone, Ross' head hug low, his bright orange hair flowed with the ambient breeze around us.

I stopped.

Though my powers wanted it, I forced my arm to lower as it shook, fighting me.

I couldn't put him in harm's way.

"Well," my hand found its way into my pocket, "while this is fun," my fingertips met something cool and smooth inside, "I have to go fuck up Cyrus so," pulling the stone Kasper gave me from my pocket, its sobering electric blue glow pierced the air, "excuse me."

Throwing the stone down, as it plummeted to the ground below me, my eyes followed it until they caught on Ross. When the stone met with the ground, its blue light exploded, illuminating my little brother's features.

Tears welling in my eyes despite my smile, I promised him that I'd defeat these powers before they defeated me and ended the world so that he could live on in it.

He deserved so much more, but that was the best I could do.

A blue portal swam on the ground below me, the lights ebbing and flowing, electric strings splashed up out of it into the air. Eyes raising to The Three as they scrambled up, my brow raised as they darted toward me. Dropping from the air, my posture remained as I fell, a smile taking me as I waved. One of The Three swiped at me as my feet met with the portal, barely missing me, brushing against the top of my head in a suspended moment. As blue took over everything I saw beyond the dark haze beneath their hood and, in that moment, I saw blue reflect in human eyes.

Blue became my world, erasing everything else.

Shot back out the other side of the portal, I had expected to land or something, but no, I was thrown right into a fucking wall.

Stiff as pain caused my body to seize, I fell backward away from the stone, flat to the ground. Air knocked out of me with the impact, my ears rang as my nose stung. Goddamn piece of shit portal. Hand up to my face, a curse beneath my cough, that's when the tickle of grass met my ears. Eyes slowly opening beneath furrowed brow, they focused on the sky above. Orange raging behind the sprinkling of clouds, it corrupted the twilight, tinting the park that surrounded me.

My heart pounded against my ribs with one, vengeful beat.

Hissing, my other hand tightened in the grass beneath me. Body locking up as my teeth grit, my eyes closed under the pressure.

My colors wanted out.

My heart pounded again.

They wanted to destroy everything.

And again.

But I couldn't let them out.

Again.

Not here.

The grass beneath me caught fire.

Not yet.

Something cold and a little bit wet brushed up against the side of my face.

Eyes flying open, they were met with a purple sky. Head slowly turning to the side, the grass suspended, standing straight like the hairs on the back of my neck, my gaze met orange.

My heart stopped, and with it, a shockwave took out every nearby tree.

Swimming in the air, weaving through the blades of grass, unbothered by the flames, was a ghost, a little ghost. Slightly transparent, it didn't dull their color as they hid behind a bit of grass when they noticed me staring. Purple turning to something else as I slowly sat up, I only saw her for a moment more before my vision turned to glass.

"Margo?"

When I blinked the tears from my eyes, rain deluged from the sky, instantly drenching me and putting out the fires. With a little flash of movement, she crashed into my chest. Though I could barely feel her impact, as my shaking hands raised, I could feel a warmth she didn't carry in life, not even when her blood dripped through my fingers.

She snuggled into my chest, her contact lessening the swell beneath my ribs.

The rain stopped.

What was once careening out of control began to quell, though still untamed, as my heart began to steady, surrounded by scorched grass, fallen trees, and rain sizzling with the smoke.

As I held her close, my wide eyes slowly raised to the now clear sky.

Jesus fucking Christ.

Mind clearing a bit with the clouds, I took a shaking breath. I was going to have to get the brooch back before I completely lost control. My eyes drifted down to the wall I had impacted with. Cracked and damaged, bits of it fell to the ground. Gaze catching beyond it, I was met with the Limbo castle. I just needed to get to Kasper, needed to get to Cyrus, then this would all be over.

Nox's wish would finally be granted.

Shaking as I stood, holding Margo close, my body fought every move, as if my muscles had been fried. Glasses falling from my face, they hit the singed grass. Staring down at them as they rested there, throwing up some ash in the impact, their metal bent and lenses cracked, I realized I could see them clearly. Blinking, I looked up and around. Nothing was even a bit blurry. Eyes dropping down to Margo as she cuddled me, the sky grew yellow above.

A rock fell from the wall next to me, making me jump away, the sky flashing purple. Heart racing, I'm sure Margo could feel it as a shaking breath escaped me. I couldn't lose it. Eyes catching on an entrance to the castle, I didn't know why I had calmed some, but I wasn't going to waste my moment of clarity. Holding Margo close, I took off running, stepping on my glasses in my hurry.

Retracing the steps I took accompanied by Phantasmal, I ran past the outer wall, through the courtyard, and toward the castle. Legs threatening to buckle with every step, out of breath, I entered the shadow of the castle as I approached the stairs. Stumbling on every other incline, I nearly fell but I couldn't stop. Something had calmed my powers down enough for me to think, I couldn't waste a moment. Coughing as I made it to the top of the stairs, I ran toward the towering front doors. Not taking a moment to catch my breath, I ran into the doors.

And I suppose I must have just like, assumed that when I became the most powerful being in the fucking universe that doors would light up and magically open for me or whatever.

But I was wrong.

Stumbling back, I nearly fell back down the stairs when the doors didn't even budge upon my impact. One hand up to my nose as my face stung, tears welling in the corners of my closed eyes, when they opened, the door was too.

Eyebrow twinging up, I stared into the dark passage for a moment before bolting in.

With every step I took the ground rumbled, every candle on the wall I passed in the main hall lit a different color. Eyes locked on the next set of doors as colorful light surrounded me, I held Margo up to my chest against my heart.

"Kasper!" My voice cracked as I nearly slipped on the marble floor.

The door gained a blue glow the moment before I would have run into it, busting open just in time. Stumbling forward into the throne room, I almost tripped over myself, panting so hard I felt like I was going to be sick. Battery acid in my veins, blood draining from my head, numbness washed through me as I doubled over. Ears ringing, I was tired, so, so tired, but I couldn't stop.

Lifting my head, disheveled bangs hanging in my face, my chest heaved as my eyes met his. Standing a few steps in front of me, as if he had just seen a ghost, Kasper brought his hands up to his hair.

"Igor," running to me, Kasper stopped at my side, bending over to look into my eyes, "what happened?"

Coughing, one hand up to my mouth, my head dropped again as other footsteps raced toward us. "Cyrus," I could barely speak, but between the pants, I forced the words out, "Cyrus killed Nox."

Oliver's voice came from my other side, "He claimed he killed you too."

A laugh stifled my panting as I straightened, "He's going to wish he had."

Flipping my hair out of my face, I was met with Phantasmal, Kasper, and Oliver all staring back at me. Salem, Jack, Hugo and the others stayed a few steps behind Oliver, his arm extended to stop them as Kasper looked me up and down, a slow caution to him.

Jack stepped forward a bit, stopped by Oliver before he could get any closer, "If Cyrus killed Nox and took your brooch, then how are you…"

"I don't know," eyes drifting to Jack, I could only look at him for a moment before they flew away, one random candle in the oom lighting red in the background, "but I need to get to Cyrus." Taking a deep breath, I tried to gather myself enough to stand straight, "Will you help me?"

When Kasper said nothing, brow furrowed, eyes taking me in, the hesitation that took him suspended my breath in my chest. Hugo looked between Kasper and I, waiting on every word, Salem eyeing me from his side. Jack stood, arms crossed over his chest clad in lengthy white lab coat while the other two members stood back, unengaged. When my eyes met Hugo's, I could see it, the silence was killing him.

"Please," I ran my free and through my hair, leaving it there, "I figured it out, I've met the seventh color and I know Nox's wish," lowering my hand, my hair fell back into place, "and I need to grant it, or this cycle will continue."

Eyes widening, I saw something light in Kasper.

A slight smile took him.

"Alright."

Hugo cheered, breaking the ice of the room. Kasper tried to hide his laugh as he turned to face Edgar. Instructing him to send us to Netherside, they exchanged quiet words that were drowned out by Hugo's footsteps as he ran toward me. Salem and Jack following close behind, the smiles they wore made me forget the dire situation for a moment.

Hugo had his mouth open, about to say something to me when his hand met my back. The kid must have not known his own strength because when he pat me, he sent me stumbling forward. A laugh took me, for a moment, but then Margo was knocked from my grip and the moment she left my hands, my heart stopped.

The candles roared, rainbow fire screaming up the walls as my body seized.

An explosion screamed from me, sending everyone flying. Dropping to my knees, crushed beneath the weight of my powers, my arms wrapped around my chest as my forehead met the floor. Searing, they blurred my vision as tears streamed from my eyes, turning the marble floor beneath me into a kaleidoscope. Wind ripping around, in the eye of a storm, my colors warped my surroundings, muddying as they corrupted everything around me.

What happened?

The ground cracked beneath me.

I may have yelled under the weight, I couldn't hear it through the ringing of my ears, but I did taste the blood as I was crushed. I was so close, I just needed to get to Cyrus, to end this, before it ended me.

Blue flashed through the warping colors, clearing a space in the storm before me. Landing on his knees at my side, Kasper's hand met my back. The storm lessened, though its howling winds quieted, they were overtaken by Kasper's yell. Shaking as I turned my head to the side, I looked up to him through pained eyes and disheveled hair. Teeth grit, writhing above me, Kasper's hand glowed blue on my back, my colors flashing beneath his skin.

What was he doing.

His head dropped as his other hand met my back.

Every color flashed through my mind, meeting orange and yellow and green and blue and red and purple and black, the images became overwhelming. Raging and laughing and falling and sobbing and loving and fighting and grieving, Cyrus and Finnegan and Valor and Abraxas and Anton and Kasper and everyone, it was so much.

He collapsed against me, his grip unfading.

I was too much.

Black flashed over us and a moment later, two more hands met my back.

Pressure sharply dropping, the storm began to not only quiet, but calm as I looked up to see Hugo and Salem kneeling with me, hands on my back, in obvious pain. Running through the windy haze, Jack met us and without hesitation joined. As my vision blurred, exhaustion taking me, the last thing I saw before my eyes forced themselves shut was Oliver and the others as they came running up to me, too.

More hands met my back.

Everything became still.

A quiet so loud, it made my ears hum.

Panting, forehead against the ground, body too weak to pick itself up, enough hands to carry a casket on my back, my body finally relaxed. The pressure dripping from me, I was left with nothing but exhaustion.

Picking himself up from my back, Kasper's hand remained, and though I couldn't manage to move and look at him, I could sense it as he lowered his head near mine, his voice soft, "Yeah, that's about what I was expecting, how were you keeping it together until now?"

"That's way too much to be carrying on your own," Hugo's hand rubbed my back, "I don't know what I did, but I'm like 94% sure that was my fault, I'm real sorry."

"The fish," Jack's voice made my heart jump a bit, bringing some life back to me as he went on, "you noticed it too, right, Salem?"

"Yes," Salem's hand was so dainty I could barely feel it as he kept it on my shoulder, "Say, Igor, Cyrus killed Nox, but did that include every incarnation?"

All I could do was nod, forehead still pressed into the floor, doubled over on my knees, arms wrapped around my chest.

I heard it, Kasper's sharp intake. "You're all alone now, aren't you?"

I tried to keep myself gathered, but failed, as I nodded again.

"He's not alone," Edgar said, making me tense a bit, "look at what we just did. He was gonna end the world or somethin' but because he has us to help take some of the brunt, he was okay."

"This is not sustainable, though," Oliver said, his hand the coldest on my back, "what, are we just going to waltz into the Netherside castle like this? We will not even fit through a door."

A beat dragged by, one in which I could feel my pulse beating through all of them though their hearts no longer lived. They had done what Cyrus used to do on his own, what Nox was doing from behind the scenes without my knowledge. These powers were too big for me, but apparently weren't too big for company.

Jack hummed, his hand starting to slide from my back, but before he lost contact, he paused, "Igor, I'm going to remove my hand, be prepared, but if my guess is right, then it should only hurt for a moment."

Taking a breath, I managed to say, "Okay."

hen Jack's hand slid completely from my back, I felt it, a jolt of power shoot through all of us. Muffled groans scattered through the group, I could feel them tense beneath the brunt. I was hurting them. But then, a moment later, the weight was lessened, distributed again.

"Fantastic," I could hear Jack's smile, "okay, I have a plan. Hugo, take Kasper's hand, but leave your other on Igor until you do."

This time, when Hugo's hand left me, I didn't feel any change. One at a time, I listened to Jack instruct everyone until only one hand was left on my back. Sliding his hand up my back to my shoulder, Kasper's fingers trailed down my arm until his hand met mine. Face surely red, I did my best not to shiver as I knelt there staring at the ground. Taking grip of my hand, Kasper pulled me up.

Eyes wide as they met everyone else, I barely had enough strength to hold myself up. Kneeling in a line, a chain of held hands, Kasper, Hugo, Salem, Ash, Edgar, Jack, and Oliver looked back at me. Margo floated around, swimming about everyone until she swam right up to me. Hovering before my eyes, though she had no expressions, being a fish and all, it almost felt like she was smiling at me. Landing on my shoulder, when she made contact, relief took everyone.

Energy returning to me, I could still feel the powers, but they weren't so heavy, not demanding to break free from my ribs just to be seen any longer. Glancing around, my eyes took in what I had done. Windows shattered, the castle a mess, my powers spared nothing. Taking a deep breath that turned up with his smile, Kasper's glassy eyes glowed a bit brighter as his grip on my hand tightened. As he stood, the others followed behind him. Straightening, he looked down to me, his crown fading into existence above his head. Hand in mine as I knelt before him, Kasper smiled at me.

If only the people who bullied him in school could have seen the king he had become.

Pulling me to my feet, Kasper yanked me into his arms. As Edgar's shadow stretched out beneath us, taking the entire floor, Kasper buried his head in my shoulder. The floor disappeared beneath us, sending us dropping into darkness. As we fell, the moment before we were taken away, I heard Kasper's voice.

"That was scary, I don't want to lose you."

Dropping into the strings of shadow, I saw the glistening of a tear that flew from my eyes in the fall.

My arms tightened around him.

Thrown out the other end of the shadow, everyone else caught their footing and kept me from losing mine. Surrounded in embraces, it took me a moment to gather myself, arms wrapped around me, my face buried in Kasper's chest. Pulling myself back as Kasper's hand slid from my back, down my arm, then to my hand, my vision glassed a bit. At Kasper's side, silent but eyes speaking volumes, Salem smiled at me.

Smiling back at him, I didn't deserve them, but I think I had found myself in the company of friends.

The air spiked cold, a shared shudder taking everyone. When their eyes flew up behind me, I watched everyone's color drain, even Kasper's, as they caught on something. Slowly turning around, my eyes met the Netherside castle, or what once was. The structure warped, barely solid, as if one could poke it and it would liquify, hemorrhaging a river. The silver moat boiling, the surrounding topiary burned as the sky raged, galaxies birthing and dying within flashing moments above.

Eyes lowering, they caught on the chaotic center of it all. On the roof, the platform I had watched him fall from, the throne he stood before was visible from all the way down there. His laugh, it echoed, a distorted ring from what it once was as he stood above it all.

Father Cyrus Glory.

Though, from that name, he was about to fall.

With a roar of thunder and a strike of lightning, the front doors to the Netherside castle shattered, its singed shards pouring into the foyer. Cracking beneath my shoes as I ran in, pulling Kasper and the others behind me, I took a sharp turn into an outer hall. Deserted, the castle sat in ruin around us as we took a corner. Running down the hall, they kept up with me, even as my every step grew faster. Every candle we passed on the wall lit a different color, the flame roaring. Rounding another corner, I retraced my steps until we were met with just another one of the candles, mounted to the wall above a drip tray.

Stopping behind me, my chain of support, they never seemed to run out of breath, but I did as I struggled to catch it. Reaching my free arm up to the candle mounted above me, my hand wrapped around the metal neck. Chest heaving, my head dropped as I pulled down on it. With a click and a rumble, dust knocked loose, raining around us. Coughing as my fingers slid from the neck, I looked up through my messy bangs as a door slid open from the stone wall in front of us.

A gasp from behind me broke the dramatics of the moment, "See, they know what's up," Jack went on as I turned to look at him from over my shoulder, "as far as I can tell, there isn't a single secret door in your castle and that's a shame."

Laughing, Hugo ran his hand through his hair.

Staring at Jack for a moment too long as Salem and Edgar heckled Kasper about how boring all the limbo castles were, I took one more shaking breath before I turned back to face the dark passage. Dimly lit spiral stairs before me, atop them stood Cyrus. One way or another, the story Nox was writing, the story he never finished, would end on that rooftop. Closing my eyes for a moment, my grip on Kasper tightened.

Pulling them into the darkness, my shoes thudded against the wooden stairs. As we ran up the spiral, every candle we passed lit another color, but as we grew closer to the top, they all turned purple.

"Hey, Kasper?"

"Yeah?"

The echoing of our steps filled the beat until we reached the top of the stairs. Facing the door that didn't close properly, a sliver of light pouring from the threshold, I struggled to catch my breath. Kasper close at my side, I turned to him, looking between his eyes.

"Nox's wish, it was," Leaning in, I lowered my voice to a whisper, and as I finished my sentence, Kasper's grip tightened on my hand.

His intake shook, "Why are you-"

Stepping away from him, I looked back to the door. "I don't plan on losing to myself, but," I glanced back over my shoulder to see his glowing blue eyes furrowed in the dark, "if it comes to that, promise that you'll tell the next incarnation what I just told you?"

Blue eyes widening in the darkness, he stared at me for a moment, "You promised me you wouldn't make me do that."

"I know," I raised my hand to the door, "and it's only if," Bringing my forehead to the door, I closed my eyes for a moment, "I just don't want to hurt anybody."

With a harsh breath, he looked away from me, "I promise."

Smiling, as I stood from the door, it lit purple and a moment later, it exploded off its hinges, blinding even me with the flash. Hand slipping from Kasper's, I felt him try to keep me, but decided to set me free.

Margo floated up from my shoulder.

With my first step into the dust, the roof cracked beneath my shoe.

With my second through the dust, I took a deep breath in.

And with my third step out of the dust, I exhaled.

A smile took me.

The deafening ring after a bomb, I let it, the swell inside pounding on my ribs, break out.

Roaring from me, they took the air with them as the colors poured, bleeding. Warping the world, distorting our surroundings further as I stood, head crooked, smile tearing across my face, tears in my eyes, the dust cleared. Succumbed to their totality, when I wasn't fighting them, my colors didn't hurt me.

Partially turned to face us, Cyrus' raging red eyes widened only the slightest bit as a brow raised. His briefest moment of surprise passed, his features twisting with his laugh. Perhaps he was confused to see my colors, under the impression that he had stolen my powers, not only the object through which they were managed. Possessing but an echo of my colors, they were still too much for him. This wasn't the movie star I knew, it wasn't the zombie I had exhumed, or the boyish underdog with a job to do, no, this person, warped from power, was nothing more than the reflection of a six-hundred-year misconception at his breaking point. Though, as I took my next step toward him, I could see it, that breaking point reached over and over again.

Being killed but never dying, it was his specialty.

And no matter what he said, no matter what act he put on, as I took another step, I saw right through him.

"Goddamn," Cyrus swayed around, unhinged as his words were more laughter than anything else, "you must be a glutton for punishment, I saved you, finally freed you of these colors, and what do you do? Not only get them back, somehow, but also waltz yourself right back to me, after you saw what I am willing to do?" throwing his head back as he stood before the throne, he didn't even move as I closed the space between us, "Don't tell me you have a death wish, too."

Not sparing him a word, my colors warping my surroundings as I walked up to him, I could barely look at Cyrus, any dignity he once possessed thrown to the wind. As glass threatened to take my eyes, I stopped right before him. Pity, that was all I was left with as he leaned forward to look me in the eyes, his smirk leaving him unrecognizable.

It didn't have to come to this.

I'm sure in all his years of being alive Cyrus had accumulated enough money to afford a therapist.

Snorting, brow raised as his head crooked, it appeared that my lack of reaction stoked the flames of his meltdown as another laugh took him. Looking him up and down, his whole body shaking, about to burst at the seams, he may have been a threatening villain, if he could have handled it.

But at his core, Cyrus was truly the kindest person I had ever met.

Though he had done his best to hide it, my powers betrayed him, turning red as he killed Nox. At first, I wasn't sure how it could have been an act of love, but as I stood there, eyes locked on his, it all made sense. Though his reasons were unknown to me, one thing was true, in every life time, Cyrus was there, helping us, caring for us, loving us, each and every incarnation, for exactly who they were, exactly where they were at, determined to save us, to save Nox. Despite his curse of immortality, despite being the one who killed Nox in the first place, Cyrus never faltered, and even now, as he turned to fully face me, a monster of a man, I could still see it in him, as he died at the hands of our powers over and over, he'd do it all again.

He'd hold every incarnation as they died, he'd smile at the next, he'd do his best to save them, he'd do anything for Nox, he'd grant Nox's wish, even if that meant killing him, no matter how much he didn't want to. He'd take our powers to keep them from hurting us, he'd erase my memories, he'd send me away, he'd sentence himself to eternal torture, just to end this, to free Nox, to save me. He may have gotten away with it, had it not been for his wish.

His resolve must have been shaky, as he wished my memories away, his heart betraying him. Because for a spell bestowed by the strongest powers in the universe, it was pretty easy to break.

Father Cyrus Glory, he wasn't Cyrus at all.

Out of the corner of my eye I could see them, Kasper, Oliver, and Phantasmal standing back, Kasper's arm out to stop them, keeping them at standby. His eyes locked on me, my every move under his scrutiny. I'm sure he was looking for it, the moment I snapped, the moment he'd need to jump in and banish me before I destroyed everything, the moment I'd make him break our promise.

Mouth opening, likely to mock me again, whatever stupid ass thing Cyrus was going to say would forever remain unsaid as everyone watched me raise my hand from my side. When my fingers met his head, his word turned into a croak, dying in his throat as they laced through his hair. Sky turning red, it became the only color in the world as it drowned everything else out, all consuming. Stepping right up to him, eyes locked, I felt my powers in him as they seared up through my arm. Grip tightening in his hair, I earned a sound from him as I pressed my body up against his, backing him into the throne. Twisting his head toward mine, our lips hovered but an inch apart. His entire body tense, eyes wide, face redder than the world around us, his quivering brows brought a teary need to his crimson. Though he'd never say it, he didn't need to, because I could hear it in his eyes.

He needed help.

Slowly moving in, I watched his eyes close as I stopped, our lips barely touching.

A smile tugged up on the line of my mouth.

My grip tightened in his hair.

Twisting my wrist, the snaps that followed flattened the air.

Ripping my arm out to the side, I tore his head clean off with it.

The splashing of his black blood took the moment as it spewed from his neck's stalk, his head left dangling, disembodied, in my hand out to my side. The sound of his crown hitting the ground rang over all else. Blood rolling down my cheek, my yellow shirt stained in it, my exhale turned into a chuckle. His body dropped to its knees before me as my chuckle turned to a laugh. Head flying back, I looked into the sky, losing myself to the moment.

Tears streaming down my face, laugh echoing over the kingdom, my colors stormed around, warping the word.

I heard it, the moment it all came to head, the one in which I snapped.

And just like that, every feeling I could have ever felt came to me, every laugh I could have shared with my family, the annoyance of every stupid thing a customer had said, every tear I never got to shed, every flutter of my heart I never got to experience, the exhilaration of every youthful endeavor I never got to ride, the panic of every unknown I could have faced. Then, as my laugh began to cripple me, my body shaking with the power, with the lost time and normalcy of the numbness of the past, something else came.

Something I had never met before.

These powers, these emotions, they roared, they screamed and cried and yearned and yelled, begged for attention, to be noticed, to be felt. But, as they came to a crescendo, through them, through the lost time and never-to-bes, came black once more.

I had denied my role in this story, that I was the next incarnation of Nox, rebuked all that Cyrus had said. I had clashed with it, wrestled a losing fight with my powerlessness and lack of agency. I did what was expected of me, under the expectation that it was an exchange, a bargain. I did anything I could to turn the tides of the enviable.

My eyes closed, tears breaking loose from them.

And here I was, at the other end of it all.

I thought black was all that there was left, the black of Finnegan's betrayal, the black of Nox's death, the black of Cyrus' broken heart, but, as black grew brighter, I met something else.

White.

Through the grief of what was never to be, it was then, in that moment as I met my feelings in their true totality, that I found acceptance in what I was meant to be.

Heart thudding, my eyes flew open.

Fighting with my body as my powers seared through my muscles, I dropped my head back down. Met with Cyrus' bleeding body on its knees before me, my eyes stopped on the brooch pinned to the knot of his tie. Arm shaking as I forced it forward, it fought with every stiff movement. Hand trembling as my fingers quivered, they desperately tried to extend toward the brooch as it sat, dripping in Cyrus' black blood.

The tips of my fingers met the brooch, and as they dug behind it, I had to choke my laugh back, had to force every move, if I didn't, Nox's wish would never come true, these powers never sated.

Pulling the brooch from Cyrus' bloodied tie, it was a welcome weight on my fingertips. Bringing it up to myself, I hesitated only for the briefest moment before pinning it to the knot of my bowtie. In that moment, that final moment, I took it in, the unhindered might of Nox's legacy, free of any catalysis.

The line of my mouth turned up.

Pinning the brooch to myself, the colors retracted back into me in an instant, leaving a quiet, still vacuum behind as the air hummed in the silence. My breath shook as the tension drained from my body. The mania had ended, but what I was left with was also a lot. Dropping my head with my shoulders, I took another breath as normal sensation began to return to me, albeit a bit numb after how heightened everything had been. The colors on my brooch lit to life, brighter than they had been, and I could see them, reflected in Cyrus' blood, completed by the center gem glowing black.

I heard a stifled breath at my side.

Slowly looking up to my left, my right arm remaining extended out, my eyes met metal.

Raised above my head, stopped mid swing, Kasper's glowing sword was but a moment from decapitating me. Beneath it, breath catching in his throat, eyes wide and teary, Kasper was white as a ghost as panic cracked into something else. Chest heaving as tears broke from his eyes, he hard averted them as he let go of his sword. Turning to glitter above me before it could make contact, the sword disappeared entirely.

Turning away from me, a curse beneath his breath, Kasper brought his hands up to the sides of his head, lacing them through his hair. "Jesus fucking christ, Igor, what was that? I almost banished you."

Before I could say anything to him, as my colors settled in my bones, my eyes met the others who had come with me. Standing there, staring, every single one of them looked as if they had watched a cold-blooded murder. I didn't know why even Salem was looking at me like that until-

My eyes widened.

Oh.

"Don't worry, I'm sure it hurt but," I brought my right arm back around, "he's okay."

Cyrus stared back at me, his hair a clump in my hand as I held his dismembered head before me, blood dripping from his neck. He was ridiculous, he didn't even fight back, an anticlimactic villain. Though, as he rolled his eyes away from me, it was obvious that he hadn't wanted to be, he just had to save me. He just had to grant what he thought was Nox's wish, he just had to free me from the fate my powers surely held, he just had to send me back to live and die in a way he never could. I don't think he wanted to, but he had no choice if he wanted to remain true to who he was and what he stood for, all he's ever done and all he'll ever do.

To truly love Nox.

Irises calmly red again, his charming features were now recognizable, no longer corrupted, "That wasn't fair, I thought you were going to kiss me."

Raising a brow as the rainbow from my brooch illuminated him, I held his helpless, decapitated head, dangling in my grip right before mine. Before I could laugh, I closed the space. His sound of surprise muffled by my lips meeting his, tears budded in my closed eyes as I kissed him. When he kissed me back, I parted his lips. The sound he made when I kissed him again surely turned the sky red as my other hand found its way to the side of his face.

Jack cleared his throat, sending ice through my blood as his footsteps approached.

Kissing Cyrus one last time, I savored it before pulling back.

Eyes wide on me, brow raised and face red, Cyrus stared as his head dangled in my hand. When I loosened my grip in his hair, his soft waves sliding out between my fingers, his body reached up to catch his head. Holding it above his neck as his body beneath started to slither together, reattaching the bone, nerves, and flesh, he didn't look away from me. When his head was attached enough to let go, his middle finger met his forehead, lowered to the center of his chest, then tapped each of his shoulder before he swallowed, on his knees before me.

Submission looked good on him.

Which was great, because I was mad.

Bringing up my shoe, I pressed it against his chest, making him fall back, barely catching himself on one of hands behind him. His crown scratched against the stone as his other hand met it. Leaning down, pressing all my weight into him, I could feel his arms shake under the pressure as my eyes met his. His gaze drifted down and when it met the brooch, it widened. Jack stopping at my side, we exchanged looks for a moment before my view lowered again.

There Cyrus was, beneath me, defeated. Though we had only been separated for hours perhaps, it felt like eons as Netherside came to peace around us, the sky no longer storming. It was him, it had always been him, the cause of it all. And though I could perhaps forgive him eventually for what he had done to me because I knew somewhere he was trying to save me, operating under false assumptions because he didn't pay attention to Nox's explanation of the brooch six-hundred-some-odd years ago, I could never forgive Father Glory for what he did to Nox in his first life. But, as my eyes searched his, something didn't add up. Not a single lifetime had passed me by since in which Cyrus wasn't there, supporting me, loving me, caring for me, not even the very first reincarnation.

I had so many questions, though as they churned in my mind, I knew that the answer to one of them would answer all but one.

"Cyrus," I pressed into him a bit more, my shoe digging into his chest as he fought to keep himself up, "what the fuck do you think Nox's wish was?"

Blinking at me, his teeth grit as his brow trembled low as he struggled under my weight, "He wished me immortal so that I could watch him die over and over again."

Staring at him and his wavy disheveled hair and exhausted crimson eyes, all I could do was sigh, "You're an idiot." I leaned down further, pushing his muscles to the limit, "Nox's wish was to-"

A booming laugh cut me off, echoing so loud it made my ears ring as I felt the weight of the sound on my shoulders. Teeth grit as I looked up and around, I couldn't see the source of the laugh. But as it turned into feedback, a laugh track playing over itself, I knew who it belonged to.

I looked down to Cyrus as he looked up to me.

"That's Anton, it's it?"

He nodded, just once.

Sighing as I ran my hand through my hair, head turning to the side, I closed my eyes, "Of course it is."

A sonic boom tore through the air, rattling me down to my bones as I stepped back from Cyrus. Shoe catching, I tripped, and as I fell back toward Jack, my eyes met the sky. Careening toward me, but a moment from colliding, a black form with piercing white, glowing eyes stared into my soul. The sky flashed purple, my heart hitting the floor with my stomach and blood, as that moment passed, the final moment before that monster would end me. Crashing into Jack's chest in my stumble, when his hands found my shoulders, my eyes closed, cringing away from the impending impact.

But then, when I heard Jack's breath hitch, my eyes flew open.

Staring straight into the dark form, less than a centimeter away from my face, it sat, suspended. Eyes darting down to Cyrus as he remained on the ground, eyes wide on the form above him, he didn't move. Looking over my shoulder to the others, Kasper bringing his sword up, Oliver and Hugo about to jump into action, Salem opening a small black book, Edgar and Ash looking to one another, they were still, frozen in time.

World put on pause, my breath caught as I slowly looked behind me.

The green of his wide eyes churning from behind his glasses, Jack didn't look at me.

A sharp sting caused me to seize, shrieking down my back from my shoulders. When my eyes met his hands on me, they were gone, but forms, covered in a raging static. Infecting me, the static started to overtake where he touched. Eyes lurching to me, I watched alarm take Jack when he saw the static. Pulling me back, he sent us both stumbling out of the way of the dark form. Falling away from me, the moment his hands lost contact with me, the world snapped back into place.

Colliding with the ground exactly where I had been standing, the form tore up the stone, shaking the castle with its impact like a fallen satellite. Dust overtaking the air as the world rumbled, the dark form exploded, quickly outgrowing the smoke. Struggling to stand up, I wasn't given the chance as darkness swiped through my vision, meeting my middle. In a blur of movement, I was yanked up into the air, a dark, smoky tentacle wrapped around my chest. Hair thrown into my face, obstructing my view as I was yanked around, I heard the others yell as the tentacle tightened, squeezing the air from my lungs.

"Finally," Anton's voice took over the air, "god, that took forever didn't it? Forty-nine incarnations was a bit excessive."

Flinging me roughly to the side, he knocked the hair from my eyes, revealing the scene before me. Held, tens of feet in the air above the roof of the castle, a massive, dark, smoky, Lovecraftian horror of a being before me, Anton stood in the middle of it as tentacle after tentacle came from beneath him, whipping around in the air. The others ensnared, I looked around to them as they struggled in his grip, arms, pinned to their sides, their fight fruitless.

The tentacle holding me became still.

Pulling me in, the air blew my hair back as the tentacle reeled me toward Anton. Stopping suddenly, it threw my hair back into my face as it tightened enough to earn a sound from me, teeth grit as my body became cold.

A hand met my hair, raking it back. Grip tightening atop my head, Anton held me, hostage, eyes locked on mine. Taking me in, his comedic persona eroding with the smoke that shed from him to feed the monster, a smirk twisted his wrinkled features.

"I knew there was something special about you, you even conquered black." Twisting my head to the side, he leaned in, lowering his voice as he hovered next to my ear, "I've waited so long, I'm starving."

Tentacle climbing up my body, it split off into smaller ones, wrapping around my arms and legs, keeping a tight hold on my core, as one slithered up and around my neck. Letting go of me, Anton threw me back and the tentacle reeled away. Holding me up above the others, the tentacles tightened, subduing my struggle, on display above the kingdom. Tears budding in my eyes, darkened by my furrowed brow, one tentacle slid up to my brooch, but hesitated before touching it, hovering, crooked like a little hook, thin tip pointing right at my face.

Through the glass in my eyes, I saw them. Kasper as a storm brewed above, lightning dancing over the tentacle to no avail. Oliver as blue fire roared, burning his tentacle away just a bit slower than it could regenerate around him. Salem as he remained calm, eyes carefully taking in the situation. Jack as he didn't fight, green eyes wide on Anton, the darkness of the tentacle staining the white of his long lab coat. Hugo as he tried to overpower the grip on him, the tentacle starting to give against his strength. Ash as they were able to slide their arms out from the grip, and Edgar as his shadow shot up to help him.

Then I saw him, as the tentacle hovered closer to my face, Cyrus.

While everyone else looked at the monster, Cyrus didn't, he looked at me.

Blonde, wavy hair blowing in the storm, not putting up a fight, pained beneath the strength of the tentacle wrapped around his chest, his eyes, no matter how much he was thrown about, never left me. I had something to tell him, something he needed to know, otherwise this would never end.

I opened my mouth to yell it, the one truth that pulled the entire story together, but then, as I took a shaking breath, the tentacle shot forward. Violating me, the tentacle crawled into my mouth, clawing its way further, choking me as it dug into my throat. Tears breaking from my eyes as my yell was muffled by my gag, my fight was nothing against the strength of the tentacles as it felt as if they sucked away my strength with every moment of contact.

It was then, as my body begged to throw up but couldn't, that I remembered something Cyrus had said.

Incubus.

Anton's chuckle split the air.

"While Cyrus' little show was something, I'm not a moron." Extending his arms, Anton looked up into the sky, "I know I can't raw dog your powers, so there would be no point in me taking your brooch, not that it ever held anything more than a ghost of your true powers anyway." Dropping his head to the side, his eyes met mine, "I'll just keep you like this, a living battery, powering my continued reign of Netherside for all time."

As the tentacle dug deeper into me, tears streaming down my jawline, the monster exploded with my power, tightening its grip and earning yells from everyone.

When I heard it, the sound he made Cyrus make, the sky turned orange.

In an explosion of orange so hot it incinerated the tentacle, turning it to ash before my eyes, I heard Anton yell. Suspended in that moment, hand flying to my mouth as I gagged, my eyes met his, tears falling from my furrowed brow. Hands up to his head, Anton writhed as the other tentacles flailed in a panic.

Dropping, I fell from above the kingdom.

Falling, I was always falling.

I fell for Cyrus and that Brooklyn accent; I fell for his lies and right into his plan.

Hand reaching above me as I dropped below the roof of the castle, all I could see was the stars.

I fell for Finnegan and the way they lit something in me; I fell for their façade and greed.

Hair blowing into my face, I felt the pull of gravity on my ribs as I plummeted.

I fell for Netherside, for its charm and people.

My eyes closed as my shaking breath left me.

I fell for these powers, for the colors they showed me.

I fell for it all.

Now all that was left was to hit the ground.

A hand met mine.

Eyes flying open, black crossed my vision.

The beat of wings stopped my heart.

Above me, dark robe flailing out around him, over his shoulders like a cape, hand holding mine, two beautiful, feathered black wings extended out behind him, Salem

Willow smiled at me. Staring up at him, suspended in that moment midair, my eyes widened.

A sign of the times.

With another beat of his wings, the dark angel pulled me up with him. The monster coming back into view as we raised, Anton fought to keep the others subdued. Letting go of my hand, Salem dropped me to the roof. Falling to a knee upon impact, I looked up to him. Flying up above everything, Salem stood in midair, looking down upon Anton. Taking a book out from a leather strap harness hanging at his side, Salem opened it. Eyes glancing down, a slight smile tugged up on the fine line of his mouth. Opening it, when he spoke, it was too quiet for me to hear.

A dark glow exploded from the ground around us, massive runes coming to life, creating a circle that trapped us all. When the two lines of the circle came racing around, connecting behind me to complete the circuit, a black wall exploded up, surrounding us as it came to a head above, sealing a dark dome. Hair whipping in the wind as everything grew darker, illuminated by the black glow, I looked back to Anton.

He no longer smiled.

I heard Kasper smirk.

With a blinding strike of lightning and a roar of thunder so loud it made my ears scream, I heard it above everything else, the metal zing of a sword unsheathed. Flying up into the air, free of the grip of a tentacle, electricity snapped over his every appendage as his raging blue eyes became the brightest thing in the dark dome. Glowing sword above his head, he brought it down into the tentacle holding Hugo. Cutting it with a strike of lightning, it turned to ash as it disappeared around Hugo. Dropping into the darkness below, I felt it when Hugo landed.

Two clicks split the air, like a stove trying to light.

Then, on the third, it did.

Black flames exploded around us, meeting the ritualistic circle, trapping everything within as their glow brought light back into the dome. Standing in the middle of it, right hand ablaze in black fire, letterman jacket flowing around him, Hugo's red eyes smiled at me as he turned to look my way.

Lightning lit around, and with each flash, Anton yelled out.

My shadow ripped away from me, catching on every one it passed as it grew, a dark form on the ground. Edgar landed, the ash of the tentacle that had held him dissipating around him as he straightened. Glancing back to me, his eyes had gone completely black. With a gesture of his arm, the shadow raged toward Anton. Raising his arm, he commanded it to climb Anton, wrapping around him as he stood in the center of the chaos. Fighting against it, Anton quickly became subdued as Edgar's hair slowly danced in the air.

Anton about to yell something, another thud of someone's shoes met the ground as he took his gasping, angry breath, but before whatever it was could come out on it, he was cut off by a scythe. Protruding from the darkness behind him, the blade hooked around his neck, pulled tight. Though, despite Ash pulling back on the blade with all their might, it only drew blood, and nothing more.

Falling to his knees when he dropped, Jack remained there, head low. Running to him, I put my hand on his back. Looking up to me in the chaos, his eyes caught on something behind me. Turning, I saw a tentacle shooting toward us.

Blue fire exploded before us, incinerating the tentacle.

Landing with grace, Oliver's long orange hair flowed among the blue flames shedding from him. Looking back to us, he nodded, though there was an edge to his usual reservation, a smile I could tell he was fighting.

Anton yelled out, fighting against Edgar's shadows and Ash's scythe, surrounded by Hugo's flames and trapped under Salem's spell. An explosion of tentacles raged out, whipping around without aim, recklessly, trying to destroy everything.

Kasper landing at Oliver's side, hair electrified, as they stood between Anton and I, they looked to each other. With nothing but silence passed between them, they jumped in opposite directions. Sword materializing in Oliver's hands, it burned orange as he swung it down, slicing through one of the tentacles. Sword disappearing from his hands as he landed, it reappeared with Kasper as he jumped, cracking blue as he took out another tentacle. Back and forth, orange and blue, as one jumped and the other fell, the sword disappeared and reappeared, keeping the onslaught of tentacles at bay.

Straightening, pulling Jack with me, I stood in the center of it all, the eye of the storm, in the midst of chaos.

One more set of shoes hit the floor.

Running in front of me, shoes skidding to a stop from the speed, his golden hair bounced with the movement, crown glistening from its place back atop his head. Pulling something from his pocket, Cyrus brought his hands together in front of him in prayer. Rosary glinting in the fiery light as it dangled between his hands, Cyrus looked up to Anton. Saying something under his breath, a white glow joined the ritualistic runes beneath us, making Anton cry out.

"Igor," Kasper yelled as he appeared above another tentacle, slicing it with his sword before it disappeared, "we have him contained."

"Wreck his shit," Hugo raised his hand and with it, the flames roared up the sides of the dome.

Salem turned the page in his book, saying something under his breath before looking down to me, "end this story."

"You have to do it," Cyrus glanced at me from over his shoulder, his hair blowing around in the storm, "you're the only one strong enough to banish him."

Standing there, despite being in profound company, despite everything they were doing, somehow, they still needed me? Shoved forward by a kind hand, I looked back to Jack as he smiled at me. Turning forward, I looked Anton up. My first step toward him accompanied by a flash of orange as Oliver cut another tentacle, the next was followed by blue as Kasper did the same, the air laced with electricity, heated by the flames, weighed down by the shadows, and chilled by the light reflecting off the scythe. Bringing up my hand, I could feel the weight of my brooch. A light beginning to come to life in my palm, it started off small.

Orange.

I stepped closer.

Yellow.

A tentacle shot toward me.

Green.

Kasper cut the tentacle before it could reach me.

Blue.

I began to close the space.

Red.

My hair flared about in the wind.

Purple.

I stopped before Anton.

Black.

Looking down to my hand and the colors that sat in it, I watched as they danced with one another, mixing into different shades until they swelled, changing into one, unified color.

White.

Looking back up to Anton and his teary eyes, his rough, erratic angry huffs as he struggled against the shadows, and his blood dripping down his neck from the scythe, I was going to do it, end the story about the boy who could feel nothing.

I brought my hand to his chest.

As the white grew near, so did his panic.

Eyes locked, tears began to bud in mine, despite my smile.

White had been Nox's color all along.

Shoving my hand into his abdomen, the moment it made contact, it burned through his ribs, pushing into the cavity of his chest. White was more than me, it was every thought, every feeling, of the incarnations that came before. As it grew inside him, it was every ungranted wish that was about to come true, it was every time Cyrus came into our lives, it was the moment each of them died. Cracking him from the inside, the light swelled, turning his yell into the ring of a bell. As it grew and grew, the intensity shaking the world, I didn't know how to control it, if one even could.

Bringing my other hand up to my wrist in an attempt to steady the shaking, my teeth grit.

Eyes struggling to stay open as the white burned a dark hole in my vision, a wish came to me.

Shoving my hand into Anton further, I wished for one last thing.

A happy ending.

The darkness around him exploded into white, the tentacles eroding to ash. As the light began to bleach everything out, eating up every last trembling inch of him, it climbed up his being, disappearing his limbs and torso, making its way up his neck, creeping up his face, until all that was left were his eyes.

When they met mine, my heart lurched.

Darkening, I saw something in them.

Throwing himself forward, I couldn't yank myself away before the white engrossing him took me too.

Exploding, I felt everything, then suddenly nothing, all at once. I heard the others yell, their shadowed forms thrown away too, tumbling violently through the air. Flying back, everything around me erased, my ears ringing out, my body was cold. As my eyes started to fall shut, everything limp, the ringing in my ears began to take form, creating words I could almost hear. When my eyes closed, everything went black.

"Thank you for taking time to meet with me this evening," Anton's voice took over my mind, though it was different than the one I knew, calmer, but still had that edge, "Father Glory."

A scene faded to life before me in my mind's eye. Dimly lit, a small chapel, lined in pews and few candles, it was modest, the air stuffy, dust particles visible through the setting sun as it poured its last light through the one window above the altar.

"Of course," Cyrus' voice met me as I watched him walk down the aisle. As he passed, I could see it, the blue of his eyes as they met Anton, "what did you wish to discuss?"

Leaning up against the altar, arms crossed over his chest, Anton watched as Cyrus stopped before him. Standing in pause, it was long, filled by the loud silence of a quiet church, ghostly echoes of hymns since passed lingering in the air. A sigh took him as he pushed himself up from the altar.

"They've caught on, the town's people." Stepping down the one stair toward Cyrus, Anton stopped right before him, "They confided in me this morning, so I cannot allow you and Nox to continue your operation."

Eyes wide, I watched the color drop from Cyrus as he stood, stiff and silent.

"I was willing to look the other way as long as you didn't cause me any trouble, your little show did bring great donations to our humble church, but now that they know," walking around Cyrus, Anton folded his arms behind him, "or rather, now that they know I know, well," Anton stopped behind Cyrus, back to his, "I'm sure you can gather where this is going. I can't have my reputation ruined. It would be ages before I got another town wrapped around my finger like this, and you know me, I don't fancy being hungry."

Cyrus spun around, about to say something, tears budding in his beautiful blue eyes, when Anton cut him off.

"It's too late, you cannot run. They are already at your house in the woods, likely burning it down as we speak." Slowly looking up over his shoulder to Cyrus as tears rolled down his face, Anton stood in that moment, "And as we don't know what Nox will do, the one who will execute him, will be you." Turning away, he started toward the door, and with every step the scene started to fade away, "but don't worry, you will be soon to follow, too."

As Anton left the chapel, the image fell into obscurity, the last image remaining that of Cyrus as he dropped to his knees, his sobs echoing as everything fell away. But they didn't disappear, only grew louder, closer, until suddenly I heard him say.

"Igor!"

Eyes slowly opening, I couldn't feel anything, my legs especially numb. Too blurry to see anything, I had to blink a couple times to get my eyes to focus enough to even sort of see. Coming into clarity above me, tattered, covered in soot, smeared in his own black blood, crown over his head, tears in his eyes, it was Cyrus.

"Igor," his word more of a sob when his eyes met mine, his hand found the side of my face.

I couldn't feel it.

As my vision grew clearer, Oliver came into view at my side, glowing hands on my chest. Kneeling around me, I was met with tears and struggling fronts. Salem kneeling in next to Cyrus, Hugo at his side, Jack knelt between Oliver and Kasper at my other. Edgar stood behind them, turned away, hand up to his face as Ash stood at his side, barely able to look at me.

All ripped to shit, tattered and torn, it wasn't Anton who had done that to them, no, it was me and my inability to control my colors.

But despite that, none of them appeared mad at me.

Laying on the ground among rubble and ruins, the castle in the sky behind them, no sign of Anton, I was confused. Why were they all crying?

Didn't we win?

Why, as my eyes lowered and struggled to drift over them all, why were they looking at me like that?

When my eyes drifted down further, they widened.

Oh.

Protruding through my chest, a structural beam dripped in my blood as it blossomed over my shirt, turning the yellow of my retail button-down red. Staring down at it as coldness started to take me, all I could do was laugh. Coughing as I choked, alarm shot over everyone as I coughed up blood. Unable to move my arms, I couldn't wipe it away as it dripped from my mouth and down my jawline.

"Igor," Cyrus looked between my eyes, tears in his, "please hold on, Oliver is healing you."

Smiling up at him, as every piece of the story of the boy who could feel nothing fell into place, peace found me. Everything Cyrus ever did, he did out of love. He did it, despite not knowing the truth, despite thinking Nox had cursed him, he never gave up, he never stopped loving, never stopped trying. Even when he killed Nox, he did so with red, an act of love, doing what he thought Nox wanted, subjecting himself to eternal torture to spare me. He pulled that lever six-hundred-years ago, knowing what Nox would think, and despite wanting nothing more than death, all he's done is live for Nox.

And that's what he'd have to keep on doing.

As my eyes struggled to remain focused, I could tell that despite surely doing his best, Oliver was fighting a losing war. It was so absurd it was funny, I survived not one, not two or three or four or five or six or even seven, but eight different colors, lived through surges of power strong enough to destroy all the realms, and here I was, undone by a fucking pole.

Taking a breath that was more of a death rattle, even the taste of iron started to fade from my mouth, "Cyrus."

Hand on my face, kneeling close at my side, a moment from shattering, Cyrus didn't reply.

"I have a message for the next incarnation."

"No," Cyrus shook his head, tears falling from his dimming red eyes, "there won't be a next, you're going to be the last, you're going to be okay," his words broke, "you have to be."

Looking up at him, I knew I was about to die with a smile on my face, "I did my best, but I fell short. Jack knows the secret to helping keep the powers from destroying the next one, I believe together you'll save him." Coughing, with each one my hearing rang more, "But, you have to tell him something for me, please," I looked between Cyrus' eyes as he barely contained his panic, "you have to promise me."

Looking between my eyes, jaw tight, intake shaking, it took him a moment, but he nodded.

"Nox's wish, my zombie," smiling at him, tears welled in my eyes, "was to spend forever, with you."

It was the only thing that made sense, the only reason he would keep incarnating, the only reason Cyrus could never die, the reason that no matter where or when, their paths would cross time and time again. Watching the dots connect behind Cyrus' eyes as they widened, glassing over, I could feel it, the end.

"Don't worry," my smile threatened to fade as my voice cracked, "I'll see you again soon."

Shaking his head, Cyrus fell onto me, holding me close.

I wished I could have felt him.

Warmth met me as my eyes began to close, the faint sensation of his trembling breath taking me. A little smile remaining on my face as my world became fuzzy, my dying wish had been granted. As my eyes fell shut, Cyrus' warmth all that I had left, I wondered what the next incarnation would be like and if it would be my turn to wait for them by the tree, surrounded by white.

"The crown," I heard Jack's faint voice, so far away, "Cyrus, the crown."

"What, no," I felt it, the moment Cyrus' warmth pulled away, leaving me cold, "that would make him immortal, I can't-"

"He's dying," Kasper's voice cracked, "please."

I felt it as my heart started to stumble, fighting with every beat.

"You're the only one who can grant it," Jack's voice became fuzzy, "Nox's wish."

The conversation dulled out of my ears, Salem's voice inaudible to me as my breathing ceased. The last thing I felt was my hair shifting, brushed by something. In that moment, my last moment, I wasn't scared. I knew that they had a better chance, now more than ever, to save the realms, to help Nox. I didn't know how they'd sustain until then, but they'd find a way, Cyrus always did. He would take the brooch back as he had every time before me, and when the next Nox came, then they'd know how to save him, how to grant his wish and end the cycle, all because of me.

Like falling asleep, I dropped.

My heart stopped.

thirteen

the Graveyard Shift

My eyes opened.

Blinded by white, my hands flew to my face as I stumbled back. Hissing through my teeth as I rode out the sting, feeling started to return to me. Lowering my hand as my eyes adjusted, my breath caught. Stepping around, I looked out as far as the eye could see in every direction, but I was alone, it was just me. Looking down to my shoes, I didn't have a shadow in the white abyss.

Looking back up as a deep breath took me, I stood in the silence, my only company.

But then, as every truth of my reality settled, a smile came to be.

I'd be here for the next, just as Nox had been here for me.

Looking down to my yellow button-up shirt, I smoothed it with my hands, tucking it in nicely beneath my belt. I was no stranger to the monotony. Hand lingering on my chest, it was then that I noticed it, I no longer had a heartbeat. Bringing my hand up to my hair, I raked my fingers through it, but as it fell back into place, orange caught the corner of my eye. Pulling my bangs out as far as I could, I stared up at them. Met with my fiery, natural orange hair just like my mother's and brother's, I guess black hair dye didn't follow you into the afterlife. Lowering my hand to my brooch at the center of my bowtie, I straightened it.

A cool breeze brushed by me.

Jumping, I turned around.

Floating slightly above the ground, dark smoke pouring from every opening of their cloaks, The Three met me. Turning fully to face them, the absence of a racing heart in my chest roared as I straightened.

I was opening my mouth to say something bratty when the one on the right spoke first, "I would congratulate you on a job well done, however, you put me out a significant amount."

Stopping, voice creaking to death in my throat, I blinked as I stepped back, "What?"

The Three started to float toward me as the one on the left spoke, "It's not his fault you bet against him," breaking off from the formation, that figure floated right up to me, leaning down to be eye-level, "but I always believed in you so thank you, I am a bit richer now."

Staring into the darkness churning beneath the hood, I had no words.

"We have seen it all, Igor," the one in the middle said, "read every book there ever has been, watched every narrator fight their way to the end of their story. But in all the novels we've read, every main character we've witnessed, not a single one has been quite like you." They floated up to me, the other figure moving to the side to make space, "I didn't believe Nox when he said you'd be entertaining, it takes a lot to occupy us, but he was right."

Floating to my either side, the other two got in a bit too close, "We're excited to see what else you do."

Finally finding my voice, I stepped back and away from them, "What do you mean, didn't my story end here?"

Staring back at me, The Three's hovering came to a pause until one said, "What lies ahead is uncharted waters, not a single incarnation, not even Nox, has awakened and conquered every color that you have. Your powers will likely grow as you do, becoming more complex with time. Without Nox to help, you will inevitably succumb to them if you're not very careful."

One floated back next to the first, "Though the fragment of Nox that lived within you has died, there are many others, scattered in everyday objects granting everyday wishes."

The last returned to their formation, "Jinx continues to work to unify him once more, they will need your help."

"But," the one in the middle floated toward me, "you mustn't fret about that yet, the time will come for that story. Now, Netherside needs you."

Eyes widening as glass began to take them, I looked over The Three, "You're going to send me back?"

"No, we hold no jurisdiction over you any longer, you have far surpassed us in power," a little laugh took them, until the one in the middle continued, "It wasn't us who saved you." Lifting their arm toward me, the smoke that poured from the opening of the sleeve began to take form, "Anton is gone, you banished him beyond even our reach. However," the smoke turning into a hand, it landed on my shoulder. Its touch was kinder than I could ever imagine.

"We believe he may have hidden some of himself Flipside, creating a vortex in a parking lot in a red-light district for some reason. We will keep an eye on it, but all I want you to worry about right now is taking care of yourself."

One floated up to their left, "That's the only way you will be able to take care of everyone else." Raising their arm, they waved it over my head, "King Igor."

As the smoke passed by, something came to form above me. Looking up, my eyes widened on the crown Cyrus had been wearing. Looking back down to The Three, though I couldn't see their faces, I could just tell they were smiling at me.

That was it, the crown of immortality.

"Now," The one on the left raised their arm toward me, hand taking form before meeting my other shoulder, "get back to him, I'm sure he's worried."

Raising their arm, the one on the right held it up, crooking their head at me, "Quite some time has passed, we apologize for keeping you so long."

"But," the one in the middle bent down, the smoke in their hood dissipating before me. Met with warm galaxy eyes and sun-kissed skin, sharply chopped bobbed silver hair poured from her hood as a woman winked at me, "it isn't every day that we get to fuck with Cyrus Glory."

Mouth open, eyes wide, I didn't have the breath to speak as the last of The Three placed their hand on me.

Dropping into the white floor beneath me, I looked up as darkness surrounded me to see The Three, waving. Enveloped in the fall, I dropped and dropped, faster and faster, like an asteroid reentering orbit, just as I had fallen into Nearside the night that started it all. But this time, I didn't fight the fall. Though, as it started to come to a slow, the colors of my brooch lighting up brighter in the dark, there was one color that had dulled.

Green.

Coming to a sudden stop, I jumped awake, gasping. Hitting my head on something soft in darkness, disorientation ruled me until I heard it.

The ring of a bell.

Legend had it that, once upon a time, it wasn't unheard of to be buried alive, so to combat this, the peoples of old would tie a string to the wrist of the deceased, feed it six feet up, and attach it to a bell so that, in the event they woke up, the person working the graveyard shift would hear the ringing and exhume them.

The colors of my brooch bringing a glow to my surroundings, I was met with beautiful velvet walls, flowers laying around me in the enclosed space. As I brought my hands up to the lid of the box, I pushed on it as another muffled ring met me. A slight tug on my wrist caught my attention. Pulling it closer to my face in the dimly lit space, another ring came from above as the glow of my brooch reflected off a thin, silver string tied around my wrist.

An occupying thought, though snobs will say the phrase was coined much later and held no such connection.

A thump from above startled me, shifting my space as dirt was knocked loose from the lid. Laying there, lowering my wrist as I stared up at the velvet door above me, the bell rang out again. With each thump it got closer and closer, knocking more dirt loose, clouding the air around me. When it suddenly fell quiet, my breath sat, suspended in my chest. Faint jingling of metal came from the side and a moment later, the seal popped.

Air came pouring in with the dirt, blinding me as my hands came up to my face. Dirt obscuring the air in the moonlight as the lid fell to the side with a thud, I coughed. As the dirt started to settle, I forced my eyes open. The first thing that broke through the haze was a glow, crimson like a fine wine, aged but robust. A hand extended to me, chest heaving and eyes full of glass, his wavy locks caught the

moonlight as the dust cleared between us.

Smiling, I accepted his hand.

"It's you."

They call it

the Graveyard Shift

"While I have all eternity," they extended their hand, "you don't. I can only sustain you for so long, so you'll need to make your choice."

Staring at their hand, it wasn't a hard choice to make.

Who wouldn't want to be a vampire?

Dainty in my enthusiastic grip, their hand was the warmest thing I had ever felt as I shook it.

"What's your name?" They asked as the handshake stopped, though they didn't let go of my hand.

"Ross."

"Ross," they way they said it, filtered through the faintest echoes of a French accent, it absolutely stopped my fucking heart as I stared at them, "It's wonderful to meet you," their smile lit up that dark place, "My name is Archduke Finnegan van Serifino."

-HELL'S BELLS AND BUCKETS OF BLOOD-

-COMING SOON-

www.ingramcontent.com/pod-product-compliance
Lightning Source LLC
Chambersburg PA
CBHW071130010826
48975CB00018B/1341